TERMS OF ENGAGEMENT

BY
ANN MAJOR

M&B policy is to use papers that are natural, renewable and
roducts and made from wood grown in sustainable forests. The
manufacturing processes conform to the legal environmental
of the country of origin

bound in Spain
it CPI, Barcelona

MILLS
BOON

Published in Great Britain 2012
by Mills & Boon, an imprint of Harlequin (UK) Limited,
Eton House, 18-24 Paradise Road, Richmond, Surrey TW9 1SR

© Ann Major 2012

ISBN: 978 0 263 89180 5
ebook ISBN: 978 1 408 97188 8

51-0612

Harlequin (U   K) policy   pa
recyclable pr
logging and
regulations o

Printed and b
by Blackprin

Ann Major lives in Texas with her husband of many years and is the mother of three grown children. She has a master's degree from Texas A&M at Kingsville, Texas, and is a former English teacher. She is a founding board member of the Romance Writers of America and a frequent speaker at writers' groups.

Ann loves to write—she considers her ability to do so a gift. Her hobbies include hiking in the mountains, sailing, ocean kayaking, traveling and playing the piano. But most of all, she enjoys her family. Visit her website at www.annmajor.com.

To Ted, with all my love.
And as always I must thank my editor, Stacy Boyd, and
Shana Smith, along with the entire Desire team
for their talented expertise.
I thank as well my agent, Karen Solem.

One

No good deed goes unpunished.

When would she ever learn? Kira wondered.

With her luck, never.

So, here she sat, in the office of oil billionaire Quinn Sullivan, too nervous to concentrate on her magazine as she waited to see if he would make time for a woman he probably thought of as just another adversary to be crushed in his quest for revenge.

Dreadful, arrogant man.

If he did grant her an audience, would she have any chance of changing his mind about destroying her family's company, Murray Oil, and forcing her sister Jaycee into marriage?

A man vengeful enough to hold a grudge against her father for twenty years couldn't possibly have a heart that could be swayed.

Kira Murray clenched and unclenched her hands. Then

she sat on them, twisting in her chair. When the man across from her began to stare, she told herself to quit squirming. Lowering her eyes to her magazine, she pretended to read a very boring article on supertankers.

High heels clicked rapidly on marble, causing Kira to look up in panic.

"Miss Murray, I'm so sorry. I was wrong. Mr. Sullivan *is* still here." There was surprise in his secretary's classy, soothing purr.

"In fact, he'll see you now."

"He will?" Kira squeaked. *"Now?"*

The secretary's answering smile was a brilliant white.

Kira's own mouth felt as dry as sandpaper. She actually began to shake. To hide this dreadful reaction, she jumped to her feet so fast she sent the glossy magazine to the floor, causing the man across from her to glare in annoyance.

Obviously, she'd been hoping Quinn would refuse to see her. A ridiculous wish when she'd come here for the express purpose of finally meeting him properly and having her say.

Sure, she'd run into him once, informally. It had been right after he'd announced he wanted to marry one of the Murray daughters to make his takeover of Murray Oil less hostile. Her father had suggested Jaycee, and Kira couldn't help but think he'd done so because Jaycee was his favorite and most biddable daughter. As always, Jaycee had dutifully agreed with their father's wishes, so Quinn had come to the ranch for a celebratory dinner to seal the bargain.

He'd been late. A man as rich and arrogant as he was probably thought himself entitled to run on his own schedule.

Wounded by her mother's less-than-kind assessment of her outfit when she'd first arrived—"Jeans and a torn shirt? How could you think that appropriate for meeting a man so important to this family's welfare?"—Kira had stormed out of the house. She hadn't had time to change after the crisis at her best friend's restaurant, where Kira was temporarily waiting tables while looking for a museum curator position. Since her mother always turned a deaf ear to Kira's excuses, rather than explain, Kira had decided to walk her dad's hunting spaniels while she nursed her injured feelings.

The brilliant, red sun that had been sinking fast had been in her eyes as the spaniels leaped onto the gravel driveway, dragging her in their wake. Blinded, she'd neither seen nor heard Quinn's low-slung, silver Aston Martin screaming around the curve. Slamming on his brakes, he'd veered clear of her with several feet to spare. She'd tripped over the dogs and fallen into a mud puddle.

Yipping wildly, the dogs had raced back to the house, leaving her to face Quinn on her own with cold, dirty water dripping from her chin.

Quinn had gotten out of his fancy car and stomped over in his fancy Italian loafers just as she got to her feet. For a long moment, he'd inspected every inch of her. Then, mindless of her smudged face, chattering teeth and muddy clothes, he'd pulled her against his tall, hard body, making her much too aware of his clean, male smell and hard, muscular body.

"Tell me you're okay."

He was tall and broad-shouldered, so tall he'd towered over her. His angry blue eyes had burned her; his viselike fingers had cut into her elbow. Despite his overcharged emotions, she'd liked being in his arms—liked it too much.

"Damn it, I didn't hit you, did I? Well, say something, why don't you?"

"How can I—with you yelling at me?"

"Are you okay, then?" he asked, his grip loosening, his

voice softening into a husky sound so unexpectedly beautiful she'd shivered. This time, she saw concern in his hard expression.

Had it happened then?

Oh, be honest, Kira, at least with yourself. That was the moment you formed an inappropriate crush on your sister's future fiancé, a man whose main goal in life is to destroy your family.

He'd been wearing faded jeans, a white shirt, his sleeves rolled up to his elbows. On her, jeans looked rumpled, but on him, jeans had made him ruggedly, devastatingly handsome. Over one arm, he carried a cashmere jacket.

She noted his jet-black hair and carved cheekbones with approval. Any woman would have. His skin had been darkly bronzed, and the dangerous aura of sensuality surrounding him had her sizzling.

Shaken by her fall and by the fact that *the enemy* was such an attractive, powerful man who continued to hold her close and stare down at her with blazing eyes, her breath had come in fits and starts.

"I said—*are you okay?*"

"I was fine—until you grabbed me." Her hesitant voice was tremulous…and sounded strangely shy. "You're hurting me, really hurting me!" She'd lied so he would let her go, and yet part of her hadn't wanted to be released.

His eyes narrowed suspiciously. "Sorry," he'd said, his tone harsh again.

"Who the hell are you anyway?" he'd demanded.

"Nobody important," she'd muttered.

His dark brows winged upward. "Wait…I've seen your pictures… You're the older sister. The waitress."

"Only temporarily…until I get a new job as a curator."

"Right. You were fired."

"So, you've heard Father's version. The truth is, my professional opinion wasn't as important to the museum director as I might have liked, but I was let go due to budget constraints."

"Your sister speaks highly of you."

"Sometimes I think she's the only one in this family who does."

Nodding as if he understood, he draped his jacket around her shoulders. "I've wanted to meet you." When she glanced up at him, he said, "You're shivering. The least I can do is offer you my jacket and a ride back to the house."

Her heart pounded much too fast, and she was mortified that she was covered with mud and that she found her family's enemy exciting and the prospect of wearing his jacket a thrill. Not trusting herself to spend another second with such a dangerous man, especially in the close quarters of his glamorous car, she'd shaken her head. "I'm too muddy."

"Do you think I give a damn about that? I could have killed you."

"You didn't. So let's just forget about it."

"Not possible! Now, put my jacket on before you catch your death."

Pulling his jacket around her shoulders, she turned on her heel and left him. Nothing had happened, she'd told herself as she stalked rapidly through the woods toward the house.

Nothing except the enemy she'd feared had held her and made her feel dangerously alive in a way no other man ever had.

When she'd reached the house, she'd been surprised to find him outside waiting for her as he held on to her yapping dogs. Feeling tingly and shyly thrilled as he handed her their tangled leashes, she'd used her muddy clothes again as an excuse to go home and avoid dinner, when her father would formally announce Quinn was to marry her sister.

Yes, he was set on revenge against those she loved most, but that hadn't been the reason she couldn't sit across the table from him. No, it was her crush. How could she have endured such a dinner when just to look at him made her skin heat?

For weeks after that chance meeting, her inappropriate attachment to Quinn had continued to claim her, causing her much guilt-ridden pain. She'd thought of him constantly. And more than once, before she'd returned his jacket to Jaycee, she'd worn it around her apartment, draped over her shoulders, just because his scent lingered on the soft fabric.

Now, retrieving the magazine she'd dropped, she set it carefully on the side table. Then she sucked in a deep breath. Not that it steadied her nerves.

No. Instead, her heart raced when Quinn Sullivan's secretary turned away, saying, "Follow me."

Kira swallowed. She'd put this interview off to the last possible moment—to the end of the business day—because she'd been trying to formulate a plan to confront a man as powerful and dictatorial and, yes, as dangerously sexy, as Quinn Sullivan.

But she hadn't come up with a plan. Did she ever have a plan? She'd be at a disadvantage since Sullivan planned everything down to the last detail, including taking his revenge plot up a notch by marrying Jaycee.

Kira had to sprint to keep up with the sleek, blonde secretary, whose ridiculous, four-inch, ice-pick, gold heels clicked on the polished gray marble. Did *he* make the poor girl wear such gaudy, crippling footwear?

Quinn's waiting room with its butter-soft leather couches and polished wainscoting had reeked of old money. In truth, he was nothing but a brash, bad-tempered upstart. His long hallway, decorated with paintings of vivid minimalistic splashes of color, led to what would probably prove to be an obscenely opulent office. Still, despite her wish to dislike everything about him, she admired the art and wished she could stop and study several of the pictures. They were elegant, tasteful and interesting. Had he selected them himself?

Probably not. He was an arrogant show-off.

After their one encounter, she'd researched him. It seemed he believed her father had profited excessively when he'd bought Quinn's father out of their mutually owned company. In addition, he blamed her father for his father's suicide—if suicide it had been.

Quinn, who'd known hardship after his father's death, was determined to make up for his early privations, by living rich and large. Craving glamour and the spotlight, he never attended a party without a beauty even more dazzling than his secretary on his arm.

He was a respected art collector. In various interviews he'd made it clear nobody would ever look down on him again. Not in business; not in his personal life. He was king of his kingdom.

From the internet, she'd gleaned that Quinn's bedroom had a revolving door. Apparently, a few nights' pleasuring the same woman were more than enough for him. Just when a woman might believe she meant something to him, he'd drop her and date another gorgeous blonde, who was invariably more beautiful than the one he'd jilted. There had been one woman, also blonde, who'd jilted him a year or so ago, a Cristina somebody. Not that she hadn't been quickly forgotten by the press when he'd resumed chasing more beauties as carelessly as before.

From what Kira had seen, his life was about winning,

not about caring deeply. For that purpose only, he'd surrounded himself with the mansions, the cars, the yachts, the art collections and the fair-haired beauties. She had no illusions about what his marriage to Jaycee would be like. He had no intention of being a faithful husband to Kira's beautiful, blonde sister.

Rich, handsome womanizer that he was, Kira might have pitied him for being cursed with such a dark heart—if only her precious Jaycee wasn't central in his revenge scheme.

Kira was not gifted at planning or at being confrontational, which were two big reasons why she wasn't getting ahead in her career. And Quinn was the last person on earth she wanted to confront. But the need to take care of Jaycee, as she had done since her sister's birth, was paramount.

Naturally, Kira's first step had been to beg her father to change his mind about using her sister to smooth over a business deal, but her father had been adamant about the benefits of the marriage.

Kira didn't understand the financials of Quinn's hostile takeover of Murray Oil, but her father seemed to think Quinn would make a brilliant CEO. Her parents had said that if Jaycee didn't walk down the aisle with Quinn as agreed, Quinn's terms would become far more onerous. Not to mention that the employees would resent him as an outsider. Even though Quinn's father had been a co-owner, Quinn was viewed as a man with a personal vendetta against the Murrays and Murray Oil. Ever since his father's death, rumors about his hostility toward all things Murray had been widely circulated by the press. Only if he married Jaycee would the employees believe that peace between the two families had at last been achieved and that the company would be safe in his hands.

Hence, Kira was here, to face Quinn Sullivan.

She was determined to stop him from marrying Jaycee, but how? Pausing in panic even as his secretary rushed ahead, she reminded herself that she couldn't turn back, plan or not.

Quickening her pace, Kira caught up to the efficient young woman, who was probably moving so quickly because she was as scared of the unfeeling brute as Kira was.

When his secretary pushed open Quinn's door, the deep, rich tones of the man's surprisingly beautiful voice moved through Kira like music. Her knees lost strength, and she stopped in midstep.

Oh, no, it was happening again.

She'd known from meeting him the first time that he was charismatic, but she'd counted on her newly amassed knowledge of his despicable character to protect her. His edgy baritone slid across her nerve endings, causing warm tingles in her secret, feminine places, and she knew she was as vulnerable to him as before.

Fighting not to notice that her nipples ached and that her pulse had sped up, she took a deep breath before daring a glance at the black-headed rogue. Looking very much at ease, he sat sprawled at his desk, the back of his linebacker shoulders to her as he leaned against his chair, a telephone jammed to his ear.

She couldn't, wouldn't, be attracted to this man.

On his desk she noted a silver-framed photograph of his father. With their intense blue eyes, black hair and strongly chiseled, tanned features, father and son closely resembled each other. Both, she knew, had been college athletes. Did Quinn keep the photo so close out of love or to energize him in his quest for revenge?

"I told you to buy, Habib," he ordered brusquely in that

too-beautiful voice. "What's there to talk about? Do it."
He ended the call.

At least he was every bit as rude as she remembered.
Deep baritone or not, it should be easy to hate him.

His secretary coughed to let him know they were at the
door.

Quinn whirled around in his massive, black leather
chair, scowling, but went still the instant he saw Kira.

He lifted that hard, carved chin, which surprisingly
enough had the most darling dimple, and, just like that,
dismissed his secretary.

His piercing, laser-blue gaze slammed into Kira full
force and heated her through—just like before.

Black hair. Bronze skin. Fierce, brilliant eyes… With a
single glance the man bewitched her.

When his mouth lifted at the edges, her world shifted as
it had that first evening—and he hadn't even touched her.

He was as outrageously handsome as ever. Every bit as
dark, tall, lean and hard, as cynical and untamed—even
in his orderly office with his efficient secretary standing
guard.

Still, for an instant, Kira thought she saw turbulent grief
and longing mix with unexpected pleasure at the sight of
her.

He remembered her.

But in a flash the light went out of his eyes, and his
handsome features tightened into those of the tough, heart-
less man he wanted people to see.

In spite of his attempt at distance, a chord of recognition
had been struck. It was as if they'd seen into each other's
souls, had sensed each other's secret yearnings.

She wanted her family, who deemed her difficult and
frustrating, to love and accept her for herself, as they did
her sister.

He had longings that revenge and outward success had failed to satisfy. What were they? What was lacking in his disciplined, showy, materialistic life?

Was he as drawn to her as she was to him?

Impossible.

So how could he be the only man who'd ever made her feel less alone in the universe?

Hating him even more because he'd exposed needs she preferred to conceal, she tensed. He had no right to open her heart and arouse such longings.

Frowning, he cocked his dark head and studied her. "I owe you an apology for the last time we met," he drawled in that slow, mocking baritone that turned her insides to mush. "I was nervous about the takeover and the engagement and about making a good impression on you and your family. I was too harsh with you. A few inches more…and I could have killed you. I was afraid, and that made me angry."

"You owe me nothing," she said coolly.

"I don't blame you in the least for avoiding me all these weeks. I probably scared the hell out of you."

"I haven't been avoiding you. Not really," she murmured, but a telltale flush heated her neck as she thought of the family dinners she'd opted out of because she'd known he'd be there.

If only she could run now, escape him. But Jaycee needed her, so instead, she hedged. "I've been busy."

"Waitressing?"

"Yes! I'm helping out Betty, my best friend, while I interview for museum jobs. Opening a restaurant on the San Antonio River Walk was a lifetime dream of hers. She got busier faster than she expected, and she offered me a job. Since I waited tables one summer between college semesters, I've got some experience."

He smiled. "I like it that you're helping your friend

realize her dream even though your career is stalled. That's nice."

"We grew up together. Betty was our housekeeper's daughter. When we got older my mother kept hoping I'd outgrow the friendship while Daddy helped Betty get a scholarship."

"I like that you're generous and loyal." He hesitated. "Your pictures don't do you justice. Nor did my memory of you."

His blue eyes gleamed with so much appreciation her cheeks heated. "Maybe because the last time I saw you I was slathered in mud."

He smiled. "Still, being a waitress seems like a strange job for a museum curator, even if it's temporary. You did major in art history at Princeton and completed that internship at the Metropolitan Museum of Art. I believe you graduated with honors."

She had no idea how she'd done so well, but when her grades had thrilled her father, she'd worked even harder.

"Has Daddy, who by the way, has a bad habit of talking too much, told you my life history?"

For a long moment, Quinn didn't confirm her accusation or deny it.

"Well, is that where you learned these details?"

"If he talked about you, it was because I was curious and asked him."

Not good. She frowned as she imagined her parents complaining about her disappointments since Princeton during all those family dinners she'd avoided.

"Did my father tell you that I've had a hard time with a couple of museum directors because they micromanaged me?"

"Not exactly."

"I'll bet. He takes the boss's side because he's every bit

as high-handed and dictatorial. Unfortunately, one night after finishing the setup of a new show, when I was dead tired, the director started second-guessing my judgment about stuff he'd already signed off on. I made the mistake of telling him what I really thought. When there were budget cuts, you can probably guess who he let go."

"I'm sorry about that."

"I'm good at what I do. I'll find another job, but until I do, I don't see why I shouldn't help Betty. Unfortunately, my father disagrees. We frequently disagree."

"It's your life, not his."

Her thoughts exactly. Having him concur was really sort of annoying, since Quinn was supposed to be the enemy.

In the conversational lull, she noticed that his spectacular physique was elegantly clad in a dark gray suit cut to emphasize every hard sinew of his powerful body. Suddenly, she wished she'd dressed up. Then she caught herself. Why should she care about looking her best for a man she should hate, when her appearance was something she rarely thought about?

All she'd done today was scoop her long, dark hair into a ponytail that cascaded down her back. Still, when his eyes hungrily skimmed her figure, she was glad that she'd worn the loosely flowing white shirt and long red scarf over her tight jeans because the swirls of cloth hid her body.

His burning gaze, which had ignited way too many feminine hormones, rose to her face again. When he smiled as he continued to stare, she bit her bottom lip to keep from returning his smile.

Rising, he towered over her, making her feel small and feminine and lovely in ways she'd never felt lovely before. He moved toward her, seized her hand in his much larger one and shook it gently.

"I'm very glad you decided to give me a second chance."

Why did his blunt fingers have to feel so warm and hard, his touch and gaze so deliciously intimate? She snatched her hand away, causing his eyes to flash with that pain he didn't want her to see.

"That's not what this is."

"But you *were* avoiding me, weren't you?"

"I *was*," she admitted and then instantly regretted being so truthful.

"That was a mistake—for both of us."

When he asked her if she wanted coffee or a soda or anything at all to drink, she said no and looked out the windows at the sun sinking low against the San Antonio skyline. She couldn't risk looking at him any more than necessary because her attraction seemed to be building. He would probably sense it and use it against her somehow.

With some difficulty she reminded herself that she disliked him. So, why did she still feel hot and clammy and slightly breathless, as if there were a lack of oxygen in the room?

It's called chemistry. Sexual attraction. It's irrational.

Her awareness only sharpened when he pulled out a chair for her and returned to his own. Sitting down and crossing one long leg over the other, he leaned back again. The pose should have seemed relaxed, but as he concentrated on her she could see he wasn't relaxed—he was intently assessing her.

The elegant office became eerily silent as he stared. Behind the closed doors, she felt trapped. Leaning forward, her posture grew as rigid as his was seemingly careless.

His hard, blue eyes held her motionless.

"So, to what do I owe the pleasure of your visit this afternoon…or should I say this evening?" he asked in that pleasant tone that made her tremble with excitement.

She imagined them on his megayacht, sailing silently across the vast, blue Gulf of Mexico. Her auburn hair would blow in the wind as he pulled her close and suggested they go below.

"You're my last appointment, so I can give you as much time as you want," he said, thankfully interrupting her seduction fantasy.

Her guilty heart sped up. Why had she come at such a late hour when he might not have another appointment afterward?

The sky was rapidly darkening, casting a shadow across his carved face, making him look stark and feral, adding to the danger she felt upon finding herself alone with him.

Even though her fear made her want to flee, she was far too determined to do what she had to do to give in to it.

She blurted out, "I don't want you to marry Jaycee." Oh, dear, she'd meant to lead up to this in some clever way.

He brought his blunt fingertips together in a position of prayer. When he leaned across his desk toward her, she sank lower in her own chair. "Don't you? How very strange."

"It's not strange. You can't marry her. You don't love her. You and she are too different to care for each other as a man and wife should."

His eyes darkened in a way that made him seem more alive than any man she'd ever known. "I wasn't referring to Jacinda. I was talking about you…and me and how strange that I should feel…so much—" He stopped. "When for all practical purposes we just met."

His eyes bored into hers with that piercing intensity that left her breathless. Once again she felt connected to him by some dark, forbidden, primal force.

"I never anticipated this wrinkle when I suggested a marriage with a Murray daughter," he murmured.

When his eyes slid over her body again in that devouring way, her heart raced. Her tall, slim figure wasn't appealing to most men. She'd come to believe there was nothing special about her. Could he possibly be as attracted to her as she was to him?

"You don't love her," she repeated even more shakily.

"Love? No. I don't love her. How could I? I barely know her."

"You see!"

"Your father chose her, and she agreed."

"Because she's always done everything he tells her to."

"You, however, would not have agreed so easily?" He paused. "Love does not matter to me in the least. But now I find myself curious about his choice of brides. And...even more curious about you. I want to get to know you better." His tone remained disturbingly intimate.

She remembered his revolving bedroom door and the parade of voluptuous blondes who'd passed through it. Was he so base he'd think it nothing to seduce his future wife's sister and then discard her, too?

"You've made no secret of how you feel about my father," she whispered with growing wariness. "Why marry his daughter?"

"Business. There are all these rumors in the press that I want to destroy Murray Oil, a company that once belonged to my beloved father."

"It makes perfect sense."

"No, it doesn't. I would never pay an immense amount of money for a valuable property in order to destroy it."

"But you think my father blackened your father's name and then profited after buying your father out. That's why you're so determined to destroy everything he's built, everything he loves…including Jaycee."

His lips thinned. Suddenly, his eyes were arctic. "My father built Murray Oil, not yours. Only back then it was called Sullivan and Murray Oil. Your father seized the opportunity, when my dad was down, to buy him out at five cents on the dollar."

"My father made the company what it is today."

"Well, now I'm going to take it over and improve upon it. Marriage to a Murray daughter will reassure the numerous employees that family, not a vengeful marauder, will be at the helm of the business."

"That would be a lie. You are a marauder, and you're not family."

"Not yet," he amended. "But a few Saturdays hence, if I marry Jaycee, we will be…family."

"Never. Not over my dead body!" She expelled the words in an outraged gasp.

"The thought of anything so awful happening to your delectable body is hateful to me." When he hesitated, his avid, searching expression made her warm again.

"Okay," he said. "Let's say I take you at your word. You're here to save your sister from me. And you'd die before you'd let me marry her. Is that right?"

"Essentially."

"What else would you do to stop me? Surely there is some lesser, more appealing sacrifice you'd be willing to make to inspire me to change my mind."

"I…don't know what you mean."

"Well, what if I were to agree to your proposal and forgo marriage to your lovely sister, a woman you say is so unsuited to my temperament I could never love her—I want to know what I will get in return."

"Do you always have to get something in return? You wouldn't actually be making a sacrifice."

His smile was a triumphant flash of white against his deeply tanned skin. "Always. Most decidedly. My hypothetical marriage to your sister is a business deal, after all. As a businessman, I would require compensation for letting the deal fall through."

Awful man.

His blue eyes stung her, causing the pulse in her throat to hammer frantically.

"Maybe…er…the satisfaction of doing a good deed for once in your life?" she said.

He laughed. "That's a refreshing idea if ever I heard one, and from a very charming woman—but, like most humans, I'm driven by the desire to avoid pain and pursue pleasure."

"And to think—I imagined you to be primarily driven by greed. Well, I don't have any money."

"I don't want your money."

"What do you want, then?"

"I think you know," he said silkily, leaning closer. "*You. You* interest me…quite a lot. I believe we could give each other immense pleasure…under the right circumstances."

The unavoidable heat in his eyes caused an unwanted shock wave of fiery prickles to spread through her body. She'd seriously underestimated the risk of confronting this man.

"In fact, I think we both knew what we wanted the moment we looked at each other today," he said.

He wanted her.

And even though he was promised to Jaycee, he didn't have a qualm about acknowledging his impossible, unsavory need for the skinnier, plainer, older sister. Maybe the thought of bedding his future wife's sister improved upon his original idea of revenge. Or maybe he was simply a man who never denied himself a female who might amuse him, however briefly. If any of those assumptions were true, he was too horrible for words.

"I'm hungry," he continued. "Why don't we discuss your proposition over dinner," he said.

"No. I couldn't possibly. You've said more than enough to convince me of the kind of man you are."

"Who are you kidding? You were prejudiced against me before you showed up here. If I'd played the saint, you would have still thought me the devil…and yet you would have also still…been secretly attracted. And you are attracted to me. Admit it."

Stunned at his boldness, she hissed out a breath. "I'm not."

Then why was she staring at his darling dimple as if she was hypnotized by it?

He laughed. "Do you have a boyfriend?" he asked. "Or dinner plans you need to change?"

"No," she admitted before she thought.

"Good." He smiled at her as if he was genuinely pleased. "Then it's settled."

"What?"

"You and I have a dinner date."

"No!"

"What are you afraid of?" he asked in that deep, velvet tone that let her know he had much more than dinner in mind. And some part of her, God help her, wanted to rush toward him like a moth toward flame, despite her sister, despite the knowledge that he wanted to destroy her family.

Kira was shaking her head vehemently when he said, "You came here today to talk to me, to convince me to do as you ask. I'm making myself available to you."

"But?"

He gave her a slow, insolent grin. "If you want to save your sister from the Big Bad Wolf, well—here's your chance."

Two

When they turned the corner and she saw the gaily lit restaurant, Kira wished with all her heart she'd never agreed to this dinner with Quinn.

Not that he hadn't behaved like a perfect gentleman as they'd walked over together.

When she'd said she wanted to go somewhere within walking distance of his office, she'd foolishly thought she'd be safer with him on foot.

"You're not afraid to get in my car, to be alone with me, are you?" he'd teased.

"It just seems simpler…to go somewhere close," she'd hedged. "Besides, you're a busy man."

"Not too busy for what really matters."

Then he'd suggested they walk along the river. The lovely reflections in the still, brown water where ducks swam and the companionable silences they'd shared as they'd made their way along the flagstones edged by lush vegetation, restaurants and bars had been altogether too enjoyable.

She'd never made a study of predators, but she had a cat, Rudy. When on the hunt, he was purposeful, diligent and very patient. He enjoyed playing with his prey before the kill, just to make the game last longer. She couldn't help but think Quinn was doing something similar with her.

No sooner did Quinn push open the door so she could enter one of the most popular Mexican restaurants in all of San Antonio than warmth, vibrant laughter and the heavy beat of Latin music hit her.

A man, who was hurrying outside after a woman, said, "Oh, excuse us, please, miss."

Quinn reached out and put his strong arm protectively around Kira's waist, shielding her with his powerful body. Pulling her close, he tugged her to one side to let the other couple pass.

When Quinn's body brushed against hers intimately, as if they were a couple, heat washed over her as it had the afternoon when she'd been muddy and he'd pulled her into his arms. She inhaled his clean, male scent. As before, he drew her like a sexual magnet.

When she let out an excited little gasp, he smiled and pulled her even closer. "You feel much too good," he whispered.

She should run, but the March evening was cooler than she'd dressed for, causing her to instinctively cling to his hot, big-boned body and stay nestled against his welcoming warmth.

She felt the red scarf she wore around her neck tighten as if to warn her away. She yanked at it and gulped in a breath before she shoved herself free of him.

He laughed. "You're not the only one who's been stunned by our connection, you know. I like holding you as much as you like being in my arms. In fact, that's all I want to do…hold you. Does that make me evil? Or all too human because I've found a woman I have no will to resist?"

"You are too much! Why did I let you talk me into this dinner?"

"Because it was the logical thing to do, and I insisted. Because I'm very good at getting what I want. Maybe because *you* wanted to. But now I'd be quite happy to skip dinner. We could order takeout and go to my loft apartment, which isn't far, by the way. You're a curator. I'm a collector. I have several pieces that might interest you."

"I'll bet! Not a good idea."

Again he laughed.

She didn't feel any safer once they were inside the crowded, brilliantly lit establishment. The restaurant with its friendly waitstaff, strolling mariachis, delicious aromas and ceiling festooned with tiny lights and colorful banners was too festive, too conducive to lowering one's guard. It would be too easy to succumb to temptation, something she couldn't afford to do.

I'll have a taco, a glass of water. We'll talk about Jaycee, and I'll leave. What could possibly go wrong if I nip this attraction in the bud?

When told there was a thirty-minute wait, Quinn didn't seem to mind. To the contrary, he seemed pleased. "We'll wait in the bar," he said, smiling.

Then he ushered them into a large room with a high-beamed ceiling dominated by a towering carved oak bar, inspired by the baroque elegance of the hotels in nineteenth-century San Antonio.

When a young redheaded waiter bragged on the various imported tequilas available, Quinn ordered them two margaritas made of a particularly costly tequila he said he had a weakness for.

"I'd rather have sparkling water," she said, sitting up straighter, thinking she needed all her wits about her.

"As you wish," Quinn said gallantly, ordering the water as well, but she noted that he didn't cancel the second margarita.

When their drinks arrived, he lifted his margarita to his lips and licked at the salt that edged the rim. And just watching the movement of his tongue across the grit of those glimmering crystals flooded her with ridiculous heat as she imagined him licking her skin.

"I think our first dinner together calls for a toast, don't you?" he said.

Her hand moved toward her glass of sparkling water.

"The tequila really is worth a taste."

She looked into his eyes and hesitated. Almost without her knowing it, her hand moved slowly away from the icy glass of water to her chilled margarita glass.

"You won't be sorry," he promised in that silken baritone.

Toying with the slender green stem of her glass, she lifted it and then tentatively clinked it against his.

"To us," he said. "To new beginnings." He smiled benevolently, but his blue eyes were excessively brilliant.

Her first swallow of the margarita was salty, sweet and very strong. She knew she shouldn't drink any more. Then, almost at once, a pleasant warmth buzzed through her, softening her attitude toward him and weakening her willpower. Somewhere the mariachis began to play "La Paloma," a favorite love song of hers. Was it a sign?

"I'm glad you at least took a sip," he said, his gaze lingering on her lips a second too long. "It would be a pity to miss tasting something so delicious."

"You're right. It's really quite good."

"The best—all the more reason not to miss it. One can't retrace one's journey in this life. We must make the most of every moment…because once lost, those moments are gone forever."

"Indeed." Eyeing him, she sipped again. "Funny, I hadn't thought of you as a philosopher."

"You might be surprised by who I really am, if you took the trouble to get to know me."

"I doubt it."

Every muscle in his handsome face tensed. When his eyes darkened, she wondered if she'd wounded him.

No. Impossible.

Her nerves jingled, urging her to consider just one more sip of the truly delicious margarita. What could it hurt? That second sip led to a third, then another and another, each sliding down her throat more easily than the last. She hardly noticed when Quinn moved from his side of the booth to hers, and yet how could she not notice? He didn't touch her, yet it was thrilling to be so near him, to know that only their clothes separated her thigh from his, to wonder what he would do next.

His gaze never strayed from her. Focusing on her exclusively, he told her stories about his youth, about the time before his father had died. His father had played ball with him, he said, had taken him hunting and fishing, had helped him with his homework. He stayed off the grim subjects of his parents' divorce and his father's death.

"When school was out for any reason, he always took me to his office. He was determined to instill a work ethic in me."

"He sounds like the perfect father," she said wistfully. "I never seemed to be able to please mine. If he read to me, I fidgeted too much, and he would lose his place and his temper. If he took me fishing, I grew bored or hot and squirmed too much, kicking over the minnow bucket or snapping his line. Once I stood up too fast and turned the boat over."

"Maybe I won't take you fishing."

"He always wanted a son, and I didn't please Mother any better. She thought Jaycee, who loved to dress up and go to parties, was perfect. She still does. Neither of them like what I'm doing with my life."

"Well, they're not in control, are they? No one is, really. And just when we think we are, we usually get struck by a lightning bolt that shows us we're not," Quinn said in a silken tone that made her breath quicken. "Like tonight."

"What do you mean?"

"Us."

Her gaze fixed on his dimple. "Are you coming on to me?"

He laid his hand on top of hers. "Would that be so terrible?"

By the time they'd been seated at their dinner table and had ordered their meal, she'd lost all her fear of him. She was actually enjoying herself.

Usually, she dated guys who couldn't afford to take her out to eat very often, so she cooked for them in her apartment. Even though this meal was not a date, it was nice to dine in a pleasant restaurant and be served for a change.

When Quinn said how sorry he was that they hadn't met before that afternoon when he'd nearly run her down, she answered truthfully, "I thought you were marrying my sister solely to hurt all of us. I couldn't condone that."

He frowned. "And you love your sister so much, you came to my office today to try to find a way to stop me from marrying her."

"I was a fool to admit that to you."

"I think you're sweet, and I admire your honesty. You were right to come. You did me one helluva favor. I've been on the wrong course. But I don't want to talk about Jacinda. I want to talk about you."

"But will you think about...not marrying her?"

When he nodded and said, "Definitely," in a very convincing manner, she relaxed and took still another sip of her margarita with no more thoughts of how dangerous it might be for her to continue relaxing around him.

When he reached across the table and wrapped her hand in his warm, blunt fingers, the shock of his touch sent a wave of heat through her whole body. For a second, she entwined her fingers with his and clung as if he were a vital lifeline. Then, when she realized what she was doing, she wrenched her hand free.

"Why are you so afraid of me, Kira?"

"You might still marry Jaycee and ruin her life," she lied.

"Impossible, now that I've met you."

Kira's breath quickened. Dimple or not, he was still the enemy. She had to remember that.

"Do you really think I'm so callous I could marry your sister when I want you so much?"

"But what are you going to do about Jaycee?"

"I told you. She became irrelevant the minute I saw you standing inside my office this afternoon."

"She's beautiful...and *blonde*."

"Yes, but your beauty affects me more. Don't you know that?"

She shook her head. "The truth isn't in you. You only date blondes."

"Then it must be time for a change."

"I'm going to confess a secret wish. All my life I wished I was blonde...so I'd look more like the rest of my family, especially my mother and my sister. I thought maybe then I'd feel like I belonged."

"You *are* beautiful."

"A man like you would say anything…"

"I've never lied to any woman. Don't you know how incredibly lovely you are? With your shining dark eyes that show your sweet, pure soul every time you look at me and defend your sister? I feel your love for her rushing through you like liquid electricity. You're graceful. You move like a ballerina. I love the way you feel so intensely and blush when you think I might touch you."

"Like a child."

"No. Like a responsive, passionate woman. I like that… too much. And your hair…it's long and soft and shines like chestnut satin. Yet there's fire in it. I want to run my hands through it."

"But we hardly know one another. And I've hated you…"

"None of the Murrays have been favorites of mine either…but I'm beginning to see the error of my ways. And I don't think you hate me as much as you pretend."

Kira stared at him, searching his hard face for some sign that he was lying to her, seducing her as he'd seduced all those other women, saying these things because he had some dark agenda. All she saw was warmth and honesty and intense emotion. Nobody had ever looked at her with such hunger or made her feel so beautiful.

All her life she'd wanted someone to make her feel this special. It was ironic that Quinn Sullivan should be the one.

"I thought you were so bad, no…pure evil," she repeated.

His eyebrows arched. "Ouch."

If he'd been twisted in his original motives, maybe it

had been because of the grief he'd felt at losing someone he loved.

"How could I have been so wrong about you?" Even as she said it, some part of her wondered if she weren't being naive. He had dated, and jilted, all those beautiful women. He had intended to take revenge on her father and use her sister in his plan. Maybe when she'd walked into his office she'd become part of his diabolical plan, too.

"I was misguided," he said.

"I need more time to think about all this. Like I said…a mere hour or two ago I heartily disliked you. Or at least I thought I did."

"Because you didn't know me. Hell, maybe I didn't know me either…because everything is different now, since I met you."

She felt the same way. But she knew she should slow it down, reassess.

"I'm not good at picking boyfriends," she whispered.

"Their loss."

His hand closed over hers and he pressed her fingers, causing a melting sensation in her tummy. "My gain."

Her tacos came, looking and smelling delicious, but she hardly touched them. Her every sense was attuned to Quinn's carved features and his beautiful voice.

When a musician came to their table, Quinn hired him to sing several songs, including "La Paloma." While the man serenaded her, Quinn idly stroked her wrist and the length of her fingers, causing fire to shoot down her spine.

She met his eyes and felt that she had known him always, that he was already her lover, her soul mate. She was crazy to feel such things and think such thoughts about a man she barely knew, but when dinner was over, they skipped dessert.

An hour later, she sat across from him in his downtown

loft, sipping coffee while he drank brandy. In vain, she tried to act unimpressed by his art collection and sparkling views of the city. Not easy, since both were impressive.

His entrance was filled with an installation of crimson light by one of her favorite artists. The foyer was a dazzling ruby void that opened into a living room with high, white ceilings. All the rooms of his apartment held an eclectic mix of sculpture, porcelains and paintings.

Although she hadn't yet complimented his stylish home, she couldn't help but compare her small, littered apartment to his spacious one. Who was she to label him an arrogant upstart? He was a success in the international oil business and a man of impeccable taste, while she was still floundering in her career and struggling to find herself.

"I wanted to be alone with you like this the minute I saw you today," he said.

She shifted uneasily on his cream-leather sofa. Yet more evidence that he was a planner. "Well, I didn't."

"I think you did. You just couldn't let yourself believe you did."

"No," she whispered, setting down her cup. With difficulty she tried to focus on her mission. "So, what about Jaycee? You're sure that's over?"

"Finished. From the first moment I saw you."

"Without mud all over my face."

He laughed. "Actually, you got to me that day, too. Every time I dined with Jacinda and your family, I kept hoping I'd meet you again."

Even as she remembered all those dinner invitations her parents had extended and she'd declined, she couldn't believe he was telling the truth.

"I had my team research you," he said.

"Why?"

"I asked myself the same question. I think you intrigued

me…like I said, even with mud on your face. First thing tomorrow, I will break it off with Jacinda formally. Which means you've won. Does that make you happy? You have what you came for."

He was all charm, especially his warm, white smile. Like a child with a new playmate, she was happy just being with him, but she couldn't admit that to him.

He must have sensed her feelings, though, because he got up and moved silently toward her. "I feel like I've lived my whole life since my father's death alone—until you. And that's how I wanted to live—until you."

She knew it was sudden and reckless, but she felt the same way. If she wasn't careful, she would forget all that should divide them.

As if in a dream, she took his hand when he offered it and kissed his fingers with feverish devotion.

"You've made me realize how lonely I've been," he said.

"That's a very good line."

"It's the truth."

"But you are so successful, while I…"

"Look what you're doing in the interim—helping a friend to realize her dream."

"My father says I'm wasting my potential."

"You will find yourself…if you are patient." He cupped her chin and stared into her eyes. Again she felt that uncanny recognition. He was a kindred soul who knew what it was to feel lost.

"Dear God," he muttered. "Don't listen to me. I don't know a damn thing about patience. Like now… I should let you go…but I can't."

He pulled her to him and crushed her close. It wasn't long before holding her wasn't enough. He had to have her lips, her throat, her breasts. She felt the same way. Shedding her shirt, scarf and bra, she burst into flame as he kissed her. Even though she barely knew him, she could not wait another moment to belong to him.

"I'm not feeling so patient right now myself," she admitted huskily.

Do not give yourself to this man, said an inner voice. *Remember all those blondes. Remember his urge for revenge.*

Even as her emotions spiraled out of control, she knew she was no femme fatale, while he was a devastatingly attractive man. Had he said all these same wonderful things to all those other women he'd bedded? Had he done and felt all the same things, too, a thousand times before? Were nights like this routine for him, while he was the first to make her feel so thrillingly alive?

But then his mouth claimed hers again, and again, with a fierce, wild hunger that made her forget her doubts and shake and cling to him. His kisses completed her as she'd never been completed before. He was a wounded soul, and she understood his wounds. How could she feel so much when they hadn't even made love?

Lifting her into his arms, he carried her into his vast bedroom, which was bathed in silver moonlight. Over her shoulder she saw his big, black bed in the middle of an ocean of white marble and Persian carpets.

He was a driven, successful billionaire, and she was a waitress. Feeling out of her depth, her nerves returned. Not knowing what else to do, she pressed a fingertip to his lips. Gently, shyly, she traced his dimple.

Feeling her tension, he set her down. She pushed against his chest and then took a step away from him. Watching her, he said, "You can finish undressing in the bathroom if you'd prefer privacy. Or we can stop. I'll drive you to your car. Your choice."

She should have said, "I don't belong here with you,"

and accepted his gallant offer. Instead, without a word, she scampered toward the door he'd indicated. Alone in his beige marble bathroom with golden fixtures and a lovely, compelling etching by another one of her favorite artists, she barely recognized her own flushed face, tousled hair and sparkling eyes.

The radiant girl in his tall mirror *was* as beautiful as an enchanted princess. She looked expectant, excited. Maybe she did belong here with him. Maybe he was the beginning of her new life, the first correct step toward the bright future that had so long eluded her.

When she tiptoed back into the bedroom, wearing nothing but his white robe, he was in bed. She couldn't help admiring the width of his bronzed shoulders as he leaned back against several plumped pillows. She had never dated anyone half so handsome; she'd never felt anything as powerful as the glorious heady heat that suffused her entire being as his blue eyes studied her hungrily. Still, she was nervy, shaking.

"I'm no good at sex," she said. "You're probably very good... Of course you are. You're good at everything."

"Come here," he whispered.

"But..."

"Just come to me. You could not possibly delight me more. Surely you know that."

Did he really feel as much as she did?

Removing his bathrobe, she flew to him before she lost her nerve, fell into his bed and into his arms, consumed by forces beyond her control. Nothing mattered but sliding against his long body, being held close in his strong arms. Beneath the covers, his heat was delicious and welcoming as she nestled against him.

He gave her a moment to settle before he rolled on top of her. Bracing himself with his elbows against the mattress, so as not to crush her, he kissed her lips, her cheeks, her brows and then her eyelids with urgent yet featherlike strokes. Slowly, gently, each kiss was driving her mad.

"Take me," she whispered, in the grip of a fever such as she'd never experienced before. "I want you inside me. Now."

"I know," he said, laughing. "I'm as ravenous as you are. But have patience, darlin'."

"You have a funny way of showing your hunger."

"If I do what you ask, it would be over in a heartbeat. This moment, our first time together, is too special to me."

Was she special?

"We must savor it, draw it out, make it last," he said.

"Maybe I want it to be over swiftly," she begged. "Maybe this obsessive need is unbearable."

"Exquisite expectation?"

"I can't stand it."

"And I want to heighten it. Which means we're at cross-purposes."

He didn't take her. With infinite care and maddening patience he adored her with his clever mouth and skilled hands. His fevered lips skimmed across her soft skin, raising goose bumps in secret places. As she lay beneath him, he licked each nipple until it grew hard, licked her navel until he had all her nerve endings on fire for him. Then he kissed her belly and dived even lower to explore those hidden, honey-sweet lips between her legs. When she felt his tongue dart inside, she gasped and drew back.

"Relax," he whispered.

With slow, hot kisses, he made her gush. All too soon her embarrassment was gone, and she was melting, shivering, whimpering—all but begging him to give her release.

Until tonight she had been an exile in the world of love. With all other men, not that there had been that many, she had been going through the motions, playing a part, searching always for something meaningful and never finding it.

Until now, tonight, with him.

He couldn't matter this much! She couldn't let this be more than fierce, wild sex. He, the man, couldn't matter. But her building emotions told her that he did matter—in ways she'd never imagined possible before.

He took her breast in his mouth and suckled again. Then his hand entered her heated wetness, making her gasp helplessly and plead. When he stroked her, his fingers sliding against that secret flesh, she arched against his expert touch, while her breath came in hard, tortured pants.

Just when she didn't think she could bear it any longer, he dragged her beneath him and slid inside her. He was huge, massive, wonderful. Crying out, she clung to him and pushed her pelvis against his, aching for him to fill her even more deeply. *Yes! Yes!*

When he sank deeper, ever deeper, she moaned. For a long moment he held her and caressed her. Then he began to plunge in and out, slowly at first. Her rising pleasure carried her and shook her in sharp, hot waves, causing her to climax and scream his name.

He went crazy when she dug her nails in his shoulder. Then she came again, and again, sobbing. She had no idea how many climaxes she had before she felt his hard loins bunch as he exploded.

Afterward, sweat dripped off his brow. His whole body was flushed, burning up, and so was hers.

"Darlin' Kira," he whispered in that husky baritone that could still make her shiver even when she was spent. "Darlin' Kira."

For a long time, she lay in his arms, not speaking, feeling too weak to move any part of her body. Then he leaned over and nibbled at her bottom lip.

The second time he made love to her, he did so with a reverent gentleness that made her weep and hold on to him for a long time afterward. He'd used a condom the second time, causing her to realize belatedly that he hadn't the first time.

How could they have been so careless? She had simply been swept away. Maybe he had, too. Well, it was useless to worry about that now. Besides, she was too happy, too relaxed to care about anything except being in his arms. There was no going back.

For a long time they lay together, facing each other while they talked. He told her about his father's financial crisis and how her father had turned on him and made things worse. He spoke of his mother's extravagance and betrayal and his profound hurt that his world had fallen apart so quickly and brutally. She listened as he explained how grief, poverty and helplessness had twisted him and made him hard.

"Love made me too vulnerable, as it did my father. It was a destructive force. My father loved my mother, and it ruined him. She was greedy and extravagant," he said. "Love destroys the men in our family."

"If you don't want to love, why did you date all those women I read about?"

"I wasn't looking for love, and neither were they."

"You were just using them, then?"

"They were using me, too."

"That's so cynical."

"That's how my life has been. I loved my father so much, and I hurt so much when he died, I gave up on love. He loved my mother, and she broke his heart with her unrelenting demands. When he lost the business, she lost interest in him and began searching for a richer man."

"And did she find him?"

"Several."

"Do you ever see her?"

"No. I was an accident she regretted, I believe. She couldn't relate to children, and after I was grown, I had no interest in her. Love, no matter what kind, always costs too much. I do write her a monthly check, however."

"So, my father was only part of your father's problem."

"But a big part. Losing ownership in Sullivan and Murray Oil made my father feel like he was less than nothing. My mother left him because of that loss. She stripped him of what little wealth and self-esteem he had left. Alone, without his company or his wife, he grew depressed. He wouldn't eat. He couldn't sleep. I'd hear the stairs creak as he paced at night.

"Then early one morning I heard a shot. When I called his name, he didn't answer. I found him in the shop attached to our garage. In a pool of blood on the floor, dead. I still don't know if it was an accident or...what I feared it was. He was gone. At first I was frightened. Then I became angry. I wanted to blame someone, to get even, to make his death right. I lived for revenge. But now that I've almost achieved my goal of taking back Murray Oil, it's as if my fever's burned out."

"Oh, I wouldn't say that," she teased, touching his damp brow.

"I mean my fever for revenge, which was what kept me going."

"So," she asked, "what will you live for now?"

"I don't know. I guess a lot of people just wake up in the morning and go to work, then come home at night and drink while they flip channels with their remote."

"Not you."

"Who's to say? Maybe such people are lucky. At least they're not driven by hate, as I was."

"I can't even begin to imagine what that must have felt like for you." She'd always been driven by the need for love.

When he stared into her eyes with fierce longing, she pulled him close and ran her hands through his hair. "You are young yet. You'll find something to give your life meaning," she said.

"Well, it won't be love, because I've experienced love's dark side for too many years. I want you to know that. You are special, but I can't ever love you, no matter how good we are together. I'm no longer capable of that emotion."

"So you keep telling me," she said, pretending his words didn't hurt.

"I just want to be honest."

"Do we always know our own truths?"

"Darlin'," he whispered. "Forgive me if I sounded too harsh. It's just that…I don't want to hurt you by raising your expectations about something I'm incapable of. Other women have become unhappy because of the way I am."

"You're my family's enemy. Why would I ever want to love you?"

Wrapping her legs around him, she held him for hours, trying to comfort the boy who'd lost so much as well as the angry man who'd gained a fortune because he'd been consumed by a fierce, if misplaced, hatred.

"My father had nothing to do with your father's death," she whispered. "He didn't."

"You have your view, and I have mine," he said. "The important thing is that I don't hold you responsible for your father's sins any longer."

"Don't you?"

"No."

After that, he was silent. Soon afterward he let her go and rolled onto his side.

She lay awake for hours. Where would they go from here? He had hated her family for years. Had he really let go of all those harsh feelings? Had she deluded herself into thinking he wasn't her enemy?

What price would she pay for sleeping with a man who probably only saw her as an instrument for revenge?

Three

When Kira woke up naked in bed with Quinn, she felt unsettled and very self-conscious. Propping herself on an elbow, she watched him warily in the dim rosy half light of dawn. All her doubts returned a hundredfold.

How could she have let things go this far? How could she have risked pregnancy?

What if… No, she couldn't be that unlucky.

Besides, it did no good to regret what had happened, she reminded herself again. If she hadn't slept with him she would never have known such ecstasy was possible.

Now, at least, she knew. Even if it wasn't love, it had been so great she felt an immense tenderness well up in her in spite of her renewed doubts.

He was absurdly handsome with his thick, unruly black hair falling across his brow, with his sharp cheekbones and sculpted mouth. She'd been touched when he'd shown her his vulnerability last night. Just looking at him now was enough to make her stomach flutter with fresh desire.

She was about to stroke his hair, when, without warning, his obscenely long lashes snapped open, and he met her gaze with that directness that still startled her. Maybe because there were so many imperfections she wanted to keep hidden. In the next instant, his expression softened, disarming her.

"Good morning, darlin'." His rough, to-die-for, sexy baritone caressed her.

A jolt sizzled through her even before he reached out a bronzed hand to pull her face to his so he could kiss her lightly on the lips. Never had she wanted anyone as much as she wanted him.

"I haven't brushed my teeth," she warned.

"Neither the hell have I. I don't expect you to be perfect. I simply want you. I can't do without you. You should know that after last night."

She was amazed because she felt exactly the same. Still, with those doubts still lingering, she felt she had to protect herself by protesting.

"Last night was probably a mistake," she murmured.

"Maybe. Or maybe it's a complication, a challenge. Or a good thing. In any case, it's too late to worry about it. I want you more now than ever."

"But for how long?"

"Is anything certain?"

He kissed her hard. Before she could protest again, he rolled on top of her and was inside her, claiming her fiercely, his body piercing her to the bed, his massive erection filling her. When he rode her violently, she bucked like a wild thing, too, her doubts dissolving like mist as primal desire swept her past reason.

"I'm sorry," he said afterward. "I wanted you too much."

He had, however, at the last second, remembered to use a condom. This time, he didn't hold her tenderly or make small talk or confide sweet nothings as he had last night. In fact, he seemed hellishly annoyed at himself.

Was he already tired of her? Would there be a new blonde in his bed tonight? At the thought, a sob caught in her throat.

"You can have the master bathroom. I'll make coffee," he said tersely.

Just like that, he wanted her gone. Since she'd researched him and had known his habits, she shouldn't feel shocked or hurt. Hadn't he warned her he was incapable of feeling close to anyone? She should be grateful for the sublime sexual experience and let the rest go.

Well, she had her pride. She wasn't about to cling to him or show that she cared. But she did care. Oh, how she cared. Her family's worst enemy had quickly gained a curious hold on her heart.

Without a word, she rose and walked naked across the vast expanse of thick, white carpet, every female cell vividly aware that, bored with her though he might be, he didn't tear his eyes from her until she reached the bathroom and shut the door. Once inside she turned the lock and leaned heavily against the wall in a state of collapse.

She took a deep breath and stared at her pale, guilt-stricken reflection, so different from the glowing wanton of last night.

She'd known the kind of guy he was, in spite of his seductive words. How could she have opened herself to such a hard man? Her father's implacable enemy?

What had she done?

By the time she'd showered, brushed her hair and dressed, he was in the kitchen, looking no worse for wear.

Indeed, he seemed energized by what they had shared. Freshly showered, he wore a white shirt and crisply pressed dark slacks. He'd shaved, and his glossy black hair was combed. He looked so civilized, she felt the crazy urge to run her hands through his hair, just to muss it up and leave her mark.

The television was on, and he was watching the latest stock market report while he held his cell phone against his ear. Behind him, a freshly made pot of aromatic coffee sat on the gleaming white counter.

She was about to step inside when he flicked the remote, killing the sound of the television. She heard his voice, as sharp and hard as it had been with the caller yesterday in his office.

"Habib, business is business," he snapped. "I know I have to convince the shareholders and the public I'm some shining white knight. That's why I agreed to marry a Murray daughter and why her parents, especially her father, who wants an easy transition of power, suggested Jacinda and persuaded her to accept me. However, if the older Murray sister agrees to marry me instead, why should it matter to you or to anyone else…other than to Jacinda, who will no doubt be delighted to have her life back?"

Habib, whoever he was, must have argued, because Quinn's next response was much angrier. "Yes, I know the family history and why you consider Jacinda the preferable choice, but since nobody else knows, apparently not even Kira, it's of no consequence. So, if I've decided to marry the older sister instead of the younger, and this decision will make the shareholders and employees just as happy, why the hell should you care?"

The man must have countered again, because Quinn's low tone was even more cutting. "No, I haven't asked her yet. It's too soon. But when I do, I'll remind her that I told her yesterday I'd demand a price for freeing her sister. She'll have to pay it, that's all. She'll have no choice but to do what's best for her family and her sister. Hell, she'll do anything for their approval."

One sister or the other—and he didn't care which one. That he could speak of marrying her instead of Jaycee as a cold business deal before he'd even bothered to propose made Kira's tender heart swell with hurt and outrage. That he would use her desire for her family's love and acceptance to his own advantage was too horrible to endure.

Obviously, she was that insignificant to him. But hadn't she known that? So why did it hurt so much?

He'd said she was special. Nobody had ever made her feel so cherished before.

Thinking herself a needy, romantic fool, she shut her eyes. Unready to face him or confess what she'd overheard and how much it bothered her, Kira backed out of the kitchen and returned to the bedroom. In her present state she was incapable of acting rationally and simply demanding an explanation.

He was a planner. Her seduction must have been a calculated move. No longer could she believe he'd been swept off his feet by her as she had by him. She was skinny and plain. He'd known she desired him, and he was using that to manipulate her.

Last night, when he'd promised he'd break it off with her sister, she'd never guessed the devious manner in which he'd planned to honor that promise.

She was still struggling to process everything she'd learned, when Quinn himself strode into the bedroom looking much too arrogant, masterful and self-satisfied for her liking.

"Good, you're dressed," he said in that beautiful voice. "You look gorgeous."

Refusing to meet the warmth of his admiring gaze for fear she might believe his compliment and thereby lose her determination to escape him, she nodded.

"I made coffee."

"Smells good," she whispered, staring out the window.

"Do you have time for breakfast?"

"No!"

"Something wrong?"

If he was dishonest, why should she bother to be straight with him? "I'm fine," she said, but in a softer tone.

"Right. That must be why you seem so cool."

"Indeed?"

"And they say men are the ones who withdraw the morning after."

She bit her lip to keep herself from screaming at him.

"Still, I understand," he said.

"Last night is going to take some getting used to," she said.

"For me, as well."

To that she said nothing.

"Well, the coffee's in the kitchen," he said, turning away.

Preferring to part from him without an argument, she followed him into the kitchen where he poured her a steaming cup and handed it to her.

"Do you take cream? Sugar?"

She shook her head. "We don't know the most basic things about each other, do we?"

"After last night, I'd have to disagree with you, darlin'."

She blushed in confusion. "Don't call me that."

He eyed her thoughtfully. "You really do seem upset."

She sipped from her cup, again choosing silence instead of arguing the point. Was he good at everything? Rich and strong, the coffee was to die for.

"For the record, I take mine black, very black," he said.

"Without sugar. So, we have that in common. And we have what we shared last night."

"Don't…"

"I'd say we're off to a great start."

Until I realized what you were up to, I would have agreed. She longed to claw him. Instead, she clenched her nails into her palms and chewed her lower lip mutinously.

The rosy glow from last night, when he'd made her feel so special, had faded. She felt awkward and unsure…and hurt, which was ridiculous because she'd gone into this knowing who and what he was.

Obviously, last night had been business as usual for him. Why not marry the Murray sister who'd practically thrown herself at him? Did he believe she was so smitten and desperate for affection she'd be more easily controlled?

Why had she let herself be swept away by his looks, his confidences and his suave, expert lovemaking?

Because, your stupid crush on him turned your brain to mush.

And turned her raging hormones to fire. Never had she felt so physically and spiritually in tune with anyone. She'd actually thought, at one point, that they could be soul mates.

Soul mates! It was all an illusion. You were a fool, girl, and not for the first time.

"Look, I'd really better go," she said, her tone so sharp his dark head jerked toward her.

"Right. Then I'll drive you, since you left your car downtown."

"I can call a cab."

"No! I'll drive you."

Silently, she nodded.

He led the way to stairs that went down to the elevator and garage. In silence, they sped along the freeway in his silver Aston Martin until he slowed to take the off-ramp that led to where she'd parked downtown. After that, she *had* to speak to him in order to direct him to her small, dusty Toyota with several dings in its beige body. She let out a little moan when he pulled up behind her car and she saw the parking ticket flapping under her windshield wipers.

He got out and raced around the hood to open her door, but before he could, she'd flung it open.

"You sure there isn't something wrong?" he asked.

She snatched the ticket, but before she could get in her car, he slid his arms around her waist from behind.

He felt so solid and strong and warm, she barely suppressed a sigh. She yearned to stay in his arms even though she knew she needed to get away from him as quickly as possible to regroup.

He turned her to face him and his fingertips traced the length of her cheek in a tender, burning caress, and for a long second he stared into her troubled eyes with a mixture of concern and barely suppressed impatience. He seemed to care.

Liar.

"It's not easy letting you go," he said.

"People are watching us," she said mildly, even as she seethed with outrage.

"So what? Last night was very special to me, Kira. I'm sorry if you're upset about it. I hope it's just that it all happened too fast. I wasn't too rough, was I?"

The concern in his voice shook her. "No." She looked away, too tempted to meet his gaze.

"It's never been like that for me. I…I couldn't control myself, especially this morning. I wanted you again… badly. This is all happening too fast for me, too. I prefer being able to plan."

That's not what he'd said on the phone. Quinn seemed to have damn sure had a plan. Marry a Murray daughter. And he was sticking to it.

"Yes, it is happening…too fast." She bit her lip. "But… I'm okay." She wanted to brush off his words, to pretend she didn't care that he'd apologized and seemed genuinely worried about her physical and emotional state. He seemed all too likable. She almost believed him.

"Do you have a business card?" he asked gently.

She shook her head. "Nope. At least, not on me."

He flipped a card out of his pocket. "Well, here is mine. You can call me anytime. I want to see you again…as soon as possible. There's something very important I want to discuss with you."

The intensity of his gaze made her heart speed up. "You are not going back on your word about marrying Jaycee, are you?"

"How can you even ask? I'll call it off as soon as I leave you. Unfortunately, after that, I have to be away on business for several days, first to New York, then London. Murray Oil is in the middle of negotiating a big deal with the European Union. My meeting tonight in New York ends at eight, so call me after that. On my cell."

Did he intend to propose over the phone? Her throat felt thick as she forced herself to nod. Whipping out a pen and a pad, she wrote down her cell phone number. "Will you text me as soon as you break up with my sister?"

"Can I take that to mean you care about me…a little?" he asked.

"Sure," she whispered, exhaling a pent-up breath. How did he lie so easily? "Take it any way you like."

She had to get away from him, to be alone to think. Everything he said, everything he did, made her want him—even though she knew, after what she'd heard this morning, that she'd never been anything but a pawn in the game he was playing to exact revenge against her father.

She wasn't special to him. And if she didn't stand up for herself now, she never would be.

She would not let her father sell Jaycee *or* her to this man!

Four

"You're her father. I still can't believe you don't have a clue where Kira could be. Hell, she's been gone for nearly three weeks."

Shaking his head, Earl stalked across Quinn's corner office at Murray Oil to look out the window. "I told you, she's probably off somewhere painting. She does that."

Quinn hated himself for having practically ordered the infuriating Murray to his office again today. But he was that desperate to know Kira was safe. Her safety aside, he had a wedding planned and a bride to locate.

"You're sure she's not in any trouble?"

"Are *you* sure she didn't realize you were about to demand that she marry you?"

Other than wanting Kira to take Jaycee's place, he wasn't sure about a damn thing! Well, except that maybe he'd pushed Kira too fast and too far. Hell, she could have overheard him talking to Habib. She'd damn sure gotten quiet and sulky before they parted ways.

"I don't think—"

"I'd bet money she got wise to you and decided to let you stew in your own juices. She may seem sweet and malleable, but she's always had a mind of her own. She's impossible to control. It's why she lost her job. It's why I suggested you choose Jaycee in the first place. Jaycee is biddable."

Quinn felt heat climb his neck. He didn't want Jaycee. He'd never wanted Jaycee. He wanted Kira...sweet, passionate Kira who went wild every time he touched her. Her passion thrilled him as nothing else had in years.

The trouble was, after he'd made love to her that morning, he'd felt completely besotted and then out of sorts as a result. He hadn't wanted to dwell on what feeling such an all-consuming attraction so quickly might mean. Now he knew that if anything had happened to her, he'd never forgive himself.

"I couldn't ask her to marry me after our dinner. It was too soon. Hell, maybe she did figure it all out and run off before I could explain."

"Well, I checked our hunting lodges at the ranch where she goes to paint wildlife, and I've left messages with my caretaker at the island where she paints birds. Nobody's seen her. Sooner or later she'll turn up. She always does. You'll just have to be patient."

"Not my forte."

"Quinn, she's okay. When she's in between museum jobs, she runs around like this. She's always been a free spirit."

"Right." Quinn almost growled. He disliked that the other man could see he was vulnerable and crazed by Kira's disappearance. The need to find her, to find out why she'd vanished, had been building inside him. He couldn't go on if he didn't solve this mystery—and not just because the wedding date loomed.

His one night with Kira had been the closest thing to perfection he'd known since before his dad had died. Never had he experienced with any other woman anything like what he'd shared with Kira. Hell, he hadn't known such closeness was possible. He'd lost himself completely in her, talked to her as he'd never talked to another person.

Even though she'd seemed distant the next morning, he'd thought she'd felt the same wealth of emotion he had and was running scared. But no—something else had made her vanish without a word, even before he'd told her she'd have to marry him if Jaycee didn't. Thinking back, all he could imagine was that she'd felt vulnerable and afraid after their shared night—or that she *had* overheard him talking to Habib.

Then the day after he'd dropped her at her car, Quinn had texted her, as he'd promised, to let her know he'd actually broken it off with Jacinda. She'd never called him back. Nor had she answered her phone since then. She'd never returned to her tiny apartment or her place of employment.

Kira had called her friend Betty to check in, and promised she'd call weekly to keep in touch, but she hadn't given an explanation for her departure or an estimation for when she'd return.

Quinn had to rethink his situation. He'd stopped romancing Jacinda, but he hadn't canceled the wedding because he planned to marry Kira instead. Come Saturday, a thousand people expected him to marry a Murray daughter.

Apparently, his future father-in-law's mind was running along the same worrisome track.

"Quinn, you've got to be reasonable. We've got to call off the wedding," Earl said.

"I'm going to marry Kira."

"You're talking nonsense. Kira's gone. Without a bride, you're going to piss off the very people we want to reassure. Stockholders, clients and employees of Murray Oil. Not to mention—this whole thing is stressing the hell out of Vera, and in her condition that isn't good."

Several months earlier, when Quinn had stalked into Earl's office with enough shares to demand control of Murray Oil, Earl, his eyes blurry and his shoulders slumped, had sat behind his desk already looking defeated.

The older man had wearily confided that his wife was seriously ill. Not only had Earl not cared that Quinn would soon be in charge of Murray Oil, he'd said the takeover was the answer to a prayer. It was time he retired. With Murray Oil in good hands, he could devote himself to his beloved wife, who was sick and maybe dying.

"She's everything to me," he'd whispered. "The way your father was to you and the way your mother was to him before she left him."

"Why tell me—your enemy?" Quinn had asked.

"I don't think of you as my enemy. I never was one to see the world in black or white, the way Kade, your dad, did—the way you've chosen to see it since his death. Whether you believe me or not, I loved your father, and I was sorry about our misunderstanding. You're just like him, you know, so now that I've got my own challenge to face, there's nobody I'd rather turn the company over to than you.

"Vera doesn't want me talking about her illness to friends and family. She can't stand the thought of people, even her daughters, thinking of her as weak and sick. I'm glad I finally have someone I can tell."

Quinn had been stunned. For years, he had hated Earl, had wanted revenge, had looked forward to bringing the man to his knees. But ever since that conversation his feelings had begun to change. The connection he'd found with Kira had hastened that process.

He'd begun to rethink his choices, reconsider his past. Not all his memories of Earl were negative. He could remember some wonderful times hunting and fishing with the blunt-spoken Earl and his dad. As a kid, he'd loved the stories Earl had told around the campfire.

Maybe the bastard had been partially responsible for his father's death. But maybe an equal share of the blame lay with his own father.

Not that Quinn trusted his new attitude. He'd gone too far toward his goal of vengeance not to seize Murray Oil. And he still believed taking a Murray bride would make the acquisition run more smoothly.

"I will get married on Saturday," Quinn said. "All we have to do is convince Kira to come back and marry me."

"Right. But how? We don't even know where she is."

"We don't have to know. All we have to do is motivate her to return," Quinn said softly.

Seabirds raced along the beach, pecking at seaweed. Her jeans rolled to her knees, Kira stood in the shallow surf of Murray Island and wiggled her toes in the cool, damp sand as the wind whipped her hair against her cheeks. Blowing sand stung her bare arms and calves.

Kira needed to make her weekly phone call to Betty after her morning walk—a phone call she dreaded. Each week, it put her back in touch with reality, which was what she wanted to escape from.

Still, she'd known she couldn't stay on the island forever. She'd just thought that solitude would have cleared her head of Quinn by now. But it hadn't. She missed him.

Three weeks of being here alone had changed nothing. None of her confusion or despair about her emotional entanglement with Quinn had lifted.

Maybe if she hadn't been calling Betty to check in, she would be calmer. Betty had told her about Quinn's relentless visits to the restaurant. Thinking about Quinn looking for her had stirred up her emotions and had blocked her artistically. All she could paint was his handsome face.

Well, at least she was painting. When she'd been frustrated while working at the museum, she hadn't even been able to hold a paintbrush.

Since it was past time to call Betty again, she headed for the family beach house. When she climbed the wooden stairs and entered, the wind caught the screen door and banged it behind her.

She turned on her cell phone and climbed to the second floor where the signal and the views of the high surf were better.

Betty answered on the first ring. "You still okay all alone out there?"

"I'm fine. How's Rudy?"

She'd packed her cat and his toys and had taken him to Betty's, much to his dismay.

"Rudy's taken over as usual. Sleeps in my bed. He's right here. He can hear your voice on speakerphone. He's very excited, twitchin' his tail and all." She paused, then, "I worry about you out there alone, Kira."

"Jim's around. He checks on me."

Jim was the island's caretaker. She'd taken him into her confidence and asked him not to tell anyone, not even her father, where she was.

"Well, there's something I need to tell you, something I've been dreadin' tellin' you," Betty began.

"What?"

"That fella of yours, Quinn…"

"He's not my fella."

"Well, he sure acts like he's your guy when he drops by. He's been drillin' the staff, makin' sure you weren't datin' anyone. Said he didn't want to lay claim to a woman who belonged to another."

Lay claim? Kira caught her breath. Just thinking about Quinn in the restaurant looking for her made her breasts swell and her heart throb.

Darn it—would she never forget him?

"Well, today he comes over just as I'm unlocking the door and launches into a tirade about how he's gonna have to break his promise to you and marry your sister, Jaycee! This Saturday!

"I thought it right funny at first, him sayin' that, when he comes by lookin' haunted, askin' after you all the time, so I said up front I didn't buy it. Called him a liar, I did.

"He said maybe he preferred you, but you'd forced his hand. He had to marry a Murray daughter for business reasons, so he would. Everything is set. He told me to read the newspapers, if I didn't believe him. And I did. They're really getting married. It's all over the internet, too."

"What?"

"Tomorrow! Saturday! I know he told you he broke off his wedding plans, but if he did, they're on again. He's every bit as bad as you said. You were right to go away. If I was you, I'd never come back."

So, since he'd never cared which Murray sister he married, he was going to marry Jaycee after all.

Well, she'd stop him. She'd go back—at once—and she'd stop him cold.

Five

A sign in front of the church displayed a calendar that said Murray-Sullivan Wedding: 7:30 p.m.

It was five-thirty as Kira swung into the mostly empty parking lot.

Good. No guests had arrived. She'd made it in time.

The sun was low; the shadows long; the light a rosy gold. Not that she took the time to notice the clarity of the light or the rich green of the grass or the tiny spring leaves budding on the trees. Her heart was pounding. She was perspiring as she hit the brakes and jumped out of her Toyota.

The drive from the coast hadn't taken much more than three hours, but the trip had tired her. Feeling betrayed and yet desperate to find her sister and stop this travesty before it was too late, Kira ran toward the back of the church where the dressing rooms were. Inside, dashing from room to room, she threw open doors, calling her sister's name. Then, suddenly, in the last room, she found Jaycee, wearing a blue cotton dress with a strand of pearls at her throat. With her blond hair cascading down her back, Jaycee sat quietly in front of a long, gilt mirror, applying lipstick. She looked as if she'd been carefully posed by a photographer.

"Jaycee!" Kira cried breathlessly. "At last… Why aren't you wearing…a wedding dress?"

Then she saw the most beautiful silk gown seeded with tiny pearls lying across a sofa and a pair of white satin shoes on the floor.

"Oh, but that's why you're here…to dress… Of course. Where's Mother? Why isn't Mother here to help you?"

"She's not feeling well. I think she's resting. Mother and Quinn told me to wait here."

Odd. Usually when it came to organizing any social affair, their mother had endless reserves of energy that lasted her until the very end of the event.

"Where are your bridesmaids?"

Turning like an actress compelled by her cue, Jaycee pressed her lips together and then put her lipstick inside her blue purse. "I was so worried you wouldn't come," she said. "I was truly afraid you wouldn't show. We all were. Quinn most especially. But me, too. He'll be so happy you're here. I don't know what he would have done if you hadn't gotten here in time. You don't know how important you are to him."

Right. That's why he's marrying you without a qualm.

As always, Jaycee worried about everyone she loved. Kira very much doubted that Quinn would be happy with her once she finished talking to Jaycee.

Guilt flooded Kira. How would she ever find the words to explain to her trusting sister why she couldn't marry Quinn? Jaycee, who'd always been loved by everybody, probably couldn't imagine there was a soul in the world who wouldn't love her if she tried hard enough to win him. After all, Daddy had given his blessing.

"You can't marry Quinn today," Kira stated flatly.

"I know that. He told me all about you two. When Daddy asked me to marry Quinn, I tried to tell myself it was the right thing to do. For the family and all. But…when I found out he wanted to marry you…it was such a relief."

"Why did you show up here today if you knew all this?"

"Quinn will…explain everything." Jaycee's eyes widened as the door opened. Kira whirled to tell their visitor that this was a private conversation, but her words died in a convulsive little growl. Quinn, dressed in a tux that set off his broad shoulders and stunning dark looks to heart-stopping perfection, strode masterfully into the room.

Feeling cornered, Kira sank closer to Jaycee. When he saw her, he stopped, his eyes flashing with hurt and anger before he caught her mood and stiffened.

"I was hoping you'd make it in time for the wedding," he said, his deep baritone cutting her to the quick.

"Damn you!" Her throat tightened as she arose. "Liar! How could you do this?"

"I'm thrilled to see you, too, darlin'," he murmured, his gaze devouring her. "You do look lovely."

Kira, who'd driven straight from the island without making a single stop, was wearing a pair of worn, tight jeans and a T-shirt that hugged her curves. She hadn't bothered with makeup or a comb for her tangled hair. She could do nothing but take in a mortified breath at his comment while she stared at his dark face, the face she'd painted so many times even when images of him had blurred through her tears.

"What is the meaning of this?" she screamed.

"There's no need for hysterics, darlin'," he said calmly.

"Don't *darlin'* me! You have no right to call me that!"

she shrieked. "I haven't even begun to show you hysterics! I'm going to tear you limb from limb. Pound you into this tile floor... Skin you alive—"

"Kira, Quinn's been so worried about you. Frantic that you wouldn't show up in time," Jaycee began. "Talk about wedding jitters. He's had a full-blown case..."

"I'll just bet he has!"

"I see we misunderstand each other, Kira. I was afraid of this. Jacinda," he said in a silky tone that maddened Kira further because it made her feel jealous of her innocent sister, "could you give us a minute? I need to talk to Kira alone."

With a quick, nervous glance in Kira's direction, Jaycee said, "Kira, are you sure you'll be okay? You don't look so good."

Kira nodded mutely, wanting to spare Jaycee any necessary embarrassment. So Jaycee slipped out of the room and closed the door quietly.

Her hand raised, Kira bounded toward him like a charging lioness ready to claw her prey, but he caught her wrist and used it to lever her closer.

"Let me go!" she cried.

"Not while you're in such a violent mood, darlin'. You'd only scratch me or do something worse that you'd regret."

"I don't think so."

"This storm will pass, as all storms do. You'll see. Because it's due to a misunderstanding."

"A misunderstanding? I don't think so! You promised you'd break up with my sister, and I, being a fool, believed you. Then you slept with me. How could you go back on a promise like that after what we—"

"I wouldn't. I didn't." His voice was calm, dangerously soft. "I've kept my promise."

"Liar. If I hadn't shown up, you would have married my sister."

"The hell I would have! It was a bluff. How else could I get you to come back to San Antonio? I was going mad not knowing where you were or if you were all right. If you hadn't shown up, I would have looked like a fool, but I wouldn't have married your sister."

"But the newspapers all say you're going to marry her. Here. Today."

"I know what they say because my people wrote the press releases. That was all part of the bluff—to get you here. We'll have to write a correction now, won't we? The only Murray sister I plan to marry today is you, darlin'. If it'll help to convince you, I'll repeat myself on bended knee."

When he began to kneel, she shrieked at him, "Don't you dare…or I'll kick you. This is not a proposal. This is a farce."

"I'm asking you to marry me, darlin'."

He didn't love her. He never would. His was a damaged soul. He'd told her that in plain, hurtful terms right after he'd made love to her.

The details of the conversation she'd overheard came back to her.

"Let me get this straight," she said. "You always intended to marry a Murray daughter."

"And your father suggested Jaycee because he thought she would agree more easily."

"Then I came to your office and asked you not to marry her, and after dinner and sex, you decided one sister was as good as the other. So, why not marry the *easy* sister? Is that about it?"

"Easy?" He snorted. "I wish to hell you were easy, but no, you disappeared for weeks."

"Back to the basics. Marrying one of the Murray daughters is about business and nothing more to you?"

"In the beginning…maybe that was true…"

"I repeat—I heard you talking to Habib, whoever the hell he is, the morning after we made love. And your conversation made it seem that your relationship with me, with any Murray daughter, was still about business. Your voice was cold, matter-of-fact and all too believable."

"Habib works for me. Why would I tell him how I felt when I'd only known you a day and was still reeling, trying to figure it out for myself?"

"Oh, so now you're Mr. Sensitive. Well, I don't believe you, and I won't marry you. I've always dreamed of marrying for love. I know that is an emotion you despise and are incapable of feeling. Maybe that's why you can be so high-handed about forcing me to take my sister's place and marry you. I think you…are despicable…and cold. This whole situation is too cynical for words."

"It's true that our marriage will make Murray Oil employees see this change of leadership in a less hostile way, as for the rest—"

"So, for you, it's business. I will not be bought and sold like so many shares of stock. I am a human being. An educated, Western woman with a woman's dreams and feelings."

"I know that. It's what makes you so enchanting."

"Bull. You've chosen to ride roughshod over me and my family. You don't care what any of us want or feel."

"I do care what you feel. I care too damn much. It's driven me mad these last few weeks, worrying about you. I wished you'd never walked into my office, never made me feel… Hell! You've made me crazy, woman."

Before she had any idea of what he was about to do, he

took a long step toward her. Seizing her, he crushed her against his tall, hard body.

His hands gripping her close, his mouth slanted across hers with enough force to leave her breathless and have her moaning…and then, dear God, as his masterful kiss went on and on and on, she wanted nothing except more of him. Melting, she opened her mouth and her heart. How could she need him so much? She'd missed him terribly—every day they'd been apart.

Needle-sharp thrills raced down her spine. His tongue plunged inside her lips, and soon she was so drunk on his taste and passion, her nails dug into his back. She wanted to be somewhere else, somewhere more private.

She'd missed him. She'd wanted this. She hadn't been able to admit it. His clean, male scent intoxicated her. The length of his all-too-familiar body pressing against hers felt necessary. Every second, asleep and awake, she had thought of him, craved him—craved this. Being held by him only made the need more bittersweet. How could she want such a cold man so desperately?

"We can't feel this, do this," she whispered in a tortured breath even as she clung to him.

"Says who?"

"We're in a church."

His arms tightened their hold. "Marry me, and we can do all we want to each other—tonight…and forever," he said huskily. "It will become a sacred marital right."

How could he say that when he didn't care which Murray sister walked down the aisle as long as it saved him a few million dollars?

The thought hissed through her like cold water splashed onto a fire.

Her parents' love had carried them through many difficulties. Her dad was a workaholic. Her mother was a perfectionist, a status-seeking socialite. But they had always been madly in love.

Kira had grown up believing in the sanctity of marriage. How could she even consider a marriage that would be nothing more than a business deal to her husband?

A potential husband who had lapped up women the way she might attack a box of chocolates. Maybe he temporarily lusted after her, but he didn't love her and never could, as he'd told her. No doubt some other woman would soon catch his fancy.

Even wanting him as she did, she wasn't ready to settle for a marriage based on poor judgment, a momentary sexual connection, shallow lust, revenge and business.

She sucked in a breath and pushed against his massive chest. His grip eased slightly, maybe because the handsome rat thought he'd bent her to his will with his heated words and kisses.

"Listen to me," she said softly. "Are *you* listening?"

"Yes, darlin'."

"I won't marry you. Or any man who could dream up such a cold, cynical scheme."

"How can you call this cold when we're both burning up with desire?" He traced a fingertip along her cheek that made her jump and shiver before she jerked her head away.

"Cheap tricks like that won't induce me to change my mind. There's nothing you can say or do that will convince me. No masterful seduction technique that you honed in other women's bedrooms will do the job, either."

"I wish I had the time to woo you properly and make you believe how special you are."

Special. Now, *there* was a word that hit a nerve. She'd always wanted to feel beloved to those she cared about. How did he know that? It infuriated her that he could guess her sensibilities and so easily use them to manipulate her.

"What you want is revenge and money. If you had all of eternity, it wouldn't be long enough. I won't have you or your loveless deal. That's final."

"We'll see."

His silky baritone was so blatantly confident it sent an icy chill shivering down her spine.

Six

"You told him—the enemy—that Mother might be dying, and you didn't tell me or Jaycee! And you did this behind my back—weeks and weeks ago!"

Kira fisted and unfisted her hands as she sat beside her father in the preacher's library. Rage and hurt shot through her.

"How could you be so disloyal? I've never felt so completely betrayed. Sometimes I feel like a stray you picked up on the side of the road. You didn't really want me—only you have to keep me because it's the right thing to do."

"Nonsense! You're our daughter."

He blanched at her harsh condemnation, and she hung her head in guilt. "I'm sorry," she muttered.

She wanted to weep and scream, but she wouldn't be able to think if she lost all control.

"You know your mother and how she always wants to protect you. I thought only of her when I confided in him."

"First, you sell Jaycee to him because, as always, she's your first choice."

"Kira…"

"Now, it's me."

"Don't blame me. He wants *you!*"

"As if that makes you blameless. Why didn't either of my parents think about protecting their daughters from Quinn?"

"It's complicated. Even if your mother weren't sick, we need someone younger at the top, someone with a clearer vision of the future. Quinn's not what you think. Not what the press thinks. I knew him as a boy. This can be a win-win situation for you both."

"He grew into a vengeful man who hates us."

"You're wrong. He doesn't hate you. You'll never make me believe that. You should have seen how he acted when you disappeared. I think he'll make you a good husband."

"You don't care about that. You don't care about me. You only care about Murray Oil's bottom line, about retiring and being with Mother."

"How can you say that? I care about you, and I care about this family as much as you do. Yes, I need to take care of your mother now, but like I said—I know Quinn. I've watched him. He's good, smart, solid. And he's a brilliant businessman who will be the best possible CEO for Murray Oil during these tumultuous economic times. He's done great things already. If I had time, I'd fill you in on how he helped organize a deal with the EU while you were gone. He's still in the middle of it at the moment."

"For years he's worked to destroy you."

"Hell, maybe he believed that's what he was doing, maybe others bought it, too, but I never did. I don't think *he* knew what was driving him. This company is his heritage, too. And I saw how he was when you were gone.

The man was beside himself. He was afraid you were in trouble. I don't know what happened between the two of you before you ran away, but I know caring when I see it. Quinn cares for you. He's just like his father. You should have seen how Kade loved his wife, Esther. Then you'd know the love Quinn is capable of."

"You think Quinn will come to love me? Are you crazy? Quinn doesn't believe he can love again. The man has lived his life fueled by hate. Hatred for all of us. How many times do I have to repeat it?"

"Maybe so, but the only reason his hatred was so strong was that the love that drove it was just as strong. You're equally passionate. You just haven't found your calling yet." Her father took her hands in his as he continued, "You should have seen him the day he came to tell me he had me by the balls and was set to take over Murray Oil. He could have broken me that day. Instead, he choked when I told him about Vera because he's more decent than he knows. He's ten times the man that his father ever was, that's for sure. Maybe you two didn't meet under ideal circumstances, but he'll make you a good husband."

"You believe that only because you want to believe it. You're as cold and calculating as he is."

"I want what's best for all of us."

"This is a deal to you—just like it is to him. Neither of you care which daughter marries Quinn today, as long as the deal is completed for Murray Oil."

"I suggested Jaycee primarily to avoid a scene like the one we're having, but Quinn wants you. He won't even consider Jaycee now, even though he was willing to marry her before you meddled."

"Oh, so this fiasco is my fault."

"Someday you'll thank me."

"I'm not marrying him. I won't be sacrificed."

"Before you make your decision, your mother wants to talk to you." He pressed a couple of buttons on his phone, and the door behind him opened as if by magic. Her mother's perfectly coiffed blonde head caught the light of the overhead lamp. She was gripping her cell phone with clawlike hands.

She looked so tiny. Why hadn't Kira noticed how thin and colorless her once-vital mother had become? How frail and tired she looked?

"Dear God," Kira whispered as she got up and folded her precious mother into her arms. She felt her mother's ribs and spine as she pressed her body closer. Her mother was fading away right before her eyes.

"Please," her mother whispered. "I'm not asking you to do this for me, but for your father. I need all my strength to fight this illness. He can't be worried about Murray Oil. Or you. Or Jaycee. I've always been the strong one, you know. I can't fight this if I have to worry about him. And I can't leave him alone. He'd be lost without me."

"I—I…"

"I'm sure your father's told you there's a very important international deal with the EU on the table right now. It can make or break our company."

"*His* company."

"Your father and I and the employees of Murray Oil need your help, Kira. Your marriage to Quinn would endorse his leadership both here and abroad. Have I ever asked you for anything before?"

Of course she had. She'd been an ambitious and very demanding mother. Kira had always hoped that when she married and had children, she'd finally be part of a family where she felt as if she belonged, where she was accepted, flaws and all. How ironic that when her parents finally needed her to play a role they saw as vital to their survival,

their need trampled on her heartfelt dream to be at the core
of her own happy family.

Would she ever matter to her husband the way her
mother mattered to her father? Not if the man who was
forcing her to marry him valued her only as a business
prize. Once Quinn had Murray Oil under his control, how
long would she be of any importance to him?

Still, what choice did she have? For the first time ever,
her family really needed her. And she'd always wanted that
above all things.

"I don't want to marry you! But yes!" she spat at Quinn
after he had ushered her into one of the private dressing
rooms. She'd spun around to face him in the deadly quiet.
"*Yes!* I will marry you, since you insist on having your
answer today."

"Since I insist we marry today!"

Never had she seemed lovelier than with her dark, heavily lashed eyes glittering with anger and her slender hands
fisted defiantly on her hips. He was so glad to have found
her. So glad she was all right. So glad she'd agreed without
wasting any more precious time. Once she was his, they'd
get past this.

"Then I'll probably hate you forever for forcing me to
make such a terrible bargain."

Her words stabbed him with pain, but he steeled himself not to show it. She looked mad enough to spit fire and
stood at least ten feet from him so he couldn't touch her.

Looking down, staring anywhere but at her, he fought
to hide the hurt and relief he felt at her answer, as well as
the regret he felt for having bullied her.

Bottom line—she would be his. Today. The thought
of any man touching her as Quinn had touched her their

one night together seemed a sacrilege worthy of vengeful murder.

"Good. I'm glad that's finally settled and we can move on," he said in a cool tone that masked his own seething passions. "I've hired people to help you get ready. Beauticians. Designers. I selected a wedding gown that I hope you'll like, and I have a fitter here in case I misjudged your size."

"You did all that?" Her narrow brows arched with icy contempt. "You were that sure I'd say yes? You thought I was some doll you could dress up in white satin…"

"Silk, actually, and no, I don't think you're some doll—" He stopped. He wasn't about to admit how desperate he'd felt during the dark days of her absence, or how out of control, even though his silence only seemed to make her angrier.

"Look, just because you bullied me into saying yes doesn't mean I like the way you manipulated my family into taking your side. And, since this is strictly a business deal to all of you, I want you to know it's nothing but a business deal to me, too. So, I'm here by agreeing to a marriage in name only. The only reasons I'm marrying you are to help my father and mother and Murray Oil and to save Jaycee from you."

His lips thinned. "There's too much heat in you. You won't be satisfied with that kind of marriage…any more than I will."

"Well, I won't marry you unless you agree to it."

He would have agreed to sell his soul to the devil to have her. "Fine," he said. "Suit yourself, but when you change your mind, I won't hold you to your promise."

"I won't change my mind."

He didn't argue the point or try to seduce her. He'd

make the necessary concessions to get her to the altar. He'd pushed her way too far already.

He was willing to wait, to give her the time she needed. He didn't expect it would be long before he'd have her in his bed once more. And perhaps it was for the best that they take a break from the unexpected passion they'd found.

Maybe he wanted her to believe his motive for marrying her was business related, but it was far from the truth. Need—pure, raw, unadulterated need—was what drove him. If they didn't make love for a while, perhaps he could get control over all his emotions.

After they'd made love the last time, he'd felt too much, had felt too bound to her. Her power over him scared the hell out of him. She'd left him just as carelessly as his own mother had left his father, hadn't she?

He needed her like the air he breathed. Kira had simply become essential.

But he wasn't about to tell her that. No way could he trust this overwhelming need for any woman. Hadn't his father's love for Quinn's own mother played the largest part in his father's downfall? And then his own love for his father had crushed him when his father died.

Grief was too big a price to pay for love. He never wanted to be weak and needy like that again.

Seven

"You look...absolutely amazing," her mother said, sounding almost as pleased as she usually did when she complimented Jaycee. "Don't frown! You know you do!"

In a trancelike daze, Kira stared at the vision in the gilt mirror. How had Quinn's beauty experts made her look like herself and yet so much better? They'd tugged and pulled, clipped and sprayed unmercifully, and now here she was, a sexy, glowing beauty in a diaphanous silk gown that clung much too revealingly. The dress flattered her slim figure perfectly. How had he known her exact size and what would most become her?

All those blondes, she told herself. He understood glamour and women, not her. The dress wasn't about her. He wanted her to be like them.

Still, until this moment, she'd never realized how thoroughly into the Cinderella fantasy she'd been. Not that she would ever admit that, on some deep level, he'd pleased her.

"How can I walk down the aisle in a dress you can see straight through?"

"You're stunning. The man has flawless taste."

"Another reason to hate him," Kira mumbled, brushing aside her mother's hard-won approval and pleasure for fear of having it soften her attitude toward Quinn.

"Haven't I always told you, you should have been playing up your assets all along," her mother said.

"Straight guys aren't supposed to know how to do stuff like this."

"Count yourself lucky your man has such a rare talent. You'll have to start letting him dress you. Maybe he knows how to bring out your best self in other areas, as well. If he does, you'll amaze yourself."

The way he had during their one night together. A shiver traced through her. "May I remind you that this is not a real marriage?"

"If you'd quit saying that in such a sulky, stubborn tone, maybe it would become one, and very soon. He's very handsome. I'll bet there isn't a single woman in this church who wouldn't trade places with you."

"He doesn't love me."

"Well, why don't you start talking to him in a sweet voice? More like the one that you always use with that impossible cat of yours?"

"Maybe because he's not my loyal, beloved pet. Maybe because being bullied into a relationship with him does not make me feel sweet and tender."

"Well, if you ask me, the men you've chosen freely weren't much to brag about. Quinn is so well educated and well respected."

A few minutes later, when the wedding march started, Kira glided down the aisle in white satin slippers holding on to her father's arm. When she heard awed gasps from

the guests, she lifted her eyes from the carpet, but in the
sea of faces it was Quinn's proud smile alone that made her
heart leap and brought a quick, happy blush to her cheeks.

Then her tummy flipped as their souls connected in that
uncanny way that made her feel stripped bare. Fortunately,
her father angled himself between them, and she got a brief
reprieve from Quinn's mesmerizing spell.

Not that it was long before her father had handed her
over to her bridegroom where she became her awkward,
uncertain self again. As she stood beside Quinn at the altar,
she fidgeted while they exchanged rings and vows. With
a smile, he clasped her hand in his. Threading her fingers
through his, he held them still. Somehow, his warm touch
reassured her, and she was able to pledge herself to him
forever in a strong, clear voice.

This isn't a real marriage, she reminded herself, even
as that bitter truth tore at her heart.

But the tall man beside her, the music, the church and
the incredibly beautiful dress, combined with the memory
of her own radiance in the mirror, made her doubt what she
knew to be true. Was she a simple-minded romantic after
all, or just a normal girl who wanted to marry a man she
loved?

After the preacher told Quinn he could kiss his bride,
Quinn's arms encased her slim body with infinite gentleness. His eyes went dark in that final moment before he
lowered his beautifully sculpted mouth to hers. Despite her
intention not to react to his lips, to feel nothing when he
kissed her, her blood pulsed. Gripping his arms, she leaned
into him.

"We'd better make this count because if you have your
way, it will probably be a while before I convince you to
let me kiss you again," he teased huskily.

She threw her arms around his warm, bronzed neck, her

fingers stroking his thick hair, and drew his head down. Fool that she was, it felt glorious to be in his arms as he claimed her before a thousand witnesses.

Such a ceremonial kiss shouldn't mean anything, she told herself. He was just going through the motions. As was she.

"Darlin'," he murmured. "Sweet darlin' Kira. You are incredibly beautiful, incredibly dear. I want you so much. No bridegroom has ever felt prouder of his bride."

The compliment brought her startled eyes up to his, and his tender expression fulfilled her long-felt secret desire to be special to someone. For one shining instant, she believed the dream. If a man as sophisticated as he was could really be proud of her and want her...

He didn't, of course... Oh, but if only he could...

Then his mouth was on hers. His tongue inside the moist recesses of her lips had her blood heating and her breath shuddering in her lungs. Her limbs went as limp as a rag doll's. When she felt his heart hammering against her shoulder blade, she let him pull her even closer.

The last thing she wanted was to feel this swift rush of warm pleasure, but she couldn't stop herself. How could a single, staged kiss affect her so powerfully?

He was the first to pull away. His smile was slow and sweet. "Don't forget—the last thing I want is for our marriage to be business-only," he whispered against her ravaged lips. "You can change your mind anytime, darlin'. Anytime. Nothing would please me more than to take you to my bed again."

"Well, I won't change my mind! Not ever!" she snapped much too vehemently.

He laughed and hugged her close. "You will. I should warn you that nothing appeals to me more than a challenge."

After a lengthy photography session—she was surprised that he wanted photos of a wedding that couldn't possibly mean anything to him—they were driven by limousine to the reception, held at his opulent club in an older section of San Antonio.

Once again he'd planned everything—decorations in the lavish ballroom, the menu, the band—with enough attention to detail that her critical mother was thoroughly impressed and radiantly aglow with pride. Vera sailed through the glittering throng like a bejeweled queen among awed subjects as she admired the banks of flowers, frozen sculptures and the sumptuous food and arrangements. Kira was secretly pleased Quinn had at least married her under circumstances that gave her mother, who loved to impress, so much pleasure.

With a few exceptions, the majority of the guests were employees and clients of Murray Oil. The few personal friends and family attending included Quinn's uncle Jerry, who'd been his best man, and her friend Betty. The guest list also included a few important people from the Texas art world, mostly museum directors, including Gary Whitehall, the former boss who'd let her go...for daring to have an opinion of her own.

Since the wedding was a business affair, Kira was surprised that Quinn had allowed his employees to bring their children, but he had. And no one was enjoying themselves more than the kids. They danced wildly and chased each other around the edges of the dance floor, and when a father spoke harshly to the little flower girl for doing cartwheels in her long velvet gown, Quinn soothed the child.

Watching the way the little girl brightened under his tender ministrations, Kira's heart softened.

"He's very good with children," Betty whispered into her ear. "He'll make a wonderful father."

"This is not a real marriage."

"You could have fooled me. I get all mushy inside every time he looks at you. He's *so* good-looking."

"He's taken over my life."

"Well, I'd be glad to take him off your hands. I think he's hunky. And so polite. Did I tell you how nice he was to Rudy after he found out the reason the beast wouldn't stop meowing was because he missed you? He sat down with that cat and commiserated. Made me give the beast some tuna."

"I'll bet he got you to feed him, too."

"Well, every time Quinn came to the restaurant he did sit down with me and whoever was waiting tables, like he was one of us. He bragged on my pies."

"Which got him free pies I bet."

"His favorite is the same as yours."

"Your gooey lemon meringue?"

"I thought he was sweet to remember to invite me to the wedding. He called this evening after you showed up."

Betty hushed when Quinn appeared at his bride's side and stayed, playing the attentive groom long after his duties in the receiving line ended. Even when several beauties—one a flashy blonde he'd once dated named Cristina, whom he'd apparently hired as a junior executive—came up and flirted boldly, he'd threaded his fingers through Kira's and tucked her closer.

For more than an hour, ignoring all others, he danced only with Kira. He was such a strong partner, she found herself enjoying the reception immensely as he whirled her around the room. She could see the admiring glances following them. He smiled down at her often, no doubt to give the appearance that she delighted him. The women who'd flirted with him watched him with intense interest, especially Cristina, whose lovely mouth began to pout.

"I've never been much of a dancer," Kira confessed during a slow number.

"You could've fooled me. Just goes to show that all you need is a little self-confidence."

Had his attentiveness given her that, at least briefly? When Gary Whitehall's gaze met hers over Quinn's broad shoulder, he smiled tightly. As Quinn's wife, she'd taken a huge step up in the art world. Was Gary wishing he'd let someone else go other than her when the budget had been tight? Why had Quinn included him on the guest list?

After a fast number, when Kira admitted she was thirsty, Quinn left her to get champagne. Seeing his chance, Gary rushed up to her.

"You look lovely," he said, smiling in the way he used to smile at major artists and important donors. How rare had been the smiles and compliments he'd bestowed on his lowly curator for her hard work. "I'm very happy for you," he said.

She nodded, embarrassed to be so pleased that her marriage had won his respect.

"If I can do anything for you, anything at all, just call me. I am rewriting your letter of recommendation. Not that you'll need to work now."

"I intend to work again. I loved my job."

"Your husband has been most generous to the museum. We value his friendship and expertise almost as much as we will value yours—as his wife," he gushed. "I have a feeling we may have a position for a curator opening up soon. If so, I'll give you a call."

She thought about what Gary had said about a position possibly being available and was surprised she was so pleased. Maybe…she would consider working for him again…if he made her the right offer. She would, however, demand to have more power.

Stunned, she stared at him. Then Quinn returned with her champagne. The two men shook hands and exchanged pleasantries. When Quinn made it clear he preferred his bride's conversation to art talk, Gary quickly eased himself back into the crowd. But every time after that conversation, when their eyes met, Gary smiled at her.

For a man who supposedly hated her family, Quinn was excessively attentive to her mother and father and Jaycee. He talked to them, ordered them wine and appetizers, acted as if he actually wished to please them. He was especially solicitous of her mother, who positively glowed.

Kira watched him during dinner, and his warm smiles and polite comments rang with sincerity. If she hadn't known better, she wouldn't have believed he was simply acting a part in order to reassure oil company clients and executives that Murray Oil was in good hands.

Never had a bridegroom appeared more enthusiastic, even when his uncle Jerry congratulated him on his marriage.

"Kira, he's had his nose to the grindstone so long, we were beginning to think that's all he'd ever do," Jerry said. "We'd given up on you, son. Now I see you just hadn't met the right girl. Sooner or later, if we're lucky, love comes our way. The trick is to know it and appreciate it. When you fall in love, wanting to spend the rest of your life with the same woman doesn't seem that hard to imagine."

Quinn stared at her as if he agreed. The two men shook hands again and laughed. But since Quinn's heart wasn't really in their marriage, she wondered how soon he'd give up trying to pretend to people like his uncle. After that, when she felt herself too charmed by one of Quinn's thoughtful smiles or gestures, she reminded herself that she'd be a fool if she fell for his act. Their marriage was a business deal. She didn't matter to him. She never would.

All too soon the dinner and dancing came to an end, and she and Quinn had changed into street clothes and were dashing out to his limo while cheering guests showered them with birdseed. When someone threw seeds straight at her eyes, and a tear streamed down her cheek, Quinn took out his monogrammed handkerchief and dabbed her face while everybody cheered.

She expected to be driven to his loft. Instead, the limo whisked them to his sleek private jet, which had been prepared for flight and was waiting outside a hangar at the San Antonio International Airport.

"Where are we going?" she asked as he helped her out into the blinding glare of dozens of flashes.

"Honeymoon," he whispered, his mouth so close to her ear she felt the heat of his breath. Her heart raced until she reminded herself he was only staging a romantic shot for the press.

Putting his arm around her, he faced the reporters, who asked him questions about his pending international oil deal as well as his marriage.

With abundant charm and smiles, he answered a few and then, grabbing her by the elbow, propelled her into his jet.

"Surely a honeymoon isn't necessary," she said when they were safely on board.

He smiled down at her. "A man only marries once."

"Like that reporter asked—how can you afford the time when you're working on that important EU deal?"

"You have to make time...for what's important."

"So, why did you notify the press about our honeymoon? Was it only so the EU people would know you married into the Murray family?"

"Why don't you relax? Step one, quit asking so many questions. Step two, just enjoy."

"You're thorough. I'll have to give you that. Even so,

how can I leave town when I haven't even packed for a trip," she said. "Besides, I have a cat—Rudy. I promised Betty I'd relieve her… He's been crying for me."

"I know. Rudy's all taken care of. Jacinda's going to look after him at your apartment. So, he'll be on his own turf. I bought him a case of tuna."

"You shopped for Rudy?"

"Okay—so I sent my assistant. And your mother helped me shop and pack for you."

"I'll bet she loved that."

"She did—although I did make certain key choices."

"Such as?"

"The lingerie and bikinis."

"Lingerie? I'm not much for lingerie! Or bikinis!"

"Good. Then you'll be exquisite in nothing. You slept in my arms like that all night, remember."

Hot color flooded her face. "Don't!"

"With your legs wrapped silkily around me," he added. "You were so warm and sweet, I can't believe you really intend to sleep alone tonight."

The images he aroused in her, coupled with his warm gaze and sexy grin, made her blood hum.

"I meant I feel bad about going away again so soon without telling Betty."

"Already done. Betty's fine with the idea."

"You *are* thorough."

When her temples began to throb, Kira squeezed her eyes shut. "Did everyone, absolutely everyone, know I was getting married to you today before I did?"

"Not me, darlin'. I was scared sick you wouldn't turn up or that you'd order me straight to hell after I proposed."

Had he really felt that way? Did he care a little?

No! She couldn't let herself ask such questions.

Or care at all what the answers might be.

Eight

An hour later, after a flight to the coast and a brief but exciting helicopter ride over Galveston Island, they dropped out of the night sky onto the sleek, upper deck of the white floating palace he kept moored at the Galveston marina. She took his arm when the rotors stopped and sucked in a breath as he helped her onto his yacht. Gusts of thick, humid air that smelled of the sea whipped her clothes and hair.

Promising to give her a tour of the megayacht the next day, the captain led them down a flight of steep, white stairs and through a wood-lined corridor to Quinn's master stateroom. Clearly the captain hadn't been told that they would not be sharing a room. Crewmen followed at a brisk pace to deliver their bags.

Once alone with Quinn in his palatial, brass-studded cabin, her brows knitted in concern as she stared at the mountain of bags.

"Don't worry. If you really insist on sleeping alone, I'll move mine."

Shooting a nervous glance toward his big bed, she felt her body heat.

Above the headboard hung a magnificent painting of a nude blonde by an artist she admired. The subject was lying on her tummy across a tumble of satin sheets, her slender back arched to reveal ample breasts. Long-lashed, come-hither eyes compelled the viewer not to look away. Surely such a wanton creature would never send her husband away on their wedding night.

"Last chance to change your mind," he said.

Feeling strangely shy, Kira crossed her arms over her own breasts and shook her head. "So, where will you sleep?"

"Next door." There was a mesmerizing intensity in his eyes. "Would you like to see my room?"

She twisted her hands. "I'll be just fine right here. So, if that's settled, I guess we'll see each other in the morning."

"Right." He hesitated. "If you need anything, all you have to do is punch this button on your bedside table and one of the staff will answer. If you want me, I'll leave my door unlocked. Or, if you prefer me to come to you, you could ring through on that phone over there."

"Thanks."

He turned, opened the door, shoved his bags into the passageway and stepped outside. When the door slammed behind him, and she was alone with his come-hither blonde, a heavy emotion that felt too much like disappointment gripped her.

To distract herself, she studied the painting for another moment, noting that the artist had used linseed oil most effectively to capture the effect of satin.

Feeling a vague disquiet as she considered the nude,

she decided the best thing to do was shower and get ready for bed. As she rummaged in her suitcase, she found all sorts of beautiful clothes that she never would have picked out. Still, as she touched the soft fabrics and imagined her mother shopping for such things without her there to discourage such absurd purchases, she couldn't help smiling. Her mother had always wanted to dress Kira in beautiful things, but being a tomboy, Kira had preferred jeans and T-shirts.

What was the point of fancy clothes for someone who lived as she had, spending time in art vaults, or painting, or waiting tables? But now, she supposed, for however long she was married to a billionaire with his own jet and mega-yacht, she would run in different circles and have fundraisers and parties to attend. Maybe she did need to upgrade her wardrobe.

Usually, she slept in an overlarge, faded T-shirt. In her suitcase all she found for pajamas were thin satin gowns and sheer robes, the kind that would cling so seductively she almost regretted she wouldn't be wearing them for Quinn.

Instead of the satin gown, which reminded her too much of the blonde above the bed, she chose black lace. Had he touched the gown, imagining her in it, when he'd picked it out? As the gossamer garment slipped through her fingers she shivered.

Go to bed. Don't dwell on what might have been. He's ruined enough of your day and night as it is.

But how not to think of him as she stripped and stepped into her shower? What was he doing next door? Was his tall, bronzed body naked, too? Her heart hammered much too fast.

Lathering her body underneath a flow of warm water, she imagined him doing the same in his own shower. Leaning against the wet tile wall, she grew hotter and hotter as the water streamed over her. She stood beneath the spray until her fingers grew too numb to hold the slippery bar of soap. When it fell, she snapped out of her spell.

Drying off and then slipping into the black gown, she slid into his big bed with a magazine. Unable to do more than flip pages and stare unseeingly at the pictures because she couldn't stop thinking about Quinn, she eventually drifted to sleep. But once asleep, she didn't dream of him.

Instead, she dreamed she was a small child in her pink bedroom with its wall-to-wall white carpet. All her books were lined up just perfectly, the way her mother liked them to be, in her small white bookcase beneath the window.

Somewhere in the house she heard laughter and hushed endearments, the sort of affection she'd never been able to get enough of. Then her door opened and her parents rushed inside her bedroom. Only they didn't take her into their arms as they usually did. Her mother was cooing over a bundle she held against her heart, and her father was staring down at what her mother held as if it were the most precious thing in the world.

She wanted them to look at her like that.

"Kira, we've brought your new baby sister, Jaycee, for a visit."

A baby sister? "Where did she come from?"

"The hospital."

"Is that where you got me?"

Her mother paled. Her father looked as uneasy as her mother, but he nodded.

What was going on?

"Do you love me, too?" Kira whispered.

"Yes, of course," her father said. "You're our big girl now, so your job will be to help us take care of Jaycee.

She's *our* special baby. We're all going to work hard to take very good care of Jaycee."

Suddenly, the bundle in her mother's arms began to shriek frantically.

"What can I do?" Kira had said, terrified as she ran toward them. "How can I help? Tell me what to do!"

But they'd turned away from her. "Why don't you just play," her father suggested absently.

Feeling lonely and left out as she eyed her dolls and books, she slowly backed away from them and walked out of her room, down the tall stairs to the front door, all the while hoping their concerned voices would call her back as they usually did. She wasn't supposed to be downstairs at night.

But this time, they didn't call her. Instead, her parents carried the new baby into a bedroom down the hall and stayed with her.

They had a new baby. They didn't need her anymore.

Kira opened the big front door. They didn't notice when she stepped outside. Why should they? They had Jaycee, who was special. They didn't care about Kira anymore. Maybe they'd never really cared.

Suddenly, everything grew black and cold, and a fierce wind began to blow, sweeping away everything familiar. The house vanished, and she was all alone in a strange, dark wood with nobody to hear her cries. Terrified, she ran deeper into the woods.

If her family didn't love her anymore, if nobody loved her, she didn't know what she would do.

Hysterical, she began sobbing their names. "Mother! Daddy! Somebody! Please…love me. I want to be special, too…"

Quinn opened her door and hurled himself into her stateroom.

"Kira!" He switched on a light. She blinked against the blinding glare of gold with heavy-lidded eyes.

"Are you okay?" he demanded. "Wake up!"

"Quinn?" Focusing on his broad shoulders, she blinked away the last remnants of that terrifying forest. He was huge and shirtless and so starkly handsome in the half shadows she hissed in a breath.

Her husband. What a fool she'd been to send him away when that was the last thing she really wanted.

When he sat down on the bed, she flung herself against his massive bare chest and clung. He felt so hard and strong and hot.

Snugging her close against his muscular body, he rocked her gently and spoke in soothing tones. "There...there..."

Wrapped in his warmth, she almost felt safe...and loved.

"I was a little girl again. Only I ran away and got lost. In a forest."

He petted her hair as his voice soothed her. "You were only dreaming."

She stared up at his shadowed face. In the aftermath of her dream, she was too open to her need of him. Her grip on him tightened. She felt his breath hitch and his heart thud faster. If only *he* loved her...maybe the importance of her childhood fears would recede.

"Darlin', it was just a dream. You're okay."

Slowly, because he held her, the horror of feeling lost and alone diminished and reality returned.

She was on his megayacht. In Galveston. He'd forced her to marry him and come on a honeymoon. She was in his bed where she'd been sleeping alone. This was supposed to be their wedding night, but she'd sent him away.

Yet somehow *she* was the one who felt lonely and rejected.

She liked being cradled in his strong arms, against his

virile body. Too much. She grew conscious of the danger of letting him linger in her bedroom.

"You want me to go?" he whispered roughly.

No. She wanted to cling to him…to be adored by him…. Another impossible dream.

When she hesitated, he said, "If you don't send me packing, I will take this as an invitation."

"It's no invitation," she finally murmured, but sulkily. Her heart wasn't in her statement.

"How come you don't sound sure?" He ran a rough palm across her cheek. Did she only imagine the intimate plea in his voice? Was he as lonely as she was?

Even as she felt herself softening under his affectionate touch and gentle tone, she forced herself to remember all the reasons she'd be a fool to trust him. Squeezing her eyes shut, she took a deep breath. "Thanks for coming, but go! Please—just go."

She felt his body tighten as he stared into her eyes. Time ticked for an endless moment before he released her.

Without a word he got up and left.

Alone again, she felt she might burst with sheer longing. When she didn't sleep until dawn, she blamed him for not going farther than the room next to hers. He was too close. Knowing that all she had to do was go to him increased her frustration. Because he'd made it clear he would not send her away.

Twisting and turning, she fought to settle into slumber, but could not. First, she was too hot for the covers. Then she was so cold she'd burrowed under them.

It was nearly dawn when she finally did sleep. Then, after less than an hour, loud voices in the passageway startled her into grouchy wakefulness. As she buried her head in her pillow, her first thought was of Quinn. He'd probably slept like a baby.

When the sun climbed high and his crewmen began shouting to one another on deck, she strained to hear Quinn's voice among theirs shouts, but didn't.

Sitting up, alone, she pulled the covers to her throat. Surely he couldn't still be sleeping. Where was he?

A dark thought hit her. Last night he'd left her so easily, when what she'd craved was for him to stay. Had she already served her purpose by marrying him? Was he finished with her?

Feeling the need for a strong cup of coffee, Kira slipped into a pair of tight, white shorts and a skimpy, beige knit top. Outside, the sky was blue, the sun brilliant. Normally, when she wasn't bleary from lack of sleep, Kira loved water, boats and beaches. Had Quinn been in love with her, a honeymoon on his luxurious yacht would have been exceedingly romantic. Instead, she felt strange and alone and much too needily self-conscious.

Was his crew spying on her? Did they know Quinn hadn't slept with her? Did they pity her?

Anxious to find Quinn, Kira grabbed a white sweater and left the stateroom. When he didn't answer her knock, she cracked open his door. A glance at the perfectly made spread and his unopened luggage told her he'd spent the night elsewhere. Pivoting, she stepped back into the corridor so fast she nearly slammed headlong into a crewman.

"May I help you, Mrs. Sullivan?"

"Just taking a private tour," she lied. On the off chance he'd think she knew where she was going, she strode purposefully past him down the wood-lined passageway.

Outside, the gulf stretched in endless sapphire sparkle toward a shimmering horizon. Not that she paid much attention to the dazzling view. Intent on finding Quinn, she was too busy opening every door on the sumptuously appointed decks. Too proud to ask the numerous crew members she passed for help, she averted her eyes when she chanced to meet one of them for fear they'd quiz her.

The yacht seemed even bigger on close inspection. So far she'd found six luxury staterooms, a cinema, multiple decks, a helipad and a grand salon.

Just when she was about to give up her search for Quinn, she opened a door on the uppermost deck and found him slumped over a desk in a cluttered office. Noting the numerous documents scattered on chairs, desks, tables and even the floor, she crossed the room to his side. Unfinished cups of coffee sat atop the jumbled stacks. Obviously, he'd worked through the night on a caffeine high.

At the sight of his exhausted face, her heart constricted. Even as she smoothed her hand lightly through his rumpled hair, she chastised herself for feeling sympathy for him. Hadn't he bullied her into their forced, loveless marriage?

Now that she knew where he was, she should go, order herself coffee and breakfast, read her magazine in some pristine chaise lounge, sunbathe—in short, ignore him. Thinking she would do just that, she stepped away from him. Then, driven by warring emotions she refused to analyze, she quickly scampered back to his side.

Foolishly, she felt tempted to neaten his office, but since she didn't know what went where, she sank into the chair opposite his. Bringing her knees against her chest, she hugged them tightly and was pleased when he slept another hour under her benevolent guardianship. Then, without warning, his beautiful eyes snapped open and seared her.

"What the hell are you doing here?" he demanded.

She nearly jumped out of her chair. "He awakens—like a grumpy old bear," she teased.

Managing a lopsided grin, he ran a hand through his

spiked, rumpled hair. "You were a bit grumpy...the morning after...you slept with me in San Antonio, as I recall."

"Don't remind me of that disastrous night, please."

"It's one of my fondest memories," he said softly.

"I said don't!"

"I love it when you blush like that. It makes you look so...cute. You should have awakened me the minute you came in."

"How could I be so heartlessly cruel when you came to my rescue in the middle of the night? If you couldn't sleep, it was my fault."

When his beautiful white teeth flashed in a teasing grin, she couldn't help smiling back at him.

"I could bring you some coffee. Frankly, I could use a cup myself," she said.

He sat up straighter and stretched. "Sorry this place is such a mess, but as I'm not through here, I don't want anybody straightening it up yet."

She nodded. "I sort of thought that might be the case."

"What about breakfast...on deck, then? I have a crew ready to wait on us hand and foot. They're well trained in all things—food service...emergencies at sea..."

"They didn't come when I screamed last night," she said softly. "You did."

"Only because you didn't call for their help on the proper phone."

"So, it's my fault, is it?" Where had the lilt in her light tone come from?

Remembering how safe she'd felt in his arms last night, a fierce tenderness toward him welled up in her heart. He must have sensed what she felt, because his eyes flared darkly before he looked away.

Again, she wished this were a real honeymoon, wished that he loved her rather than only lusted for her, wished that she was allowed to love him back. If only she hadn't demanded separate bedrooms, then she would be lying in his arms looking forward to making love with him again this morning.

At the thought, her neck grew warm. She'd been wishing for the wrong stuff her whole life. It was time she grew up and figured out what her life was to be about. The sooner she got started on that serious journey, one that could never include him, the better.

Nine

Breakfast on deck with his long-limbed bride in her sexy short shorts was proving to be an unbearable torture. She squirmed when his gaze strayed to her lips or her breasts or when it ran down those long, lovely legs.

If only he could forget how she'd clung to him last night or how her big eyes had adored him when he'd first woken up this morning.

"I wish you wouldn't stare so," she said as she licked chocolate off a fingertip. "It makes me feel self-conscious about eating this and making such a mess."

"Sorry," he muttered.

He tried to look away, but found he could not. What else was there to look at besides endless sapphire dazzle? Why shouldn't he enjoy watching her greedily devour her fresh-baked croissants and *pain du chocolat?* The way she licked chocolate off her fingers made him remember her mouth and tongue on him that night in his loft. *Torture.*

Even though he was sitting in the shade and the gulf breeze was cool, his skin heated. His bride was too sexy for words.

If he were to survive the morning without grabbing her like a besotted teenager and making a fool of himself, he needed to quickly get back to his office and the EU deal.

But he knew he wouldn't be able to concentrate on the deal while his forbidden bride was aboard. No. He'd go to the gym and follow his workout with a long, cold shower. Only then would he attempt another try at the office.

Dear God, why was it that ever since she'd said no sex, bedding her was all he could think about?

With the fortitude that was so much a part of his character, he steeled himself to endure her beauty and her provocative sensuality, at least until breakfast was over and they parted ways.

"So, are we heading somewhere in particular?" she asked playfully.

"Do you like to snorkel?"

"I do, but I've only snorkeled in lakes and shallow coves in the Caribbean."

"Once we get into really deep water, the gulf will be clear. I thought we'd snorkel off one of my oil rigs. It's always struck me as ironic the way marine life flourishes around a rig. You're in for a treat."

Her brief smile charmed him. "I read somewhere that rigs act like artificial reefs." She stopped eating her orange. "But you don't need to interrupt your precious work to entertain me."

"I'll set my own work schedule, if you don't mind."

"You're the boss, my lord and master. Sorry I keep forgetting that all-important fact." Again her playful tone teased him.

"Right." He smiled grimly. What could he say?

They lapsed into an uncomfortable silence. Focusing on his eggs and bacon, he fought to ignore her. Not that he didn't want to talk to her, because he did. Very much. But small talk with his bride was not proving to be an easy matter.

"I'd best get busy," he said when he'd finished his eggs and she her orange.

"Okay. Don't worry about me. Like I said, I can entertain myself. I love the water. As you know, I spent the past few weeks on Murray Island. I don't know where we are, but we probably aren't that far from it."

Scanning the horizon, he frowned. He didn't like remembering how much her stay at her family's isolated island had worried him.

How had he become so attached—or whatever the hell he was—to her so fast? They'd only had one night together!

Biting out a terse goodbye that made her pretty smile falter, he stood abruptly. Pivoting, he headed to his gym and that icy shower while she set off to her stateroom.

The gym and shower didn't do any good. No sooner did he return to his office on the upper deck than who should he find sunbathing right outside his door practically naked but his delectable bride.

She lay on a vivid splash of red terry cloth atop one of his chaise lounges, wearing the white thong bikini he'd picked out for her while under the influence of a lurid male fantasy.

He'd imagined her in it. Hell, yes, he had. But not like this—not with her body forbidden to him by her decree and his unwillingness to become any more attached to her. He would never have bought those three tiny triangles if he'd had any idea what torture watching her would give him.

Clenching his fists, he told himself to snap the blinds shut and forget her. Instead, mesmerized, he crossed his office with the long strides of a large, predatory cat and stood at a porthole, staring at her hungrily, ravenous for whatever scraps of tenderness the sexy witch might bestow. He willed her to look at him.

She flipped a magazine page carelessly and continued to read with the most maddening intensity. Not once did she so much as glance his way.

Damn her.

She was on her tummy in the exact position of the girl in the painting over his bed. He watched her long, dark hair glint with fiery highlights and blow about her slim, bare shoulders. He watched her long, graceful fingers flip more pages and occasionally smooth back flying strands of her hair. Every movement of her slim wrist had her dainty silver bracelet flashing.

Was she really as cool and collected as she appeared?

How could she be, when she'd given herself to him so quickly and completely that first night? Her eyes had shone with desire, and she'd trembled and quivered at his touch. She hadn't faked her response. He'd bet his life on it. He would never have forced her to marry him if he'd thought her cold and indifferent.

And last night he'd definitely felt her holding on to him as if she didn't want to let go.

So, she must be clinging to her position of abstinence out of principle. Wasn't she turning those pages much too fast? Was she even reading that magazine? Or was she as distracted as he was? Did she sense him watching her and take perverse delight in her power over him?

Damn the fates that had sent her to him!

Always, before Kira, he'd gone for voluptuous blondes with modern morals, curvy women who knew how to dress, women who thought their main purpose was to please a man. Women with whom he'd felt safe because they'd wanted his money and position more than they'd valued his heart.

This slim, coltishly long-limbed girl hadn't yet learned what she was about or even how to please herself, much less how to seduce a man. But her innocence in these matters appealed to him.

Why?

Again, he told himself to forget her, but when he went to his desk, he just sat there for a full half hour unable to concentrate. Her image had burned itself into his brain. She had his loins hard and aching. The woman lured him from his work like the Sirens had lured Ulysses after Troy.

He began to worry that she hadn't put on enough sunblock. Weren't there places on that long, slim body she couldn't reach?

Hardly knowing what he was about, he slammed out of his office and found himself outside, towering grimly over her. Not that she so much as bothered to glance away from her damn magazine, even though she must have heard his heavy footsteps, even though he cast a shadow over the pages.

He felt like a fool.

"You're going to burn," he growled with some annoyance.

"Do you think so? I've got lotion on, and my hat. But maybe you're right. I need to turn over for a while." She lowered her sunglasses to the tip of her nose and peered up at him saucily with bright, dark eyes.

Was she flirting with him? Damn her to hell and back if she was.

"Since you're out here, would you mind being a dear and rubbing some lotion on my back for me?"

He sank to his haunches, his excitement so profound at the thought of touching her that he didn't worry about her request for lotion on her back being illogical. Hadn't she forbidden his touch? And didn't she just say she intended to turn over onto her back?

He didn't care.

The lotion was warm from the sun, and her silky skin was even warmer as he rubbed the cream into it.

A moan of pure pleasure escaped her lips as his large palm made circular motions in the center of her back, and his heart raced at her response. He felt a visceral connection to her deep in his groin.

"You have strong hands. The lotion smells so deliciously sweet. Feels good, too," she whispered silkily, stretching like a cat as he stroked her.

"Thanks," he growled.

She rolled over and lay on her towel. Throwing him a dismissive glance, she lifted her magazine to shut him out.

"You can go now," she whispered.

Feeling stubborn and moody, he didn't budge. Only when he saw his oil rig looming off the starboard side did he arise and ask his crew to assemble their diving gear: fins, wet suits, marker floats and masks.

So much for working on the EU deal...

Later, when he and she stood on the teak diving platform at the stern of the yacht in their wet suits, she noticed nobody had thrown out an anchor.

"What if your yacht drifts while we're in the water?"

"She won't," he replied. "*Pegasus* is equipped with a sophisticated navigational system called dynamic positioning. On a day this calm she'll stay exactly where we position her. Believe me, it's much better than an anchor, which would allow her to swing back and forth."

"You plan so much that you think of everything. Does your planning and your fortune allow you to have everything you want?"

"Not quite everything," he murmured as he stared hungrily at her trim body.

Didn't she know she had changed everything?

For years, he'd been driven to avenge himself against her father, but no sooner had he been poised to seize his prize than he'd learned of Vera's illness. From that moment, his victory had begun to feel hollow.

Just when he'd wondered what new challenge could ever drive him as passionately as revenge once did, Kira had walked into his office to fight for her sister. He'd known he had to have her.

Trouble was, he was beginning to want more than he'd ever allowed himself to dream of wanting before. He wanted a life with her, a future, everything he'd told himself he could never risk having.

Kira stood on the platform watching Quinn in the water as he adjusted his mask.

"Come on in," he yelled.

She was removing her silver jewelry because he'd told her the flash of it might attract sharks.

"You know how I told you I've mainly confined my snorkeling to lakes or shallow lagoons," she began. "Well, the gulf's beginning to seem too big and too deep."

"I'll be right beside you, and Skip and Chuck are in the tender."

"I've seen all the *Jaws* movies."

"Not a good time to think about them."

She squinted, searching the vast expanse of the gulf for fins.

"Are you coming in or not?" he demanded.

Despite her doubts, she sucked in a deep breath and jumped in.

As she swam out to him, the water felt refreshingly cool.

After she got her mask on she and Quinn were soon surrounded by red snapper and amberjack. She was enjoying their cool, blue world so much that when he pointed out a giant grouper gliding by, she stared in awe instead of fear. Quinn's sure presence beside her in the water instilled in her a confidence she wouldn't have believed possible.

Snorkeling soon had her feeling weightless. It was as if she were flying in an alien world that dissolved into endless deep blue nothingness. As he'd promised, Quinn stayed beside her for nearly an hour. Enjoying herself, she forgot the vast blue darkness beneath them and what it concealed.

Just when she was starting to relax, a tiger shark zoomed out of the depths straight at Quinn. In her panic, she did exactly what she shouldn't have done. Kicking and thrashing wildly, she gulped in too much water. Choking, she yanked off her mask. As the fin vanished, Quinn ordered her to swim to the yacht.

In seconds, the fin was back, circling Quinn before diving again. Then the shark returned, dashing right at Quinn, who rammed it in the nose and made a motion with his arm for her to quit watching and start swimming. Staying behind her so he could keep his body between hers and the shark, he headed for the yacht, as well.

A tense knot of crewmen on the platform were shouting to them when she finally reached the yacht.

"Quinn," she yelled even as strong arms yanked her on board. "Quinn!" She barely heard his men shouting to him as she stood on the teak platform panting for breath. Then the dorsal fin slashed viciously right beside Quinn, and her fear mushroomed.

"Get him out! Somebody do something! Quinn! *Darling!*" she screamed.

Quinn swam in smooth, rapid strokes toward the stern. When he made it to the ladder, his crewmen sprang forward and hauled him roughly aboard, slamming him onto the teak platform.

Quinn tore off his mask. When he stood up, he turned to Kira, who took the desperate glint in his eyes as an invitation to hurl herself into his arms.

"You're as white as bleached bone," he said, gripping her tightly. "You're sure you're okay?"

The blaze of concern in his eyes and his tone mirrored her own wild fears for him.

"If you're okay, I'm okay," she whispered shakily, snuggling closer. She was so happy he was alive and unhurt.

"You're overreacting. It would take more than one little shark—"

"Don't joke! He could have torn off your arm!"

"He was probably just curious."

"Curious! I saw the movies, remember?"

He stared down at her in a way that made her skin heat. "In a funny way I feel indebted to the shark. Because of him, you called me darling."

"Did not!"

"Did, too," he drawled in that low tone that mesmerized her.

When she wrenched free of him, he laughed. "Okay. It must have been wishful thinking on a doomed man's part. Guess it was Chuck who let out the *d*-word."

She bit her lip to keep from smiling.

After they dressed, they met on the upper deck where they'd had breakfast earlier. Quinn wore jeans and a blue Hawaiian shirt that made his eyes seem as brilliant as the dazzling sky.

He ordered pineapple and mangoes and coffee. She was still so glad he was alive and had all his body parts she couldn't take her eyes off him.

"I have an idea," she said. "I mean…if we're looking for a less exciting adventure."

"What?"

"I could show you Murray Island."

"Where is it?"

"South of Galveston. Since I don't know where we are, I can't tell you how to get there. But it's on all the charts."

He picked up a phone and talked to his captain. When he hung up, he said, "Apparently, we're about forty nautical miles from your island. The captain says we could run into some weather, but if you want to go there, we will."

"What's a raindrop or two compared to being lunch for Jaws?"

"I love your vivid imagination."

In little over an hour, *Pegasus* was positioned off the shore of Murray Island, and Kira and Quinn were climbing down into the tender together. After Quinn revved the outboard, they sped toward the breaking surf, making for the pass between the barrier islands and the tiny harbor on the island's leeward side.

The bouncy ride beneath thickening gray storm clouds was wet and choppy. Heedless of the iffy weather, she stared ahead, laughing as the spray hit them. Quinn's eyes never strayed from his course—except when they veered to her face, which secretly thrilled her. She knew she shouldn't crave his attention so much, but ever since the shark incident, her emotions refused to behave sensibly.

He's alive. I have this moment with him. It's our honeymoon. Why not enjoy it? Why not share this island sanctuary I love with him?

Ten

Quinn watched his beachcombing bride much too avidly for his liking. He hated feeling so powerfully attracted to her. It was incomprehensible. She was Earl's daughter, a woman he barely knew, a wife who wouldn't even share his bed.

She'd slept with him once and then she'd left him, causing a pain too similar to what he'd felt after his father's death. The tenderness he continued to feel for her put him on dangerous ground, but still she possessed him in a way no other woman ever had.

It was the shark. Before they'd snorkeled, he'd been able to tell himself that he was under a temporary spell, that he could vanquish his burning need for her simply by staying out of her bed.

But he'd been afraid for her when she'd been swimming for the boat, more afraid than he'd ever been in his life.

Then he'd seen her bone-white face and the wild terror in her eyes when she'd imagined him in danger.

Once he'd been safely on board, her slim face had become luminous with joy. She'd hurled herself into his arms so violently she'd all but knocked them both back into the water again.

Nobody had ever looked at him like that.

Surely his father had loved him more, but she was here, and so beautiful, and so alive, and his—if only he could win her.

The prevailing southeasterly wind, cooler now because of the dark gray clouds, licked the crests of the waves into a foaming fury and sent her dark chestnut hair streaming back from her face as she scampered at the surf's edge. Every few steps, she knelt, not caring if a wave splashed her toes. Crouching, she examined the beach debris: tangles of seaweed, driftwood and shells.

Her long slim feet were bare, her toenails unpolished. Flip-flops dangled from her left hand.

For twenty years, his determination to succeed and get revenge had made time seem too valuable for him to waste on a beach with a woman. Most nights he'd worked, and most mornings, he'd left for his office before dawn. Driven by his dark goals, he'd often worked through entire weekends and holidays. His main sources of relaxation had been the gym or a willing woman and a glass of scotch before he hit his bed or desk again. He'd been more machine than human.

But that was before Kira.

Memories, long suppressed, stirred. As a child, he'd looked forward to the hour when his father's key would turn in the lock and he'd holler Quinn's name.

Quinn would race into his father's arms. After hugging him close, his father would lift him so high in the air

Quinn could touch the ceiling. So high, he'd felt as if he was flying. Then his dad would set him down and ruffle his hair and ask him about his day.

Never had his father been too tired to pass a football around the yard or take him to the park to chase geese. His father had helped with Quinn's homework, helped him build models, played endless games with him. His mother, on the other hand, had always been too busy to play. Then his father had died, and Quinn had known grief and loneliness.

For the first time, while indulging in this simple walk on the beach with Kira, Quinn felt a glimmer of the warmth that had lit his life before his father's death.

His father would want him to stop grieving, he realized. He'd want him to choose life, to choose the future.

Kira didn't realize she was beautiful, or that her lack of pretention and artifice made her even more attractive. Her every movement was graceful and natural. On the beach, she seemed a lovely wild thing running free.

This island was her refuge. For however long they were together, he would have to accept her world if he wanted her to accept his. No doubt, she would need to come here again from time to time.

He frowned, not liking the thought of her leaving him to stay out here all alone. Anyone could beach a small boat or tie up at her dock. Jim, the island's caretaker, had the faraway look of a man who'd checked out of life a long time ago. Quinn wasn't about to trust a dropout like him as her protector. No, he would have to get his security team to figure out how to make her safe here without intruding on her privacy. She was a free spirit, and Quinn wanted her to be happy, the way she was now, but safe, as well.

The sky was rapidly darkening from gray to black. Not that Kira seemed concerned about the gathering storm as she leaned down and picked up a shell. When she twisted, their gazes met. At her enchanting smile, his heart brimmed with way too much emotion. Then she ran over to show him her newfound treasure. When she held it up, her eyes shone, and the tiny window that had opened into his soul widened even further.

"Look, it's a lightning whelk," she cried.

"It's huge," he said, turning the cone-shaped shell over in his hand to properly admire it.

"At least a foot long. I've never seen one so big. And it's in perfect condition. Did you know it's the state shell of Texas?"

Shaking his head, he shot a glance at the darkening sky before he handed it back to her. "Do you collect shells?"

"Not really, but I'd like to give you this one. So you can remember Murray Island."

And *her,* he thought. "As if I could ever forget," he said. "I'll cherish it."

"I'm sure." She attempted a laugh and failed. "A new gem for your art collection."

"It's already my favorite thing."

Stronger now, the wind whipped her hair, and the sand bit into his legs.

"We should take cover," he said. "Storm's coming in. Fast. I think we'd better make a run for the house!"

"I'll race you!" Giggling as she danced on her toes, she sprinted toward the house, and because he liked watching her cute butt when she ran, he held back and let her win.

Darting from room to room as the wind howled and the frame structure shuddered, she gave him a quick tour of the house. A shady front porch looked out onto the raging gulf. Two bedrooms, a bath and a kitchen were connected by screened breezeways to each other and to the porch.

The southern bedroom had a wall of windows. "This is my favorite room," she said. "There's always a breeze, so I usually sleep here."

When she cracked a window, the room cooled instantly as storm gusts swept through it.

Deliberately, he stared outside at the rain instead of at her narrow bed. Since it was much too easy to imagine her long, lithe body on that mattress beneath him, he concentrated on the fat raindrops splatting on sand.

"With all the doors and windows open, the prevailing breezes cool the house on the hottest summer days," she said.

"If you open everything up, doesn't that make you vulnerable to a break-in?"

"No one usually comes here except me and Jim."

All anybody had to do was slit a screen to get inside. She would be defenseless. If Quinn had known how vulnerable she was while she'd been gone, he would have been even crazier with worry.

"Would you like some tea?" she said. "While we wait out the weather?"

"Sure."

When he nodded, she disappeared into the kitchen, leaving him to explore the room. A violent gust hit the house as the storm broke with full force. Somewhere, a breezeway door slammed so hard the entire house shook. Then papers fluttered under her bed. Curious, he knelt and pulled them out.

To his amazement, he discovered dozens of watercolors, all of himself, all ripped in two. He was trying to shove the entire collection back under the bed, when he heard her light footsteps at the doorway.

"Oh, my God," she said. "I forgot about those. Don't think… I mean… They don't mean anything!"

"Right."

You just painted picture after picture of me with violent, vivid brushstrokes. Then you shredded them all. For no reason.

"You obviously weren't too happy with me," he muttered.

"I really don't want to talk about it."

"Did you paint anything else…besides me?"

"A few birds."

"How many?"

"Not so many. One actually." She turned away as if uncomfortable with that admission.

Obviously, she was just as uneasy about her feelings for him as he was about his obsession with her.

"Why don't we drink our tea and go back to the yacht," he said brusquely.

"Fine with me."

"I shouldn't have pulled those pictures out," he said.

"We said we were going to forget about them."

"Right. We did." So, while he'd been obsessing about her absence, maybe she'd done a bit of obsessing herself. He took a long breath.

They sat on the porch drinking tea as the gray fury of the storm lashed the island. Now that he wanted to leave, the weather wasn't cooperating. To the contrary. Monstrous black waves thundered against the beach while rain drummed endlessly against the metal roof. No way could he trust his small tender in such high seas.

"Looks like we're stuck here for the duration," he said. So much for distracting himself from his bride anytime soon.

She nodded, her expression equally grim. "Sorry I suggested coming here."

The squalls continued into the night, so for supper she

heated a can of beans and opened cans of peaches and to-
matoes. Happily, she produced a bottle of scotch that she
said she kept hidden.

"We have to hide liquor from the pirates," she told him
with a shy smile.

"Pirates?" he asked.

"We call anyone who lands on the island pirates. We
leave the house open so they don't have to break in. Because they will if we don't."

"So, you're not entirely unaware of the dangers of being
here all alone?"

"Jim's here."

"Right. Jim."

Quinn poured himself a drink and toasted good old Jim.
Then he poured another. When he'd drained the second,
she began to glow. Her smile and eyes looked so fresh and
sparkly, he saw the danger of more liquor and suggested
they go to bed.

"Separate bedrooms, of course," he said, "since that's
what you want."

Nodding primly, she arose and led him to the guest bedroom. When she left him, he stripped off his shirt and lay
down. She wouldn't leave his thoughts. He remembered her
brilliant eyes lighting up when she saw him hauled safely
onto *Pegasus*. He remembered how shyly she'd blushed
every time she'd looked at him in his office, when she'd
faced him down to ask him not to marry her sister. He remembered her breasts in the skimpy T-shirt she'd worn
today and her cute butt and long legs in her white shorts
as she'd raced him across the deep sand back to the house.

With the scotch still causing visions of her to warm his
blood, he couldn't sleep for thinking of her on her narrow
bed in the next room. Would she sleep curled in a ball like

a child or stretched out like a woman? Was she naked? Or in her bra and panties? Did she desire him, too?

Remembering all the things she'd done to him in his loft in San Antonio, he began to fantasize that she was in the bed with him, her long legs tangled with his. That got him even hotter.

If only they were on board the yacht so he could hide out in his office on the upper deck and bury himself in paperwork. Here, there was nothing to think about but her lying in the bed next door.

At some point, he managed to fall asleep only to dream of her. In his dream, she slipped as lightly as a shadow into his bedroom. Slim, teasing fingers pulled back his sheet. Then, calling his name in husky, velvet tones, she slid into bed beside him. Her eyes blazed with the same fierce passion he'd seen when she'd realized he was safely back on board the yacht, away from the shark's teeth.

His heart constricted. Was this love? If it wasn't, it felt too dangerously close to the emotion for comfort. Even in his dream he recoiled from that dark emotion. Love had ruined his life and the life of his father. Hadn't it?

Then, in the dream, she kissed him, her sensual mouth and tongue running wildly over his lips and body while her hands moved between his legs and began to stroke. Soon he forgot about the danger of love and lost all power to resist her.

Lightning crashed, startling him. When his eyes flew open he heard the roar of the surf. He was alone in a strange, dark bedroom with sweat dripping from his long, lean body onto damp sheets, aching all over because he wanted to make love to his forbidden wife.

She was driving him crazy. On a low, frustrated groan, he hurled himself out of bed and stalked onto the breezeway in the hope that the chill, damp wind whipping

through the screens would cool his feverish body and re-
store his sanity.

"Quinn!" came Kira's soft, startled cry, the sexy sound
setting his testosterone-charged nerves on high alert.

He whirled to face her just as a bolt of lightning flashed.
Her hair streaming in the wind, she leaned against a post
some ten feet away, in the shadows. Momentarily blinded
from the lightning, he couldn't make her out in the darkness. Imagining the rest of her, his blood notched a degree
hotter.

"You'd better get back to your room," he rasped.

"What's the use when I couldn't sleep even if I did?
Storms like this are exciting, aren't they?"

"Just do as I said and go."

"This is my house. Why should I do what you say, if I
prefer watching the storm…and you?" she said in a low,
breathless tone.

"Because if you plan to keep me in a separate bedroom,
it's the smart thing to do."

"Used to giving orders, aren't you? Well, I'm not used to
taking them. Since I'm your wife, maybe it's time I taught
you that. I could teach you a lot…"

Thunder rolled, and rain slashed through the breezeway furiously, sending rivulets of water across the concrete
floor.

"Go," he muttered.

"Maybe I will." But her husky laughter defied him.
"Then, maybe not."

When she turned, instead of heading across the breezeway toward her bedroom, she unlatched a screen door
behind her and ran onto the beach. As she did, a blaze of
white fire screamed from the wet black sky to the beach.

Hell! She was going to get herself fried if he didn't bring
her back.

"Kira!" he yelled after her.

When she kept running, he heaved himself after her, his bare feet sinking deeply into the soft, wet sand and crushed shells as he sprinted. Sheets of rain soaked him through within seconds.

She didn't get more than twenty feet before he caught her by the waist and pulled her roughly into his arms. She was wet and breathless, her long hair glued to her face, her T-shirt clinging to her erect nipples.

Quinn closed his eyes and willed himself to think of something besides her breasts and the light in her eyes. But as the cold rain pounded him, her soft warmth and beauty and the sweetness of her scent drew him. He opened his eyes and stared down at her. Slowly, she put her arms around him and looked at him as she had in his dreams, with her heart shining in her eyes.

Laughing, she said, "Have you ever seen anything so wild? Don't you love it?"

He hadn't deliberately stood in the rain or stomped in a puddle since he'd been a kid, when his dad had encouraged him to be a boy, as he'd put it. Hell, maybe that was his loss. Maybe it wasn't right for him to control himself so tightly.

As the torrents washed them, he picked her up and spun her crazily, high above his head. Then he lowered her, slowly, oh, so slowly. He let her breasts and tummy and thighs slide against his body, which became even harder in response to hers.

If only she'd stop looking at him with such fire in her eyes… She made him crave a different kind of life…. One of brightness, warmth and love.

"Kiss me," she whispered, pressing herself into his rock-hard thighs, smiling wantonly up at him when she felt his impressive erection.

So—she wanted him, too.

Kissing her so hard she gasped, he plunged his tongue into her mouth. The rain streamed over their fused bodies and the lightning flashed and the thunder rolled. He knew he should take her inside, but she tasted so good that, for the life of him, he couldn't let her go.

He would regret this, he was sure. But later. Not now, when she smelled of rain. Not when the wild surf roared on all sides of them. Not when his blood roared even louder.

Tonight, he had to have her.

Eleven

When he stripped her and laid her on the bed, she closed her eyes. With her face softly lit by an expectant smile and her damp hair fanning darkly across her pillow, she looked too lovely and precious for words.

"I wanted you to come to me… Even before…you appeared in the breezeway," she admitted, blushing shyly. "I know I shouldn't have…but I just lay on my bed craving you."

"Imagine that. We're on the same page for once."

"I don't want to want you…"

"I know exactly how you feel."

Thank God, he'd thought to stuff some condoms into his wallet before they'd left the yacht—just in case. Thinking about them now made him remember the first time— the one time he'd failed to protect her—and the little clock ticking in the back of his mind ticked a little louder.

She could be pregnant.

Part of him hoped she *was* pregnant…with a son. His son… No, *their* son. A little boy with dark hair who he could play ball with as his father had played with him. They would call him Kade. Quinn would come home, call his name, and the boy would come running.

Foolish dream.

Stripping off his wet jeans and Jockey shorts, he pulled the condoms out of his wallet and laid them on the bedside table. Still thinking she could very well be pregnant and that he wouldn't mind nearly as much as he should, he stroked the creaminess of her cheek with his thumb. When her eyes sparked with anticipation, he kissed each eyelid and then her smiling mouth.

"Such tiny wrists," he said as he lifted them to his lips. He let his warm breath whisper across her soft skin. "Your heart is beating faster than a rabbit's. So, you did want me…my darlin'. Feed my bruised ego—admit it."

She laughed helplessly. "Okay—I'm tingling in so many places, I feel weak enough to faint."

He touched her breasts, her slender waist, the thatch of silken curls where her thighs were joined. He pressed his lips to all those secret places so reverently that his kisses transcended the physical.

"Better." He smiled. "I told you that you'd change your mind about sex." Triumphantly, he skimmed his mouth along her jawline. With each kiss that he bestowed, she claimed another piece of his heart.

"That you did. Are you always right? Is that how you became so rich?"

He kissed her earlobe, chuckling when she shivered in response.

"Focus is the key in so many endeavors. It only took a day, and I didn't once try to seduce you, now, did I?"

"Stop crowing like a rooster who's conquered a henhouse! I see you brought plenty of protection…which means you intended this to happen."

"I was hopeful. I usually feel optimistic about achieving my goals." He trailed the tip of his tongue along her collarbone.

She moved restlessly beneath him. "You're rubbing it in, and I said don't gloat." When he licked her earlobe again, she shuddered, causing a blazing rush of fire to sizzle through him. "Just do it," she begged.

"Why are you always in such a hurry, sweet Kira?"

Because she was unable to take her eyes from his face, she blew out a breath. Except for clenching her fingers and pressing her lips together, she lay still, as if fighting for patience.

"After all," he continued, "for all practical purposes, this is our wedding night."

Her quick scowl made him wonder why the hell he'd reminded them both of the marriage he'd forced her into.

Before she could protest, he kissed her lips. Soon her breathing was deep and ragged, and it wasn't long until she was quivering beneath his lips and begging him for more.

Her hands moved over his chest and then lower, down his torso and dipping lower still. When her fingers finally curled firmly around the swollen length of his shaft, he shuddered. Soon she had him as hot and eager to hurry as she was. He was out of control, completely in her thrall.

"I bet we're on the same page now," she said huskily, a triumphant lilt in her husky tone.

"Sexy, wanton witch." Unwrapping a condom, he sheathed himself.

Compelled to claim her as his, he plunged into tight, satiny warmth. Stomach to stomach. Thigh to thigh. The moment he was inside her, she wrapped her legs around his waist and urged him even deeper.

"Yes," she whispered as a tortured moan was torn from her lips.

"Yes," he growled, holding her even closer.

Then, some force began to build as he stroked in and out of her, his rhythm growing as hard and steady as the surf dancing rhythmically against the shore. His blood heated; his heart drummed faster. When he fought to slow down, she clung tighter, writhing, begging, urging him not to stop—shattering what was left of his fragile control.

With a savage cry, he climaxed. She felt so good, so soft, so delectable. Grabbing her bottom, he ground himself into her, plunging deeper. As she arched against him, he spilled himself inside her.

She went wild, trembling, screaming his name, and her excitement sent him over the fatal edge he'd vowed never to cross. Walls inside him tumbled. He didn't want to feel like this—not toward her, not toward any woman.

But he did.

Long minutes after he rolled off her, he lay beside her, fighting for breath and control.

"Wow," she said.

Even though sex had never felt so intense before, he didn't trust his feelings. Why give her any more power than she already had by admitting them? But though he confessed nothing, her sweet warmth invaded him, soothing all the broken parts of his soul.

She sidled closer and touched his lips with feverish fingertips, her eyes alight with sensual invitation. As she stroked his mouth and cheek teasingly, desire sizzled through him. He was rock-hard in another instant.

No way in hell would one time suffice. For either of them. With one sure, swift movement, he slid nearer so that his sex touched hers. When she stared up at him hungrily, he kissed her brow, her eyelids and then the tip of her pert nose. Then he edged lower, kissing her breasts and navel. Spreading her legs, he went all the way down, laving those sweet forbidden lips that opened to him like the silken petals of a warm flower. The tip of his tongue flicked inside, causing her to moan.

"Darlin'," he said softly. "You're perfect."

"I want you inside me. So much."

He wanted that, too, so he eased into her, gently this time, and held her tight against him. How could she feel so wonderful in his arms? So right? Like she belonged there, always, till the end of time? How could this be? She was Earl's daughter, a woman he'd coerced into marriage.

"How can this be?" she asked, her words mirroring his dark thoughts.

He took his time, and when it ended in violent, bitter-sweet waves of mutual passion, he felt again the inexplicable peace that left no space for hate or thoughts of revenge. He simply wanted her, wanted to be with her. He didn't want to hurt anything or anybody she loved.

"You're dangerously addictive," he whispered against her earlobe.

Her sweet face was flushed; her lips bruised and swollen from his kisses.

"So are you," she said with a tremulous smile even as her wary eyes reminded him that she hadn't married him for this. "This wasn't supposed to happen, was it? You didn't want this connection any more than I did."

"No…" His mood darkened as he remembered she didn't believe this was a real marriage.

His old doubts hit him with sweeping force. Tomorrow… if it would make her happy, he'd swear to her he'd never touch her again. But not tonight. Tonight, he had to hold her close, breathe in her scent, lose himself in her…dream of a different kind of life with her.

Just for tonight she was completely his.

Hugging him close, she sighed and fell asleep. Beside her, he lay awake for hours watching her beautiful face in the dark, longing and…wishing for the impossible.

When Kira awoke, her arms and legs were tangled around Quinn's. She'd slept so well. For a fleeting instant she felt happy just to be with him.

Last night he'd made her feel precious and adored. Until…the end. With a frown, she remembered how tense and uncertain he'd seemed right before he'd crushed her close and she'd fallen asleep in his arms.

How could she have thrown herself at him? Begged him? He was determined never to love again. Sex, even great sex, would not change his mind.

Despite regrets and misgivings, the gray morning was beautiful. Rain was falling softly, scenting the island with its freshness. A gentle breeze whirred in the eaves while dazzling sunlight splashed the far wall with vivid white.

Had she been sure of Quinn's love, it would have felt romantic to be nestled so warmly in his strong arms. She would have reveled in the sensual heat created by his breath stirring her hair.

But wrapped in cocoonlike warmth with him when she knew he couldn't ever care for her only aroused longings for forbidden things like friendship and affection.

He was going to break her heart. She knew it.

Slowly, she shifted to her side of the bed. Careful not to wake him, she eased herself to her feet. When he smiled in his sleep, she couldn't help thinking him the most stunningly handsome man she'd ever seen.

He looked so relaxed. So peaceful. Last night, he'd taken great care to make her happy in bed. Longing to brush his thick hair away from his brow filled her. Because of what they'd shared, she simply wanted to touch him.

No… She had to remember his experience. He was probably just a great lover and had taken no special pains with her.

Fearing she'd accidentally awaken him if she didn't stop gaping at his virile, male beauty, she tiptoed onto the breezeway where salty air assaulted her. When her tummy flipped violently, causing a brief dizzy spell, she sank against the doorjamb.

After a deep breath, the dizziness loosened its hold. She wasn't sick exactly, but her face felt clammy and she was queasy in a way she'd never been before.

Alarmed, she swallowed. Shakily, she smoothed her damp hair back from her face.

Again, she remembered that Quinn hadn't used a condom their first time in bed. In her head, she began to count the days since her last period, which she already knew was a little late. It was time…past time…for her period to start…and under the circumstances, her odd light-headedness made her anxious.

What if she were pregnant? How would Quinn react? He had not married her because he loved her or wanted a family. Quite the opposite. He'd used protection every single time since that first lapse. She'd never want to force him to stay married to her because of a baby. She wanted love, acceptance. Making their marriage of convenience a permanent situation was the best way to guarantee she'd never find it.

Quickly, she said a little prayer and decided not to borrow trouble just yet. Why upset him until she knew for sure? Still, no matter how she denied it, a seed of worry had taken root.

By the time Quinn had awakened, yanked on his jeans

and called for her, Kira had had her first cup of coffee and felt almost calm enough to face him. As she sat on the front porch, she watched the last gusts of the storm whip the high waves into a frenzy and hurl them against the shore.

At the sound of his approaching footsteps her belly tightened. Then she reminded herself there had only been one lapse…so there really wasn't much danger of pregnancy, was there?

"Kira?"

Concentrating on the angry seas, she wondered how soon the waves would calm down enough for them to leave. When she heard Quinn turning away from the porch, maybe because she hadn't answered, and stomping around somewhere inside the kitchen calling her name, she sensed he was out of sorts, too.

The door behind her creaked.

"Why didn't you answer when I called you?" His low voice was harsh, uncertain. "Avoiding me, are you?"

She didn't turn around to look at him. "Maybe I didn't hear you."

"Maybe you did."

"The seas are still so high, it may be a while before we can leave," she said.

"I see. After last night, you're too embarrassed to talk about anything but the weather. Are you blaming me because I didn't stick to our no-sex deal?"

Hot color climbed her cheeks. "No. I know that what happened was as much my fault as yours."

"But you don't like it."

"Look, what I don't like is being bullied into this marriage in the first place."

"Right."

"If you hadn't forced me to marry you, we wouldn't be

trapped on this island together. Then last night wouldn't have happened."

"Okay, then. So, am I to assume from your mutinous expression that you want to go back to our no-sex deal?"

Why were men always so maddeningly literal? All she wanted was a little reassurance. Instead, he'd launched into the blame game.

Well, she wasn't about to admit she'd craved him last night or that she'd enjoyed everything they'd done together. Nor would she admit that despite everything, she still wanted him. That the last thing she wanted was their no-sex deal. To admit any of that would prove her irrational and give him too much power over her.

When she sat staring at the stormy gulf in silence, he squared his shoulders. "It's too bad the waters are so rough and you're stuck with me, but if we've waited it out this long, I don't intend to push our luck by trying to take the tender out when we could capsize. I'm hungry. Do you want to share that last can of pork and beans with me for breakfast or not?"

The mere thought of canned pork and beans made her mouth go dry and her tummy flip. Within seconds, she began to perspire.

"Or not," she whispered, shaking her head fiercely as she inhaled a deep breath to settle her stomach.

"Are you all right? You look a little pale," he said, stepping closer. "Sick almost."

"I'm fine," she snapped, turning away so he couldn't read her face.

"I wasn't too rough last night, was I?" he asked, the genuine concern in his low tone touching her.

"The less said about what happened the better!"

With a weary look, he nodded. "I talked to my captain via satellite phone. *Pegasus* held up well under the rough seas and squalls. The crew had a bit of a bad night, but other than a case or two of seasickness, all is well."

"I'm glad."

"Look, for what it's worth, I'm sorry I reneged on our bargain and made love to you."

She knotted her hands and unknotted them.

"I took advantage."

"No, you didn't! I was the one who ran out in the storm and lured you after me!" She jumped up. Hugging herself, she walked over to the window. "I'm sure any man would have done the same."

"Look, I'm not just some guy you picked up off the street who is out to get what he can get."

She whirled on him. "Whatever you may think because of that night we shared in San Antonio, I don't do one-night stands, either!"

"I know that. I believe that. I wouldn't have married you otherwise."

"I wonder. Did anything besides my last name really matter to you?"

His face went cold. "I'm your husband. Last night I knew what you wanted and what you didn't want. But in the end, it didn't matter."

"You told me you'd have me in your bed in no time, and you did. So why don't you chalk up another win for your side in your little plan to get revenge against my father."

"Damn it. Because that's not how I feel about it! Or about you!"

"Don't romanticize what happened! We were bored and trapped. Big deal. It's over."

"The hell it is."

"Ours is only a marriage of convenience."

"Do you have to constantly remind me of that?"

"Why not, if it's the truth?"

"Is it? Does it have to be?"

"Yes! Yes!"

He was silent for a long moment. "If that's really how you feel, I won't sleep with you again. You can have your marriage of convenience—permanently. I hope it makes you happy!"

His cold announcement chilled her. Not that she was about to let him see how hurt she felt.

"Great! Now that that's settled, go! Eat your beans and leave me alone!"

"All right. And after I eat them, I'm going out. For a walk. To check on the tender. And I won't be back till the storm's over."

"Great! Perfect!"

When he slammed out of the porch and stalked toward the kitchen, her stomach twisted sharply. She felt ill, really ill. Clutching her stomach, she ran out the back door so he wouldn't see, knelt on the damp sand in the lightly falling rain, and was sick.

She *was* pregnant. She just knew she was.

His strides long and quick because he was anxious to get as far from the house—and from her—as fast as he could, Quinn stalked down the beach toward the dock. As his heels thudded into the deep sand, his head pounded viciously. Their quarrel had given him the headache from hell.

How different he felt now than he had when he'd first woken up. The air had smelled so fresh. He'd lain in bed, his eyes closed, drinking in a contentment he hadn't known in years. Then, he'd reached for her and discovered cool sheets instead of her warm, silky body, and some part of him had gone cold.

He didn't regret his harsh words because she'd smashed

his heart. He didn't regret the sex, either. She'd been sweet, and she'd felt too good—so good that just thinking of her naked and writhing in his arms, her shining eyes big as she'd begged for more had him brick-hard all over again.

When he saw the dock up ahead and the tender riding the waves, he felt intense relief.

He wasn't used to second-guessing himself or feeling the slightest guilt or confusion after sex. In his whole life he'd never awakened beside a woman who hadn't wanted him. Quite the opposite. They always clung, wanting more than he could give. Then he'd be the one to pull away. With her, he felt different. That's probably why he'd been fool enough to marry her.

From the moment Kira had shown up in his office to beg him not to marry her sister, he'd changed all the rules he'd lived by for so long. She'd tangled his emotions into a painful knot.

For some insane, ridiculous reason, he wanted to please her. He'd actually hoped she'd be happier with him after last night, so her obvious misery this morning ate at him all the more.

In his frustration, he broke into a jog. His marriage be damned. The sooner he ended this farce of a honeymoon and got back to business the better.

From now on, their marriage would be as she wished—all for show. He'd ignore the hell out of her except when there were in public.

When he reached the dock, he grabbed the stern line. After snugging the tender closer, he sprang on board.

Crafted of teak for the turbulent waters of the North Sea, she was an efficient, self-bailing craft. Maybe that was why she hadn't sunk. Also, the dock was on the leeward side of the island and in a well-protected cove.

He started the engine and smiled grimly when it purred

to life. Once he made sure the tender was sound, he shut it off, sat down and let the wind buffet him.

In no mood to return to the house or to his wife, he kept an eye on the distant horizon. As soon as the seas calmed, he'd take his bride home and get back to work. He'd lose himself in negotiations with the European Union and forget all about Kira.

His marriage was turning out to be the last thing from convenient, whatever Kira might say to the contrary.

Twelve

Quinn spoke to her as little as possible now.

If Kira had wondered how long Quinn would pretend to be interested in her, she had her answer and was miserable as a result.

No sooner had they returned to San Antonio than he'd made it clear he intended to live as he had before his marriage—working nearly every waking hour.

"The EU deal is going to command my full attention, so I won't be around much for a while," he'd said.

"Fine. I understand."

"Jason will come promptly at ten every morning to take care of you and the house."

"Jason?"

"My houseman. He's at your command. You'll find him highly competent."

Quinn had ensconced her in his fabulous loft apartment, and yes, he'd given her the master bedroom. Now she slept alone in the vast bed they'd shared that first night. As for himself, their first evening home, he'd packed a suitcase and moved his things into a second bedroom. Then he'd politely bid her a terse good-night, gone to bed early and left for work the next morning hours before she'd woken up.

That first morning Jason, a much older man, who was thin-lipped and skeletal, had greeted her so haughtily in the kitchen, she'd felt she was invading his territory.

"I'm Jason," he'd said with a vague sneer in his upper-class tone. "I'm here for whatever you need, cleaning, shopping, cooking—anything. It is my duty and privilege to please you, madam."

Madam?

"Wow! I'm really not used to being waited on. I can't think of a thing for you to do. I mean, I can pour my own cereal out of a box, can't I?"

"Cereal?" He scowled briefly. "Would you prefer an omelet?" he'd suggested with a contemptuous lift of his brows.

"Well, why not," she'd whispered, sensing they were getting off to a bad start. She wanted to be agreeable, yet she despised herself for giving in to him when he was supposed to be serving her. The man made her feel more out of place in Quinn's home than she'd felt before.

Jason had cooked a very good ham-and-vegetable omelet, and she'd dutifully eaten it. Then she'd rushed off to Betty's restaurant to help out while one of the waitresses was away, and the kitchen smells had bothered her way more than usual.

The rest of the week followed the same pattern with Quinn leaving early and returning late. Jason cooked her breakfast and made her dinner, and she began to feel grateful for his presence since it meant she wasn't totally alone.

Since Quinn was gone all the time, she might hardly have noticed she was married if she hadn't missed him so much. She was on her own, as she had been before her marriage, but because her husband was a man she found exceedingly attractive, she felt rejected and constantly unsettled. If he was home behind his shut door, she thought of him every minute.

When he was gone, she felt lost. With every passing day she grew more acutely sensitive to odors, which made her increasingly worried that he'd made her pregnant. She wanted to talk to Quinn about the situation, but she dreaded the conversation, especially now that he was so intent on avoiding her.

On the eighth day of their return, when her period still hadn't started and she was queasier than ever, she called her doctor and made an appointment for the next morning. She'd agreed to take her mother to a routine chemo treatment the same afternoon.

Jaycee had called her earlier in the week, begging her to pick up their mother for her appointment as a favor because escorting her mother for treatment made Jaycee so sad.

"So, how's it going with Quinn?" Jaycee had asked after Kira agreed.

"Fine."

"Fine? Hmm? Well, they do say the first few months are an adjustment."

"I said we're fine."

"I know you don't believe this, but he cares about you. He wanted to marry you."

"Right."

"He bought you that beautiful wedding dress, and you should have seen him when you were gone and nobody knew where you were."

"Well, he's ignoring me now," Kira confided.

"Did you two have a fight?"

She didn't answer.

"If you did, and I think you did, you need to find a way to kiss and make up."

"Why bother to make up, if we have no future?"

Kira changed the subject to her cat, Rudy, and asked if Jaycee minded keeping him a while longer. "I don't want him attaching himself to Quinn…if we're just going to break up."

"He's only a cat."

"Rudy's sensitive."

"And Quinn's not? If I were you, I'd worry more about your husband."

She was; she just wasn't going to admit it.

When Jaycee hung up, Kira had marked her mother's appointment on her calendar. She was glad to have something other than Quinn and her possible pregnancy to concentrate on.

Hours later, she was in bed that night with her light out when she heard Quinn at the door. Throwing off her covers, she started to go out and greet him. Then, pride made her stay where she was.

Wishing he'd knock on her door, she counted his approaching footsteps as he walked across the great room before he made his way down the hall.

When he paused at her door her heart beat very fast. But after a minute, he resumed walking to his own bedroom.

When his door slammed, a strangled sob rose in her throat. With a little cry, she got out of bed and ran to her window. Staring out at the brilliant city, she imagined other married couples, happier couples, slipping into bed together, snuggling close, talking about their day or their children, taking such blissful marital pleasures for granted.

Suddenly, Kira felt as lonely as a butterfly trapped in a child's glass jar.

Pulling on her robe, she wandered out into the great room. Baby or not, she could not live like this, with a husband who didn't want her.

Behind her, she heard a floorboard creak. Whirling, she caught her breath at the sight of Quinn standing barechested in the dark. His shadowed eyes looked haunted.

"You okay?" His low, harsh voice made her shiver. She wanted to be held, loved and crushed against him.

"I'm fine. And you?"

"A little tired, but the deal with the EU seems to be coming together. I'll be going to London for a few days."

"Oh."

"A car's coming for me at 5:00 a.m. Don't worry. I'll be careful so as not to wake you."

How could he be so obtuse? Was he just indifferent? Or was he still angry with her for their harsh exchange on the island?

She wanted to scream at him that he should kiss her goodbye properly. She wanted to drive him to the airport herself. But she kept such foolish thoughts to herself, and he only stared at her from the dark with his intense, burning gaze. She thought he was watching her, waiting—but for what?

Jaycee had advised her to kiss and make up. But how? To what purpose, when he so clearly had his mind on more important things?

After a few minutes of staring at each other in stony silence, he said good-night.

The next morning, when she heard the front door close behind him, she got up. Throwing away all pride, she rushed from her room into the foyer that was filled with crimson light, managing to catch up to him as he waited for the elevator.

"Sorry to wake you," he murmured, concern in his eyes.

"Don't be. I had to say goodbye and wish you a safe journey, didn't I," she whispered, surprised that she could sound so calm, so normal when she felt so incredibly depressed. "I'll miss you."

His dark brows arched warily. "Will you now?"

"I will," she said.

After another long moment spent considering her, he sighed and drew her close against his long, hard body. "I'll miss you, too." He paused. "Sorry about the last week or so."

"I'm sorry, too."

"Habib will call you later and give you all the numbers where I can be reached. I'll think of you in London. I really will miss you. You know that, don't you?" he murmured.

Would he really?

Wrapping her closer, he kissed her hard. She clung to him, probably revealing more of her real feelings than was wise. Then the elevator pinged, and he was forced to let her go or be late. Holding her gaze, he picked up his suitcase and strode through the doors.

She couldn't turn away or stop looking at him or take even one step toward the loft until the door shut.

Pregnant! Needing a moment to take in that news, Kira clenched the steering wheel of her Toyota as she sat in the parking lot of the medical complex and kneaded her forehead with her knuckles.

After a brief exam, the doctor had ripped off his latex gloves and confirmed she was pregnant.

"How do you know? You haven't even tested me."

"When you've been doing this as long as I have, young lady, you just know."

Within minutes, a pregnancy test administered in his office confirmed his opinion.

After the office visit, she felt both numb and tingly as she sat in her car. Biting her lip, she pulled out the slip of paper where she'd written all the numbers Habib had given her earlier. After calculating the time difference between the U.K. and Texas, she grabbed her cell phone and started dialing. Then she stopped. Quinn was probably extremely busy or in an important meeting. Her news would distract him from what was all-important to him—the deal. Better to share the news with him in person when she was sure she had his full attention and could gauge his reaction.

Still, her heart felt as if it was brimming over. She was bursting to tell someone…who would be every bit as excited as she was.

Mother. Suddenly, she was very glad she would be taking her mother to treatment today. Who better to confide in than her precious baby's grandmother? Nobody adored babies, anybody's babies, more than her mother did. Her mother would be happier about this news than anyone, and goodness knew, with all she was going through, she needed a cheerful future to contemplate.

"Oh, my dear," her mother gushed, setting her flowered china teacup aside and seizing Kira's hand in both of her thin ones. Kira had waited until after her mother's treatment, when they could sit down together at Betty's, to share the news.

How weak her mother's grasp felt, even if her eyes were alight with joy.

"Such wonderful news! The best ever! Unbelievable! And it was so easy for you two! And so soon!"

A fierce rush of pride swamped Kira. Never had her mother been so pleased with her. Such rapture had always been reserved for Jaycee's accomplishments.

"Have you told Quinn yet?" her mother asked.

"I started to call him. Then I thought I'd wait…until he comes home, until he's not so distracted."

"So, I'm the first!" Her mother beamed so brightly she almost looked as she had before the illness. Her grip strengthened. "I'm going to beat this thing and live for a very long time. I have to…if I'm to see my darling grand-baby grow up."

Kira's gaze blurred, and she had to turn away to hide her emotion. She felt exhilarated and proud, and a big part of her pleasure had to do with the fact that for once she'd trumped Jaycee.

Oh, why hadn't she ever felt sure of her parents' love?

The river sparkled beside their table outside Betty's. Kira was thrilled her mother's fighting spirit was intact and that she felt reasonably strong. But most of all, she couldn't help being glad that she'd been the one to make her mother so happy.

"Your father will be just as excited as I am. He's very up on Quinn's successes in London, too. So this will be a doubly great day for him."

"Oh, so he's already heard from Quinn?" Kira whispered, feeling more than a little hurt that Quinn had called her father and not her.

"Yes, and it sounds like things are going very well," her mother replied. "Am I to assume by the way you're biting your lip that *you* haven't spoken to him?"

"He texted me, saying he'd arrived in London safely. I'm not hurt. Not in the least."

After studying her for a long moment, her mother looked

dubious. "Well, I'm sure he'll be so happy to hear your exciting news."

Would he be? Oh, how she hoped so, but her doubts soon had her biting her lower lip again.

"Don't do that, dear. How many times have I told you that biting your lip like that chaps your beautiful mouth?"

"When I was a child, Mother!"

"Well, just the same, I know you want to be beautiful for Quinn when he comes home, now, don't you?"

"Right. I do." She glanced at the muddy green river and tried to focus on a white duck. "Frankly, I'm a little worried about telling him. You know…we didn't marry under the best of circumstances."

"I wish you wouldn't make so much of that. I really think it means something when a couple gets pregnant so easily," her mother said almost enviously.

"What are you saying?"

"Sometimes it doesn't work that way… Earl and I had a terrible time getting pregnant with…with you. But let's not go there."

Did she only imagine the shadow that passed over her mother's thin face?

"Is anything wrong, Mother?"

"No, dear."

But her mother looked away and something in her manner and stiff posture rang alarm bells inside Kira. When the silence between them lengthened and grew more strained, she was sure her mother was worrying about something.

"What's wrong? Have I upset you?"

Her mother stared at her, hesitating. "I guess…it's only natural that your news would stir up the past."

"When you were pregnant with me?"

A single tear traced down her mother's cheek. "No…" She clenched her napkin.

"Did the doctor tell you something when you were alone with her that has you upset? Bad news of some kind?"

"Dear God, no!" Her mother took her hand. "No. It's not that. It's nothing like that. It's about you…" Her mother's eyes filled with some unfathomable emotion. "I was never pregnant with you."

"What?"

"I…*we* tried so hard, your father and I, to have a baby. So dreadfully hard. You know how I am. I took my temperature all the time. Ten times a day. But I didn't…I couldn't get pregnant…no matter what I did. We went to so many specialists, and they told us that it was my fault, not your father's. Some hormone imbalance. And then…we never told anyone, not even you, the truth."

"What truth?" Under the table Kira's hands fisted so tightly her nails dug bloody crescents into her palms.

"I couldn't conceive, so, in the end, we adopted."

"What?"

"You're adopted. Please don't look so upset! I could never have had a daughter of my own as wonderful as you. You've always been so sweet. Like now. Coming with me for my treatment when poor Jaycee couldn't bear it. She hates thinking of me being sick. She's too much like me, you see. I'm strong in some ways, but weak in others. Until now, I could never admit, not to anyone, that you weren't my biological child. It represented my biggest imperfection as a woman."

"Oh, my God." Kira felt overwhelmed, hollow. Suddenly she remembered all the little things that had never added up in her life. The rest of her family members were blond and blue-eyed, while she had dark eyes and hair. She was tall and slim, while her mother and Jaycee were more petite and curvy.

She'd never been as interested in style or fashion as they were. She'd been wired more emotionally and hadn't thought as logically as they did. Maybe this was why she'd always felt as if she hadn't belonged in her family. Maybe she'd always sensed this huge falsehood in her life.

"I felt like such a failure," her mother continued. "As a woman. For not being able to conceive a child. And then suddenly, inexplicably, when you were two years old, I became pregnant with Jaycee...without even trying. When she was so perfect, so gorgeous, I felt I'd achieved something grand by giving birth. But really, having you was always just as big an achievement. Only I never appreciated it until now. Illness like this can change you, make you wiser somehow.

"I was silly and so unsure when I was young. I know I haven't always understood you, but you are very precious to me."

Kira could say nothing. She was as overwhelmed as a stage actress in a drama who'd forgotten all her lines. Her mind had gone blank.

"I'm so glad you have Quinn. We all suffered so much when Kade died right after selling the company to us. Your father loved Kade like a brother. And then, all these years later, to have Quinn take over the company at the best possible moment for us was a fortunate irony. And now this baby. This wonderful baby will make everything right again. I just know it will.

"I'll get well, and you'll be happy with Quinn. You'll quit...doubting you belong together because you'll have this baby to love together. Nothing can bring a couple closer than a child."

"If only life were that simple."

"Sometimes it is."

Kira couldn't think about her adoption and what it meant right now. So she focused on finding out more about Quinn's past.

Squeezing her eyes shut, she reopened them. "Mother, why did Quinn blame Daddy for his father's death?"

"Your father and Kade Sullivan created Murray Oil. Well, back then it was Sullivan and Murray Oil. Esther Sullivan was extravagant, but Kade adored her. Of course, he was always borrowing from Earl, always needing more… because of her, you see. Esther's needs were insatiable. In time, Kade began to gamble on the side and play the market. For years he was lucky, but then one day his luck ran out.

"When money went missing at the company, from accounts he was responsible for, your father asked him some pointed questions. Kade got angry. The money was found eventually, but the misunderstanding had caused a rift between them.

"Kade said he wanted out, so Earl bought him out. But when times got better and the stock price took off, Kade got hard feelings and started drinking and bad-mouthing your father, especially to Quinn, I think. Around that time, Esther divorced Kade and took whatever he had left.

"Not too long afterward, Earl made a deal that tripled the worth of Murray Oil. Kade claimed the deal had been his idea and wanted compensation, so he sued. He lost the suit, and Quinn discovered his father's body in his shop off the garage. Supposedly Kade had been cleaning his shotgun and it went off. Accidentally. But who knows? Not that Kade ever seemed like the kind of man who'd kill himself. In fact, your father definitely believes it was an accident.

"Oh, my darling, let's not talk of such depressing things.

I much prefer to think about my future grandbaby. Do you want a boy or a girl?"

"A little boy," she whispered. "A little boy with blue eyes who looks just like Quinn and Kade."

"So, you're beginning to love him a little."

With all her heart. Yet she wasn't ready to admit that, not even to her mother.

But her mother saw the truth. "I told you so," she said triumphantly. "And no wonder. He's everything any woman with half a brain would want in a husband."

Not quite everything. He could never return her love, Kira thought.

Thirteen

Quinn remained in London for a week, during which time Kira ached for him. She didn't know how she could miss a man who'd worked so hard to ignore her before he'd left, but she did.

Then, suddenly he sent her a brief text informing her of his flight information for the next day. He said he'd hired a driver to pick him up. Then, right before he boarded his plane, he called her cell while she was still asleep. When she didn't answer, he left a message saying he'd called to remind her of a company party they were attending that evening an hour after his flight was scheduled to land.

So, there would be no private time together his first night home.

"You can call my secretary to find out what to wear," he'd said over the phone. Then his voice had lowered. "Missed you...worse than I thought I would," he'd whispered before ending the call.

Damn. Damn. Damn. What rotten luck that she'd missed his call. What else might he have said if they'd actually talked? She replayed his message several times just to hear his mesmerizing voice say he'd missed her.

A lump formed in her throat. Why had she muted her phone before laying it on her bedside table?

Dialing his secretary, she asked what she should wear to the party.

"It's formal, but Mr. Sullivan did tell me to suggest you wear something red."

"Why red?"

"He didn't say. The deal he pulled off with the EU will have far-reaching consequences for Murray Oil, hopefully positive. Since he's returning in triumph, the party's important to him. I'd suggest you go with his color choice, in case it fits with a bigger plan."

Her heart thumping wildly, Kira took off early from Betty's to indulge in a shopping spree with her mother in search of the perfect sexy red dress. Then she rushed home, with her low-cut scarlet gown and a pair of new heels, so she could take special pains getting dressed.

After the party, if Quinn was in a good mood, she would tell him she was pregnant.

At six, while she was combing her hair, his driver called to tell her Quinn's plane had just landed. "I'll have him home soon."

"Can I please talk to him?"

"He's on the phone. Business. But I'll tell him to call you as soon as he finishes."

When Quinn's key turned in the lock, Kira hurried to the door to greet him. His luggage thumped heavily on the floor. Then he strode through the foyer with his phone still pressed to his ear.

His voice rang with authority as he stepped into the living room. When she met his hard, dark eyes, she saw the shadows of weariness under them. Even if he hadn't bothered to call her from the car, she was so thrilled he was home, her heart leaped with pure joy.

"Gotta go," he said abruptly. "We'll wrap this up in the morning." He flipped his phone shut and stared at her. "Sorry about the phone call. Business."

"Of course. I understand." She smiled tremulously.

His mouth curved, but his smile played out before it reached his eyes.

She wanted to rush into his arms, and it was only with great effort that she remained where she was. No matter how eager she felt, she would not throw herself at him.

"You look pale," he said. "Thinner. Are you okay?"

She hadn't been eating as regularly due to her morning sickness, but she couldn't tell him that. At least, not now.

"I'm fine," she whispered.

"Right. Why is that answer always your first line of defense?"

She didn't know what to say to him. If only he would take her in his arms and kiss her, maybe that would break down the barriers between them.

His eyes burned her, and his hands were clenched. Was being married to her so difficult for him?

"I like the dress. It becomes you," he murmured.

She blushed, pleased.

"I bought you something." He tossed a box onto the sofa carelessly. "Open it and see if you like it." He spoke casually, as if the gift was a token and nothing more.

When he turned sharply and walked down the hall to his bedroom, she felt a sickening sensation of loss. How foolish she'd been to dream they might have a new beginning.

Sinking onto the sofa, she opened the black box and let

out a pleased cry when a necklace and earrings of rubies and diamonds exploded in fiery brilliance. He'd tucked his business card inside the box. On the back of it, scrawled in bold black ink, she read, "For my beautiful wife."

Tears filled her eyes as she hesitantly touched the necklace. She quickly brushed the dampness away. The necklace was exquisite. Nobody had ever given her anything half so lovely.

In the next breath, she told herself the gift meant nothing. He was wealthy. It was for show. He'd bought the jewels to impress Murray Oil's clients, stockholders and employees. He'd probably had someone pick them up for her. The gift wasn't personal.

"Do you like it?" Tall and dark, he stood in the doorway looking gravely handsome in his elegant black suit.

"It's too beautiful," she whispered. "You shouldn't have, but thank you."

"Then stand up, and I'll help you put it on. You have no idea how many necklaces I looked at. Nothing seemed right until I found this one."

"You shopped for it yourself?"

"Indeed. Who could I possibly trust to select the right gift for my bride? The wrong necklace could overpower you."

He let her secure the earrings to her ears before he lifted the necklace from the black velvet box and fastened it around her neck.

At the warmth of his fingertips against her nape, her skin tingled and her heart beat wildly. Was it possible to have an orgasm from sheer longing?

"With your dark hair, I thought rubies would become you, and they do," he said, staring so long at the sparkle on her slim neck his gaze made her skin burn. "I imagined you wearing them and nothing else."

In spite of herself, she giggled. *This was more like the homecoming she'd fantasized about.* In another moment, he would kiss her.

He stepped back to admire her and shot her an answering grin. Why, oh, why hadn't he kissed her?

She pursed her lips, touched her hand to her throat.

His face grew guarded again; his lips set in that firm line she'd come to dread. Instead of taking her in his arms, he backed away almost violently. "Shall we go?" he said, his tone rough and deliberately impersonal.

Cut to the quick, she didn't dare look at him as she nodded. During the short drive, he didn't speak to her again.

As soon as they arrived at the party, he put his arm around her as executives and clients rushed up and surrounded him, all clamoring to congratulate Quinn on his successes in London.

Black silk rustling, Cristina was among the first who hurried to his side. Barely managing a cool smile for Kira, she placed a bejeweled, exquisitely manicured hand on Quinn's cheek with practiced ease and kissed him lightly.

"I'm *so* proud of you," she gushed in a low, intimate tone. "I knew you'd pull it off. See—everybody loves you now. Worries over."

Clearly, he'd taken the time to inform *her* personally of his successes.

"So the deal went well?" Kira whispered into his ear when the lovely Cristina glided away.

He nodded absently as he continued shaking everybody's hand.

"Why didn't you tell me?"

"You know now, don't you?"

"But I'm your wife…"

"Unwillingly, as you keep reminding me. Which is why

I've been working hard not to burden you with too much attention."

Stung, her eyes burning and her heart heavy, she turned away. Why did it hurt that he saw no need to share the things that mattered to him when she'd known all along their marriage was for show?

She was sure he had a duty to mingle, so she was surprised when Quinn stayed by her side. When she noticed a dark-skinned man talking animatedly to her family, she asked Quinn who he was.

"Habib."

"The man you were talking to after we made love that first time?"

He nodded. "I thought you two had met...at the wedding."

"No, but we've talked on the phone this past week. Why did he think you should marry Jaycee instead of me?"

"Whatever he thought, he was wrong. What difference does it make now?"

"My mother told me today that I was adopted."

When Quinn's blue eyes darkened, she sensed that he knew more than he wanted to let on.

"Something you said that morning made me wonder if you and he somehow knew that," she persisted.

He stiffened warily.

"I thought that if you had known, maybe you assumed my family cared more about her...and maybe that was why Habib concurred with my father that she was the better choice...?"

"Habib's research did indicate a partiality on your father's part for Jacinda."

Her chest constricted. That truth was one of the reasons being loved in her own right by her husband was something that was beginning to matter to Kira more than anything.

"I preferred you from the first," he countered.

He kept saying that. Could she dare to believe him?

"Doesn't that count for something?" he asked.

"Our marriage was a business deal."

"So you keep reminding me."

"You only married me to make taking over Murray Oil go more smoothly, and now that you've made a place for yourself, your need for me is at an end."

"I'll decide when my need for you is at end. What do you say we end this depressing conversation and dance?" He took her hand. "Shall we?"

"You don't really want to dance with me— I'm just—"

"Don't put yourself down," he growled as he pulled her into his hard arms. "You're my wife."

"So, dancing with me at the company party is expected?" she said.

"I suppose." His grip strengthening, he smiled grimly down at her. "Did it ever occur to you that I might want to dance with you even if it wasn't expected?"

She was aware of people watching them and reminded herself that he was only dancing with her to make the guests believe their marriage was real.

From a corner, her laughing parents and a smiling Jaycee watched them, too. Looking at them, so happy together, Kira felt left out, as usual. Even being in Quinn's arms, knowing she was pregnant with his child, gave her no joy. How could it? Had he touched her other than for public viewing, or shown her any affection since he'd returned? Their marriage was a business deal to him, and one that wasn't nearly as important as the one he'd just concluded in London.

"Quit thinking dark, mutinous thoughts, and just dance," he whispered against her ear. "Relax. Enjoy. You're very beautiful, you know, and I'd seize any excuse to hold you in my arms."

Despite her determination to resist his appeal, his words, his nearness and his warm breath against her earlobe had her blood beating wildly.

She knew it was illogical, but being held in his arms reassured her. Soon she almost forgot dancing with him was just for show. Everyone in the gilded room blurred except her handsome husband.

They didn't speak again, but his eyes lingered on her lips as the music washed through her. Did he want to kiss her? She wanted it so much, she felt sick with longing. Surely he knew it. If so, he gave no indication, and, after a while, all the spinning about began to make her feel dizzy and much too hot.

She didn't want to be sick. Not now...not when he was finally holding her, when he seemed almost happy to be with her. Still, she couldn't take another step or she'd faint.

"I need some air," she whispered.

"All right." He led her round along the shadowy edges of the room until they came to a pair of tall French doors that opened onto a balcony overlooking the sparkling city. Gallantly, he pulled her outside. The night was mild, pleasant even. Once they were alone, his grip around her tightened in concern and he pressed her close.

"You look so strained and pale. Are you sure you're okay?"

She gulped in a breath of air. And then another. "I'm perfectly fine," she lied, believing that surely in a minute or two she would be.

"Obviously, even being in my arms is an ordeal."

"No!"

"You don't have to lie. I know well enough that I've given you ample reason to dislike me."

"I don't dislike you."

"But you don't like me. How could you? I was your father's enemy."

"Quinn—"

"No, hear me out. Since the island, I've kept my distance in order to make our marriage less onerous to you. I know I pushed you into this situation too hard and too fast, and I took advantage of you the night of the storm. I'm not proud of that. But do you have any idea how difficult it's been to stay away from you ever since?

"I wanted to give you your precious space and time to get used to our arrangement. I prayed that a week's separation would give me the strength to resist you when I returned," he muttered. "So, I didn't call you from London, and when I came home, I tried to be the cold husband you desire. But after our days apart, when you looked so ethereal and beautiful in your flashy red dress, my vow not to touch you drove me crazy. God help me, ever since the first day I saw you at your parents' ranch, you've obsessed me."

"But I don't desire a cold husband. I've wanted you, too," she whispered, wishing her feet felt a little steadier beneath her. Despite the fresh air, she was beginning to feel light-headed again.

"You have?"

Whatever encouragement he sought in her eyes, he found. Instantly, his lips were on hers, but when he crushed her closer, holding her tightly and kissing her, her dizziness returned in a sickening rush.

"I've wanted you so much," he murmured. "Missed you so much. You have no idea. Darlin', tell me you missed me, at least a little?"

Her heart beat violently even as she gulped in another breath. "Of course I did," she managed to say even as his dear face blurred and the walls of the building and the twinkling lights beneath them whirled dizzyingly like bright colors dancing in a kaleidoscope.

She willed herself to be strong, to fight the dizziness. "I did... But there's something I have to tell you, Quinn. Something...wonderful."

Little blue stars whirred. *Not good.* On the next beat the bottom dropped out of her tummy, and try as she might to save herself by gulping in mouthfuls of air, she couldn't get her breath.

"Quinn—"

Her hands, which had been pushing frantically against his hard chest, lost their strength. She was falling into a heavy darkness that was hot and swirling and all-enveloping.

The last thing she saw was Quinn's anxious face as his arms closed around her.

Fourteen

When Kira regained consciousness, Quinn was leaning over her in a small room, pressing a cool rag to her brow. To his right, a tall blond man with an air of grave authority had a finger pressed to her wrist while he studied his watch.

"Dennis is a doctor, and he wants me to ask you if…if you could possibly be pregnant," Quinn said.

"I wanted to tell…you. First thing… I really did."

"What?"

"Yes!" She blushed guiltily as Quinn stared down at her. "Yes. I'm pregnant. "I…I think that's why I got too hot while we were dancing. I've been having morning sickness while you were gone."

"That's why you were so pale. Why didn't you call me? Or tell me when I got home?" Quinn's hand tightened on her arm, and his expression grew grim. "Because you were unhappy about the baby? Were you planning to end the pregnancy without telling me?"

"No!" she exclaimed, horrified.

Quinn turned to the doctor and grilled him about her condition. The man quickly reassured him that her pulse and blood pressure were just fine. Still, he advised that she see her own doctor the next day, just to make sure.

"We're going home," Quinn said. "You're going to bed. No wonder I thought you looked thin. You should have told me."

"I was going to…"

"When?" he demanded so coldly she couldn't answer him.

That was the last word either of them said until they reached his loft. In the car, he gripped the steering wheel with clenched fists, while his profile seemed fashioned of unyielding granite. Never once did he look her way. Deliberately, he shut her out. The walls between them thickened and grew taller. Would she ever be able to reach him again?

Once inside the loft, he lingered in the crimson shower of light by the door while she fled to the master bedroom.

Alone in the vast room, she stared at the bed they'd shared. Silently, she kicked off her heels and pulled off the red dress and then slipped into a frothy white nightgown.

This wasn't the way she'd imagined telling him about the baby.

The rubies on her neck felt heavy, unbearable, but when she went to undo the clasp, her fingers shook too badly for her to manage it. The weight on her heart was even heavier. How could he have thought, even for one second, she might want to end her pregnancy? How could she go to bed when heartbreak was suffocating her?

She had to talk to him, to at least try to make things

right. Without remembering to grab a robe, she raced to the huge living room. It was empty, so she tiptoed back down the hall to his bedroom door, which he'd shut against her. She called his name, softly at first. When he didn't answer, she knocked.

His door swung open and he stood before her, his powerful, bare-chested body backlit by the lamp on his nightstand. He looked so glorious, she caught her breath. For a long moment, she could only stare at his bronzed muscles with bemused fascination. He was so fit and hard. If only she could throw herself into his arms and tell him she loved him and his baby.

But she knew he didn't want her love.

"I want this baby, and I was going to tell you," she whispered.

She watched his magnificent muscles cord as he pushed the door wider. "When?" he muttered roughly, disbelieving her.

"Just before I passed out at the party. I wanted to tell you in person, and… It was just that I was scared," she continued breathlessly. "I—I…couldn't believe you'd want my baby, too."

"Our baby," he corrected in a tight tone. "Couldn't the baby give us something more positive to build on?"

"How? If you regret marrying me. And blame our child for trapping you into a permanent involvement with a woman you don't want.

"Quinn, if you'd planned to dissolve our marriage after your takeover of Murray Oil, you don't have to stay with me because of this. I hope you know that. This doesn't have to change the businesslike nature of our arrangement."

He sucked in a breath. "Damn it. Are you ever going to quit telling me what I feel?"

"But isn't that…how you feel?"

For a long moment he was silent. "Would you listen to me for once, instead of being so sure you've got me pegged?"

"Yes. All right."

After another lengthy interval, his expression softened. "I guess I'm a little scared by your news," he said simply.

"Because you know our marriage isn't real?"

His mouth tensed. "No! Because babies are a lifetime commitment. Because they are so little...and so helpless. Because they know how to turn their parents into doting sots—and they do it with charm, in no time flat. Anything could happen to a baby." He caught her hand, and when she didn't struggle, he pulled her into his arms. "Or to you... while you're pregnant. I couldn't bear it." He kissed her brow.

It was bliss to be in his arms.

So he didn't love her, couldn't love anybody. But he cared. She was sure he cared, at least a little. He was holding her as if he did.

"But nothing will happen because we'll take good care of the baby...and me," she said reassuringly.

"My father was strong, and he died. We're all only a heartbeat away from death." There was so much grief and passion in his voice she felt hot tears sting the back of her eyelids.

"Which is why we have to live each moment to the fullest," she whispered. In a burst of tenderness, she raised her fingertips to stroke his temples in consolation. "We don't have a second to waste. We might as well be dead if we're afraid to live." To love, she wanted to add.

Quinn's arms tightened around her. He lowered his face and this time it was her mouth he sought. When he found it, he kissed her long and deeply. She opened her lips and sighed. She'd wanted him to kiss her like this for hours, days. Maybe that was why she couldn't help shivering in delight and giving him everything—all her love, even her soul—when she kissed him back.

"Oh, Kira…" For an endless time, he couldn't seem to stop kissing her. Then, suddenly, he let her go and jerked free of her embrace.

"Forgive me. I forgot—you don't want me pawing you. That's what made you sick, earlier." His dark face was flushed and his breathing ragged.

"No… I told you… I've had morning sickness. Only sometimes it's not just in the morning."

"Go to your own room. We can talk tomorrow." Even as his harsh rejection wounded, his eyes continued to hungrily devour her.

He wanted her. He was pushing her away *because* he desired her so much. And because she'd made him promise not to sleep with her.

She'd been wrong, impossible from the first. She'd missed him while he was away. She was carrying his child.

Everything had changed for them.

If she had to beg, she would.

"Don't make me sleep alone tonight," she pleaded. "Because I won't sleep. I'll just lie there…wanting you."

"I won't sleep, either. Still, in the morning you'll regret it if you don't go." His expression darkened. "Like you did before…on the island."

But she hadn't regretted it. He had.

"I don't think so," she said. "You did say we should focus on the positive…for the baby's sake. Am I right?"

His sensual mouth quirked ever so charmingly, and the heat in his gaze soon had her bones melting.

"How do you make me break every rule that allowed me to survive during my long, dark years of grief?"

"I get that you don't want to love anybody ever again.

Especially not me," she whispered. "But I'm not asking for your love tonight."

When he would have protested, she sealed his lips with a fingertip. "I'm not asking for anything you can't give. I just want to be with you."

"My father loved my mother too much, and…she destroyed him…when she left. I can't help thinking you're just waiting for the right moment to walk out."

Don't you know how much I love you? Don't you know that if only you loved me, I would never leave you?

Her knees were so weak with desire, she could barely stand. No way did she possess the courage to voice her true thoughts. She was afraid they would only drive him further away.

Her hold on him was tenuous, and only sexual. She had to accept that, use it and hope that someday she could build on that foundation.

Reaching toward him, she splayed her fingertips against his massive chest. Flesh and bone and sinew felt solid and warm beneath her open palm. When she ran her fingers over his nipples and through the dark hair that matted his torso, he groaned, which pleased her.

"Kira. Darlin'." On a shuddering sigh, he pulled her close and teased her lips and jawline with his mouth and tongue.

Lifting her, he carried her to the bed. There, he slid off his belt and slacks and pushed her nightgown down her shoulders. As it pooled onto the floor, he pulled her against him and pushed inside her slick satin warmth. Riding their mutual passion, they let it carry them like a charging black steed, faster and faster, until they soared together in torrid surrender. Afterward, as she held on to him, her sated body melted into his.

"You've ruined me," he whispered.

"Whiner," she teased.

"Seriously. I'll never be able to move again," he said.

She laughed. "Sure you will. And it better be sooner than you think. Because I'm going to be wanting more… very soon. You've neglected me…you know."

"Have I now? And whose fault was that, darlin' Kira?"

For an entire hour, he held her against his body as if she was precious to him. When she kissed his rough cheek, his throat, his nipples, he muttered huskily, "You weren't kidding, were you?"

"I've missed you."

"Slave driver."

But he smiled and ran his hands through her hair as he pulled her close.

This time his love was sweeter, and slower, and afterward, when he kissed her belly gently, he showed her that his intense passion included their precious child.

"So, you want my baby, do you?" he whispered.

"So much, too much," she admitted in a breathless whisper as she pressed his dark head against her flat stomach. "More than anything. In fact, I hope the baby's a boy and that he looks just like you."

He laughed in husky delight and nuzzled her tummy with his feverish lips. "Be careful what you wish for. He'll be a handful, I assure you."

"I can't wait."

When he held her close like this and was so teasingly affectionate, she could almost forget he didn't love her, that he never could. She could almost forget how inadequate and uncertain she'd always felt.

Almost…

He was a handsome billionaire, who could have any woman he wanted. What could she do to hold him?

Nestled in his arms, she fell into a restless sleep and

dreamed. She was a child again, standing beside her parents as they cheered Jaycee and her basketball team to victory. Then she was sitting in her room alone. The house was empty because her mother and father had driven Jaycee to a slumber party.

Older now, Kira was walking across the stage at Princeton where she'd graduated with honors. As she posed for photographs, she smiled brightly through her disappointment. None of her family was in the audience because Jaycee had a conflicting high school event. The picture was all they'd have to remember this huge milestone in Kira's life.

"Remember to smile," her mother had commanded over the phone. "You never smile." A pause. "Oh, how I wish I could be there to see you graduate!"

"Couldn't Daddy stay with Jaycee?"

"You know your father. He's no good at those high school functions without me."

The dream darkened into a nightmare. Quinn was standing in a shower of crimson light, holding Cristina against his long, lean body. "I have to marry *her,* don't you understand? I don't want to. You're the one who's special to me. Don't ever forget that my marriage to her is strictly business. You're the woman who really matters. Who will always matter. Nothing will change between us. You'll see."

Then he kissed Cristina as those awful words repeated themselves in her mind. "Strictly business…"

Kira woke up crying that phrase even as Quinn wrapped his arms around her and held her close.

"Hush. It's okay, baby. You were only dreaming."

Was she? Or were her dreams where she faced the harsh truths she denied when awake?

"I'm fine," she murmured, pushing him away. "You

don't have to comfort me. I can take care of myself—just like I always have. I didn't ask you to love me—did I?"

"No, you damn sure didn't."

Strictly business.

God, if only Quinn could feel that way, too, maybe then he'd survive this nightmare.

As soon as Kira's breathing had become regular again and Quinn was sure she was asleep, he'd tossed his own covers aside and shot out of bed.

Groping clumsily for his slacks on the dark floor, he yanked them on and stalked out of the bedroom in bare feet. When he got to the bar, he splashed a shot of vodka into a glass.

Strictly business.

Damn her! Not that he didn't feel sorry for her, because he did. Even now, her stricken cries echoed in his mind. She was no happier than he was.

He'd been right to think she'd regret the sex. So, why the hell had she slept with him when he'd given her an out?

He'd never figure her out. She might regret what had happened, but he couldn't. She'd been too sweet, and he'd craved her too desperately. Hell, it embarrassed him to think of how needy he'd felt all week without her in London.

Frowning as he stared into his glass, he remembered how he'd grabbed his cell phone at least a dozen times in his eagerness to call her, only to shove it back in his pocket. All he'd wanted was to hear her soft voice. Without her, he'd felt cut off, alone, alienated in a city he usually enjoyed.

Once in San Antonio, he'd rushed home. And when he'd seen her, he'd wanted nothing except to sweep her into his arms and kiss her endlessly. But she'd been pale and with-drawn.

Every day his obsession for her increased. If she could not reciprocate, they were shackled together on the same fatal course his own parents had traveled. He would not endure that kind of marriage.

His father had given his mother everything, and it hadn't been enough.

He would not make the same mistake.

Fifteen

Quinn's side of the bed was ice-cold.

Nothing had changed.

He was gone.

It wasn't the first time Kira had woken up alone in Quinn's bed, but this morning, she felt needier than usual. Maybe because of what they'd shared the night before, or maybe because of her bad dreams, she wanted a good-morning kiss. And maybe breakfast together punctuated with a lot more kisses.

But he'd left her for work, which was all-important to him. Hadn't business been the sole reason he'd married her?

To him, last night must have been about sex and nothing more. She'd known that, hadn't she? Still, as she lay in bed, her body sore from making love, she felt lonely. Would it always be like this?

Stretching, she rolled onto his side of the bed where his

scent lingered and hugged his pillow. Then, realizing what an idiot she was, she hurled his pillow at the wall. It struck an etching, which crashed to the floor.

Footsteps in the corridor brought a quick blush to her face.

"Mrs. Sullivan? Is that you? Do you need my assistance?" Jason sounded so stiff and formal, she cringed. She wanted her husband, not some uptight houseman with high-class British airs.

"I'm fine," she cried.

How was she going to get from Quinn's room to hers in her sheer nightie without Jason seeing her wrapped in a blanket? Such an encounter would be embarrassing for both of them.

When five minutes passed without another sound, she cracked the door. There was no sign of him, so she ripped a blanket off the bed, covered herself and shot down the hall on flying tiptoes. Once inside her bedroom, she bolted the door.

As she dressed, taking her time because it was hours before she needed to be at Betty's, she turned on the television. Murray Oil and the EU deal were all over the news.

Both the local news channels and the national ones were full of stories about Quinn's heady successes. In too many shots, a beaming Cristina stood so close to Quinn the pair seemed joined at the hip. Why hadn't Quinn told her that Cristina had gone to London with him?

Cristina worked for him. Surely he'd taken other executives. It was no big deal.

But in her fragile mood, and after her dream last night, it felt like a big deal to her.

You can't blame a man for something you dreamed!

Maybe not, but she still had to ask him about Cristina and his reasons for taking the woman to London. So, when the phone rang, she rushed to pick it up, hoping it was Quinn.

"Hello!" she said a little too brightly.

"Kira? You don't sound like yourself."

The critical male tone was very familiar. Still, because she was focused on Quinn, it took her a second to place the voice. Then it came to her: Gary Whitehall, her former boss.

"Hi, Gary."

"Are you still looking for a job?"

"I am," she said.

"Even though you're Quinn Sullivan's wife?"

"Yes, even though. He's a very busy man, and I love doing what I'm trained to do."

"Well, Maria is retiring because she needs more time to help her daughter. The minute she told me she wanted to play grandmother, well, naturally, we all thought of you."

She lifted a brow. *And Quinn.*

"You could have your old job back... Although, like I said, I wasn't at all sure you'd be interested now that you're *the* Mrs. Sullivan."

"Well, I am, so...this is wonderful news."

"Then you'll make yourself available for a meeting? No hurry, though. Don't want to pressure you."

"I'm available. In fact, I'm free for an hour or two this afternoon."

They agreed upon a time and hung up.

The call boosted her mood until she remembered how Quinn had rushed off to work this morning without even a goodbye. Until she remembered what a gorgeous couple he and Cristina had made on television. They were both so stylish and good-looking. They had business concerns in common, too.

With an effort, she quit thinking about Cristina and refocused on Gary's offer. She was glad Gary had called, even if it was her marriage to Quinn that had made her more attractive as a job applicant.

On a whim, she decided to call Quinn and run the job idea by him just to see what he'd say.

Oh, be honest, Kira, you just want to hear his sexy voice and distract him from Cristina.

Kira made the call, only to be deflated when his secretary told her, "I'll have him return your call. He's in a meeting."

"With whom?"

"Cristina Gold. They're taking a last look at the contracts for the EU deal before everything is finalized."

Don't ask a question if you don't want the answer.

"Would you please tell him…that I'll be on my cell."

"Are you all right, Mrs. Sullivan?"

"I'm fine," she whispered as she hung up.

Perfectly fine.

Clutching the phone to her breast, she sank onto her bed. She didn't feel fine. She felt more uncertain than ever.

Leave it alone. Cristina works for him. That's all there is to it. Go to Betty's. Do the interview with Gary. Forget your stupid nightmare.

But being pregnant had her feeling highly emotional. She couldn't leave it alone. She had to see him. After last night, she had to know how he felt.

Dressing hurriedly, she was in his office in less than an hour. The same beautiful blonde secretary who'd greeted her on her first visit greeted her again, more warmly this time.

"Mr. Sullivan told me you two are expecting a baby. He sounded so happy about it. Congratulations."

"Thank you."

"Would you like coffee? Or a soda?"

"I just want to talk to my husband. He didn't call me back, and since I was in the neighborhood…"

"I'm afraid he's still going over those contracts."

"With Miss Gold?"

The young woman nodded. "I'm afraid the documents are long and very complicated. A mistake could cost millions. Miss Gold is one of our attorneys, you see. She had several concerns."

"Please tell him I'm here."

After the young woman buzzed him, she looked up almost immediately. "He says he'll see you. Now."

Intending to lead her down the hall, she arose, but Kira held up a hand. "I remember the way."

When Kira reached his office, Cristina was just exiting with a thick sheaf of documents. She tossed Kira a tight smile. Behind Cristina, Quinn leaned negligently against the doorjamb.

When he opened the door, Kira said, "I hope I'm not interrupting."

"Glad that meeting's over. And doubly glad to see you." He shut the door. "I needed a break."

Despite the welcoming words, when their eyes met, she felt a sudden unbearable tension coming from him.

"Sorry I left so early this morning, but I had a couple of urgent texts."

"From Cristina?"

"One was. Unfortunately, I still have a lot of balls in the air related to the EU deal," he said.

"No problem."

"You look upset." His voice was flat.

"I didn't realize Cristina went to London with you… until I saw some of the news coverage on television."

A cynical black brow lifted. "I took a team of ten. She

was part of the team. She's very talented at what she does, or I never would have hired her."

"Not only is she talented, but she's beautiful, too."

He stood very still. "I imagine her looks are part of why she made it into so many of the TV shots. Look, there's no need for you to be jealous of her...if that's what this is."

"I'm not."

"I'm married to you, and whether you believe it or not, that means something to me."

What did it really mean if he could never love her?

"Since you obviously want to know more about Cristina and me," he began in the maddening, matter-of-fact tone of a lawyer presenting his case, "I'll clarify our relationship. We dated briefly. The press gave our romance more attention than it deserved.

"Then she broke up with me—for another man with whom she's still seriously involved. At the time, she complained I never had time for her. He did. Naturally, I was angry, but since then I've realized she was right."

"A vengeful man might have held what she did against her," she said coolly. "Why did you hire her?"

"We worked together on several projects before we dated. She will do a lot for Murray Oil."

"So, as always, business is all-important to you? Does nothing else ever matter? Not even your own injured feelings?"

He shrugged. "They weren't that injured. I got over her pretty quickly."

Would he get over Kira and be this matter-of-fact about it? At the thought, Kira cringed.

"Business will always be an important part of my life. I don't deny that. It's part of who I am. I hired her...before I met you." He paused. "What is it you want from me this morning, Kira?"

"Right. I'm interrupting you. You're a busy man. You probably have many more important meetings to get through today. All those balls in the air. And here I am, your pregnant, overly emotional wife needing reassurance."

He studied her warily. "What do you want, Kira?"

Why couldn't she be as cool and logical as he was? Because everything in her life was out of balance. She was pregnant and feeling needy. There were too many unanswered questions in their relationship, and she was still reeling from the discovery that she'd been adopted.

She wanted to belong somewhere, to someone. She wanted to matter to *Quinn*. If she'd been more important to him, wouldn't he have kept her in the loop while he was gone? Wouldn't he have shared more details concerning his oil deal?

"I guess I want the impossible," she blurted out. "I want a real marriage."

"Now you want a real marriage, when all along you've said that's the last thing you want? Last night you woke up crying from some dream, apparently about me, demanding 'strictly business.' You pushed me away as if you wanted nothing to do with me. If I give you space it's wrong. If I push myself on you it's wrong."

"I know I'm not making sense," she said. "Our marriage was never based on love, mutual understanding or anything that makes up a true partnership. I guess I'm upset because…because I don't know… I just know I can't go on like this!"

"As soon as I complete this deal, I'll have more time…"

"How will that matter if you don't want the same kind of marriage I do? Now, maybe because of the baby and finding out I was adopted, I have this huge need for things to be right between us. I want more. I've wanted more my whole life. I don't want to feel left out anymore. Most of all, I want to count to my husband."

"If you wanted to belong in this marriage, then why did you tell me from the first that you didn't want to sleep with me?"

"I guess to protect myself…from ever feeling like I feel now—needy…confused. I knew this marriage was only a business deal for you. I didn't want to get my heart broken," she whispered.

"What are you saying?"

"What we have isn't enough. Not for me…or for you."

"You're pregnant. We can't just walk away from each other. It's not about you and me anymore, or even Murray Oil. We have a child to think about now."

"That's all the more reason I don't want us trapped in a loveless marriage. I want a husband who can love me. I want my child to grow up in a loving home. After the deal you just made, the executives at Murray Oil trust you. You don't need to be married to me anymore. You can divorce me and date somebody who understands you, someone who can make you happy…someone like Cristina."

"Damn it. I don't want a divorce. Or Cristina. Like I said—if you'd ever once listen to me—she's practically engaged."

"But you don't love me…"

"Well, I damn sure don't love anyone else. And I'm not lusting after anybody else. I'm focused solely on you! You're very important to me, Kira. Vital. Still, it's true that I'm not sure I'll ever be capable of loving anyone—even you. Maybe I've been hard and dark and driven for too long."

"Well, I want a man who will commit his heart to me, or I want out."

"Okay," he said in a tone that was cold, infuriatingly

logical and final. "Now that our marriage has served its purpose, you want out. Well, I don't want out, and I'm not ready to let you go. But if that's what you want, I won't hold you against your will any longer."

"What?"

"I'll give you what you say you want. You're free to leave. But understand this—I intend to take an active role in raising our child."

"Of course," she whispered, feeling shattered.

"Then so be it," he said.

He stared at her, waiting for her to walk out the door, and, for a brief moment, his guard fell. She saw longing and pain flash in his eyes.

Suddenly, she realized just how much she'd wanted him to fight for her, for them.

After stumbling blindly out of his office, she sat behind the wheel of her car, clenching her keys in her hand. All her life she'd wanted someone to fight for her, someone to put her first. She'd had a right to push for more from her marriage.

He wasn't willing to fight for her as he'd fought for his oil deal in London, so she would do the fighting.

She would fight for her self-respect, and she would teach their child to fight for his, too.

Kira had been in no condition to be interviewed by Gary the afternoon she'd parted from Quinn, so she'd rescheduled.

Two miserable days later, she still didn't feel strong enough, but here she sat, facing Gary across his wide, cluttered desk in his flashy corner office that overlooked the museum grounds and the busy street that fronted the modern building.

If only she could stop thinking about Quinn and how

bereft she'd felt ever since he'd agreed to end their marriage.

Concentrating on Gary, who wasn't the most fascinating man, was difficult. Lately, everything had been difficult. Returning to Quinn's gorgeous loft, packing the beautiful clothes that she would no longer need and then moving back into her cramped apartment with her dead plants and resentful cat had been full of emotional hurdles.

Rudy wouldn't sit on her lap or use his scratching post. Only this morning he'd peed on her pillow just to show her how much he resented being abandoned.

"Quit feeling sorry for yourself! I'm the one who got married and pregnant...and separated," she'd yelled at him.

Swishing his tail, he'd flattened his ears and stalked indifferently to his bowl where he'd howled for more tuna.

She tried to pay attention to Gary, she really did, but her mind constantly wandered to her miserable new separated state and to Quinn and how cold he'd been right before he'd watched her walk away.

Suddenly, she found Gary's droning insufferable and longed to be anywhere else, even home alone with her sullen cat. If she didn't interrupt Gary, he might easily rant on for another half an hour.

"Gary, this is all very fascinating, but I need to ask a question."

He frowned.

"Is this job offer contingent on me remaining married to Quinn?"

"What?"

"Let me be blunt."

His mouth tightened. "You do that so well."

"Quinn and I have separated. Do you still want me for this job? "

His face fell. "Separated?" Flushing, he pushed himself

back from his desk. "Well, that does change things." Recovering quickly, he ran a nervous hand through his hair. "Still, I want you to work here, of course."

Her voice was equally silky as she leaned toward him. "*Of course.* I'm so glad we understand each other."

A few minutes later he hastily concluded the interview. "I'll call you," he said.

She left, wondering if he would.

As she stood on the curb outside the museum, about to cross the street, Jaycee called her on her cell.

"How are things going?"

"I've been better," Kira replied. "The interview with Gary went okay, I guess."

"And Rudy?"

"He peed on my pillow this morning."

"Well, you abandoned him. He's still mad at you."

"I guess. Hold on—"

Pressing the phone against her ear, she looked both ways to cross the street. But just as she jumped into the crosswalk a motorcycle made a left turn, going too fast.

She felt a surge of panic, but it was too late. In the next moment, she was hurled into the air.

It was true what they said about your life flashing before your eyes.

She saw Quinn's darkly handsome face and knew suddenly, without a doubt, that she loved him.

It didn't matter that he could never love her. Or maybe she knew, on some deep level, that he must love her, too—at least a little.

She remembered all the times he'd looked at her and she'd felt her soul join to his.

She'd been an idiot to walk out on the man she loved, to

abandon a man so afraid of love that he denied what was in his own heart. He needed her.

She wanted to get up and run back to his office. She wanted to beg him for another chance. But when she tried to sit up, her body felt as if it were made of concrete.

Someone knelt over her, but she couldn't see his face.

"Quinn," she cried. "I want Quinn."

The man spoke, but she couldn't hear what he said.

Then everything went black.

"A Jerry Sullivan is here to see you," Quinn's secretary informed him crisply. "Says he's family."

"Show him in," Quinn ordered in a dull voice as he set the lightning whelk Kira had given him back on the shelf. "He's my uncle. He'll want coffee with cream and sugar."

Uncle Jerry didn't wait for Quinn's secretary to return with his coffee before he pounced.

"Sorry to interrupt you, but I just heard you separated from your beautiful wife. I'd ask you to tell me it isn't true, but since you look like something my dog dragged in from the gutter, I won't bother."

"Good to see you, too, Uncle J."

"What the hell did you do to drive her away?"

"I never should have married her in the first place."

"If you let her go, you'll be making the biggest mistake of your life. You've already wasted too many years of your life alone."

"Let me be, why don't you?"

"You're still in love with her. I can see it!"

"The hell I am. Did anybody ever tell you to mind your own business?"

"Sure. You. Plenty of times. Good thing I've got better sense than to listen to the likes of an upstart nephew who doesn't have a clue about what's good for him."

"I think some men are better off single. And I'm probably one of them."

"Bull. I saw the way you were with her. You're like your father. He was the most loving man I ever knew."

"And what did it get him—other than a broken heart and an early grave?"

"You're not your father. Kira's not Esther. Kira's the real thing. Esther was a beautiful woman who knew how to play your dad. And, yes, your dad foolishly loved her with all his heart—just like he loved you. But when you get down to it, even when you're wrong about the people you love, loving is still the best way to live. That's why we still miss Kade. He loved us all so much!"

"My father killed himself because my mother left him."

"You'll never make me believe that! Kade wouldn't ever deliberately walk out on you. You were everything to him. His death was an accident."

"Uncle Jerry, thanks for coming by."

"Great. Now you're giving me the brush-off."

"I know you mean well...but I'm a grown man—"

"Who has the right to screw up his life royally and who's doing a damn good job of it."

"If you've said your piece, I've got work to do."

"You've always got work to do! Maybe it's time you got a life." Uncle Jerry smiled grimly. "Okay, I'll leave you to it, not that it's any fun watching my favorite nephew walk out on the best thing that ever happened to him."

"I didn't walk out on her! Damn it! She left me!"

"So, quit sulking, and go after her!"

"If only it were that easy!"

"Trust me—it is. The only thing stopping you is your damn arrogance."

"Get the hell out of here!"

Holding a silver tray with a coffee cup, Quinn's secre-

tary pushed the door open and would have entered except
Quinn held up a hand. "Uncle Jerry won't be having coffee
after all. He's leaving."

For some time after his uncle had gone, Quinn sat in his
office and seethed. Slowly, as he cooled down, everything
the older man had said began replaying in his mind. Since
his father's death, Uncle Jerry was the one person Quinn
had been able to count on.

Quinn walked over to the shelf where he'd placed the
lightning whelk. How full of hope he'd felt when she'd
given it to him. He remembered her shining eyes, her glowing beauty.

Turning away, he grabbed his cell phone. For a long
moment he just held it.

Quinn didn't just want to call Kira for his own selfish
reasons. He was genuinely worried about her and the baby.
The longer he went without talking to her, the more worried
he grew. Would it be so wrong to call just to make sure she
and the baby were all right? Would it? Even if they never
got back together, she was the mother of his future child.

Swallowing his pride, he lifted his phone and punched
in her number. As he waited for her to answer, his gut
clenched.

Then, on the third ring, a man answered.

"I want Kira," Quinn thundered. "I need to speak to my
wife."

"Sir, I'm so sorry. I'm terribly afraid there's been an accident…"

The man introduced himself as someone working at the
local hospital. He said something about a motorcycle hit-
ting Kira and that Kira had been taken to his emergency
room by ambulance. After getting the specifics, Quinn
hung up and was grabbing his jacket and on his way to the
door, when Earl Murray rang his cell phone.

Quinn picked up on the first ring. "I just heard Kira's been hurt."

"Apparently, Jaycee was talking to her when the motorcycle hit her... I don't know anything else."

"Then I'll meet you at the hospital," Quinn said. His heart was in his throat as he bolted out of his office in a dead run, praying he wouldn't be too late.

Sixteen

Quinn had never been as scared in his life as he was when he stood over Kira watching the IV drip clear liquid into her veins. Her narrow face had the awful grayish tint Quinn had seen only one time before—on his father's face as he'd lain in a pool of his own blood.

"Tell me she's going to be all right. Tell me the baby's all right."

"I've told you," the doctor repeated patiently. "Apparently, she was thrown onto the pavement, but seems to have suffered only a concussion and a few bruises. After a night or two of rest, she and the baby will be fine. She's one lucky young lady."

"You're sure?" For some reason, the facts weren't sticking in Quinn's head as they usually did.

"As sure as I can be under the circumstances."

"When will she wake up?"

"Like I told you before—soon. You just have to be patient."

An hour later, the longest hour of Quinn's life, her long lashes fluttered. Sensing that she was struggling to focus on him, Quinn gripped her hand and leaned forward.

"Kira… Darlin'…"

"Quinn… I wanted you to come. I wanted it so much."

"Kira, you're in a hospital. You're going to be okay. The baby, too."

"I love you," she said softly. "I was such a fool."

Rather than terrifying him, those three words brought a rush of joy.

"I love you, too. More than anything." He squeezed her hand tightly. "So much it scares the hell out of me."

It had only taken her admission to make him brave enough to admit his own feelings for her.

With glistening eyes, she laughed softly. "You really love me?"

"Yes. Maybe even from the first moment I saw you. I just didn't know what had hit me." He paused. "Jaycee's here, along with your parents. We've all been so scared for you and the baby. Half out of our minds."

"They're all here, too?"

"Of course we're here," her father roared.

Kira smiled radiantly up at them. "It's almost worth getting hit by a motorcycle to have all of you all here… together, knowing…knowing that you love me."

They moved closer, circling her bed. Holding hands, they smiled down at her. "Of course we love you," her father said. "You're our girl."

"You gave us a terrible scare," her mother said. "You're very important to all of us."

"I'm so happy," Kira whispered. "I've never been happier."

"By the way," her father said, "your old boss called and said you'd better get well soon because you've got a big job at the museum waiting for you. So, no more waitressing…"

Kira smiled weakly. "I guess that's good news…but not nearly as good as all of you being here." Her grip on Quinn's hand tightened as she looked up at him. "I never, ever want to let go of you again."

"You won't have to."

Quinn needed no further encouragement to lean forward and kiss her. Very carefully, so as not to hurt her, he pressed his mouth to her lips.

As always, she gave her entire being to him, causing warmth and happiness to flow from her soul into his.

She was everything to him. He would love her and cherish her always, or at least until the last breath left his body.

"Darlin'," he whispered. "Promise me you'll never leave me again."

She nodded. "Never. I swear it. Like I said, I was a fool."

Circling his neck with her hands, she brought his face down to hers and kissed him again.

Epilogue

One Year Later
July the Fourth
Wimberley, Texas

Kira looked across the green lawns that sloped down to cypress trees shading the sparkling river. The air stirring through the leaves was warm, while the water was clear and icy.

Kira couldn't believe her happiness. Ever since that afternoon in the hospital, when she'd awakened to Quinn and her family gathered around her bed, her happiness had grown a little every day.

Despite the pain in her shoulder and back, she'd seen the love shining in all their eyes.

Love for her.

Had it always been there? Whether it had or not, all her doubts about herself, about Quinn, about her adoption, had vanished. She'd simply known that she mattered—to all of them.

She belonged.

Knowing she was truly loved, her confidence had grown in every aspect of her life, including in her career as a curator. Naturally, Gary had been thrilled that she was to remain Mrs. Sullivan. Quinn had thrilled him even more by being most generous to the museum, stipulating with every donation that his wife be in charge of the funds.

This lazy summer afternoon on the grounds of the Sullivans' new weekend home on the Blanco was perfect for a July Fourth celebration that included friends, family and business associates. The star of the show was only a few months old.

Thomas Kade Sullivan fulfilled his mother's most fervent hopes as he sat on his red-and-blue quilt by the water, holding court. He shook his rattle while Aunt Jaycee laughed and held up a stuffed bunny rabbit. With his brilliant blue eyes, Tommy Kade was every bit as handsome as his father.

Off to one side, a band played as their guests took turns swimming in the cool waters or serving themselves barbecue.

Quinn left the men he'd been talking to and walked up to her. Grinning down at her, he circled her with his arms. Contentment made her feel soft and warm as he held her close. Never had she dreamed she'd feel this complete with anyone.

She smiled at the sight of her mother ordering the caterers about. With her illness in remission, her mother was her old formidable self. When Vera had been well enough for Kira's dad to leave her at home, Quinn had made a place for him at Murray Oil.

"Murray Oil's too big for one man to run," Quinn had said when Kira had tried to thank him.

Life was good, she thought as her husband brushed his lips against her cheek. Very good.

"Happy July Fourth," Quinn said.

"The happiest ever."

"For me, too. Because you're in my life," he murmured huskily. "You're the best thing that ever happened to me... besides Tommy Kade. And you're responsible for him, too."

"Stop. We're at a party. We have to behave."

"Maybe I don't want to behave."

He drew her away from the crowd into the shade of the towering cypress trees. Once they were hidden from their guests, he wrapped her in his arms and kissed her long and deeply.

"I love you," he whispered. "I love you, and I always will. We have a real marriage, now—wouldn't you agree?"

The most wonderful thing of all was that she knew it and accepted it—down to her bones—because she felt exactly the same way. "I would! And I love you, too," she murmured. "Oh, how I love you."

* * * * *

"It's imperative that I marry a woman who'll make a good princess. I know my requirements."

"Your requirements?" Wasn't that just like him.

"For pity's sake, Adam. You do need help."

"Not with my list or what's on it. That's non-negotiable. I just need help with being a better me and a much better date."

She shook her head. "You don't need help being a better you. You just have to let people see the real you, not the you you think you have to be."

A wry smile touched his lips. "So you'll help me?"

Had she just put her foot into a trap that was starting to close?

Dear Reader,

When I started writing this book, I thought it would be all about my heroine, Danni, teaching Adam, the somewhat reserved hero (he is a prince after all, so he is allowed to be a little reserved) to lighten up and have more fun. She did that, but what I enjoyed during the process was discovering that Adam had a lot to teach Danni, too. They weren't as dissimilar as she (and I) had first thought.

I hope you enjoy their journey.

Warmest wishes,

Sandra

LESSONS IN SEDUCTION

BY
SANDRA HYATT

Published in Great Britain 2012
by Mills & Boon, an imprint of Harlequin (UK) Limited,
Eton House, 18-24 Paradise Road, Richmond, Surrey TW9 1SR

© Sandra Hyatt 2011

ISBN: 978 0 263 89180 5
ebook ISBN: 978 1 408 97189 5

51-0612

Harlequin (UK) policy is to use papers that are natural, renewable and recyclable products and made from wood grown in sustainable forests. The logging and manufacturing processes conform to the legal environmental regulations of the country of origin.

Printed and bound in Spain
by Blackprint CPI, Barcelona

millsandboon.co.uk

Get an **EXCLUSIVE 15% OFF ORDERS***

when you order online today!

Simply enter the code **15JUN12** as you checkout and the discount will automatically be applied to your order. **BUT HURRY**, this offer ends on 30th June 2012.

All of the latest titles are available 1 MONTH AHEAD of the shops, **PLUS:**

- 🌹 **Titles available in paperback and eBook**
- 🌹 **Huge savings** on titles you may have missed
- 🌹 **Try before you buy** with Browse the Book

Shop now at **millsandboon.co.uk**

After completing a business degree, traveling and then settling into a career in marketing, **Sandra Hyatt** was relieved to experience one of life's eureka! moments while on maternity leave—she discovered that writing books, although a lot slower, was just as much fun as reading them.

She knows life doesn't always hand out happy endings and figures that's why books ought to. She loves being along for the journey with her characters as they work around, over and through the obstacles standing in their way.

Sandra has lived in both the US and England and currently lives near the coast in New Zealand with her high school sweetheart and their two children.

You can visit her at www.sandrahyatt.com.

To Gaynor and Allan.

One

Keep calm and carry on. Danni St. Claire had seen the slogan somewhere and it seemed apt. She flexed her gloved fingers before tightening them again around the steering wheel.

Her passengers, one in particular, behind the privacy partition, would pay her no attention. They so seldom did. Especially if she just did her job and did it well. In this case, that job entailed getting Adam Marconi, heir to the throne of the European principality of San Philippe, and his glamorous date for the evening, back to their respective destinations.

Without incident.

And most importantly without Adam realizing that she was driving for him. She could do that. Especially if she kept her mouth shut. Occasionally she had trouble in that department, speaking when either her timing or her words weren't appropriate or required. But she could do it tonight. How hard could it be? She'd have no cause to speak. Someone else would be responsible for opening and closing the door for him. All she had to do was drive. Which, if she did it well meant without calling attention to herself. She would be invisible. A shadow. At a stop light she pulled her father's chauffeur's cap a little lower on her forehead.

A job of a sensitive nature, the palace had said. And so she'd known her father, although he'd never admit it, would rather the job didn't go to Wrightson, the man he saw as a rival for his position as head driver. Danni still had clearance from when she'd driven for the palace before, back when she was putting herself through college. She hadn't seen Adam since that last time.

All the same she hadn't known it would be Adam she'd be driving for tonight. When she'd intercepted the call, she'd thought all she'd have to do was pick up Adam's date for the evening, a beautiful, elegant Fulbright scholar, and take her to the restaurant. But then, and she should have realized there'd be a "then" because such instructions usually came on a need-to-know basis, she had to drive them both home. It was obvious, with hindsight, that there would be something that justified the sensitivity required.

Her stomach growled. She hadn't had time for her own dinner. And her father never saw the need to keep a wee stash of food in the glove compartment. There'd be all sorts of gourmet delicacies in the discreet fridge in the back but she could hardly ask them to pass her something over. Not appropriate at the best of times. Even less so tonight. She'd had to make do with crunch-

ing her way through the roll of breath mints she kept
in her pocket.

At a set of lights she glanced in the rearview mirror
and rolled her eyes. If the palace had thought that sensitivity was required because there might be shenanigans
in the backseat, they needn't have worried. Adam and
his date were deep in conversation; both looked utterly
serious, as though they were solving the problems of the
world. Maybe they were. Maybe that was what princes
and scholars did on dates. And Danni should probably
be grateful that someone had more on their mind than
what they were going to be able to unearth for dinner
from the shelves of the fridge.

Still, she would have thought the point of the date
was to get to know one another. Not to solve the problems of the world, not to discuss topics with such utter
earnestness that they looked like two members of the
supreme court about to hand down a judgment. Danni
sighed. Who was she to know about royal protocol?
Things were different in Adam's world. They always
had been. Even as a teen he'd seemed to carry the
weight of the world on his shoulders. Had taken his
responsibilities and his duties seriously. Too seriously,
she'd thought.

What she did know was that Adam was on the lookout for a suitable wife.

And one of the prospective candidates was in the
backseat with him.

At thirty-one years old, he was expected—by his
father and by the country, if the media were to be believed—to do the right thing. The right thing meant
getting married, settling down and providing heirs,

preferably male, to continue the Marconi line and to ensure succession.

If anyone had cared to ask Danni, she'd have happily shared her opinion that what the prince needed was to shake things up a little, not to settle down. She'd always thought the narrow focus of his life stopped him from seeing what was really there—the variety and opportunities. And for as long as he kept that narrow focus, it stopped anyone else from seeing who he could be, if he only let himself.

For Adam, finding the right woman meant dating. Romantic dinners like the one she'd just picked him up from in the revolving restaurant that towered above the new part of the city.

Maybe, instead of dwelling on Adam, Danni should be trying to pick up a few pointers on how a real woman comported herself on a date. She glanced in the back. Obviously sitting up straight was important, manicured hands folded demurely in the lap, polite smiles, what looked like polite laughter, occasional fluttering of long dark eyelashes, a slight tilt to the head exposing a pale slender neck.

Who was she kidding? Danni didn't do fluttering. And manicuring with the life she led—working in the motor-racing industry—was a waste of time and money.

She might sometimes wish she wasn't seen quite so much as one of the boys by all her male colleagues, but she knew she couldn't go so far as to look and behave like a Barbie clone. Scratch that, even Barbie had more personality than the woman in the backseat seemed to. Didn't they make a Pilot Barbie and NASCAR Barbie? Although she'd never heard of a Speak-Your-Mind Barbie or a Put-Your-Foot-In-Your-Mouth Barbie. Danni mentally pulled herself up. She was taking out her inse-curities and inadequacies on a woman she didn't even know.

She glanced up, again determined to think better of the couple in the backseat. No. Surely not? But yes, a second glance confirmed that Adam did indeed have his laptop out, and that both he and his date were point-ing at something on the screen.

"Way to romance a woman, Adam," she muttered.

He couldn't possibly have heard, not with the pri-vacy screen up and her speaker off, but Adam glanced up, and for a fraction of a second his gaze brushed over hers in the mirror. Danni bit her tongue. Hard. Fortu-nately there was no flicker of recognition in his dark eyes. His gaze didn't pause; it swept over hers as if she was invisible, or of no more importance than the back of her headrest. That was good. If only she could trust in it.

Because she wasn't supposed to be driving for him.

Because he'd banned her. Actually, it wasn't an offi-cial ban. He'd only intimated that he no longer wanted her to drive for him. But in palace circles an intimation by Adam was as good as a ban. Nothing official was necessary.

Though, honestly, no reasonable person would blame her for the coffee incident. The pothole had been un-avoidable. She sighed. It wasn't like she needed the job then or now. Then she'd had her studies to pursue and now she had her career as part of the team bringing a Grand Prix to San Philippe.

But, she reminded herself, her father did need the job. For his sense of self and his purpose in life, if not for the money. Close to retirement age, he'd begun to live in fear of being replaced in the job that gave his life meaning. The job that his father and his father's father before him had held.

Danni didn't look in the mirror again, not into the backseat anyway. She consoled herself with the fact that her unofficial banning had been five years ago while driving on her summer break, and surely Adam, with far more important things to think about, would have forgotten it. And definitely have forgiven her. In those intervening years he'd become a stranger to her. So she drove, taking no shortcuts, to San Philippe's premier hotel and eased to a stop beneath the portico.

"Wait here." Adam's deep voice, so used to command, sounded through the speaker system.

A hotel valet opened the rear door, and Adam and the perfectly elegant Ms. Fulbright Scholar with the endless legs exited. Clara. That was her name.

Wait here could mean anything from thirty seconds to thirty minutes, to hours—she'd had it happen before with other passengers. He was seeing a woman home from a date; Danni had no idea if it was their first or second or something more. Maybe Clara would invite him in. Maybe she'd slide his tie undone and tear that stuffy suit jacket off his broad shoulders and drag him into her hotel room, her lips locked on his, making him stop thinking and start feeling, her fingers threading into his dark hair, dropping to explore his perfectly honed chest. Whoa. Danni put the brakes on her thought processes hearing the mental screech that was in part a protest at just how quickly her mind had gone down that track and just how vividly it had provided the images of a shirtless Adam.

Danni had grown up on the palace estates, so yes,

despite their five-year age difference they'd sometimes played together, as had all the children living on the palace grounds. There was a time when she'd thought of him as almost a friend. Certainly as her ally and some-time protector. So she couldn't entirely see him as just a royal, but he would be Crown Prince one day. And she *knew* she wasn't supposed to imagine the Crown Prince shirtless. She also knew that she could too easily have gone further still with her imaginings.

Besides, Danni hadn't picked up any of those types of signals from the couple in the back, but then again, what did she know. Maybe well brought up, cultured people did things differently. Maybe they were better at hiding their simmering passions.

She eased lower in her seat, cranked up the stereo and pulled down the brim of her cap over her eyes to block out all the light from the hotel. The good thing about driving for the royal family was that at least she wouldn't be told to move on.

She leapt up again when she felt and heard the rear door open. "Holy—"

Minutes. He'd only been minutes. She jabbed at the stereo's off button. The sound faded as Adam slid back into the car.

Utterly unruffled. Not so much as a mismatched button, a hair out of place, or even a lipstick smudge. No flush to his skin. He looked every bit as serious as before as he leaned back in his seat. Nothing soft or softened about him. Even the bump on his nose that should have detracted from the perfection of his face somehow added to it. Or maybe that was just wishful thinking.

Had they even kissed?

Danni shook her head and eased away from the hotel. She shouldn't care. She didn't care.

Normally, with any other passenger she'd say something. Just a "Pleasant evening, sir?" At times a chauffeur served as a sort of butler on wheels. But Adam wasn't any other passenger, and with his head tipped back and his eyes closed, he clearly wasn't needing conversation from her. Long may the silence last. She'd have him back to the palace in fifteen minutes. Then she'd be free. She'd have pulled it off. Without incident. Her father would be back tomorrow. No one would be any the wiser.

Finally, a quarter of an hour later, she flexed her fingers as the second set of palace gates eased open. Minutes later, she drew to a sedate stop in front of the entrance to Adam's wing, the wheels crunching quietly on the gravel. Nobody knew what it cost her, the restraint she exercised, in never once skidding to a stop or better yet finishing with a perfectly executed handbrake slide, lining up the rear door precisely with the entrance. But she could imagine it. The advanced security and high-performance modules of her training had been her favorite parts.

Her smile dimmed when the valet who ought to be opening the door failed to materialize. Too late, Danni remembered her father complaining about Adam dispensing with that tradition at his private residence. Her father had been as appalled as if Adam had decided to stop wearing shoes in public. Danni didn't have a problem with it. Except for now. Now, Adam could hardly open his own door while he was asleep.

There was nothing else for it. She got out, walked around the back of the car and after a quick scan of the surroundings opened Adam's door then stood to the side, facing away from him. She'd hoped the fact that the car had stopped and the noise and motion, albeit slight, of the door being opened would wake him. When he didn't appear after a few seconds she turned and bent to look into the car.

Her heart gave a peculiar flip. Adam's eyes were still closed and finally his face and his mouth had softened, looking not at all serious and unreachable. Looking instead lush and sensuous. And really, he had unfairly gorgeous eyelashes—thick and dark. And he smelled divine. She almost wanted to lean in closer, to inhale more deeply.

"Adam," she said quietly. Right now she'd have been more comfortable with "sir" or "your highness" because she suddenly felt the need for the appropriate distance and formality, to stop her from thinking inappropriate and way too informal thoughts of the heir apparent. To stop her from wanting to touch that small bump on the bridge of his nose. But one of the things Adam had always insisted on was that the personal staff, particularly the ones who'd effectively grown up with him in the palace circles, use his name.

He was trying to be a prince of the times. Secretly she thought he might have been happier and more comfortable a century or two ago.

"Adam." She tried to speak a little louder but her voice came out as a hoarse whisper. Danni swallowed. All she had to do was wake him and then back out of the car. She leaned closer, steeling herself to try again. Ordering her voice to be normal. It was only Adam after all. She'd known him most of her life though five years and infinite degrees in rank separated them.

His eyes flew open. His gaze locked on hers and for a second, darkened. Not a hint of lethargy there. Danni's mouth ran suddenly dry. "Can I help you?" he asked, his voice low and silky with a hint of mockery as though he knew she'd been staring. Fascinated.

Disconcerted by the intimacy she'd imagined in his gaze, she responded with an unfamiliar heat quivering through her. "Yes. You can help me by waking up and getting out of my car."

"Your car, Danielle?" He lifted one eyebrow.

"Your car. But I'm the one who still needs to drive it round to the garage," she snapped. Oops. Definitely not supposed to snap at the prince, no matter how shocked at herself she was. Definitely not appropriate. But her curt response seemed almost to please him because the corners of his lips twitched. And then, too soon, flattened again.

Danni swallowed. She needed to backpedal. Fast. "We've reached the palace. I trust you had a pleasant evening." She used her blandest voice as she backed out of the car. Stick to the script. That was all she had to do.

Adam followed her and stood, towering over her, his gaze contemplative. "Very. Thank you."

"Really?" She winced. That so was not in the script. What had happened to her resolve to be a shadow?

His gaze narrowed, changing from contemplative to enquiring with a hint of accusation. "You doubt me, Danielle?" A cold breeze wrapped around her.

Well, yes. But she could hardly say that and she oughtn't to lie. She searched for a way around it. "No one would know other than yourself."

"No, they wouldn't."

She willed him to just step away from the car. Go on into the palace. Get on with saving the nation and the world. Then she could close the door and drive away and get something to eat. And it would be as if tonight had never happened. There would be no repercussions. Not for her and not for her father.

But he didn't move. He stood absolutely still. Her stomach rumbled into the silence.

"You haven't eaten?"

"I'm fine."

Again the silence. Awkward and strained. If he would just go.

He stood still. Watching her. "I didn't realize you were driving for us again. I thought you were in the States."

"I was for a while. I came back." Three-and-a-half years ago she had moved back for good. "But this is temporary, just for tonight in fact. I'm staying with Dad and he had something come up." Danni held her breath. Did he remember the ban? Would it matter now?

He nodded and she let out her breath. "Everything's all right with him?"

"Absolutely. A sick friend. He'll be back tomorrow."

"Good." Adam turned to go into the palace and then just when she thought she was free, turned back. "What was it you said?"

"He'll be back tomorrow."

"Not then. Earlier. When you were driving."

All manner of desperate, inappropriate words raced through her mind. No, no, no. He couldn't have heard.

"I can't remember." So much for her principles. She was lying through her teeth.

"It was around the time I got the laptop out to show

Clara the geographic distribution of lava from the 1300 eruption of Ducal Island."

She did roll her eyes then; she couldn't help it. He was too much. "My point exactly," she said, throwing her hand up in surrender. "I said, 'Way to romance a woman, Adam.' Really. The geographic distribution of lava?"

His expression went cold.

There was a line somewhere in the receding distance, one she'd long since stepped over. Her only hope was to make him see the truth of her assertions. "Come on, Adam. You weren't always this stuffy." She'd known him when he was still a boy becoming a man. And later she'd occasionally seen glimpses of an altogether different man beneath the surface when he'd forgotten, however briefly, who he was supposed to be and just allowed himself to act naturally.

Now wasn't that time.

His brows shot up. But Danni couldn't stop herself.

"What woman wants to talk about lava and rock formations on a date?" Too late, Danni remembered the saying about how when you found yourself in a hole the best course of action was to stop digging.

The brows, dark and heavy, drew together. "Clara is a Fulbright scholar. She studied geology. She was interested."

"Maybe she was. But surely she can read a textbook for that kind of thing. It's great if you're planning a lecture tour together but it's hardly romantic. Where's the poetry, the magic, in that? You weren't even looking into her eyes, you were looking at the screen. And did you even kiss her when you escorted her to her door?"

"I'm not sure that's any of your business, but yes." Somehow he'd made himself taller.

She wasn't going to be intimidated. "Some kiss, huh?"

"And you'd be an expert on kissing and on romance? What would you suggest? Discussing the specifications of the Bentley perhaps?"

Danni took a little step back as though that could distance her from the stab of hurt. She liked cars. She couldn't help that. Wouldn't want to, even if Adam, who she knew for a fact also liked cars, considered it a failing in a woman. "No. I'm not an expert on romance. But I am a woman."

"You're sure about that?"

This time she didn't even try to hide her mortification. She took a much bigger step back. Her heart thumped, seeming to echo in her chest. She clamped shut the jaw that had fallen open.

Her uniform—a dark jacket and pants—had been designed for men and adapted for her, the only female driver. It was well tailored but it wasn't exactly feminine. It wasn't supposed to be. And it was nothing like Clara's soft pink dress that had revealed expanses of skin and floated over her lush curves. Danni had always been something of a tomboy and preferred practicality along with comfort but she still had feelings and she had pride and Adam had just dented both. Adam, whose opinion shouldn't matter to her. But apparently did.

Shock spread over his face. Shock and remorse. He reached for her then dropped his hand. "Danni, I didn't mean it like that. I meant I still see you as a kid. It still surprises me that you're even old enough to have your license."

She shoved the hurt down, tried to replace it with defiance. "I got my license over a decade ago. And you're not that much older than me."

"I know I'm not. It just feels like it sometimes."

"True." It had always felt that way. Adam had always seemed older. Distant. Unreachable.

He sighed and closed his eyes. When he opened them again he said, "I'm sure you're a fine woman, but it hardly qualifies you to give me dating advice. I've known enough women."

"I'm sure you have," she said quietly. Of late there had been quite the string of them. All of them beautiful, intelligent and worldly, with much to recommend them for the position of future princess. But despite those apparent recommendations, he'd seldom dated the same woman twice. And never, to her knowledge, a third time. She didn't mean to keep track, but a glance at the papers on any given day, even if only when lighting the fire in her father's gatehouse, kept track for her. But it certainly wasn't her place to comment and the implied criticism would centuries ago have cost her her head.

She was thankful for the fact that beheadings hadn't been legal for several centuries because judging by the displeasure in Adam's eyes, he just might have been in favor of the practice right about now. For a moment she actually thought he might lose his legendary cool. She couldn't even feel triumph. There had been a time when, egged on by Adam's younger brother Rafe, flapping the unflappable Adam had been a pastime for the small group of children raised on the palace estate. But she was still too preoccupied with covering her own hurt to feel anything akin to satisfaction.

Adam drew himself taller. The barrier of remoteness shuttered his face, hardened his jaw. "I apologize, Danielle. Unreservedly. Thank you for your services tonight. They won't be required in future."

Sacked. He'd sacked her again.

Danni was still stung by her run-in with Adam the next night as she and her father ate their minestrone in front of the fire. Soup and a movie was their Sunday night tradition.

They finished the first half of the tradition and settled in for the movie. A big bowl of buttery popcorn sat on the coffee table and an action adventure comedy was ready to go in the DVD player, just waiting for her press of the button.

Usually, when she was in San Philippe she came round from her apartment for the evening. But her place was being redecorated so she'd been staying with her father for the last week. She had yet to tell him about the fiasco last night. Tonight would be the perfect opportunity.

But she hadn't fully recovered from the experience.

Although she pretended to herself that she was indifferent, at odd moments the latter part of the evening resurfaced and replayed itself in her head. She should have done everything so differently. Starting with keeping her mouth shut in the first place.

As head driver, her father had a right to know what had happened. Would expect to know. But she hadn't been able to tell him. Because more than head driver, he was her father and he'd be so disappointed in her. And she hated disappointing the man who'd done so much for her and who asked so little of her.

It had occurred to her that if she just kept quiet, he

need never know. It's not as if she'd ever be driving for Adam again.

Besides, her silence was justified because her father was still so saddened by the visit to his friend. She wanted to alleviate, not add, to that sorrow. At least that was her excuse. The movie they were about to watch would be the perfect tonic. The fact that it featured an awesome and realistic car chase scene would be an added bonus. And they'd both once met the main stunt driver.

It didn't matter, she told herself, if she never drove for Adam again. It was such a rare occurrence in the first place it was hardly going to make any difference. And she knew Adam wouldn't let it have any bearing on her father's position within the palace staff. No. Their exchange had been personal. He'd keep it so. That was part of his code.

She'd just found the television remote when three sharp knocks sounded at the door. Her father looked at her, his curiosity matching hers. He moved to stand but Danni held up her hand. "Stay there. I'll get it."

Visitors were rare, particularly without notice. Because her father lived on the palace grounds, in what had once been the gatehouse, friends couldn't just drop by on a whim.

Danni opened the door.

This was no friend.

Two

"Adam." Danni couldn't quite keep the shock from her voice. Was this about last night or was there some further trouble she had gotten into?

"Danielle." His face was unreadable. "I'd like to talk to you. May I come in?"

After the briefest hesitation she stepped back, giving him access. Much as instinct and pride screamed to do otherwise, you didn't refuse the heir to the throne when he asked to come in. But to her knowledge, the last time Adam had been on this doorstep looking for her was fifteen years ago when he and Rafe had turned up to invite her to join in the game of baseball they were organizing. She couldn't quite remember the reason for the game—something to do with a leadership project Rafe had been doing for school. What she remembered with absolute clarity was how badly that endeavor had ended.

Adam stepped into the small entranceway, domi-
nating the space. He smelled good. Reminding her of
last night. By rights she should loathe the scent linked
with her mortification rather than want to savor it. She
heard her father standing up from the couch in the
living room behind her.

"St. Claire." Adam smiled at her father. "Nothing
important. I wanted a word with Danielle if I may."

"Of course. I'll just pop out to the workshop."

Danni didn't want her father to hear whatever it was
Adam was about to say because despite his apparent ef-
forts at geniality it couldn't possibly be good. Nor did
she want her father to go because while he was here
Adam might actually have to refrain from saying whatever it was that had brought him here.

"Working on another project?" Adam asked.

A smile lit her father's face as he came to join them
in the foyer. "A model airplane. Tiger Moth. I should
have it finished in a few more months. A nice manage-
able project." Both men smiled.

Not long after Danni and her father's return to San
Philippe when she was five, he'd inherited the almost
unrecognizable remnants of a Type 49 Bugatti.

For years the Bugatti had been an ongoing project
occupying all of his spare time. It had been therapy
for him following the end of his marriage to Danni's
mother.

There had been nothing awful about her parents'
marriage, aside from the fact that their love for each
other wasn't enough to overcome their love for their
respective home countries. Her father was miserable in
America and her mother was miserable in San Philippe.

And for a few years, after his mother's death, Adam

had helped her father on the car. Danni too had joined them, her primary role being to sit on the workbench and watch and pass tools. And to remind them when it was time to stop and eat. Building the car had been therapy, and a distraction for all of them. She had an early memory of sitting in the car with Adam after her father had finished for the evening. Adam, probably no more than eleven, had entertained her by pretending to drive her, complete with sound effects, to imaginary destinations.

By the time Danni was fifteen none of them needed the therapy so much anymore. Adam, busy with schooling and life, had long since stopped calling around. Her father sold the still unfinished car to a collector. Parts had been a nightmare to either source or make and time had been scarce. Though Danni had later come to suspect, guiltily, that the timing of the sale may have had something to do with the fact that her mother had been lobbying for her to go to college in the States. And fees weren't cheap.

Her father shut the door behind him and she and Adam turned to face one another. Adam's gaze swept over her, a frown creasing his brow. She looked down at her jeans and sweater, her normal casual wear. Definitely not palace standard but she wasn't at the palace.

Silence loomed.

"Sit down." Danni gestured through to the living room and the couch recently vacated by her father.

"No, that's…okay." The uncertainty was uncharacteristic. Seeming to change his mind, Adam walked through to the living room and sat.

Danni followed and sat on the armchair, watching, wary.

"I have to apologize."

Not this again. "You did that."

Adam suddenly stood and crossed to the fireplace. "Not for...that. Though I am still sorry. And I do still maintain that I didn't mean it the way you took it. You're obviously—"

"Then what for?" She cut him off before he could damn her femininity with faint praise.

"For sacking you."

She almost laughed. "It's not my real job, Adam. I have the Grand Prix work. I was covering for Dad as a favor. The loss is no hardship."

"But I need to apologize because I want you to drive for me again."

This time the silence was all hers as she stared at him.

Finally she found her voice. "Thanks, but no thanks. Like I said, the loss was no hardship. I think I demonstrated why I'm the last person you want as your driver."

"Yes, you are the last person I want as my driver because you're so perceptive and so blunt you make me uncomfortable. But unfortunately I think I need you."

She made *him* uncomfortable? And he *needed* her? Curious as she was she wasn't going to ask. His statements, designed to draw her in, to lower her defenses, had all the makings of a trap. Warning bells clamored. She just wanted Adam to leave. "I don't know what you're playing at." She stood up and crossed to him, looking into his face, trying to read the thoughts he kept hidden behind indecipherable eyes. "You don't need me. There are any number of palace drivers, and I don't need the job. Seems pretty clear-cut to me."

"I could ask Wrightson," he said with obvious reluctance.

The younger man her father saw as his chief rival. "Or Dad," she suggested.

He shook his head. "I try not to use your father for the nighttime work."

She knew he did that in deference to her father's age and seniority. But her father wouldn't necessarily see it as a favor. He didn't like to think he was getting older.

"Besides, it's not just driving that I need." Adam studied her for several seconds longer and she could see him fighting some kind of internal battle. Finally he spoke again. "I called Clara this morning to ask her out again."

"You don't think that was too soon?"

"Maybe that's what it was. But I don't have time, or the inclination, for games."

"Oh." Danni's stomach sank in sympathy. This wasn't going to be good. She just knew it.

Adam rested his elbow on the mantel and stared into the fire. "She said she valued my friendship."

"Ouch."

"But that there had been no romance." A frown creased his brow. "No spark."

"Ahh." Danni didn't dare say anything more.

"That I hadn't even looked into her eyes when I was speaking to her. Not properly. That I was too uptight." He looked into Danni's eyes now, as though probing for answers.

"Mmm." She tried desperately to shield her thoughts—that he just had to look at someone with a portion of the intensity he was directing at her, and if that intensity was transformed into something like, oh say, desire, the woman at the receiving end would have only two choices, melt into a puddle or jump his bones. Danni glanced away.

"So—" he took a deep breath and blew it out "—you were right. Everything you said."

"Anyone could have seen it," she said gently.

"Sadly, you're probably right about that, too. The thing is, not anyone would have pointed it out to me. I don't know who else I can trust to be that honest with me and I can't think who else I'd trust enough to let as close as I'm going to have to let you. I can admit my weaknesses to you and you alone because you already seem to know them."

She knew being who he was had to be lonely and undoubtedly more so since Rafe, his closest confidante, had married. The fact that Rafe had married the woman intended as Adam's bride might not have helped either. But he brought much of his isolation on himself. He didn't let people close. And she shouldn't let his problems be hers. But somewhere in there, in the fact that he had a level of trust for her, was a compliment. Or maybe not. Maybe she was the next best thing to another brother.

She didn't know what to say. Her head warned her to just say no.

He was staring at the fire again. "It's imperative that I marry a woman who'll make a good princess, someone who can lead the country with me. And I know what I'm looking for in that regard. I know my requirements."

"Your requirements?" Wasn't that just like him. "Please don't tell me you have a prioritized list somewhere on your laptop."

He looked sharply at her, but spoke slowly. "All right, I won't tell you that."

Danni slapped her head. "You do, don't you?"

"I said I wouldn't tell you."

"For pity's sake, Adam."

A wry smile touched his lips.

"You do need help."

"Not with my list or what's on it. That's nonnegotiable. I just need help with being a better me and a much better date."

She shook her head. "You don't need help being a better you. You just have to let people see the real you, not the *you* that you think you have to be."

He hesitated. "So you'll help me?"

Had she just put her foot into a trap that was starting to close? "I haven't said that. I'd like to, Adam, really I would. But I don't have time. I'm only staying with Dad for a couple more weeks while I'm on leave and my apartment's being redecorated."

He raised his eyebrows. "It's that big a job? Making me into a better date? It's going to require more than a couple weeks?"

"No. I'm sure it's not."

"Then it won't take up much of your time, will it?"

She chewed her lip as she shook her head. When she was ten, Adam, who'd had a broken leg at the time, had taught her to play chess. Over the next few years when he came back on summer vacation he always made time to play her at least once or twice. But no matter how much she'd studied and practiced he'd always been able to maneuver her unawares into a corner and into checkmate.

"For so long I haven't really had to try with women

and…after Michelle I didn't really want to. I've almost forgotten how."

Michelle, whom he'd dated several years ago, well before the advent of Rafe's wife Lexie, was the last woman he'd been linked seriously with. They'd looked like the perfect couple, well matched in so many respects. An engagement had been widely expected. Then suddenly they'd broken up, and Michelle was now engaged to another member of Adam's polo team.

"What about your mystery woman?"

He frowned. Not annoyed, but perplexed. "What mystery woman?"

"Palace gossip has it that…"

"Go on." The frown deepened.

"It doesn't matter."

"Danni? What palace gossip?"

She took a deep breath. "Rumor has it that whenever you get free time, you disappear for an hour or two. When you come back you're generally in a good mood and you've often showered."

The frown cleared from his face and he threw back his head and laughed like she hadn't heard him laugh in years. The sound pleased and warmed her inordinately. "Does this mean there's no mystery woman?" she asked when he stopped laughing.

He was still doing his best to quell his amusement. "There's no woman, mysterious or otherwise."

"Then where—"

"Let's get back on track. Because there does need to be a woman, the right one, and I think you can help. This is important, Danni. All I really want is your insight and a few pointers. It won't take a lot of your time."

Danni hesitated.

"Is there something or…someone you need that time for?"

She didn't want to admit there wasn't. There had been no someone since the rally driver she'd been dating dropped her as soon as he started winning and realized that with success came women—beautiful, glamorous women.

"You'll be compensated."

He correctly interpreted her silence as admission that there wasn't anyone. But the offer of remuneration was insulting. "I wouldn't want that. You wouldn't have to pay me."

"So you'll do it?"

"But you think finding the right woman is about lists and boxes you can check off, and it's not."

"That's why I need you. Lists and tickable boxes are part of it and you'll have to accept that, but I know there's more. I want more." He paused. "I want what Rafe has."

Danni stifled a gasp. "You want Lexie?"

"No." The word was vehement and a look of disbelief and disappointment crossed his face. "I just meant he found someone to marry. Someone he could be happy with."

"She was supposed to be yours," Danni said quietly, daring to voice the suspicion she'd harbored.

"Only according to my father. We, Lexie and I, never had anything." As far as Danni could tell, Adam seemed to be telling the truth and she wanted to believe him. But it was common knowledge that Crown Prince Henri had at one point intended that the American heiress with a distant claim to the throne herself would be the perfect partner, politically, for Adam. "And to be honest," Adam continued, "I'm inclined to believe my father's later assertion that he'd always intended for Lexie and Rafe to be together. He wanted Rafe to settle down and rein in his ways, but he knew Rafe would rebel against any overt matchmaking."

Rafe had been charged with escorting Lexie to San Philippe to meet Adam. By all accounts the two had fought falling in love almost from the time they laid eyes on one another. When Rafe and Lexie finally gave in to their feelings, they utterly derailed the Crown Prince's perceived plans and Rafe's carefree bachelor existence. They'd since married and now had a beautiful baby girl. Rafe had never looked happier. And while to all outward appearances Adam had also seemed more than happy with the arrangement, Danni had always wondered. A little.

He shook his head as he watched her. "You don't believe it?"

She shrugged.

"I like Lexie." He sighed heavily as though this wasn't the first time he'd had to explain himself. "In fact, I love her. But as a sister. It was obvious from the start that it was never going to work for us. We just didn't connect."

"She's beautiful. And vivacious."

"She's both those things. But she wasn't for me. And I wasn't for her."

Danni nodded, almost, but not quite, buying it.

He must have read that shred of doubt in her eyes. "I'll tell you something on pain of death and only because it will help you believe me."

"You don't have to."

"I think I do." Adam glanced away looking almost embarrassed. "On our first date…"

A log shifted and settled in the fire as she waited for him to continue.

"I fell asleep."

She covered her mouth. "No."

"I'd been working hard, putting in some long hours. The timing was off. Dad never should have had her brought out then." He reeled off his excuses. "But anyway, we went to dinner at the same place I went with Clara, we had a lovely meal and on the drive home…" He shrugged. "It was inexcusable. But it happened."

"Was my father driving?"

Adam nodded.

"That explains why he's always been adamant that you were okay with Rafe and Lexie."

"I'm more than okay with it. But I've seen how happy they are, and Rebecca and Logan, as well."

Hard on the heels of his brother finding love his sister, Rebecca, had, as well. Her wedding to Logan, a self-made millionaire from Chicago, would be in two months. "And I wonder…"

"If you can have it, too?" Probably every single person in country had wondered the same thing, the fairy tale come true. Danni certainly had.

He sighed. "It's not realistic though. Not with the life I lead. The constraints on it, constraints that whoever marries me will have to put up with."

He'd deny himself love? Deny himself even the chance at it? And for someone as smart as he was, his reasoning was screwy. "Don't you see? That's why it's more important than ever that there's love. That she knows, whatever the constraints, that you, the real you—" She touched her fingertips just above his heart and the room seemed to shrink. She snatched her hand away. "—are worth it."

Adam's gaze followed her hand. "So, you'll help me?"

Danni hesitated.

A fatal mistake.

"I have a date on Friday." He spoke into the silence of her hesitation. "If you could drive for me then you'll be doing me and my father and the country a favor."

"So it's my patriotic duty?"

"I wouldn't quite put it like that but…" He shrugged. "I don't know if you've heard, but the doctors have told Dad to ease up on work and watch his stress levels. This is one way I can help. So, I need to expedite this process. I want a date for Rebecca and Logan's wedding, and I can't take just anyone. It has to be someone I'm seeing seriously. So that means I need to be working on it now. We've only got two months."

Danni sighed heavily. "See? Your whole approach is wrong. It's not a *transaction* that you can *expedite*. You can't put time limits on things like this."

"This is why I need your help. As a friend."

"You might think you want my help, but I remember you well enough to know that you don't take advice or criticism well. Especially not from me."

"No," he agreed. "But I'm not looking for criticism as such, just pointers."

"You might see my pointers as criticism."

"I'll try not to." Sincere, with the merest hint of a smile.

There was a time when she practically hero-worshipped Adam and would have done anything he asked of her. So she had to fight the unquestioning instinct to agree to his request. Just because it wasn't a big job and she had a little time on her hands didn't mean it was a good idea. She hadn't been this hesitant about anything since her skydiving course last year. She needed to know what she'd be getting into and she needed Adam to know she wasn't that blindly devoted girl anymore. "Normal rules would have to not apply. Because if I agree to do this, there could well be things I want to say to you that usually I absolutely wouldn't."

"This is sounding ominous."

"It won't work if I don't have the freedom to speak my mind."

He hesitated. "If you do this for me, then I'll accept that much." His dark eyes were earnest. "I'd appreciate it, Danni." When she was younger he'd called her Danni. But somewhere along the way as they'd both gotten older, and he'd gone away to school and become even more serious, formality had crept into their relationship and he'd switched to calling her Danielle with rare exceptions. Calling her Danni now brought back recollections of those easier times. He touched a finger to the small bump on his nose. Just briefly. The gesture looked almost unconscious, and she'd seen him make it before. But it never failed to make her feel guilty. Did he know that? Was it part of persuading her that she owed him?

Whether he knew it or not, it worked. "I don't know how much help I can be."

He recognized her capitulation. She could see the guarded triumph in his eyes, the almost imperceptible easing to his shoulders.

"I can't guarantee anything. Like you pointed out, I'm no expert on romance."

"But as *you* pointed out, you are a woman. And I trust you."

She sucked in a deep breath, about to make a last-minute attempt at getting out of this.

"I'll be seeing Anna DuPont. She fits all my criteria. I've met her a couple times socially and I think there's potential for us. Drive for us. Please."

He could, if he chose, all but order her to do it, make it uncomfortable for her or her father if she refused, but his request felt so sincere and so personal—just between the two of them—that the hero worship she'd once felt kicked in and she was nodding almost before she realized it. "One date," she said, trying to claim back some control. "I'll drive you for one date."

Three

On Friday, Danni pulled up to Adam's wing of the palace in the Bentley. The sandstone building towered above her, the shadows seeming to hide secrets and to mock her for how little she knew. What had she gotten herself into? There was no protocol for this situation, for being part driver, part honest adviser, part friend. She took a fortifying breath. All she could do was to stick with what she knew and maybe trust her instincts. At least she wouldn't be expected to guard her tongue quite as closely as normal.

She got out and waited by the passenger door while he was notified of her arrival. On those occasions she had driven for him in the past, he'd been scrupulously punctual. Tonight was no different. As the clock on the distant tower chimed seven, he appeared, stepping out into a pool of light.

Danni looked at him and couldn't figure out whether this was going to be ridiculously easy or ridiculously difficult.

She was still shaking her head as he stopped in front of her. "You have something to say? Already?"

"Yes. You're wearing a suit and tie."

"Yes."

"You're going to have dinner at the riverside jazz festival?"

"Yes." He managed to make that single word of agreement intimidating.

But it was clearly time for some of the honesty he'd said he trusted her to voice. "Nobody wears a suit and tie to a jazz festival."

"I do."

"Not tonight. This is not a state dinner." She held out her upturned palm. "Hand over the tie." For a moment Danni thought he might refuse. "You want my help?"

Gritting his teeth, he loosened his tie and slid it from around his neck. He dropped the strip of fabric into her hand. "Satisfied?"

She closed her fingers around the warm silk. "No."

"No?"

"The top button." She nodded at the neck of his shirt.

His lips pressed together but he reached up, undid the button then dropped his hand and looked at her patiently. Obviously waiting for her approval. But he still didn't look quite right. He still looked tense and formal. A little fierce almost.

"And the next one."

He opened his mouth, about to protest, she was certain, then closed it again and slowly undid the second button.

"Much better," she said. "Just that extra button makes you look far more relaxed, almost casual. In a good way," she added before he could object. She wanted to tousle his hair, mess it up just a little but knew that tousled hair would be a step too far for Adam. Tonight anyway. Maybe they could work on that. She settled for reaching up and spreading his collar a little wider. "See, this vee of chest?" She pointed at what she meant, at what riveted her gaze. "Women like that. It's very appealing."

"It is?"

"Definitely. And you smell really good. That's always a bonus." She was close enough to know. Without thinking she closed her eyes and inhaled. And the image of a shirtless Adam—branded in her memory—came back. The image had lurked there since the incident that had gotten her banned from driving. Her shortcut, the potholes, the spilling of his coffee that had required him to change his shirt in the back of the limo. Oh, yes. She'd seen him shirtless then. An unthinking glimpse in the rearview mirror of a broad contoured torso and sculpted abs. More than appealing. A fleeting moment of stunned and heated eye contact. It was a sight that had left her breathless and slightly dazed and slipped into her dreams. His banning her after that episode had almost been a relief.

She opened her eyes now to find him studying her, curiosity in his gaze and something like confusion. Despite the cool night Danni felt suddenly warmer. This new role was an adjustment for both of them. The normal boundaries of protocol and etiquette had blurred—they had to—but it left her floundering. Maybe she ought not to have admitted with such enthusiasm that his chest was appealing or that he smelled good. But surely if she was going to criticize and point out where she thought he went wrong, then she also needed to point out where she thought he went right.

She reached for his door, opened it wide.

She slipped his tie into her pocket, stepped back and gestured to the open door. "Let's go find your princess."

An hour later boredom was setting in. Just another reason, she reminded herself, why she'd never have made a good chauffeur. No matter how much her father would have liked it for her.

Danni fiddled with the radio again, adjusted her seat and her mirrors, and then leaned over and opened the glove compartment. A white card stood propped up inside. Definitely not regulation. Frowning, she pulled out the card. Across the front in strong sloping letters it read, "Just in case." Behind the card sat a white cardboard box. Curious, Danni pulled it out and opened it. Neatly arranged inside was a selection of gourmet snacks.

The thoughtfulness of the gesture had her grinning and taking back any uncharitable thoughts she'd ever had about Adam.

Another hour passed, during which Danni snacked and read, before Adam and his date walked out of the restaurant. Was that a hint of a stagger to the fashion-model-slender Anna's gait as she laughed and leaned against Adam? Perhaps having so little body fat meant she was just cold and needed to absorb some of his heat.

But the impression Danni got was that there had been no shortage of the champagne that they'd started—at her suggestion—on the way to the restaurant.

Anna somehow managed to stay plastered to Adam as they got into the backseat. At a nod from him—and a brief moment of eye contact, Danni drove off.

At the first set of traffic lights, she glanced in the mirror. And then just as quickly looked away.

Anna apparently had no need for eye contact or poetry. Maybe there had been enough of that in the riverside restaurant. She had undone more of Adam's buttons and had slid her hand into the opening. It certainly didn't appear that anyone was cold anymore. The screen between them blocked out most sound but Danni could hear Anna's laughter, throaty and, Danni supposed, sexy. Some men might like it. Some men apparently being Adam.

She thought of the tie still in her pocket and knew that there was something wrong with her because she wanted to pass it back to him and tell him to put it on. But really, carrying on like that, it was undignified. Then again, it was the sort of thing she'd once expected from Rafe, and never thought it was undignified in his case. But the two brothers were different. They always had been. Adam was all about barriers. And the way the woman in the back had bypassed them didn't seem right.

Danni's only consolation was that it looked like her work here was done. He'd been deluding himself if he'd thought he needed her help and she'd been deluding herself if she'd thought she had any to offer. He didn't need help at all. Anna was doing all the work. And they were both clearly enjoying themselves while she did it. Danni would be able to go home and forget all about Adam Marconi and his search for the right woman.

Her grip on the wheel tight and her jaw even tighter,

Danni pulled to a stop in front of Anna's apartment building. And maybe, just maybe, her stop wasn't quite as gentle as it ought to have been.

The couple in the backseat drew apart. Anna trailed her long red fingernails down the front of Adam's shirt. The green-and-gold-uniformed doorman stepped forward to open the car door and the couple got out, Anna still managing to drape herself over Adam. Danni wasn't sure if she was whispering into Adam's ear or trying to eat it. It looked like the latter. Danni rubbed at her own ear in sympathy.

Not wanting to watch her passengers walk to the doorway of Anna's building—public displays of affection held no appeal—she retrieved her book and reclined her seat. She hadn't even found her page when Adam reappeared and slid into the backseat.

"The palace," he said, the words terse. He lowered the privacy screen but said nothing more as she drove through the city and out toward the palace estates. She chanced the occasional glance at him in the mirror. He hadn't fallen asleep though there was a definite weariness about his eyes as he watched the city slide by.

She knew something of his schedule and so she knew that the days and evenings of the previous week had been hectic and full, meetings after functions after openings and launches.

She eased to a careful stop in front of his wing of the palace and met his gaze in the mirror.

"Better," he said.

"Better? Your date?"

"No. The date was decidedly worse. I meant your stopping. Compared to the one in front of Anna's apartment."

Ahh. "I apologize for that. My foot slipped."

"Thank you."

For apologizing or for her foot slipping in the first place? She wasn't going to ask. By the time she'd walked around the back of the car, he'd opened his door and stood. His gaze slid over her from head to toe.

Usually she was good at the whole calm, stoic thing but Danni fought the urge to squirm under his scrutiny, having no idea what he thought when he looked at her. Or maybe it was just the cold making her want to fidget. It was freezing out here tonight. Cold enough for snow.

Her gaze flicked to Adam's shirtfront, still largely unbuttoned. Frowning, as though only just remembering that they were undone, he reached for the lower buttons and slowly did them up. The movement of his fingers held her mesmerized.

It wasn't till he was finished that she remembered what she needed to say. "Thank you, too," she said. "For the food."

"It was no trouble."

And it wouldn't have been. Someone else would have prepared the food and another person would have put it in the car. But it was Adam who'd had the idea and she was still oddly touched by it.

He slid his hands into his pockets and tilted his head toward the palace. "Come in."

"To the palace?"

"Where else? I don't want to talk about the date out here."

Danni looked around. Assorted staff members stood discreet distances away, always at the ready. If she insisted on staying out here she'd only make everyone colder. Besides, she'd been into the palace before. Many times in fact, though not in the last few years. This should be no different. So she shrugged and walked with Adam, went through the door held open by a staff member she didn't recognize. As Adam led her up a flight of stairs and along a corridor hung with gilt-framed portraits, she realized where they were going.

He opened the door to the library. The room, with its floor-to-ceiling shelves of leather-bound books, and armchairs big enough to curl up in, had been her favorite when she was younger. The chess set they used to play on was still here too, nestled in a corner by a window.

Despite the fact that the room had been designed to be restful, Danni was far from relaxed. It had been years since she was last here and in that time her ease in Adam's company and her confidence in their simple friendship had vanished.

In the car she was in charge, of the car at least. Her father's gatehouse was her territory, too, and outside was…outside. A place of freedom. But here, inside the palace, where everything was governed by rules not of her making and many of them outside of her awareness, standing with the heir apparent, she was out of her depth and well out of her comfort zone.

She walked to a side table and set her cap on it then slowly peeled off her gloves, feeling oddly vulnerable without the protection her uniform afforded her. A protection that said *this is who I am and this is who you are.* We're people defined by our roles. But now, as she raked a hand through her hair, she was just Danni and he was Adam. There could never be a *just* in front of his name unless it was used in its opposite meaning.

He was *just* gorgeous. Serious, but gorgeous with those dark eyes that seemed always to be watching and thinking.

Even without the props of her uniform, she knew she had to keep focused on her reason for being here—which had nothing to do with Adam's eyes. Although maybe the eyes had helped sway her, subliminally at least. "So, your date?"

"Let's wait till after dessert."

"Dessert?"

She turned at the sound of a tap on the door. A footman walked in carrying a tray, set it on the low table between two armchairs and then left.

Danni glanced from the tray to Adam.

"I thought you might be hungry."

"Not that hungry!" She looked at the twin slices of cheesecake and the two mugs of cream-topped hot chocolate.

He smiled his first smile of the evening. "It's not all for you."

"But you've just eaten."

He shook his head. "Anna was a salad-only type of woman. No carbohydrates. No dressing. I was hardly going to eat dessert while she'd scarcely touched a thing. As it was, her pushing her lettuce around her plate all evening almost put me off my linguine. And I love linguine. So aside from it being bad manners, I was in no hurry to prolong the evening. By the time the waiter asked if we wanted to order dessert, the future chances for a relationship were crystal clear."

"You've already fed me once tonight." Her mouth watered even as she pretended that she wasn't hungry.

"It was a long evening and that was just a snack. And

unless things have changed drastically from when you were younger, you have—let's call it a healthy appetite and a sweet tooth. And cheesecake was a particular favorite." He watched her. "Have things changed?"

A grin tugged at her lips and her gaze strayed back to the cheesecake. "Apparently not all that much."

He picked up the two bowls. "Sit down then."

Once she was settled in an armchair he passed her a bowl and took the opposite chair.

Danni bit into the tart velvety cheesecake and her eyes almost rolled back in her head in ecstasy while she savored the delight. "Charlebury's still chef?" she asked once she'd opened her eyes again.

Adam laughed. "Yes."

For the next few minutes they ate in appreciative silence. Finally, sated and the dessert finished, Danni set down her bowl.

"Not licking it?" Adam asked, teasing in his tone.

"Trust me, I thought about it. I have only one complaint."

He asked the question with his eyes.

"I don't think I'm going to be able to do the hot chocolate justice now."

"You'll give it your best shot, though?"

"It would be cowardly of me not to at least try. But I think I have to stand and give it a few minutes before I make the attempt." She crossed to one of the long vertical windows. A single snowflake drifted past the narrow pane of glass, lonely and aimless.

The grounds close to the palace were well lit but farther out, the light faded to shadows illuminated only sporadically by pools of brightness for either security or decoration or both. Occasional statues and trees stood spotlighted. And in the distance a building… "I think I can see the gatehouse."

"Beyond the stand of trees to the west?"

"Yes. I don't remember being able to see it from the library."

He lifted a shoulder. "It's been a while since you were here. You're taller."

"I guess. The lights are still on," she said turning her gaze back to the window. "That probably means Dad's fallen asleep watching TV again."

"Do you remember the first time I saw you in here?"

"I try not to." Ever since he mentioned the word *taller* she'd wanted to steer the conversation in a different direction. She watched his reflection in the glass. He frowned. "I'm still a little embarrassed. I remember what I said."

His frown eased to a smile. "That just because I was taller and could reach the higher books and just because I was a prince, didn't make me any better than you."

"Yeah, that. Thanks for the reminder."

He was still smiling, with his eyes at least. "You're welcome."

"I had a little chip on my shoulder."

"No kidding."

"I was new here. Feeling out of place, and a little, no, a lot, intimidated and insecure."

"I knew that."

Danni turned back to him. "You were good to me, telling me that you were glad I didn't think of you as any different because you were a prince, because so many people did treat you differently." Danni laughed. "And then you said that maybe being taller made you a little bit better though." She pointed to a shelf. "Look.

The atlas is still up there. You helped me find America on it. Asked about where I'd come from." He had the people skills even then that made him such a good prince today, made him so well loved by his countrymen.

"I don't want to tarnish my image, but I was supposed to be studying and didn't want to. You were my excuse not to."

She remembered him sitting at the desk, books spread all over it. To her, at five years old, his ten years had made him look almost grown up. Ultimately, the fact that he became her protector and champion till she found her feet had indebted her to him.

For a long time after that she'd worshipped him, refusing to hear a hint of a bad word spoken, even in jest, about him by any of the other palace children.

"So, your date?" Danni prompted, looking back at him. That was why she was here. To help him find the right woman. Not to reminisce. She could return that favor he'd done her all those years ago.

Tension crept back into his shoulders. She ought not to be thinking about smoothing her hand over his brow, or massaging those broad shoulders. "You said the date was worse? I have to say, from where I sat, it looked to be going remarkably well."

Adam shook his head. "Appearances can be deceiving. It turned out we weren't all that compatible. I realized I'd left an important criterion off my list."

"Being?"

"A certain restraint in the consumption of alcohol."

Adam picked up the hot chocolates and carried them over to her. Danni reached for one, wrapping her fingers around the mug. "Anna could just have been nervous. She might actually be shy and reserved and conservative. Maybe she was so nervous she drank more than she would have normally. You can be intimidating."

"Not on a date. At least I try not to be," he added, forestalling her argument.

"There wasn't a lot to her, it wouldn't take much alcohol. And if she was shy…"

"That occurred to me," Adam said, standing shoulder to shoulder with her and looking out into the night. "But the suggestions she made as to how we might carry on with our date didn't seem entirely consistent with someone shy and reserved, or the least bit conservative."

Danni didn't want to imagine. "You didn't take her up on them? Because from what I saw you didn't seem entirely unhappy with the situation."

Adam turned his head and his grin had an endearing boyishness to it. "I had a beautiful woman in my lap wanting to take advantage of me. Of course I wasn't unhappy. And I didn't want to be rude."

"Of course not. Always the gentleman. But?"

The smile dimmed, turned serious. "There was no real chemistry. Not when we talked. Not even when we kissed. So, aside from the fact that she was well on her way to being drunk, there was never going to be a second date. Although she claimed that didn't bother her, it wouldn't have been…right."

Danni didn't analyze her relief or why his sense of honor pleased her quite so much. "She might not have been such a good look in a future crown princess, either."

"No."

"And your father wouldn't have approved."

"Ahh, no."

"So it worked out for the best."

"Yes."

"And clearly you don't actually need my services. Anna certainly found you attractive at least."

"Anna was drunk."

"I don't think that's necessary for a woman to find you attractive." In fact she knew it wasn't. Not a drop of alcohol had passed Danni's lips and she had no trouble finding him attractive. Too much so. His eyes, his lips, his chest—so much about him fascinated her. Which was why it might be best if they ended this arrangement.

"I know it's not. But being serious about the process certainly takes the fun out of it."

"Well of course it does if you approach it with the determination and precision of a military exercise. What was the last fun date you went on?"

"I'm not discussing past dates with you, Danni."

"You wanted my help."

"With future dates not past ones."

"But maybe if you told me about the ones that worked. Or about Michelle."

"No."

And maybe she didn't really want to know about past successful dates. She just needed to help him find a solution to his current dilemma. "So find a woman who enjoys the same things as you and do some of them together. That way you know you'll both at least have fun even if it doesn't turn into anything more."

Adam nodded as though considering her suggestion but said nothing.

"So what do you enjoy doing?" she prompted.

"I hardly remember," he said with a frown and a shake of his head that implied he didn't think it was all that important. "It's been so long since I did anything just for the fun of it. That's not what my life is about now."

"And it shows."

"Care to explain?"

Did she imagine that hint of tightness in his voice? "You don't need me to explain. And it wasn't a criticism."

"Much."

"It was a statement. You carry the weight of the world on your shoulders, you do everything you can for your family and the country, and you don't seem to do anything just for you. Just for the pure enjoyment of it. A little impulsiveness every now and then wouldn't kill you. All work and no play…"

"I play polo," he said triumphantly. "When my schedule allows," he added.

"I've seen you and the way you play—" she shook her head "—that's not anyone's definition of fun. You play as intensely as you work."

"But I enjoy it."

"It still doesn't make for much of a date for anyone else. And it's too structured. What about doing things on impulse? For laughs, for fun. Read my lips. Fun. F.U.N. Fun."

His gaze seemed to fix on her mouth as she spoke, and his frown returned. Why did he so often frown when he looked at her? She got the feeling he wasn't even listening to her.

There had been something else she was going to

add, but words and thought evaporated, replaced by an awareness she couldn't repress. Awareness of standing here with Adam. Close enough to touch. Awareness of the fact that although he'd fastened some of his buttons, he still had too many undone for her comfort, some of which he'd undone at her insistence. Awareness of that glimpse of chest, which was even more appealing than it had been earlier in the evening. And of the way he smelled—divine.

Four

Adam looked at Danni and felt himself leaning closer. He knew all about impulse—and about fighting it. Impulse told him to kiss her, to pull her into his arms and silence her with his lips on hers.

That would be pure enjoyment.

Far more even than watching her devour the cheesecake. He'd wanted some way of showing he appreciated what she was doing for him; feeding her had seemed like the perfect solution. But she ate with such uncensored sensual pleasure that he'd quickly come to regret the gesture.

The urge to kiss her now shocked him but he wouldn't let it overly concern him. His life was all about *not* acting on impulse. It was about always considering options and consequences before taking action.

But in a perverse way, it was as though since he'd

become serious about finding a wife, his subconscious was trying to thwart him, like a man looking to buy a nice safe Volvo who suddenly sees the perfect tempting Ferrari for sale.

He reminded himself that he'd known Danni since they were kids. It sent a jolt of surprise through him every time he looked at her and realized anew that she was most definitely no longer a kid.

After the evening with Anna, Danni's sparkle, her directness, her innocence were tempting him in ways that she could have no idea about. She wore no lipstick but even without her prompting to read her lips, he was most definitely thinking about them. Soft and mobile. About how the tiny smear of hot chocolate above her top lip would taste, laced with her freshness.

Her green eyes widened as he watched her and he could only hope his thoughts didn't show. Because he couldn't have thoughts like that about her. Because she was Danni.

But if she'd been any other woman, he would have reached for her and kissed that hot chocolate away.

He shook his head to clear it and stepped back, fighting the compulsion to step forward instead. Could her skin possibly feel as soft as it looked? "Danni."

Her gaze was steady on him, a measure of the confusion he felt seemed to shimmer there. She cleared her throat. "Yes."

"You have hot chocolate on your lip."

"Oh." Her quick burst of laughter held uncertainty and she glanced away. Adam passed her a napkin from the tray. "Thank you." She dabbed away the hot chocolate. He almost regretted its loss. But if it stopped him thinking about Danni's lips in ways he had no right to be thinking, then it could only be a good thing.

When he'd woken in the car the first time she drove for him the other night, with her leaning in close, smelling of mint and the cool night, he'd been swamped by an instinctive reaction of purely primal desire. The sort that had been blatantly missing from his date with Clara. It had kicked in before he'd thought to stop it.

And then, before he'd had time to rationalize it, he'd covered his unwanted response with cool civility. He'd tried to create distance and barriers. But he'd been so disconcerted that he spoke without realizing how she might interpret his words. And he'd hurt her. She was one hundred percent the woman he'd claimed he didn't see her as. No matter how desperately he wanted that claim to be true.

She watched him now, waiting for him to speak. "As for fun." That had been what they'd been talking about, hadn't it? "I don't think there's time for that right now."

She took a few steps away, putting a distance he simultaneously regretted and welcomed between them. That distance helped him think a little more clearly, and if he kept his gaze from her petite curves, it helped even more. The uniform she wore did her no favors but he'd seen those curves lovingly revealed by nothing more elegant than jeans and a soft sweater when he'd called at the gatehouse.

"You're kidding. Right?" Her eyes danced with ever-present intelligence and passion and a hint of mockery. Fortunately some things about her hadn't changed—the way she spoke her mind and the way she challenged him. Mostly he appreciated her frankness. Mostly. Other times it drove him nuts.

"This is a serious business."

"I get that," she said with a condescension he hadn't heard anybody use on him in a long time.

"Of course the woman and I need to enjoy each other's company. I want to like her, a lot, and to eventually love her, but I haven't got time to dither and get sidetracked. I'd like to be seeing someone by the time Rebecca and Logan get married. Whoever I take to that wedding will immediately come under public scrutiny. And just because I can have fun with a woman doesn't mean she's going to be suitable as a partner." If only it was that easy.

Danni sighed. "So, *fun to be with* isn't anywhere on your list of criteria."

He heard and ignored the criticism in her tone. "No."

"That explains Clara I guess."

"Clara was very nice."

"You have to admit, even if she didn't want fun, she wanted romance."

"Apparently. And I take the blame for that." He hadn't seen that one coming. "In my defense, Clara had seemed more than happy to discuss weighty issues. She was the one who introduced most of the more serious topics throughout our evening."

"Mmm-hmm." Two syllables laden with cynicism and reproof.

He sighed. Her skepticism was warranted. "The thing is, in political situations I'm good at interpreting mixed messages and subtext. I look for it. I just hadn't realized the extent to which I'd need those skills for dating. I don't *want* to have to use those skills while dating."

"It's just about listening, Adam, about not being totally fixated on your own agenda." She set down her hot chocolate. "If your work is all seriousness, then doesn't that make it more important than ever for you to have someone who can remind you to have fun occasionally, someone who's fun to be with?"

"I can see your point but you're missing mine. Besides, my list of criteria is my decision."

"You're not interviewing job candidates."

Adam said nothing.

"You're not!"

He cleared his throat. "It doesn't seem like an unreasonable way to approach it."

He could see that she wanted to argue but she bit her lip and long seconds later limited herself to a patient, "What else is on your list?"

"Just the usual."

She laughed. The sound, light and almost infectious, broke the tension. How did she make what a moment ago had seemed perfectly reasonable suddenly seem ludicrous? "There is no usual, Adam. People have preferences but they don't *usually* have such rigidly official lists of criteria in the first place."

"How on earth do they expect to find the right person?" His days and weeks were so full that he lived them by lists. They'd served him well so far.

She shrugged. "They just know. Like Rafe and Lexie just knew and Rebecca and Logan just knew. Without lists."

"It seems unreliable. I can't trust in anything as nebulous as *just knowing*."

She shook her head in reluctant defeat. "So spill—what's on your list?"

He hesitated.

"Maybe I know someone suitable."

His list made sense but he knew that Danni would somehow make it seem to not make sense. But it was his list and it didn't matter what Danni St. Claire, pest from his childhood, thought of it, so long as she helped him.

"She'll need to speak multiple languages." How had it come to this? He was sharing his dating woes with Danni. His driver. Next he'd be asking the head gardener how to manage diplomatic appointments.

"I guess I can see why you'd want that," she said.

Despite her words he didn't believe her; there was a light in her eyes he couldn't quite trust.

"You can argue and make love in a range of languages. That'll give variety, that's important. It'll keep things fresh."

He'd known she wasn't taking this seriously. "It's not for the purposes of arguing or making love. I attend endless diplomatic functions with dignitaries from around the world."

Danni was grinning at him.

"You're winding me up, aren't you?"

"You do leave yourself wide open for it. Anyway, like I said, you clearly don't need me driving for you, or giving you advice. You're managing and I don't think we're going to agree on anything important."

"No," he said slowly.

"So, I'll get going." She turned away and headed for the table to get her hat and gloves.

"I wasn't agreeing with you, I was disagreeing."

Slowly, she turned back and a smile quirked her lips. "You usually are."

Which was exactly the kind of comment he expected from her. "Anna was clearly a mistake."

"That might be one area where we agree."

"But she's not the type of woman I expect to be dating in future. I don't think there's going to be anyone else quite as…forward as her on the list. At least I hope not." If Danni didn't stop grinning at him he really was going to have to kiss her. He turned back to the window. "And I'll admit you were right about the tie." The tie she'd made him take off, practically ordering him to undress.

He shook his head sharply, disallowing the sudden image that wanted to insinuate itself there. He rested his fists on the window ledge and stared into the night. "A college education." Focus. He had to stay focused. "Preferably post graduate. Preferably international."

"Go on," he heard her say and could discern nothing of her thoughts from her voice. That was probably a good thing.

"A good conversationalist, a good hostess, diplomatic."

"Of course. Anything else?"

"She'll need to be good with the press and the public, especially children."

"What about looks?"

"Tall, slim, attractive, graceful."

"Hair color?" There was something different about her voice, something controlled. Which wasn't like Danni at all.

"It makes no difference."

"Big of you." That had definitely been a hint of anger in her voice.

He turned to see her standing with her hands on

her hips, her gaze narrowed on him and her lips thin. "What have I done now?" he asked.

She dropped her hands to her sides and shook her head. "You honestly have no idea, do you."

"I have no idea why you're suddenly so angry, like a vengeful pixie, when all I did was answer the questions you asked. You were worried about me not taking criticism well but it seems to be you who's not handling the honesty."

"I'm outraged on behalf of all women."

"Why? Because I have criteria? You can't tell me women don't do that. Must be tall, must be good-looking, must not have a beard, must drive a luxury car and be able to support the lifestyle I'd like to have."

"It's not what was on it that I objected to, it's what you left off. What about kindness, Adam? A sense of humor? What about love and someone you can just be with in the quiet moments of your life? All these criteria you have, they're just more of your barriers."

"I don't have barriers."

She laughed. At him. "You have more barriers than we'll need for the Grand Prix."

"I do not."

"You do. And they're all designed to stop people seeing the real you. You only want them to see the prince, a leader. But, trust me, you don't want to marry someone who sees you like that. You want a companion for life, not a subject. You don't want someone who's going to jump to do your bidding, who says only what you want to hear."

"Actually, that might be pleasant. Surely it would be better than living with someone who constantly challenged and provoked me."

"I give up. There's no point in me doing this, I can't help you if you won't even try."

She headed for the door. But the Danni he remembered from the days they'd played chess and the times they'd played baseball never gave up. Ever. She wasn't bluffing, she was mad. He thought quickly. "Skiing."

She stopped and looked back at him, her eyes narrowed in suspicion.

"I enjoy skiing. It's…fun." Even the word sounded frivolous and insubstantial.

Her smile reappeared and felt like a reward. "See, that wasn't difficult, was it?"

It hadn't been as easy as it should have been. Maybe she was right and he'd become a complete bore. "I'm not a frivolous person."

She crossed back toward him. "Nobody wants you to be. It's part of your appeal. But all work and no play…"

She'd used the word *appeal* or *appealing* in conjunction with him before. And she looked at him now as though there was something there that intrigued her. There was most definitely something in her that intrigued him.

And he had to quash it.

"So, you'll drive me and a date of my choice to the mountains next weekend?" Focus on the task at hand. That was all he had to do.

She shook her head. "I only agreed to drive for you once."

"I'll make it worth your while."

Her gaze narrowed on him as though she was affronted. "I'm not that mercenary."

"You used to be," he said evenly, not buying the mock offense.

Her grin slipped out. "When I was *ten* and only because my Dad never gave me pocket money and you and Rafe always had some. You'd pay for anything that you didn't want to do yourselves." She smiled, perhaps remembering the same things he was, the errands she'd run for them.

"I have more pocket money now." He winked at her.

She seemed as surprised by the gesture as he was. He hadn't winked at anyone in a very long time. But somehow Danni made the years slip away. He touched the bridge of his nose.

She sighed heavily. "I'll drive for you if you promise never to touch your nose again."

"Pardon?"

"You do it deliberately to make me feel guilty. So that I'll do what you want."

"How on earth does my touching my nose make you feel guilty?"

She rolled her eyes. "Because every time you touch that little bump, I remember how you got it in the first place."

"Really? And it makes you feel guilty? But it was an accident. As much my fault as yours." He'd been sixteen and she'd only been eleven. But she'd had a hell of a swing with the baseball bat. And he'd been distracted. He'd been arguing with Rafe instead of paying attention to a game he hadn't even really wanted to be a part of. The ball had come out of nowhere. That was the only time he'd ever seen Danni cry. Not because she'd been hurt but because she'd hurt him. And then she got mad at him for making her cry.

"I know that. But I still feel guilty about it."

"So, if I do this—" he touched the bump "—and

ask nicely, will you drive for me this weekend? Please, Danni."

"Don't. That's not fair."

He touched the bump again. "It's actually hardly noticeable. I don't see it when I look in the mirror, I can scarcely feel it."

"Adam. You're playing dirty."

"No, seriously. Touch it. It's nothing. I think you're imagining it." He reached for her, circling his fingers around her wrist—she had such delicate wrists, like the rest of her—and he lifted her hand.

Curiosity lit her eyes and she bit her bottom lip as she ever-so-tentatively touched the bridge of his nose. Her fingers were so close that he couldn't focus on them but he could see her eyes, could see a certain longing in them. Her lips were softly parted and she smelled as sweet as the promise of spring.

And, damn, there was that urge again. The one that would have him pull her into his arms. He shifted his grip from her wrist and grasped her hand instead and pressed a kiss to the back of it. That was as much as he could allow himself.

And apparently more than she wanted. She pulled her hand free. Hid it behind her back. A fierce blush heated her cheeks.

"You know, maybe it is a little sore still, you could kiss it and make it better." Where had the words come from, the teasing?

"Don't play games with me, Adam." Sudden anger tinged her voice, taking him aback. "I know I'm not sophisticated. But you know it, too. So do not make fun of me. You're better than that."

"Make fun of you? Danni, I'd never. The one time I

tried it, when you were about seven, you kicked me in the shins."

"You just did," she said. The anger had gone, only to be replaced by suspicion.

Usually he communicated well, allowing for no misunderstanding. He'd soothed ruffled diplomatic feathers on many occasions. How was he making such a mess of this when it should be so simple? "No." Making fun of her had been the very last thing on his mind. He'd wanted to kiss her and had settled, at great cost, for her hand instead. Because kissing her, when she was effectively a member of his staff, when he was on the lookout for a wife, and when she was…Danni, would be all kinds of wrong. But he could still feel the cool imprint of her skin on his lips. And that chaste, courtly gesture had stirred far more than the kiss he'd shared with Anna earlier this evening.

"I've offended you and I'm sorry." He needed time to make it better. To get their relationship back to where it ought to be, amiable and respectful.

"You haven't offended me. I'm not that soft."

He liked her indignation, the stubborn tilt to her chin.

"I have offended you, I can see it."

"You haven't. Believe me."

"Prove it. Drive for me next weekend."

She gave a little gasp and her eyes narrowed. "You've done it again, haven't you? You've manipulated me halfway to saying yes and I'm not even sure how you did it."

"I wouldn't try to manipulate you."

"I know. You do it without trying."

Had he? He hadn't meant to. "You're free to drive

for me or not. But I'd really like it if you would." She'd been right about Clara, she'd been right about the tie.

She opened her mouth.

"It'll be the last time, I promise," he said before she could deny him, because suddenly this seemed important. "You see things differently from me. In a good way. So, I'm taking your advice seriously. I'm going to go skiing and I'm going to have fun."

"Whether you like it or not?"

"Exactly." He tried to keep a straight face.

She laughed, breaking the tension he'd caused when he'd kissed her hand. The familiar sparkle returned to her eyes. "This will definitely be the last time. After that, you're on your own and you can take your fun as seriously as you like."

"You'll be able to pick me up next Friday at two?" He had to get her final commitment while he could.

"Okay."

A frown pleated her brow and she imbued that small word with a world of reluctance, but she'd agreed. That was all that mattered.

"Who are you taking?"

"I haven't decided yet. There are a number of prospective candidates."

"Hmmph. Who meet all your criteria?"

"Yes."

"Are their names in a list?"

He said nothing.

"Can I see it?"

He folded his arms.

"Why not leave earlier than two? Let the fun start sooner?"

"I have meetings in the morning."

She didn't roll her eyes, but he thought it might have taken effort on her part not to. She headed for the table and picked up her cap and gloves.

"And don't worry about the uniform. This is definitely outside of regular palace business. We'll be friends."

"That's what worries me. It feels like the ground is shifting and I don't know where I stand."

He held the door for her. "Since when did you ever *not* like a challenge?"

"Since you started using them to work against me."

She reached into her pocket and pulled out the tie he'd forgotten about. He reached for it, and for a second they were connected by that strip of silk. The fabric had been subtly warmed by her body. Her gaze flicked to his and then quickly away as she released the tie. "See you Friday."

"Thank you, Danni. You won't regret it."

She shook her head. "I already do."

Five

"There's a café up ahead." Adam's voice broke through Danni's concentration, snapping her awareness to him.

"Yes," she said warily. They'd been on the road for a little more than an hour and those were almost the first words he had spoken to her since informing her that they'd meet his date there later this evening. And the statement gave her an ominous sinking feeling sapping the pleasure she'd found in the drive. So far, he'd used the time sitting in the back making and taking calls and working on his laptop. It was an arrangement that suited her just fine and she'd hoped he was setting the tone for the whole weekend.

"Let's stop."

A glance in the mirror showed her that his laptop was now shut. Working, he was remote and safe. It was when he leaned back in his seat and focused his attention on her that things, in her head at least, became decidedly unsafe.

"Let's not stop." If she was here as more of a friend than a driver she was allowed to voice an opinion. "It's not planned. I haven't called ahead."

"They'll cope, I'm sure. I don't know what you're going to have but I only wanted a coffee. And maybe a muffin."

"I meant for security. Which you knew. They like to know in advance where we intend stopping." Now, he'd decided to tease? She didn't think much of his timing but the glint in his eyes and the lift to his lips made her stomach give a funny little lurch.

"It'll be okay," he said. "If we didn't know we were stopping, no one else could have. This whole weekend is going to be as low-key and as off-the-radar as possible."

"In that case, we shouldn't stop where people will see you and recognize you." The café loomed ahead. One more minute and they'd pass it.

"Stop the car, Danni."

Repressing a sigh, she pulled off the road and into the parking lot. There was only so far she could push the friend-versus-driver split.

"You wanted me to be more spontaneous."

So now this was her fault? "I don't think I said that, Your Highness." She used the "Your Highness" deliberately. She was desperate to get the formality back into their relationship because something fundamental had shifted that night in the library with him. When he'd kissed her hand, the press of his lips igniting a low forbidden heat. Actually, it had shifted in the seconds before when she'd touched his nose, when her eyes had met his as she did so. She'd been slammed by a desperate desire to kiss him. Properly. To slide into his arms, press herself against him and kiss the bejeebers out of him. Really, she'd been no better than Anna and hadn't even had the excuse of alcohol. If that was spontaneity, it was a bad, bad thing.

"Call me *Your Highness* again and I'll sack you on the spot."

He was joking. About the sacking part anyway. She was sure of it. Just not the "Your Highness" part. He hated that from her. "Fine. I didn't say I wanted you to be more spontaneous. Adam."

The twitch of his lips stretched into a smile. She hadn't realized it before but that smile of his could be irritating, especially when the smugness of someone who'd gotten his way—again—gleamed in his eyes. Even so it made her own lips curve in response.

"No. But you implied it," he said. "So I'm going to be spontaneous. And we're going to stop for unplanned coffee."

"Paul won't like it." Paul was the head of palace security. They'd had a half-hour meeting together before she'd picked up Adam this morning.

Everything was shifting. Even the fact that he'd insisted she not wear her uniform disturbed her. She wasn't used to driving Adam wearing jeans and a sweater. It felt…disconcerting, like she didn't quite know who she was or what role she filled. It blurred the boundaries in her mind. It allowed her to think of Adam and kissing in the same thought. Perhaps she should have packed the uniform just to be safe.

"Paul will cope. Now, are you going to come in with me, or are you going to sit out here in the car and sulk?"

"I don't sulk."

"Good. Let's go get coffee."

Danni got out and muttered a "yes, Your Highness" under her breath. By the time she'd got round to Adam's side of the car he was already standing, breathing deeply of the crisp air. "One day…" she said.

He waited for her to continue, a smile still tilting his lips.

"Yes?"

"One day I'm going to outmaneuver you."

The smile widened and stole her breath. "And on that day Satan will swap his pitchfork for a snow shovel."

She shook her head and turned away, breaking the direct line of fire of that smile. She'd forgotten, or maybe never realized because she'd known him forever, how attractive he really was. Especially when he smiled. But now wasn't when she wanted to be noticing things like that. Now, when she already felt the ground slipping and tilting beneath her. Irritation was the emotion she should be after. Irritation that he thought he could so easily best her. Irritation that it was so often true.

Inside the café they ordered drinks and chocolate muffins and sat at a booth with a view over the pine-forested hillside and up to the snow-covered mountains.

"You can see these mountains from my office in the palace," he said, leaning back in his seat after his first sip of coffee. "Every time I see them I remind myself that I ought to come up here. Rafe and Lexie have been up to the Marconi chalet several times and even Rebecca and Logan have visited. But it's been years since I made the time. So, thank you."

Danni shrugged. "Pleased to be of assistance." More pleased than she could let him know. Already he looked different, a little less strained. This could be her service to the country. Though right now she didn't care about the country, just about him and that this would be good for him. He looked relaxed and open. "So, who's the date?" She needed to remind herself what was really going on here because she was in imminent danger of forgetting. He hadn't told her anything. Just that whoever she was would already be up at the chalet.

"Claudia Ingermason."

"The figure skater?" The Claudia Ingermason Danni was thinking about had won a medal for San Philippe two winter Olympics ago and had since launched her own brand of top-of-the-line winter and ski gear. She was also stunningly beautiful with the looks of a Swedish supermodel.

He nodded. "Rebecca set it up. Claudia's an old school friend of hers. You said to try dating someone I could have fun with. We both enjoy skiing. So it should be…fun."

"You've met her before though?"

"Not exactly."

"So, this is a blind date?"

"No. I know who she is."

"Did you bully Rebecca into setting you up with someone?"

"I resent the implication that I bully people. And even if I tried, Rebecca would be the last person to stand for it. I asked her if she could think of anyone and she came up with Claudia."

"Sounds perfect." Danni set down her coffee. "So why don't we get going? The sooner I get you up there, the sooner you and Claudia can start having fun."

"There's no rush. She's tied up in a photo shoot for her next season's line. It's running behind schedule. She'll be an hour behind us at least." Adam's hands were wrapped around his mug and he didn't appear in any hurry to go. "There's just one thing I don't understand."

"What?"

"Why this still feels like work?"

"Because you're making it work. You're trying to force it."

"I'm just trying to speed things up."

She shook her head. "Relax. If you remember how. If it's meant to be with Claudia, it'll work out. And if it's not, at least you still got to go skiing. But either way I think we should get going because I don't like the look of the weather." The distant clouds seemed to have grown darker in the time they'd been sitting here.

Adam frowned. "You've had a weather update?"

"It's not supposed to snow till much later this evening or possibly tomorrow."

"That's what I thought." He shrugged and took a sip of his coffee. His eyes drifted closed in a long slow blink. And given that this was the most relaxed she'd seen him in years, Danni wasn't going to hurry him along. He'd been out till the early hours of the morning at a state function and from a comment he'd made earlier, it sounded as though he'd scarcely gone to bed because of calls to the other side of the world he'd had to take.

* * *

"What are you doing?" Danni asked, horrified, fifteen minutes later as Adam got into the front seat beside her. She'd been looking forward to the subtle reprieve from his company. Company she could like too much. Now he was beside her instead of in the back, preventing her from putting things into their proper perspective. Me driver, you passenger. Me commoner, you royalty.

Now, as he sat beside her, she had bad thoughts like me woman, you man instead.

"What does it look like?"

"It looks like you've forgotten where you're supposed to sit."

"Where I'm *supposed* to sit? It's *my* car. I can sit anywhere I want."

Definitely man, and one who thought he could do whatever he wanted. Probably because he usually could. Time for diplomacy.

"And a very nice car it is, too. But I'm your driver. And the point of having a driver is so that you can sit in the back and work. Use your time efficiently. Not have to worry about conversation." Like he had done for the first hour of their trip when he was completely oblivious to her. They had each had their space.

"We agreed that this wasn't a normal driving role. You're also here as a friend and adviser. Besides, I've finished what I need to do for the time being. Now, I thought I'd sit up here. The view's better." He looked at her as he spoke so she kept her gaze where it ought to be, trained on the road as it wound up into the mountains. Though if she was able to look at him, she might be better able to gauge what he was playing at. Or not.

She never knew with Adam. By all accounts no one did. She'd often heard his brother and sister, and even once his father—from whom he'd inherited the trait— complain of that very same thing.

He opened the glove compartment.

"What are you doing?"

"I like seeing what you keep in here."

"Nothing."

He pulled out the thriller she was reading, turned it over. "Doesn't look like nothing."

"Nothing you'd be interested in. Adam?"

"Yes?"

"You're sure you haven't got work you should be doing?"

With a smile he closed the glove compartment. "I'm sure. The truth is I'm having second thoughts about this date. Not the skiing part, but the having to get to know another woman."

"It's because you're still looking at this as work."

"It's partly that but worse than that, I've realized that if the chemistry's not right, it's just going to be a waste of my time, like getting stuck in an unproductive meeting."

"Nothing like anticipating success."

"What if it's blatantly obvious there's going to be nothing between us? I should have stuck to dinner. There's an easy escape. So, just so you know—" he folded his arms across his chest "—I'm blaming you if this goes badly."

"If that makes you feel better."

"You know I wouldn't blame you," he said a few moments later.

"I'm not so sure of it. But I can live with it."

She loved the little smile that played at his lips.

They lapsed into silence, and finally Adam seemed content to sit and absorb the beauty and serenity of their surroundings. Snow blanketed the ground and weighed on the branches of the fir trees that stretched back from the road. He spoke only once, to point out the tracks of a deer disappearing into the forest. She could almost feel the tension leeching from him.

His phone rang. The call was brief. He gave assurances to whoever was on the other end of the call that everything was fine and that there was no need to apologize. When the call ended he tipped his head back in the seat. "That solves that. Turn the car around."

Danni flicked a glance at him.

"We're going back."

"Is something wrong?"

"Claudia can't make it. The art director walked out and the photo shoot's in chaos. If she's not going to be there, then there's no point in me going. Besides now I can attend tomorrow's meeting of the Prince's Trust."

"I thought you were pleased to have a good reason not to attend."

"I was, but I don't have that reason anymore."

"But the skiing?"

"The mountain's not going anywhere. I'll come up some other time."

"You haven't in how many years?"

"I will." He wouldn't, and her heart sank on his behalf. Partly because Claudia wasn't going to be there but mainly because he'd miss out on the first day he'd taken off in nearly a year. The lines of tension and weariness showed around his eyes. "You've got competent people at the meeting for you?"

"Yes."

"Then why not stick to your half of the plan and enjoy the skiing? If you take care of your own needs, you're a better leader because of it."

"There are more important things I should be doing."

"But—"

"What?"

"Nothing." It wasn't her place to comment on his private life. He'd ignore her anyway.

"No. What were you going to say?"

"Just that I can't turn around here. There are too many blind corners. There's a place up ahead just a few minutes."

"Good." He tilted back his seat and closed his eyes. Within minutes his face softened and his breathing slowed and deepened, and now, finally asleep, he looked almost to be smiling.

It was an hour later before he opened his eyes again. And for the last half hour Danni's regret over her decision had been growing. Especially the last ten minutes during which snow had begun to fall. Earlier and more heavily than forecasted.

Adam adjusted his seat to a more upright position and looked around, frowning. "Danni?" A low warning sounded in his voice.

"Yes."

"The light is fading." He glanced at his watch. "And it's snowing."

"Yes. It's nothing the Range Rover can't handle." But she didn't like it all the same.

"And we still appear to be going up into the mountains."

"Ahh, yes, so it would seem."

"So it would seem?"

She didn't like the heavy sarcasm or the annoyance underlying his words.

"Why are we still going up?"

"Because…"

He waited—far too silently—for her to finish her explanation.

"Because that's how we get to the chalet, and now we're not so very far from it."

"The Marconi chalet?"

"You keep repeating my words."

"In an attempt to see if they make any more sense when it's not your mouth they're coming out of. Sadly, they don't. And you're going to have to explain."

"You fell asleep."

"I'm aware of that."

"And you looked so tired."

"Danni."

She couldn't ignore the warning in his tone. "And there really wasn't anywhere to turn around."

"For the last hour there's been nowhere?"

She didn't answer.

"Turn around. Now."

"I don't think it's a very good idea." They were only twenty-five minutes from the chalet.

"Clearly you don't think it's a good idea. But that doesn't concern me. What concerns me is getting back to the palace. Tonight. So that I can sleep the night in my own bed and do the things I'm supposed to be doing tomorrow." His voice was lethally quiet.

"I thought that you'd appreciate the enforced break. I thought you could use it."

"You thought wrong."

"Adam, I—"

A jolt shook the car. It shuddered and pulled to the right and at the same time an alarm sounded on the dashboard computer. All three things told her the same thing. The very last thing she wanted to happen.

A flat tire.

She pulled off to the side of the road. For a moment she sat there not daring to look at Adam. She held the wheel. "This will just take a couple of minutes. And then we'll be back on the road." She'd have it changed quicker than another vehicle could get here for assistance or to pick up Adam. She radioed in her intentions and got out.

By the time she reached the back of the car, he was already there, pushing his arms into a down jacket. "What are you doing?" She hitched up her own jacket onto her shoulders.

"I'm going to change the wheel." He spoke in a tone that indicated he would tolerate no disagreement.

She disagreed anyway. "No, you're not. I'm the driver. I'm going to change it. That's what I'm here for." Danni opened the back.

"You're here to drive me where I want to go and you weren't doing that."

"That's different."

"I'm not going to get into an argument with you." He spoke gently but implacably. "This is my car. I'm going to change the wheel." Adam reached in front of her and lifted out the spare tire.

"If I was a man, would you insist on changing it?" She grabbed the jack and the wrench and followed him to the wheel that sat heavily on its rim.

Adam set the tire down. "If you were your father I would."

Danni put the jack beside it and turned to him. She knew, and didn't like, the obstinate look in his eyes. "And he'd be just as insulted as I am."

"Deal with it. I'm not going to stand by and watch while you change the tire. What do you take me for?"

He stepped toward the jack and she insinuated herself into the sliver of space between him and the car, blocking his way.

"But you expect me to stand by and watch you? This is my job, Adam. It's what I'm here for."

"What you're here for is completely separate." He sidestepped but she moved with him.

"Not separate, because, in case you've forgotten, I drove you here. Your Highness." The title was supposed to remind him of their respective roles. It was also intended to let him know how irritated she was with him right now.

Snowflakes drifted between them. "Looks like you just solved our problem. I warned you what would happen if you called me Your Highness. You're fired. Which means you're not my driver, so stand aside."

Her temper flared. "You can't fire me without written warning." She had no idea if that restriction held true for the palace, a world that operated with its own rules. She only hoped Adam didn't know either—terms of employment for staff not being a major diplomatic concern. "So, as far as I'm concerned," she pressed on, "I'm still your driver and I'm going to change the wheel."

"No. You're not my driver and you're not going to change the wheel." He stepped closer, intimidating her with his size and his very nearness. Another inch and they'd be touching. She looked up and met the obstinate light in his eyes with what she hoped was its equal in hers. His breath mingled with hers. His warmth surrounded her. And a very different kind of warmth leaped deep within her. Her heart beat faster, her breath grew shallower. It took her a moment to register and recognize the sensation.

Desire. Need.

No. This couldn't be happening. Not with Adam. It was just the proximity. It was his very maleness, it was the insular life she led, lately devoid of male relationships that weren't purely about camaraderie.

The light in his eyes changed and darkened, the anger and stubbornness replaced by something she couldn't name. Time hung suspended. Slowly, he lowered his head. She breathed in his scent, and without meaning to, moistened her lips and swallowed. He was going to kiss her, and she shouldn't want it.

But she did.

In a single deft movement he slid his hands beneath her armpits, picked her up and set her to one side.

He smiled. Then dusted off his hands. Victorious. Satisfied with his win. Damn him.

It took seconds for her equilibrium to return, for her to get past the fact that she'd thought of Adam that way, and not just in some dim imagining, but with him right here where she could have, and almost had, reached for him. Because he was right there. She'd ached to know the taste of his lips on hers. It had seemed imperative.

And he had seen her thoughts and shunned her.

He crouched beside the wheel, positioned the jack and reached for the wrench, relegating Danni to the position of observer or at best support crew unless she wanted to tackle him out of the way. Which would get her precisely nowhere. She was left alternating between mortification at her reaction to him, and frustration at the fact that he'd so easily brushed her aside both as his driver and as a woman.

"If you fire me you'll have to drive yourself home. You'll lose all that time you could have spent working."

"With pleasure," he said, sounding as though he meant it. "At least I'll know I'll get where I want to go."

"You'll have to help yourself with your dating issues. Help yourself unwind and lighten up."

He raised his eyebrows and looked about them. "If this is your idea of helping me unwind, I can live without it."

He had a point. All she'd succeeded in achieving was to make matters worse.

Adam set to work on the wheel and Danni stood to the side and watched him. Snow dusted his head and shoulders. Petty as she knew it was, she silently tried to find fault with even the tiniest detail of how he changed the tire. He gave her no opportunity.

Usually she found strength and competence attractive. In Adam, now, coming after everything else, these traits were irrationally annoying. As he set the old tire on the ground she reached for it.

"Leave it," he said. "I'll get it when I'm done."

It sounded like an order. She ignored him, and to the sound of his sigh, wheeled it to the back of the car.

Sacked. She'd been sacked. Again. That was three times now.

If they were no longer employer and employee and they weren't friends, then what were they? Two acquaintances temporarily stranded on the side of the road as the snow began to fall more heavily. Everything was too unpredictable. Including Adam.

Maybe she should have expected his annoyance at her decision to override his request, but she hadn't expected his obstinacy over changing the wheel, and never could she have predicted that flash of awareness that passed between them as they'd faced off. Out of everything, that bothered her the most. The sudden fierceness of it had come out of nowhere.

No traffic passed by on the road. She walked back and continued watching, trying to figure him out. Adam was older, though not that much older; it had just always seemed that way. But because of that and, more importantly, their respective positions, he was untouchable. He was also supposed to be imperturbable, safe and predictable, a touch on the staid side, considered and considerate, dependable. Anything listed in the thesaurus under *safe* would do to describe him. That's who he was.

Until now.

And if Adam wasn't being Adam, it turned her world upside down.

She tucked her gloved hands beneath her arms and bounced on her toes, trying to keep warm.

He lowered the car back to the ground and began giving the wheel nuts a final tightening. "Get back in the car. You're cold."

"I'm fine." She crouched beside him and reached for the jack.

He glanced at her steadily. "Anyone ever tell you that you're stubborn?"

"A lot of people as it happens, but it's a bit rich coming from you."

"Insolent?"

"I might give you that one."

He shook his head. "Provoking?"

"No more than you."

He stood. "Exasperating?"

She stood too, glaring up at him. "Pot and kettle."

Adam looked skyward, as though seeking help from the gray and darkening sky, before his eyes met hers again. Apparently he hadn't found the help he sought because frustration tightened his features.

And there it was again, that something else in his gaze. That something that did ridiculous things to her insides, made the world seem to tilt. She studied him, trying to hide her reaction and trying to figure out what it was that had changed. If she could pinpoint it, she could deal with it.

"Way more than me," he insisted, incredulous.

"No, because I—"

His hand snaked out, cupped the back of her head and drew her to him.

Adam's lips covered hers, stealing her words, replacing them with the taste of him, overwhelming her with the feel of him, the exquisite heat of his mouth against her cold skin, and the answering heat it ignited within her. He coaxed and dominated and she gave back and gave in, welcoming and returning his fervor.

This was what she'd wanted.

He was what she'd wanted.

Danni slid her arms around him, held him and angled her head, allowing him to deepen the kiss. Allowing him to draw her deeper under his spell. She welcomed the erotic invasion of his tongue. And the flames within her leaped higher as though he'd touched a match to gasoline.

The flash point of her response told her how much more she'd wanted this than she'd ever admitted. She lost herself in sensation. Enthralled, enraptured, ensnared.

In seconds he had her backed against the car, his hands cold and thrilling against her jaw. A counterpoint to the heat of his mouth. His fingers threaded into her hair. Fierce, possessive. His body pressed against hers and she arched into it, breasts to chest, hips to hips. Meeting and matching him. Governed by hunger. Slave to sensation. He was everything she wanted and more and he was everything she'd thought—almost hoped— he wasn't. Cool reserve replaced by searing passion.

He kissed her as though starved for her and awakened the same hunger within her.

Danni groaned, weakened and empowered, aflame.

Abruptly, he broke the kiss and drew back. His eyes, passion-glazed, met hers, and she watched as shock and regret replaced that passion. He snatched his hands from her head as though burned and clenched them into fists at his side.

A terrible silence welled.

Her frantic heartbeat slowed and she fought to calm her breathing. Adam swallowed. "Danni, I—"

"Don't." She turned away from him and picked up the jack and the wrench and strode to the back of the car. She couldn't bear to hear him apologize, to voice the regret written so clearly on his face. She didn't want to hear the word *mistake* from his lips.

Gritting her teeth, she stowed the tools in the back,

mortified by her untutored and revealing response to him. And despite everything she knew, all the things about Adam that would make it impossible for him to want her, or let himself want her, she waited, hoping against hope, that he would speak—not words of regret but something else.

But she could wait only so long.

In silence, Danni headed for the driver's door. Since protocol had clearly been abandoned and left twitching in the snow, she was going to make sure she was the one behind the wheel. It was the only chance she had of control. It would remind them both of who they each were.

He got in beside her, bringing strained silence with him.

There were no guidelines for this scenario.

Danni started the car and took a deep breath as she looked out into the near darkness and the now heavily falling snow. Just as Adam was remembering who he was, she had to remember her role, too. This was not the weather to be driving back in. Visibility would be almost non-existent and the road would be icy and soon snow-covered. Common sense, much as it pained her, had to prevail. She wanted nothing more than for this to be over. She was no coward, but she wanted to run and hide. Instead she took a deep breath and said, "I don't think we should head back to the palace this evening."

Six

Adam glanced at Danni sitting stoically behind the wheel, all her attention focused ahead. The atmosphere inside the car was more frigid than outside, and it wasn't because of the snow coating her hair and shoulders. A new tension tightened her jaw that had nothing to do with the deteriorating driving conditions and everything to do with that kiss.

She'd smelled of pine and snow and tasted of the mints she kept in the car, and for a second she had melded with him, her lithe body pressing into his even through the barrier of their clothing. He'd felt her surprise. He'd caught her reciprocated desire. As surprising for her as it had been for him. And for a moment nothing else had mattered.

She had come alive in his arms, fire and light. But

perhaps that was just Danni. She probably made love that way. His groan almost escaped out loud.

He had to stop remembering and reliving the kiss.

He'd messed up. Royally. And he had to make it right. He had to find a way to get things back to the way they were before he'd kissed her.

The kiss that should never ever have happened. The kiss that, in the moment, had seemed like the only right thing in the world. The kiss that had wrenched control from him and plunged him into a place where there was no thought, only sensation and desire.

But as he watched the snow falling outside he knew they had a more immediate issue to sort out first. "How far are we from the chalet?" he asked, his question more brusque than he'd intended. The control was difficult to reclaim. Even now traces of the consuming need lingered, pulsing through him, refusing to be suppressed.

But she was Danni and he would not let himself want her.

The kiss, the desire, was an aberration.

"Twenty-five minutes," she said quietly, pressing her lips together as soon as she'd spoken.

Those lips. The compulsion to taste her had overwhelmed him. The feeble justification flitting into his mind, that, as of a few minutes ago, she was no longer officially his driver had seemed a valid excuse. And stopping that kiss had been one of the hardest things he'd ever done. Only her groan of pure desire had cut through the fog of passion, allowing a moment of sanity.

Sweet, sassy Danni kissed like a dream. The most erotic of dreams. The way she'd responded, the way her mouth had fit his, the feel of her body against his—all had felt...perfect. All had promised forbidden pleasure.

It was afterward that regret had surged in. Once that last shred of sanity had warned him to end the kiss, he'd seen the shock in her eyes and realized what he'd done, the boundaries he'd trampled over, the very wrongness of kissing Danni, no matter how right it had felt.

His responsibility, much as she'd disagree, was to protect her, not to claim her, to assault and insult her. "Let's go to the chalet." Going to the chalet was the best option given the deteriorating weather, though it carried its own risks being alone with her there. But if he kept duty to the forefront, perhaps it offered him a glimmer of a chance to make it right with her. To get things between them back to a place that was as close to normal as possible. Because otherwise once they got to the palace, they would go their separate ways and he would lose her—their relationship irreparably damaged. Because of him.

He studied her profile, searching for words. He was reputed to be diplomatic. It was failing him now. Had failed him already because that talent ought to have stopped him from getting into this situation in the first place.

He always thought before he acted or spoke.

Always.

Until that moment. And it was all to do with Danni. She stirred him up in ways he couldn't like. She made him forget to think.

"Danni—"

"I don't want to hear it, Adam."

She had to. They had to clear the air. "It was an accident."

"What, you slipped and fell and your lips landed on mine?" She shook her head and a slight smile touched her lips.

"I—"

"Just don't. I know everything you're going to say and you don't have to. It shouldn't have happened. We both know that. You're going to try to take all the blame yourself, as though it had nothing to do with me. As though I hadn't wanted it, too. Just once. Just to know. You're going to say we should forget it happened, put it behind us and move forward."

He wanted to refute her words. But she'd gotten it right.

"So let's do that," she said. "We'll forget it." She clenched her jaw and glared at the road ahead.

One of the things they had in common was that neither of them liked to admit an injury or a weakness. Perhaps that would work in their favor here. "Do you really think it's possible? That was no ordinary kiss." His head still spun, the blood still surged in his veins.

"I'll give you that, it wasn't ordinary. Far from it. And I should probably retract my implication after your date with Clara that there must be something wrong with your technique. Because clearly there's not. But we can leave it at that."

"Can we?" It was the right thing to do, the only way forward.

"Of course we can. It was a heat-of-the-moment mistake and that moment has passed. It was one minute out of all the years we've known each other. The years should count for more than the minute, don't you think?"

"Yes."

"So, if you're going to apologize for anything it should be for sacking me."

"You called me Your Highness."

"You were being a pompous ass."

"Good thing you're already fired."

She grinned, and that small flash of smile lifted a weight from him.

"That's three times now you've sacked me. Each time unjustified."

"You made me spill coffee on my shirt."

"I didn't want to hit the pothole."

The truth had nothing to do with the coffee and everything to do with the look that had passed between them when he'd taken off his shirt. The surge of desire he'd felt for her. She'd only been twenty-one, and his friend, and he hadn't wanted to feel that for her. But he'd stepped away from the friendship anyway. And he'd missed it. Not often, but sometimes in the quiet moments he thought of her.

"So can we talk about something else? Please?"

If she was prepared to try, if she was prepared to move on, then he could, too. "Tell me about the Grand Prix."

"Thank you." She sighed her relief, and filled him in on the latest developments in bringing a Grand Prix to San Philippe. And while at first there was an obvious strain to her words, over time, as they talked, it really did become easier, a little more natural. Neither of them had forgotten the kiss, but the conversation, the finding of common neutral ground, gave him hope that the damage wasn't irreversible.

After ten minutes their headlights picked out a sign through the swirling snow. It advertised an inn he didn't remember seeing before. He glanced at Danni. She wore driving gloves but he was certain that if he could see her hands, her grip would be white-knuckled. And they had another fifteen minutes of driving to go, at least, possibly longer given the speed with which conditions were deteriorating. "Let's try here."

"But—" Her argument died on her lips and she did as he suggested.

She stopped beneath the portico in front of the Austrian-style chalet. It was smaller by far than the Marconi chalet but offered respite from the driving and shelter from the weather. That was all they needed. That and somewhere he could put some space between them.

"I'll go in and check that they have rooms," she said, in the guise of chauffeur not friend, as she reached for her door. And maybe chauffeur was safer.

His hand on her arm—a new but hardly significant breach of protocol given what had already happened—stilled her before she could open her door. Despite the thaw of the last ten minutes, he at least, couldn't move on without actually apologizing.

She turned back but only enough that she could look straight ahead through the windshield. "Don't," she said, reading what was on his mind. "It never happened. We're moving on."

A sharp tapping on her window startled them both. They turned to see a hulk of a man blocking the window, his face shrouded by the hood of his coat. Danni glanced at Adam and waited for his nod before lowering her window.

"You finally made it," the man shouted against the gusting wind. "Drive around to the side. I'll open the garage door." Without waiting for a response he disappeared back inside.

Danni looked at Adam again, her eyebrows raised in inquiry, hesitation in her gaze, making it his call. He knew he should be grateful that at least she was looking at him with something other than appalled horror. He nodded. "Let's go in."

"He must be expecting someone else."

"Well, he's got us. Drive round. Unless you have a better suggestion?"

She radioed their location to the palace and then eased the car around the side of the building and into the garage.

Their host stood waiting. He'd shed his coat but he looked no less of a bear of a man than he had outside. Tall and broad, in need of a haircut and with a furrowed brow. The furrows eased as Danni and Adam got out of the car, and he smiled. "I was beginning to worry you might not make it tonight."

"We're not who you're expecting." Adam waited for recognition to dawn on the other man's face.

"That's okay. So long as you can cook."

From the corner of his eye he saw a flicker of a smile touch Danni's lips. Adam wasn't often expected to be able to cook when he arrived at an inn. "I know a couple of dishes but I have to admit, cooking's not my strong point. We were heading for a chalet further up the mountain—" he didn't say which one "—but saw your sign. And the weather's atrocious out there."

"Oh." The single word was disappointment itself. "You're not Simon?"

He shook his head. "Sadly, no."

"Well, you're here. And you can't go back out. But

the food's not going to be very good." A hint of an accent colored his words. "My name's Blake by the way. Your accidental host. Should have said that first. It's in the list of instructions in my notebook. But I keep forgetting them." He absently patted at his pockets. "I'm just looking after this place for a few days so it's all new to me and there are too many things to remember, too many proper ways and wrong ways of doing the simplest of things. They have some high-falutin' guests stay from time to time who apparently have the pickiest expectations. Everything has to be just so, and done in convoluted ways." His glance took them both in and a smile broke out. "I can tell you two aren't like that." The smile faded. "Are you?" he finished hopefully.

"Not at all," Adam said, grateful for their *accidental* host's warmth and rough charm. It covered and eased the tension. "I'm Adam and this is Danni," he said before Danni could say anything, because she'd taken a deep breath as though about to launch into an explanation. If Blake didn't know who he was, Adam was happy enough to keep it that way. Already the anonymity, when he'd been prepared for any number of different reactions, felt like one less issue to deal with.

"Come on inside. Can't have been pleasant driving in that. I'll get you a drink." Blake smiled. "That's the one instruction I never forget."

"I'll just get our bags," Danni said.

"Wouldn't hear of it. I'll get them." Blake was at the back of the car retrieving their bags before either of them had time to object. "Here, you take this one." Blake passed Danni's bag to Adam. He saw her mortification and shook his head. She didn't like him carrying her bag. But unless she wanted to fight him for it—and for a moment it looked as though she might—she'd just have to deal with it.

"What do you mean by accidental host?" he asked Blake, trying to deflect her attention.

"Crikey."

That one word told him that Blake was, as he'd suspected, Australian. Danni's smile grew.

"You wouldn't believe the rotten string of luck that's led to me being alone here," he said as he crossed the garage. "The place is owned by my sister-in-law. It's been in her family for years. She's been coping on her own these last two years since my brother died and has turned it into an inn. I was only coming over for a holiday and to give her a hand when Sabrina—"

He reached an internal door and looked back. "Nah. You don't want to know all that. All you need to know is that people have been breaking their legs and having babies when they shouldn't, and now getting waylaid by weather, so you've got me."

He led them up a flight of stairs. "We don't have any guests booked in for a couple days. I was expecting the new chef and his wife. The chef was a friend of my brother's. But I have a suspicion that if he was a friend of Jake's—and yes, I know, *Blake and Jake*, what were my parents thinking?" He barely paused for breath but his voice had a surprisingly melodic quality to it that was easy to listen to and Adam tried to focus on that rather than Danni, and the sway of her hips, as she walked up the stairs ahead of him.

Blake reached the top, set Adam's case down and turned to wait for them. "Anyway, if he's a friend of Jake's, chances are he's found himself a tavern and holed up there. And if I'm right and he has found a tavern, there's no telling when we'll see him, regardless of what the weather does. The useless—"

Blake stopped himself and grinned as Danni and Adam halted in front of him. It was a surprisingly sheepish expression for such a big man. He reached to take Danni's case from Adam. "You should know that at the very top of the list of the instructions Sabrina left for me was to not talk too much. And never ever to swear in front of guests. Written in red. Because I wasn't supposed to deal with the public, really. Simon's wife's going to do that. So, let's just get that drink I talked about. And don't worry, there'll be dinner for tonight and it'll will be warm and tasty if not fancy." He glanced from the cases at his feet to another set of stairs. "I'll take these up to your room in a jiffy."

"Rooms." Adam said with an emphasis on the *s.* "We'll need two." He said it before Danni had to. Though for a second the thought of sharing a room—a bed—with her, had stirred something fierce within him, something that had catapulted his mind back to when he was kissing her.

The kiss and the associated sensations had imprinted on him and he didn't think it was going to be possible to erase them. They would, he was certain, haunt him for a long time to come.

"Two?" Blake looked between them, frowning.

"That's not a problem, is it?"

"No," he said drawing the word out. "But seeing as I was expecting the chef and his wife, I only have one room ready. But it won't take me long to sort out. I'll do it while you're drinking your mulled wine. You will have a glass of mulled wine, won't you?" He trained a look of earnest concern on them. "I have some ready."

"We'd love to, thanks," Danni said with a smile that wiped the concern from Blake's face.

He showed them into a cavernous living room with high wooden-beamed ceilings and a roaring fire in a stone hearth. "You stay by the fire. I'll be back in two shakes of a lamb's tail."

Danni looked from Blake's departing back to Adam. "I haven't apologized for overriding your request to go back to the palace. For us ending up here."

And if she hadn't done that he wouldn't have kissed her and they wouldn't be in this mess. "It's okay. I appreciate your reasoning." He knew she'd done it for him because she'd thought he needed to take some time for himself.

"We don't have to stay here if it doesn't suit you."

"What do you mean?"

She looked around the room. "This is nice but it isn't going to be what you're used to, especially with no staff. I can get us to the Marconi chalet if you'd like."

"Okay, so now I am annoyed. What do you take me for, Danni? *This isn't what I'm used to.* You know I served in the military. I had plenty of accommodations during my time that were far less salubrious than this. Almost all of it, in fact."

"I know but…"

"I thought you were one of the few people who saw beyond the title."

"I do."

"Yet you think I'd rather send us both back out into that weather, not to mention insulting Blake, for the sake of what? A higher thread count? Someone to open doors?"

"A better meal," she suggested.

"I don't care about the food."

She looked away. "You're right. I know you're not like that." Had his kiss driven such a wedge between them that she couldn't even meet his gaze?

Another thought occurred to him. "You don't have a problem with Blake?"

"Me? No." She looked as horrified as he'd been when she'd suggested he might not consider this place up to his usual standard. But then a sudden merriment flashed in her eyes as she added, "He's gorgeous, mate."

Relief flooded through him. That was the Danni he remembered.

Her grin faded too soon. "We should tell him who you are."

Which in turn dimmed his own enjoyment in her response. "Why?"

"Because he has a right to know."

"Can you imagine what that will do to him? He's already flustered."

"But—"

"He doesn't need to know."

"Is that an order?" She raised one eyebrow.

Why did she always have to challenge and question him? He'd never figured it out. Never figured *her* out. "I don't give you orders, Danni. I never have. And not just because you wouldn't have followed them."

She did a funny little head tilt that he took to be grudging acknowledgment of the truth. "But sometimes your requests do sound a lot like orders."

He shrugged. That was his acknowledgment that

maybe there was also an element of truth in what she said. He'd learned to be careful about how he expressed his thoughts and wishes because they could be taken too seriously. But it also meant that if he wanted something done, a subtle remark was usually enough to see it accomplished.

Blake came back in carrying two cinnamon-scented glasses of mulled wine. "Here, get these down you and I'll sort out your other room. That is, if you're sure you don't want to share."

"We're sure," they said in unison.

They watched him go and Danni laughed. "I'd bet my life's savings that no one's ever handed you a drink and told you to 'get it down you' before."

"Your savings are safe." Adam raised his glass to her and looked about the room. His gaze took in an antique chess set positioned between two armchairs. The pieces set up for a game. "Do you want to play?" Anything to keep her distracted, to pull things back to where they ought to be between them.

She looked from the board to him. "I've barely played since the last time with you."

"Me neither."

"Are you lying?" she asked, suspicion narrowing her eyes.

"I might have played a time or two. What about you?"

Her lips twitched. "A time or two."

They could move on. He knew it. She'd never been one to hold grudges, preferring to live in the present.

"I'm not sure that now's the best time to get back into it though, because in all our matches that summer and the few afterward, I never won a game off you."

"I wouldn't remember."

"You remember. You're too competitive not to. But that last time I had you in check twice."

"Once. And it only lasted until my next move when I put you in checkmate."

"It was twice and it took way more moves than one to make it checkmate. I almost had you."

"Prove it." He nodded at the set.

She hesitated.

"There's nothing else for us to do. Unless you want to talk about what happened before?"

"I'm white," she said with a false cheerfulness.

Adam waited for her to sit and watched as she touched and aligned each of the intricately carved pieces. "It's a beautiful set," she said, picking up a finely carved knight and turning it slowly.

"I'm guessing it's an original Staunton." He lifted his king and looked at its base. "Ebony and boxwood made around the 1860s. And it's your move."

"I knew it would come to that," she muttered. She opened with her king's pawn. "The trouble is you taught me. You know how I play because it's how you taught me to play. It seems like an unfair advantage."

"Which means you know how I think and play, too. But you quickly developed your own strategies. Unconventional but occasionally effective."

She shook her head. "The difference now is I'm not going to let your gamesmanship put me off."

"Gamesmanship?" He feigned outrage. That had been one of the things he'd enjoyed about playing with her. The way she tried to match wits with him verbally as well as strategically.

"Gee, Danni. Are you sure you want to do that?" She

mimicked him. "'Are you sure you've thought through all the avenues? The obvious move isn't always the best one.' You turned me round in circles, like that labyrinth at the palace."

"I never gave you bad advice. Besides, you were more than capable of thinking your way out of it. And you always liked the labyrinth."

"You were five years older than me."

"You wanted to play." He mirrored her move.

"I always thought I could beat you—one day. And then we stopped playing, just as I was getting better and coming close to matching you."

"I was letting you think you were coming close because, like you said, I had five years on you. It was only fair to give you a chance."

"Says the man who taught me the French proverb, *you cannot play chess if you are kindhearted.* You weren't *letting* me come close to winning. I was doing that on my own. In fact that's probably why you stopped playing with me."

"And of course it had nothing to do with me going back to boarding school."

"That might have been a factor." She grinned.

"And if we're talking sayings, I lost count of how many times you reminded me that after the game, the king and the pawn go back in the same box."

"Still true."

And he was just as grateful now as he had been then that she thought that way. He paused with his hand on a knight. "Those chess games helped me get through that vacation."

"Only because winning makes you happy. Don't expect it tonight." Challenge and anticipation lit her eyes.

And the same sensations stirred within him. "Okay, Kasparov. Show me what you've got. But I'm thinking you're still going to make me a happy man." He hadn't intended the double entendre. But he could see by the way her eyes widened before she looked quickly back at the board that she'd read more into those words than he'd intended. And he too had thought more than he ought as soon as they were out of his mouth. In that fleeting instant he'd thought of ways Danni might make him happy and of ways he might please her, and of how she would look in the throes of pleasure. Forbidden thoughts. He had to stop them.

And he had to get his head into the game or she'd beat him. She made her next move and they played in the silence of concentration for fifteen minutes until Blake came back.

"Glad to see that being used." He nodded at the chess set. "It belonged to my grandfather. Only Jake ever played and even then not much." He stood a short distance away, his hands behind his back, and surveyed the board. "Who's winning?"

Danni met Adam's gaze then looked at Blake. "Hard to say at this point." Adam agreed with her assessment. Already she'd surprised him a couple of times. He was going to have to work for a win.

"Do you want to finish the game before I show you up to your rooms?"

Adam looked at Danni whose attention was back on the board, her hand hovering over her bishop. "This game may not finish anytime soon."

Blake shook his head. "That's the trouble with

chess," he grumbled. "Takes too long and you can't even tell who's winning."

Danni made her move and then with one last look at the board, stood and smiled at their host. Blake gestured to the door. "It took me a while to find everything. But I think I've done it right. Ticked off everything on the list anyway." The crinkling of paper sounded as he patted his pocket. "I'll show you up now and then fix your dinner. Like I said, it won't be fancy, but it'll be tasty and there'll be plenty of it. I'm more used to cooking for a shearing gang than couples on vacation. I hope you're hungry."

"I could eat a horse?" Adam said tentatively.

Clearly the right answer. Blake clapped him forcefully on the back. "That's what I like to hear," he said as he led the way up the stairs. "I've put Danni in here." He opened a door to a bedroom with a canopied four-poster bed in the center draped in a white linen coverlet, with a heart-shaped chocolate wrapped in red foil on the pillow. "It's the best room," he said proudly.

"Bathroom's over there," Blake pointed to a far door and then walked to another. "This is the adjoining door. It can be locked from either side. Or not." The man clearly thought there was something going on between them. Or that there would be soon. An idea that teased at Adam's senses no matter how he tried to repress it. But repress it he had to. There could be nothing between the two of them for a whole host of reasons. Her age and the fact that he was looking for a wife being the first two that came to mind. A wife to stand at his side now and when the time came for him to fill his father's shoes as monarch of the country. A role that wouldn't suit the adventure-loving Danni and one which he couldn't imagine her suiting in return. He knew what he needed in a partner—he had his list.

So, anything with Danni, as tempting and insistent as the idea suddenly was, would be wrong because it wouldn't be fair to her. And would ruin a relationship that he was only now coming to properly value.

She was out-of-bounds.

The room revealed by the opened door was similar though smaller than the one they stood in. The bed was a standard bed, the covers were somewhat rumpled in a testament to Blake's bed-making skills. Though here too in the center of the pillow sat a foil-wrapped chocolate.

Danni looked at him, her narrowed gaze revealing her discomfort. He was assuming the discomfort was over the disparity in their rooms rather than the proximity. He only wished he could say the same for himself. He'd never have thought having Danni St. Claire so close could be disconcerting, but he knew without a shadow of a doubt that he'd be lying in bed tonight and thinking about her on the other side of that door.

That kiss had a lot to answer for. *He* had lot to answer for. And she hadn't let him apologize for it.

Then again, maybe he'd kissed her just to stop her arguing.

No. Not true.

He'd kissed her because he'd suddenly wanted to. Needed to so badly that he hadn't been able not to. And there was a part of him, a traitorous rebellious part, that couldn't regret it, that triumphed in it.

Worst of all was the fact that she'd responded. Unequivocally. An encouragement he would have been much better off without. That instantaneous connection and heat had been like no other kiss.

Usually he made quick irrevocable decisions and seldom revisited them, seldom regretted them. This confusion, the indecision and second-guessing that assailed him was uncharted and disturbing territory.

Danni opened her mouth to protest over the room arrangement. He silenced her with a hand on her shoulder. "These look terrific," he said. "Thank you."

"I knew you'd appreciate them. Sabrina knows how to do things nicely." Their host kept talking, oblivious to the sensation rioting through Adam, and all because of the feel of her slender shoulder. "And those chocolates," Blake pointed to the pillow, "are delicious. Just had one when I was making your bed. I couldn't help it." He clapped his hands together. "So, dinner now?"

"Can you give us fifteen minutes, please?" Danni asked, stepping away from Adam's side.

"That's even better. Of course you'll be wanting a bit of private time. And I'll be able to make sure it's all properly ready and hot. Sing out if you need anything. Just come down when you're ready."

As soon as Blake left, Danni turned to Adam, her gaze earnest. He missed the feel of her close to him.

"We're swapping rooms," she said as she started for her suitcase.

Adam blocked her way. "No. We're not."

"Yes. We are." She sidestepped.

He matched her, again blocking her way with his body. "No. We're not. And that *is* an order."

"Ha. Remember what you said about me not being likely to follow your orders. You were right. My room's twice the size of yours. I wouldn't be able to sleep in it. You're the one who's a prince."

"You're only here because of me. It's very right. All it is is a bed to sleep in anyway." And no matter which bed he was in he wouldn't be getting much sleep. Not with her so close. "I'll bet you've always wanted to sleep in a four-poster bed."

Her irrepressible grin lifted one side of her mouth. "Actually, when I was younger my fantasies ran more to a racing car bed."

"But what about now? Where do your fantasies run to now?" His fantasies suddenly included her laughing lips.

They were standing close. He could see flecks of gold in her eyes. He could see the tips of her teeth revealed by her parted lips. He took a step back. "I'm sorry. That was inappropriate and not something I need to know." Her mouth closed and she bit her lip, drawing attention to its soft fullness.

He should turn and go, but he stood there staring at her, wanting her. And he could see the mirror of his wanting in her eyes.

Hope twined with desire inside him. *Hope* that she felt something of what he did, and *desire* for her, here and now. He didn't want either. He *shouldn't* want either. And together they were a fearsome combination.

Where was her outrage over his earlier kiss? The overstepping of bounds, the abuse of power? He'd settle for sympathy and a gentle admonishment that she didn't think of him that way, or even for her to laugh in his face. He could deal with any of those. Anything to remind him that the sudden attraction laying siege to him was one-sided and had to be vanquished, that kissing her could never be allowed to happen again. Because that was what was right and safe.

But it wasn't one-sided. He could see that now. It hadn't been just him in that kiss. The attraction simmered between them.

He should step away, not want to pull her closer. Her lips had a newfound power over him. He wanted, so much that it was a need, to kiss her again.

He looked away from her—her eyes, her lips, her hair, her feminine curves, everything that tempted him—so that he could think clearly. But instead he saw that big four-poster bed and pictured Danni in it. With him.

It was insanity. Lust—that's all it was—was gaining the upper hand.

He was alone here with Danni, when he'd planned a weekend with no work, no distractions, so now he was fixating on her. If his date, Claudia—he struggled to remember her name—was here that wouldn't be happening. Although he could scarcely remember what Claudia looked like. She was ostensibly a beauty but she had none of Danni's spirit and sass. And everything going on in his head was just plain wrong and he couldn't, wouldn't allow it.

Even if he'd correctly interpreted the way she'd melted into him. Even if she hadn't wanted him to stop that kiss.

His thoughts refused to be suppressed.

Danni's expression as she watched him turned thoughtful. She knew he was battling with himself. And as that realization registered, the light in her eyes changed, desire shone through. The desire that had sprung to life between them, more powerful for being mutual and forbidden. The hunger for her gnawing at him almost undid him. He could pull her to him now....

He might not have control over his thoughts or his desires but he still had control over his actions and he removed his hand from her shoulder and turned away from her.

It felt like the hardest thing he'd ever done.

He crossed the room, putting necessary distance between them. "We need to talk about what's happening here. We're alone together for the first time and I don't know how or why, but somehow it's changing things. But not everything. And what remains constant is the fact that anything between us would be wrong. It's not that I don't want...it's just all kinds of wrong."

"You think I don't know that? That you're stuck here without your duties to occupy you, or the woman who should have been here, so you're focusing on me. A convenient substitute."

She waited for him to disagree. "Yes," he said. Though it wasn't that. Not by a long shot. This attraction to her was anything but convenient. Danni was all the things that were missing in his life, things she'd pointed out, spontaneity, honesty, and this felt like his last chance to grab them. But, and it kept coming back to this, it would be wrong. Unfair to her when she deserved so much more. "So let's just go to dinner. And we are not swapping rooms." He spoke as coldly as he could. "Tomorrow we're going home. Things will be back to normal."

He crossed to the door, each step away from her heavy and determined, as though he was fighting gravity.

"Adam?"

He shouldn't respond, but he turned. And she was right there. Her hands went to his head and pulled him down and she rose up on her toes and kissed him. A kiss of contradictions. Sweet and hard. A kiss that challenged and dared, and the press of her lips to his, of her body against his, the taste of her, filled him with fire.

The kiss undid all of his resolutions, weakened him. She took and she gave and left him mindless of anything other than her.

Then she broke the kiss and strode away.

Relief and regret tore through him as he sagged against the wall.

Seven

Danni woke to a soft tapping on the door. She had no idea what time it was other than early. So she rolled over and ignored it. The tapping grew louder. "I'm fine. I don't need anything." Except maybe a glass of water but she could get that for herself.

Blake had knocked just like that last night as she was about to get into bed because he'd forgotten to check that her bathroom had everything it ought to. And although those few minutes of Blake's garrulous company after the strained torture of dinner with Adam had been a blessing, she didn't want to see him, or anybody, right now.

Adam had been polite during their meal. Too polite. And charming. Too charming. There had been nothing real or honest about their conversation. The manners and the charm masked a remoteness that seemed impossible to bridge.

She'd all but told him that she wanted him. And he'd turned her down. Supposedly hell had no fury like a woman scorned, but she wasn't feeling scorn so much as mortification.

A chasm had opened up between them and it was of her making. She'd kissed him and he'd let her walk away. He hadn't mentioned the kiss during dinner. Not once.

She'd hoped that his gentle but undeniable rebuff would quell the insane one-sided lust that had sprung from nothing and nowhere in the space of a few days. But apparently insane lust didn't work that way. And she was still hankering, twisted up on the inside with wanting him.

She'd had wine with dinner in her desperation to forget. Not much, but usually she drank nothing. The wine had given no consolation and no reprieve from her embarrassment.

He was Adam Marconi. Heir to the throne of San Philippe. She was the daughter of one of the palace drivers. He'd known her since she was five. He didn't even think of her as a woman. If only there was a way to get through this day without seeing him.

"Danni?"

Her breath caught in her chest and every muscle tensed. It wasn't Blake at the door. It was Adam. And the tapping hadn't been at the main door to her room but at the adjoining door.

"Danni? I'm coming in."

Danni burrowed farther beneath the covers. "What do you want?" She knew there was no way of completely avoiding seeing him today but surely it didn't have to start now.

He opened the door enough that he could look into the room, his gaze somewhere on the wall above her head. He didn't so much as put a toe past the threshold. "We're going skiing. Did you bring gear?"

"Yes. I'm always prepared for anything, and I wasn't going to twiddle my thumbs while you were off skiing. But I thought we were going back to the palace today?"

He opened the door a little wider. "We're going skiing first. It snowed heavily overnight again and although it's stopped now, it'll be several hours before the roads have all been cleared. So we're stuck here for a while." He was clean shaven, his dark hair slightly damp. "Blake tells me there's a small ski field a five-minute walk from here. I thought we'd try it. It's got to be better than…being cooped up in here." He didn't add, *with her*. She didn't need the reminder of what she'd done last night. "Breakfast will be ready in fifteen minutes. Can you be ready?" His gaze lowered and tracked over her rumpled bed. Rumpled because she'd tossed and turned most of the night.

"Of course I can." He was sounding a degree or two warmer than he had last night, a little more like his usual self, as though he had put yesterday and last night behind him, as though he could pretend it had never happened. Relief washed through her. She couldn't forget what she had done, her madness. But perhaps they could get back to a place of…comfort between them. A place where they both pretended. She just had to show him that she could be normal. And if normal meant spending the morning on the slopes with him to prove herself, she could do it. Skiing would be the perfect distraction and a much better alternative to staying indoors alone and stewing.

* * *

The only sound in the still morning was the quiet crunch of their boots on the snow. Danni focused on the trail lightly trampled by the few people who'd come this way already this morning. Ahead, she could make out the next three orange-tipped trail markers before their path disappeared in a gap between the pines.

The chalet had a snowmobile but she'd only been half listening to Blake's convoluted explanation as to why it wasn't available this morning. But the walk, Blake had assured them though he hadn't done it himself, was short.

"It's beautiful," Danni said. The beauty, the serenity, helped give her perspective. Her turmoil was just that, hers. And not important. Or at least she knew that one day it would seem unimportant even if that day wasn't quite here yet.

"It is," Adam agreed easily, his step keeping pace with hers.

Breakfast with him had been marginally better than dinner. They were both valiantly pretending the kisses had never happened, both trying to act normally with each other. They were managing. Just. Like bad actors in a play. She could believe it if she forced herself to.

Through a gap between some pines, Danni glimpsed the rustic buildings of the ski field farther up the hill and guessed that Blake's five-minute estimation of the trip was optimistic. "I'll bet you don't usually have to walk to your ski fields lugging your own gear," she said. She tried for a teasing tone but guilt over the fact that it was her decisions that had put him in this predicament gnawed at her. If she hadn't ignored his wishes yesterday, none of this would have happened.

"Not usually, no." He glanced at her. "But I'll bet you don't, either."

"Good point. I guess not." She looked at the markers ahead. "You know, if we skip that next marker and head straight for the one beyond it, it'll be quicker. Some of the footprints already go this way." She headed in the direction she'd suggested, not waiting for Adam to agree. Because he wouldn't. He played by the book. He didn't take shortcuts.

"Why is it you have such a poor opinion of me?" He spoke across the few feet of snow that separated them.

She glanced at him, but with his hat and glasses in the way, too little of his face was visible to gauge how serious his question had been. "I don't."

"You do. You think I'm soft and spoiled and arrogant. Not to mention boring and uptight."

"I never said those things, especially not soft." She tried to remember what she might have ever said about him.

He laughed. Loud and deep. "But that's how you think of me."

His laughter was a relief and a balm. "You're a prince Adam. You've had a life of utter privilege. Apart from a few years in the military."

"You grew up on the palace grounds. You had a lot of those same privileges and, might I add, none of the responsibilities."

Danni said nothing. She couldn't totally agree with him but she also couldn't totally disagree with him.

"It helps you, doesn't it?" he said.

"It helps me what?"

"You prefer not to see me as a normal man. It wasn't

always like that. But I am normal and that's why I have to keep my distance."

She laughed but hers was a little forced. "You're not normal. Nothing about you is normal." She didn't want to hear whatever explanation he'd come up with for rejecting her. "You wouldn't know normal if it jumped up and bit you on the—"

He waited for her to finish but she held her tongue. Too late, but she held it anyway. "You see," he said. "You won't even use words you'd usually use because you're with me. And you used to not be like that. I know that's my fault and I need to fix it. I just don't know how."

If she'd changed it was because she did see him as a normal man now. One who might have needs, one who could fill needs she didn't want to own. She deviated a little farther off the visible path, wanting to put more space between them.

"Bit me where, Danni? Go on, finish your sentence."

There was too much of a challenge in his voice for her to refuse, too much of an assumption that she wouldn't. "Bit you on your fine royal ass."

He smiled. "Thank you. For that openness and for calling my ass fine."

The way those ski pants fit him, there was no doubt about that whatsoever. Not that she was going to admit it to him. "You can also be a royal pain in the ass."

"Again, thank you."

She laughed. "You were like this when Rafe used to tease you, too. Imperturbable, unfathomable. It was totally exasperating. We jumped off the groundsman's shed roof that time just to see how you'd react. You barely batted an eyelid."

"It used to drive him nuts."

"He has my sympathy."

"He always did."

There was something she couldn't quite grasp in his tone. "Meaning?"

"Nothing. But you two were quite the team when you were younger."

"United in tormenting you."

He nodded.

"We were doing you a favor." She looked across the few feet that separated them, trying to see how he'd take that assertion.

"I don't think I ever thanked you for it."

"There's no need for sarcasm." She hid her smile. "We kept you real, and grounded. Stopped your head from getting too full with all that rubbish you insisted on cramming into it."

"By rubbish you mean…?"

Danni paused. "Maybe it doesn't seem so much like rubbish now."

"So you mean my studies? Languages?"

She nodded. "Like Latin."

"You made me teach you some of it."

"I was young and impressionable."

"It may be a dead language but it lives on in other languages it forms the basis for—"

He caught her smiling and grinned back before he looked away, shaking his head.

"See, you just can't help yours—" She squawked as she stepped into a snow drift and sank down to her thighs. She tossed her skis and boots ahead of her and tried to work her way out. Adam stopped to watch her floundering. Finally she held out a hand to him.

He set his things down beside hers, took a few steps closer and looked at her outstretched hand. "Ah, so now I can be of service to you. Now I'm not so boring for preferring to follow the trail markers. And perhaps not quite so useless, hmm?" The light teasing in his voice was invigorating.

"I'm hoping not. But it's not anything you learned in Latin that I need from you now."

"Adsisto." Testing the snow he eased forward and reached for her hand.

"Gratia," she said as she accepted his clasp. He pulled her up and toward him. In two steps she stood pressed fully against him, and he steadied her with an arm around her back. And all the sensations, all the memories, came flooding back. Time stood still. His gaze dipped and flicked up again, then he blinked, long and slow, and stepped back. Away from her.

"Do you ski much?" he asked as the field came into view a couple silent minutes later. "I should have asked earlier. I just assumed."

"You assumed right." Her heartbeat had settled back to somewhere around normal. "I go whenever I get the chance." Even her voice sounded normal, revealing nothing of the breathless, and as it turned out point-less, anticipation she'd felt pressed against him. "I love skiing. The freedom, the speed, the exhilaration." She'd wanted his kiss, had almost been able to taste it. She'd learned nothing from last night.

"I guess that's why I assumed you did. Anything that involves speed and exhilaration and the risk of break-ing your neck."

"You like it, too," she reminded him.

"Yes. I do," he agreed.

"I never thought we'd have anything in common. We're so different. Or at least you pretend you are."

"It's not me pretending I'm not like you. I freely admit who I am. It's you who's in denial. You're more like me than you want to admit."

"I'm nothing like you. You're royalty, you're a scholar, multilingual and let's face it, a bit of a geek."

"A geek? As in I like things like…chess?"

"Yes," she said slowly, seeing immediately where he was going with this, "but I only ever learned because we were both laid up that time, you with your leg and me with chicken pox. I was bored and had gone through all the other games and you'd gotten banned from everything electronic for crashing the palace network."

"The excuses won't work, Danni. Admit it, you enjoy chess."

"Yes," she admitted. "But that doesn't mean anything."

"The Lord of the Rings." Adam had given her the books and insisted she read them prior to the first of the movie adaptations coming out. He'd re-read them at the same time and they'd had many lengthy discussion about them.

"Face it, Danni. Underneath the Action Woman exterior you're part geek, too. And it's not geeky but we have skiing in common."

She focused on the buildings ahead and the chairlifts stretching up the hill before them. "Yes, but—"

"And don't forget cars. You may not like who I am and what I do, but that doesn't mean you're not like me, that we don't have things in common."

She swallowed her shock. "I never said I don't like

who you are and what you do." He couldn't possibly
think that. Could he?

"No?"

They reached the periphery of the clusters of skiers
waiting for tickets or chairs. "No. I totally admire who
you are and what you do. I always have. I can't imagine anyone better suited to it."

"I'm not sure that's a compliment."

"It is," she said quietly.

He stopped walking but because of his glasses
she couldn't read what was in his eyes. He'd opened
his mouth to say something when the sound of a sob
caught their attention. Danni looked down to see a girl
of about five or six looking woefully around, her eyes
wide and panicked. She dropped to her knees in front
of the child. "What are you looking for? Have you lost
someone?"

The girl nodded, the rabbit ears on her ski hat bob-
bing. "I can't find my daddy." Her bottom lip and her
voice trembled.

"That's okay," Danni said brightly, "because I know
how to find lost daddies."

"Do you?"

"I sure do." She passed her skis to Adam.

"There's an information kiosk just over there," he
said quietly to her.

She turned back to the girl. "Hold my hand and we'll
go to that little building." She pointed to the kiosk,
where a number of people were milling around. "They
have a special place for lost fathers."

The girl put her gloved hand into Danni's. "What's
your name?"

"Georgia."

"Come on then, Georgia. Let's go find your daddy. I'll bet he's really worried." Danni quietly prayed that Daddy had noticed the missing child and would also have gone to the kiosk.

Adam walked ahead of them, cutting a path through the crowd. At the kiosk he tapped on the shoulder of a tall man gesticulating wildly, who stopped and turned. Adam pointed out Danni and Georgia and the man came running. "Is that your daddy?" Danni asked the girl.

Georgia saw her father, said "Daddy," and promptly burst into tears. The man scooped up Georgia, enfolding her in a hug. "Are you okay, honey?"

Georgia nodded into her father's shoulder, her sobs subsiding. "The pretty lady knew how to find lost daddies."

He swung an arm around Danni and pulled her into a fierce embrace. "Thank you, thank you. I only turned around for a moment. And then she was gone." His voice was marginally steadier than his daughter's had been earlier.

"She's fine." Danni disentangled herself from father and daughter. "And a lovely girl. Enjoy your skiing." She wasn't even sure he heard, he was so busy hugging his daughter.

She turned to find Adam standing close by. "You handled that well," he said, admiration in his eyes.

"Thanks."

"Pretty lady."

"Enough with the sarcasm."

"I don't think Georgia was being sarcastic."

"I didn't mean Georgia."

"Neither did I."

And she wanted too much to believe him. "Let's see if you're still calling me *pretty lady* when I beat you to the bottom of the first run."

He tipped his head to the side. "It's all right to accept a compliment, Danni."

No. It wasn't. It wasn't all right to accept or believe in Adam's compliments. It wasn't all right to have this conversation with him. "Frightened of losing? Is that why you're being nice? So I'll go easy on you in return?"

He sighed. "Come on then. Show me what you've got."

It was late afternoon before they got back to Blake's chalet. They'd intended to return at noon. But the conditions on the slopes had been perfect. As they'd skied they'd slipped into the easy camaraderie they'd once had—at times teasing, at times earnest, always effortless. For the second part of the afternoon, when they should have been packed and departing the chalet, each time they'd made it to the bottom of a run, they'd looked at each other and one or the other of them had suggested, *one more*.

Technically Adam was a better skier than she was, a joy to watch as he swerved and swooped effortlessly down the runs, but while she couldn't quite match him in sheer skill and grace she made up for it in determination and what he'd laughingly called recklessness as she'd skidded to a stop mere inches from him at the bottom of a run.

For the afternoon, she'd allowed herself to forget who he really was, helped by the fact that if they recognized him nobody on the ski field called attention to

who he was. So, it was a day without cameras or protocol or excessive politeness and deferential or preferen-
tial treatment. He'd waited in line with her at the small
cafeteria, his hat low on his forehead and his glasses on,
and sat outside at the picnic table where they'd sipped
their hot drinks and eaten pizza before taking to the
slopes again.

"We'll head back tomorrow morning," he said as
they approached Blake's chalet.

She questioned him with a look but he gave no explanation. He never did. Not to her and, she was guessing,
seldom to anyone. Their plan, when they'd stretched out
their time on the slopes, had been to head back straight
away once they were finished. She didn't want to ask
whether he now wanted to stay because he wanted the
day—with her—to continue. Like the day at Disney-
land she'd once had as a kid, a day that she couldn't
bear to end. But perhaps he was just tired and didn't
feel like the drive, or perhaps he didn't want her driving after a day's skiing. Assuming they were ignoring
the whole *you're fired* thing and that he would let her
drive anyway. Always with Adam there were so many
questions in her head because he let no one see what
was going on in *his* head.

And the weak part of her that she'd denied for so
long was just grateful that she would get to spend more
time with him. Every minute delighting her. She wasn't
going to question that. Not yet.

They stepped inside and stowed their gear in the
drying room. But with the divestment of their outer
layers, Adam seemed to put on an invisible layer of reserve, something that had been blessedly missing all
day. He'd put it on as she'd taken off her jacket, and it

became even more noticeable as she passed by him to exit the drying room. He backed almost imperceptibly away from her.

They walked silently to the living room.

Blake welcomed them with his customary verbose good humor, insisting that he'd have mulled wine ready for them in front of the fire as soon as they'd—and he used his fingers as quotation marks—freshened up.

So she showered and thought of Adam. Thought of the deep pleasure she'd found just being with him today. She'd sat on the chairlift with him, the hum of the wheel on the cable the only sound interrupting the deep quiet that was peculiar to snow. Sometimes they'd talked on the chairs, and sometimes they'd just sat. Both ways were easy. Both were blissful.

She was a fool. And she didn't know how to stop it.

She'd had relationships before, but they'd been mutual. And clear. Superficial and uncomplicated. Nothing like this.

This one-sided wanting was so much harder to deal with, so much harder to hide. She knew he did what he thought was best for her—but he had no idea. His definition of *best* and hers were poles apart.

He was passing her door when she left her room, self-conscious in a dress and heels.

Adam, as always, looked totally at ease. A soft black cashmere sweater stretched across his shoulders and hinted at the definition of his chest. He held out his arm for her, as though it was the most natural thing in the world.

And maybe for him it was. Doubtless he had held out his arm to women to escort them to dinner almost every night. But for her, just sliding her hand onto his forearm filled her with new sensations. Made her blood rush faster. It made no sense. They'd spent the whole day together. And she'd thought she'd put yesterday's insanity behind her. They'd been close the whole day. And though she'd had wayward thoughts, they hadn't had the intensity that gripped her now. She'd been able, so long as she wasn't looking at his lips, to put their kisses from her mind and not crave more.

But they'd also had on layers and layers of clothes. And she was acutely aware that she'd never touched him before in this supposedly neutral fashion, not since she was a kid when touch meant nothing except friendship, when touch didn't light fires of connection and possibility within her.

Resting her palm on the softness of his sweater, feeling the strength and warmth beneath it, well, it did bad, bad things to her. Made her think bad, bad thoughts. She wanted to lean in, inhale more deeply of his scent, the scent of freshly showered male. And she wanted his lips on hers, and his hands on her. She wanted to know so much more about him than he let her see.

What she needed, on the other hand, was to get farther away from him. So that her brain could start functioning properly again, so that she remembered who she was. And who he was. And that he was looking for a wife. One who met his criteria. Not a temporary fling with his temporary driver.

But, a little voice whispered, *that wouldn't be so bad, would it?*

His step slowed and she looked up to see his gaze on her. "What is it? Do I have toothpaste on my lip?" She ran her tongue around her lips to check. He shook his head and looked away.

"You look—" he cleared his throat "—nice. That's all."

"Nice?"

"Lame compliment, I know. But I don't think the right word to describe you exists. And in that dress…" His gaze swept over her; it didn't linger but there was something in it that warmed her. "Your legs…I scarcely knew you had any."

Danni laughed at his uncharacteristic awkwardness. She'd brought the simple black dress because it traveled well and still made her feel feminine, as did the glint of male appreciation in Adam's eyes. "I hope that's not supposed to be a better compliment." She tried to make light of the reaction to him that was sweeping through her.

His laughter was little more than a breath. But it warmed her further and compensated somewhat for the "nice." Not the best compliment she'd ever had. But coming from Adam, who doubtless had a wealth of sophisticated flattery at the tip of his tongue, it felt honest. And making him laugh always felt like a triumph.

The laughter was still there in his eyes as they held hers for a second.

He started walking again. Oh yes. She knew how he thought of her. As a kid. Almost a sister. That was why his "nice" had felt honest. Danni slid her hand from his arm on the pretext of adjusting her dress. And didn't put it back. *Nice.* It made her realize how much more she wanted from him.

Blake met them as they came down the stairs and insisted they sit in front of the fire while he brought the mulled wine. Adam tilted his head toward the chess set and when she nodded, he shifted it so that it sat between them.

He adjusted the pieces on his side of the board and looked up. "I owe you an apology and my thanks."

"An apology *and* thanks. Wow. That's a big day for you. I'm a little shocked."

"I'm serious, Danni."

"So am I."

He shook his head but a grin tugged at his lips. "Wait till you hear me tell you that you were right."

She slapped her hand to her chest and gasped. This was how she was supposed to behave—the teasing friend, not a woman whose mind was steaming down a one-way track that ended with his bones being jumped.

His grin widened briefly before disappearing. "I haven't had a day like that, as good as that, in...I don't know how long. I skied and forgot about almost everything. Forgot about brewing diplomatic crises and security concerns and upcoming engagements and speeches. Forgot about looking for—thinking of the future." Had he been going to say looking for a wife? "And I owe you for that. You made a good decision when you brought me here."

"Thank you."

"Nobody else would have seen that or done that."

"Because they're all too scared of you."

"Scared?" He sat back in his chair, his brows drawn together. "No they're not."

"In awe, might be a better word. Though I fail to see why." He was just a man doing his job. His job happened to be fairly high profile. But it was still just a job. And a demanding one that he needed time out from occasionally. Who was she kidding? Even she felt the awe occasionally. But in her case it was because of who he was, not what he was.

"I can live with awe," he said with a faint smile.

"It's not good for you. You'll lose touch with reality. You'll get a big head."

"A big head?"

Big Head was what she used to call him when he got all superior on her when she was younger.

Now he was laughing at her. Not out loud. But inside. She just knew it. And she felt her lips twitch in response.

"Thankfully I have you to keep me humble."

And scarily, she wanted to do far more than keep him humble. Things she wasn't supposed to want to do to a prince. It was there somewhere deep inside her, a humming attraction to him. Stronger when she was closest but always there. And she didn't know how to make it go away.

"I needed today. So thank you."

He'd needed today. He'd needed the time out. But he didn't need her. She bit her lip. She shouldn't want him to need her. But wanting her, just a little, wasn't she allowed to want that?

"What about you?"

"Me?"

"You enjoyed today?"

"Yes." Way too much.

"You seem thoughtful."

"I'm fine," she said a little too brightly. "Tired. In a good way. And hungry." In a bad way.

It had happened again. Since coming back here, the ease she'd felt with him had turned to dis-ease. The stiffness and politeness that he used to keep people at a distance was creeping back.

"So, are we going to play?"

"Sure. Can't wait to whip your…"

"My?"

She loved it when he smiled like that, knowledge in his eyes. "Your fine royal ass."

"Have at it."

If only.

They'd scarcely started when Blake returned with their drinks. "Dinner will be ready in half an hour. And you'll be relieved to know that the chef finally turned up. And whatever it is he's cooking, it smells good."

They sat in front of the fire, the chess set between them. The game gave her something other than Adam to focus on. But it wasn't enough of a distraction to keep her from noticing his hands as he moved his pieces and wanting those hands on her, or the deep concentration on his face when she stole looks at him while his attention was focused on the board, and wanting it focused on her.

She was contemplating the curve of his ear when he suddenly shifted his gaze to catch her studying him. His dark eyes trapped and held hers. "Your move," he said slowly.

If it was truly her move, she'd leave her seat and trace the shape of his ear, maybe run her fingers through his hair or over his shoulders, and definitely, definitely kiss his lips, seeking the taste of him, needing to feel that softness, to inhale something of him.

They were both leaning forward over the board. His face was close and she was trapped by the depths in his eyes.

Desire. It bloomed within her. And she recognized its match in the darkening of Adam's eyes. She tried to look away. Tried and failed. And she couldn't say for certain which of them closed that small distance. She'd thought so hard about it that maybe it was her. But it didn't matter because his lips were on hers. She closed her eyes and savored the onslaught of sensation. His lips, firm yet soft, the taste of cinnamon from the mulled wine, and his encompassing warmth. She gave herself over to the kiss. Let the sensations wash through her, claim her. She felt his hand at the back of her head, his fingers threading through her hair.

Unlike their earlier desperate kisses this was achingly tender.

Eight

"Dinner's ready." They broke apart at the sound of Blake's voice. "Oh, sh—sorry. I didn't mean to interrupt."

"You weren't interrupting," Adam said.

"Looked like I was, to me. Dinner can wait if you like."

"No." Adam who was never outwardly fazed by anything spoke almost curtly. He took a breath. "We're ready now," he said a little less abruptly.

"This way. If you're sure." Blake looked from Adam to Danni.

"We're sure," Adam said.

He led them to the dining room where it would be just the two of them with candles on the table between them and soft music playing from unseen speakers. Danni, whose biggest problem was usually saying all the wrong things, could think of nothing at all to say.

They focused on their appetizers, though neither of them ate much. Finally Adam set his fork down. "I'm sorry."

And there it was, his apology, an attempt to let her down gently, to take the blame and then reassert the proper distance between them.

"Don't be," she said warily. "It's me who's sorry."

"I shouldn't have kissed you then and I shouldn't have kissed you yesterday. I can't seem to help it. But it won't happen again."

She should say nothing, but instead, "Why not?" slipped from her lips.

His eyes widened. "I don't want to ruin or lose what we have and I won't take advantage of you."

"We don't have anything to ruin or lose." Danni's fork clanged against her plate.

"Yes we do. I trust you and I value you and I like you."

Like. That was at least as bad as *nice.*

"The last thing in the world I want is to do anything to change that."

"You're too late. It's already changed."

"How do we change it back?"

"We don't. We can't. And I don't want to. And it wasn't you who kissed me just then, it was me who kissed you. So you have no right to apologize for it. Ever since we kissed yesterday—"

"We shouldn't have."

"Since before we kissed, if I'm going to be honest." She pushed on before he could stop her. "I've thought of you differently."

"We can go back to how we were."

"I don't want to."

Adam looked stricken.

"I want to go forward."

"Forward?"

"I want to see where these new feelings go. I want you to kiss me and to touch me. All over. And I want to be able to kiss you, and to touch you. All over. And I want more than that, too." She waited, her heart pounding. Why, why, could she never keep her mouth closed?

Sorrow and a shadow of horror clouded his face. "We can't, Danni."

She'd known he didn't want to think of her that way. If she'd just kept her mouth shut, she could also have kept her dignity. "I'm sorry." Heat swept across her face as she picked up her fork and stabbed at a mushroom.

"It's not that I don't want to."

She looked up. His dark eyes were troubled. "At least be honest. Making up excuses would be worse than anything. A simple 'I'm just not attracted to you' will do nicely."

"I'm more attracted to you than I can stand. I kept skiing today—past when we should have stopped and gone home—just because I wanted to prolong being with you. Just being with you. Do you have any idea how extraordinary that is? I'm happiest on my own. Or at least I thought I was. But I've discovered that's not true. I'm happier when I'm with you. I can't stop thinking about you, but…"

There had to be a *but,* because for a while her heart had hoped and soared.

"I'm not going to do anything about it."

"Why not?"

"Because I'm supposed to be looking for a woman I can marry. A woman who can stand at my side and be my princess when I take my father's place."

"And I'm not that woman?" She was the opposite of what he was looking for. She knew it, she'd always known it, so it shouldn't hurt.

"Do you want to be?"

She almost said yes, till she thought about it. Danni laughed. "No. I can't think of anything worse." Except for the part where she would get to be with him in private.

"That's why I'm not going to do anything about it."

"Because there's no future in it."

He nodded.

"What about the present?"

"It wouldn't be right. It wouldn't be fair to you."

"Who are you to decide what's fair to me?"

"I'm not having this conversation with you."

"Do you see this appetizer we're eating?"

"Yes."

"It's not dinner. It's not the main event. It'd never fill you up, but it's very nice. So just because you're looking to start dating seriously so that you can find your perfect woman doesn't mean that while we're both here we can't…" She shrugged then took a deep breath. *Don't do it,* a voice of warning cried in her head. "I want to make love with you."

He shook his head. And in his eyes was hardness. And pity. "We can't. It wouldn't be right."

She'd just propositioned him, something she'd never done to any man. And been turned down.

And still she wanted him.

* * *

In her bedroom she changed into her pajamas—
drawstring pants and a camisole—and sat on the big,
empty, four-poster bed. She had no fantasies of a four-
poster bed, only fantasies of Adam. So real she could
taste them, feel them, so real they beat inside her chest.

Senses alert, she listened to the faint precise sounds
coming through the wall of Adam getting ready for bed.
The bathroom door opening and shutting, taps running.

He was attracted to her. He'd said that much—the
admission wrung regretfully out of him.

But he wasn't going to do anything about it. That
regret was hers.

Because it wouldn't be right or fair to her. Was the
regret, the loss of something not known, never to be
known, fair? Was sitting in here alone and needing,
fair? He would do nothing about that injustice.

But could she?

A sliver of light peeped beneath the adjoining door.
Was he thinking about her? Or had he put her from his
mind? He was good at that. Deal with the issue at hand
then move on to the next, letting no overlap complicate
one or the other. He could be in there reading or working, totally focused.

But he'd said he was attracted to her. More than he
could stand. And Adam was not a man to use words
lightly.

She crossed to the door and put her ear to it but heard
nothing. She touched her fingers to its hard, unreveal-
ing, uninviting surface.

He'd already admitted that her going against his
stated wishes and bringing him here had been a good

decision. She could...seduce him. She swallowed a laugh that would have been close to hysterical.

Steeling herself, knowing that some regrets were bigger than others and some opportunities could never be recovered, she touched the handle. The beating of her heart precluded hearing anything else.

So few things in life scared her, but this...this terrified her. She deepened her breath till her fingers ceased their shaking.

She'd already made a fool of herself. She had nothing further to lose. Slowly, she turned the handle, holding her breath against the possibility that he'd locked the door from his side, and on her exhale swung the door silently open.

He sat at the small desk, his back to her and his laptop open in front of him but his head held in his hands. Trying to work? But not.

Drawn to him, to that broad back, that bent head, Danni crossed the thickly carpeted room.

Adam didn't move.

She stood behind him. His laptop had switched to its screen saver.

He straightened and held himself still, as though listening. She just had to touch him, one hand to the closest forbidding shoulder but her heart beat so hard she could scarcely move.

"No."

The single abrupt word was fierce. Sighing heavily, he rested his fingers on the keyboard and began slowly to type. A document with graphs and tables sprang to life on the screen.

That *no* was a message for her. What was she doing? She was no seductress. She was wearing her pajamas!

She didn't even own anything that could claim to be a negligee. He'd already turned her down. How much rejection did she want? Panic gripped her. She took a step backward, held still and then took another step. She backed halfway across the room on unsteady legs then turned. And she had her fingers on the edge of the door when his hand landed on her right shoulder and the shock waves reverberated through her.

"What are you doing?" His deep voice held both the question and his reluctant awareness of what her answer had to be. Given her earlier admission there could be no other.

"Nothing." She didn't turn to face him. She couldn't. Her heart thudded in her chest. Run. Run. Run. But she couldn't do that, either.

He stepped in closer. She could feel him behind her, surrounding her without touching her, except for that one touch, a heavy hand tight on her shoulder. Its grip invincible.

"Why are you in here?" His breath feathered across her neck sending warm shivers through her with the gently spoken words. Tension, beyond anything she'd known, seized her. A combination of wanting and anticipation and cowardice and fear.

He had to ask? As if her presence here wasn't obvious. She didn't doubt that women had tried to seduce him before. She was certain, however, that he'd never had to ask what they were doing. "I was going to burgle your room." Between that and seduction, burglary was surely the lesser sin.

"What were you going to take?" he asked quietly.

"Your innocence." She'd thought about making it a joke but her words came out a whisper.

His hand on her shoulder tightened and he pulled her back against him. She felt laughter reverberating through him. Okay. So maybe it had sounded like a joke. Apparently a really funny one.

But the silent laughter stilled. "My innocence is long gone, Danni," he said, utter seriousness in his quiet voice. "It's only when I'm with you that I even remember I had any."

She waited. His fingers tightened where his hand still rested on her shoulder. His breath still feathered across her neck though his breathing was shorter. And though the beat of her heart still commanded her to run, his hand and her recalcitrant feet and perhaps that whisper of breath kept her immobile.

"Maybe we should just forget I came in here."

"It's not going to be that easy."

"Nothing ever is with you."

"Why?" His other hand came to rest on her left shoulder.

"Because you never let anything just be easy. You're always analyzing life like it's a chess game."

From the floor below them came a crash and the rumble of Blake's voice.

Adam's hands slid lower till they curved around her arms, his touch gentle but unbreakable. "I meant," he said, and she imagined his smile, "why were you trying to seduce me?"

"How many reasons could there be?"

"More than you could imagine," he said quietly.

"Well apparently I don't have a very good imagination. Because as far as I can see there would only be one reason I would try to seduce you."

"Danni. Go. While you can." He moved. Closer still.

So that she felt the press of him against her back. His hands slid lower still until they wrapped around hers, holding her in direct contradiction to his words. His cheek was beside hers.

She closed her eyes and leaned against him, overwhelmed by him. His nearness, his warmth, his scent enveloped her.

Movement again, and then the gentle press of his lips against her neck. Need blossomed. Drenched her. Stole strength from her limbs so that she melted back against him, her head falling to one side to give him greater access to her neck because she needed this kiss. His kiss.

This moment of weakness might be all she would get from him. So even as the desire and delight engulfed her, she tried to catalogue the sensations. But the strength of them made cataloguing impossible.

He just was. And his touch did what it did. And called to something in her that was beyond reason.

And while his lips and touch worked magic on her, magic so powerful it needed access to no more than the bare skin of her neck, his hands moved again, sliding from her hands to her waist, sliding beneath her top. Skin to skin. His heat seared her so that her breath shuddered in her chest. She backed more firmly against him.

Hands and lips stilled.

Please don't let him stop.

She leaned farther back, trying to meld herself with him so that he couldn't let her go, couldn't push her away. And she felt the evidence of his need, heard it in the ragged hitch to his breath.

"Danni."

She heard too much in his voice. Regret and blame and apology. His hands started to slip away. He would ignore need and go with his idea of right. She gripped his wrists and his hands stilled. She guided them upward, trailing over waist and ribs till she led them where she wanted to feel them, covering her breasts. He groaned against her neck and his thumbs brushed over hardened nipples.

Her gasp matched his groan as need streaked through her, hot and fierce.

He dropped his hands and as she was about to cry out in protest he turned her around.

And kissed her.

Properly. Finally. The kiss she'd been waiting for all her life. There was no anger or regret this time. No sweet gentleness. There was only need. His lips against hers. His tongue dancing with and teasing hers, clamoring to learn her and please her. His arms wound tightly around her and his body pressed against her.

She returned his kiss. Greedily. She had wanted this for so long even while she'd denied that wanting. She'd imagined it, dreamed of it.

And it was everything that she'd imagined and dreamed only better and so much more.

And now that she was facing him, she too could touch. Lifting her hands to his face, she traced his cheekbones, his jaw, felt the rasp of beard against her palms. She slid her fingers through his hair to delight in its dark silk. But she wanted more, too. As they kissed she found the buttons of his shirt, fumbled them undone so that she could touch the warm hard planes of his abdomen, the contours of his chest, the strength of his back.

She was torn between the delight of slow exploration, the need to learn and treasure every contour, and the ravenous need to feel all of him, all at once, to fill her hands with him. She'd waited so long for this impossible reality and knew a fear that it might all vanish. It felt so much like magic, being held by him, kissed by him, that surely it could disappear as quickly as it had appeared, like a mirage in the desert.

Just as she'd feared, his hands came up, framed her face and he pulled back, breaking the kiss, ending the beauty.

He studied her and she tried to read his thoughts in his eyes. She saw turmoil and anguish. But she saw desire also. Deep, aching desire. It was there in his darkened eyes, in his parted lips and ragged breathing.

"It's not right," he whispered.

"It's very, very right," she whispered back.

And then he was kissing her again.

His attempt at restraint demolished, she could have cried in triumph.

He dropped his hands and wrapped his arms around her and carried her through the door to her bed. He set her on the floor. Torment clouded his eyes. His hands gripped her arms, their hold almost fierce. "Don't fight it, Adam. Just please tell me you have condoms."

A smile flashed across his face and he closed his eyes. "I give in. I'll be damned for it, but I give in." Relief weakened her. He was back from his bathroom within seconds and with slow wonder he peeled her camisole over her head and her pants down her legs. She helped him shed his clothes and they knelt facing each other on the bed. She helped sheath him and then Danni climbed onto his knees straddling him so that she could touch his face, trail her fingers along his nose, his jaw, over his lips. She'd wanted to touch him so badly for so long now, had done it countless times in her imagination. And the reality was everything she'd imagined and more. The hardness of muscle and bone, the silk of skin, the rasp of hair.

"Do you have any idea," he said, "how badly I want you?"

She bit her lip as she looped her hands behind his head. "I think I might." She shared that same need.

His hands rose to her breasts and a shudder rippled through her as his thumbs teased her nipples. She arched into his touch and he replaced his hands with his mouth, kissing each breast in turn, pleasuring her with lips and teeth and tongue while his hand roved, cupped her bottom and pulled her closer still so that his erection pressed against her.

He moved abruptly, swept her off him so that she was lying down and he was over her. "You are so perfect," he said, shaking his head and settling himself between her legs.

She wrapped her legs around his back. "Enough with the talking." She lifted her hips so that she felt him at her entrance. His passionate gaze locked with hers as he slid into her, stretching her, filling her as she'd ached for him to. Her body welcomed him. He stopped there, then slowly pulled out before filling her again, the pleasure exquisite. They moved together, perfectly in tune. The bliss built until it was almost unbearable. Sounds escaped her, cries of delight and need. Their rhythm built, became fiercer yet, unstoppable, till he was driving into her and she was meeting each thrust, taking him deeper still till the pleasure raging through her couldn't be contained and her orgasm ripped through her, shattering her. Adam surged against her, crying her name.

They lay, chests heaving, foreheads touching. As their breathing calmed he rolled off her but kept her in his arms. She laid her head on his shoulder, sated and dreamy.

Sanity slowly returned.

She felt and heard Adam take a breath. "Don't say anything."

"Not even, wow."

Danni laughed and he pulled her closer to him.

Adam woke and watched Danni sleeping, bathed in soft morning light. He could scarcely remember seeing her still before. Completely relaxed. Even when they played chess and she took her time thinking before making a move there was a contained restlessness to her as though she was ever ready to leap from her chair. It showed itself in the subtle tapping of her fingers or her toes.

He smiled now. She didn't share a bed well. She lay at an angle across the big bed. One arm was flung up above her head, her fingers curling gently. The pale skin of her arm looked so soft, vulnerable almost. Her eyes, usually flashing fire, were closed. Eyelashes kissed her cheeks.

She stirred and rolled. And the sheet he'd pulled up over her as she slept shifted. So beautiful. She took his breath away. Pale and lithe. More petite than he'd realized—again he blamed that restless energy that radiated for her, always making her seem…more. More than the sum of her parts. More alive than anyone else he knew. Brimming with vitality and humor.

The edge of the sheet lay across her chest, dipping low but not low enough to reveal her pert perfect breasts.

So feminine. He'd been willfully blind to that about her before. He'd focused over the years on how much of a tomboy she was, how she was his friend, at times almost a sister, to help him avoid focusing on the obvious. Danni was gorgeous. Passion personified. Nothing sultry, just an electric sensuality that called to him, like no one else.

Called to him? Like no one else? The thought stopped him cold.

He couldn't entertain thoughts like that. She was Danni. He was a brief pit stop on the race that was her life. And he had a life to lead, too. Responsibilities to live up to.

He should get out of this bed, cross back to his own room and lock the door behind him. Too late, he realized that he suddenly stood on the precipice of something unknown and dangerous.

She opened her eyes and her lips curved into a smile. That's where the danger lay. Those eyes. Just looking into them pleased him. Her smile broadened, she shifted again, arched just a little. He took back his earlier thought. Sultry. There was no other word for it. He rolled toward her. Precipice be damned.

She traced a pattern across his chest with her fingertip. "You know, French is the language of love but you never spoke French to me while we were…"

Making love? Neither of them would want to call it

that. "Because I couldn't think straight in any language. I can try now if you like?"

She grinned and her eyes sparkled.

He caught her lazily circling finger. "I'll speak words to you that will light you on fire. Words you'll understand even though you don't speak French or Italian or German." He brought that finger to his lips and kissed it. "Croissant, Citroen." He found her next finger, kissed that also. "Schnitzel, Mercedes Benz." Her fingers weren't enough. He rolled on top of her, holding his weight from her, and loved the way she wriggled to accommodate him and the heat and anticipation in her gaze.

"Go on."

He brushed her hair back from her face and kissed her forehead. "Pizza, Ferrari."

"Ohh, I think I like Italian best. Give me more."

"Demanding wench."

She rocked her hips.

And he'd give her the world. "Tiramisu, Lamborghini."

"Take me I'm yours."

He touched his lips to hers, and conscious thought, in any language, evaporated.

Nine

Adam stood with Danni and Blake under the portico of the chalet. Satisfaction thrummed through him as smoothly as the idling of the Range Rover's engine.

One night and one morning of perfection, of love-making and laughter. They'd stolen that much for themselves. As he watched Danni talking easily with Blake, he realized it was the laughter that had surprised him. He'd never laughed so much with a woman before. But Danni teased and joked, taking nothing, least of all him, too seriously. She was a revelation.

He hadn't thought she could be right when she'd said a relationship should be fun. It was one of the many lessons he'd learned from her.

Living in the moment was part of her nature. She had refused to talk about the future, about anything other than right now. And it turned out that very little talking at all was necessary and that there were far better ways than skiing to capitalize on snow on the ground outside.

The sheer compulsive energy of her had drawn him in. She'd uncovered a part of himself he'd walled over and forgotten.

He watched her now. Some of that energy had dimmed. Their time of isolated perfection was over. They were heading back. For the first time he could remember he was resisting what lay ahead.

"I hope you've enjoyed your stay," Blake said as though he was reciting lines from a script. He probably was. Several times throughout their visit, he had consulted the little red notebook that contained his instructions. Even absent, Sabrina ran a tight ship.

"Very much," Danni answered.

Blake leaned a little closer. "I didn't say anything, because I didn't want you to know." He lowered his voice. "But you were my first ever guests. I'm relieved it was you two. I don't know too much about this lark and I'll admit I was worried. I didn't know how it would go if someone important had come to stay. Sabrina would have killed me if I did anything wrong or got too familiar with guests. Or talked too much." A sheepish smile spread across his face. He winked. "If you ever see her and she asks, tell her I didn't."

"You didn't," Adam said.

"Anyway, it was a good practice run for me. We're expecting a mayor next week. I won't say who because I'm not allowed to talk about guests, but at least I've got this under my belt as a warm-up. I'll still be nervous having a local dignitary but it won't be so bad."

"Rest easy. You were the perfect host."

Blake slapped him on the shoulder with surprising force. "Thanks, mate. That means a lot to me. Oh, hey, I forgot to get you to sign the guest book."

"It's okay," Danni said. "I signed it." She tossed and caught the car keys. She knew he watched the movement. Challenge lit her eyes. He let the challenge pass. The driving was important to her.

Like him, she'd been reluctant to leave their bed this morning. But once she had, she'd approached the things they'd needed to do efficiently but almost mechanically.

They'd been on the road a few minutes when he asked, "Whose name? In the guest book."

"Just mine. And my signature's almost indecipherable. Don't worry, there'll be nothing to link you here with me." She didn't sound like the Danni of the last few days. There was a new distance and formality to her voice, and a subtle tension about her shoulders. Was this how it was going to go? Had he ruined everything by giving into the overpowering need and making love with her?

"That wasn't what I was worried about."

"No? What were you worried about then?"

"Would you believe me if I said you?"

She sighed but there was a hint of laughter behind it and her shoulders eased. "Yes. I would." The glance she flicked in his direction was almost sorrowful.

The road unwound before them, a dark damp strip between blinding white snow and dark green pines. The GPS in the dash showed what lay ahead. But there was no road map for what came next for them. And as a man who lived by plans and goals and schedules, the uncertainty and the changes they would face bothered him.

He didn't know if she realized what they'd be up

against. "You're the one who has the most to lose if this becomes public knowledge," he said. Hers was the life that would be turned upside down, its quiet privacy obliterated. He didn't want that to be the legacy for her of their brief time together.

"It won't become public knowledge. It can't. It was just one weekend." She sounded blithely unconcerned with her own fate. "Only you and I know, and I'm not telling anyone. And if you can curb your tendency to run off at the mouth," she said with pure Danni sass, "we'll be fine. Blake knows we were there together, but he doesn't know who you are. And even if he did I don't think he'd tell. Not deliberately."

"And there's always Sabrina to keep him in line." Blake had showed him a photo of the absent Sabrina, a tiny, sweet-looking woman.

"Exactly," Danni agreed with a smile. "One snow-bound weekend. We were allowed that much."

But the possibility of what they'd shared becoming public was only part of what was bothering him. The other part, the purely selfish part, was the prospect of losing her, and what they'd found, so soon after discovering it. He'd been closer to her this weekend than anyone else. Ever.

"You're saying that's it, that this is over between us?" That was supposed to be his line, but hearing it acknowledged by her made him want to fight it. He wasn't used to this kind of confusion. Usually the right thing to do was obvious, or at least felt right. But ending things with Danni, when they'd scarcely started, felt wrong in his heart at the same time as he knew in his mind it was right.

She flicked a worried glance at him. "Yes. It has to

be. You know that. We have no future. We go back to life as normal."

That was the trouble. He did know. And yet she'd turned him upside down and inside out until he couldn't think straight. Because of her, he might never think completely straight again. But what he did know was that what he used to consider normal would no longer be enough. "I'm not sure it's possible."

"We'll manage." She spoke fiercely.

Did she really believe that? They'd come together so quickly there had been no slow anticipatory buildup, no courtship. None of the romance Danni herself had once informed him women wanted. Didn't she deserve that?

"And I'm supposed to be okay with just using you for a one-night stand? You're okay with that?"

"Absolutely. And you have to be okay with me using you. It was probably wrong of me but…" She shrugged.

He shook his head. Her voice held a brittle note of falseness. "I don't know, Danni. Things have changed so quickly and so absolutely. I need time to think it through."

"No, you don't. I can see where you're going with this. You think you haven't done right by me. But you have. Very, very right."

He didn't like the sudden stubborn lift to her chin, the narrowing of her eyes.

"You'll forget about the weekend and move on." She kept her voice low and easy but he thought perhaps she had to fight for that calm. "We both will. You're being honorable. I know you don't like the thought of using anyone."

"I wasn't using you. You know I wouldn't." But had he?

"Then I guess I owe you an apology, because you wouldn't. Not intentionally. But I was using you."

"I don't believe you." He recognized the tough kid who always came up fighting in the woman beside him.

"Believe me. I thought it was mutual or I wouldn't have…"

Wouldn't have what? There had been no forethought in what had transpired between them, no stopping to consider consequences.

She swallowed. "So while your protest is sweet, it's not necessary."

He couldn't see beyond the bravado, couldn't fathom what was going on in her head. And he owed it to her to find out. Despite what she said, he did need to do right by her. It was imperative.

"Danni, we need to talk this through."

"No we don't." She looked fixedly ahead. He couldn't see her eyes, and he needed to have some idea what she really felt. Her eyes, so expressive, always gave her away. "Let's stop at that café. The one we stopped at on the way up."

"I don't think that's a good idea." And still she didn't so much as glance at him.

"If what we have is over—"

"It has to be." She made his "if" an absolute.

"Then we'll be going to go back to how it used to be between us?"

"Yes."

"So, I'll cease being your lover and go back to being a prince to you, nothing more?"

"It's for the best."

"In that case, stop at the café. It's an order. And if you really want to prove things can go back to how they were, you'll follow it."

Danni took a deep breath and consciously relaxed her shoulders and flexed her fingers before resettling them around the wheel. Adam would come to his senses soon. All she had to do was to *keep calm and carry on.* It was either that or panic and freak out. When the café came into view she slowed and pulled in to the parking lot. An obedient driver. Nothing more.

Inside, the scent of coffee filled the air and an open fire blazed in the hearth. Only a couple tables were occupied, but at first one table, and then the other, heads turned. Then each of those few people leaned in closer to their companions. And whispered.

She could have kicked herself. Getting away without Adam being recognized the first time they'd been here had been more luck than she should have hoped for. A second time was too much to ask.

But, she reminded herself, the first time they had nothing to hide, and this time needn't be any different. She was his driver. Taking him home from his weekend break. *Of fantastic sex,* a wicked, insidious voice whispered. No. She was Adam's driver for the weekend. Period. If she repeated it enough times she could almost believe it. He was a prince. She was returning him to the palace. To his life. She should have worn her uniform. Because although it made her stand out, it also made her invisible. People saw it and then dismissed her.

Without her uniform she worried that people might see the woman who had spent the weekend in bed making love with a prince. She felt so different, so sexually satisfied, it didn't seem possible that the difference wasn't obvious.

Adam's nod and smile took in the occupants and the staff, earned him smiles and gasps in return. Somehow—through years of practice most likely—he'd mastered the art of looking warm and approachable while at the same time discouraging anyone from testing that approachability. He stood at the same booth they'd occupied during their first visit and waited for her to sit.

Danni slid onto the dark leather seat. Adam sat beside her. Too close. Too intimate. She scooted around so that she sat opposite him. Like a driver might. No. Not a driver. A driver would never sit like this with a royal client. But perhaps a friend. She could live with friend.

They ordered drinks from an effusive waitress who looked as though she might almost curtsy. When she'd turned her back, Adam leaned in. "Just a few hours ago we were making love." He kept his voice low, so as not to be overheard but it made it even more seductive than normal.

Danni didn't need his reminder. It was too easy looking at him to remember all that they'd shared. But she couldn't think about them making love. And he couldn't be allowed to, either. Or at least he couldn't be allowed to talk about it.

Deep down she knew she couldn't be just friends with him. Not after they'd been so much more. So her pending grief would be for the loss of both a lover and a friend.

In the space of days, things had gone further and deeper than she should ever have let them. She should have run far and fast that first night she leaned into the car to wake him and met his gaze and felt that insistent tug of attraction, the kick of desire. She should have run before she realized how very much more lay behind it.

"I just want to know that we've thought through our options before we consign 'us' to an impossibility," he said.

"We don't have any options and there is no 'us.'"

"There are always options."

"Not always. Not this time." They couldn't have options. It ended now. She could have no part of his life. She'd remember this always as something magical. But that was all it could ever be. A memory.

She had to be ruthless with the naive unthinking part of her that craved options and possibilities, that wanted to dream of a future, no matter how short, that wanted to steal all the minutes and hours and days and nights they could. Regardless of right or wrong. Regardless of the consequences because in this case they wouldn't be hers alone.

Adam belonged to their country, he wasn't hers and he never would be.

She thought she saw a shadow of the sorrow besieging her in his eyes. Beneath the table his foot brushed against hers. A small point of contact, toe to toe, through leather. They weren't allowed even that much and yet she couldn't move her foot away.

If they weren't in a public place and he reached for her, she would too easily succumb. As it was, he rested one hand on the table near hers and she ached to hold it.

"The trouble is that I can't bear for this—" he gestured between the two of them "—to end. And I don't think you can either."

"We don't always get everything we want in life."

He sat back as the waitress approached with their coffees but his gaze never left her face.

"Don't you see," Danni said once the waitress had gone again. "It has ended. It ended when we walked out of that chalet."

His frown deepened, as though he might argue. But he knew who he was and what he owed his country and his family. He was returning to a world of responsibilities. Responsibilities that included looking for a woman to stand at his side as princess.

"I can't stand by while you search for the perfect royal wife. I'm strong, Adam, but I'm not that strong. Or that much of a masochist."

He jerked as though she'd slapped him. His hand clenched into a fist on the table. "And I'm not that much of a bastard. How could I look at another woman after you?"

"You have to."

He sat up straighter. The silence stretched and stretched, till finally he spoke quietly. "I'm stopping my search for the perfect wife."

The bottom dropped out of Danni's world.

No. She wouldn't be responsible for her country's prince postponing his search. She'd be reviled throughout the principality.

She stood, her legs far from steady. "Then you definitely don't need me."

Ten

The drive back to the palace lasted an eternity. Adam sat as silent and inscrutable as a sphinx next to her. She just wanted the trip to be over. She needed to get away from him, because being this close when she could no longer have him was torture.

She would drop him off and aides would come running with crises for him to negotiate. He would move on.

But when she finally saw the longed-for towering sandstone building, it was loss rather than relief that swamped her.

This was it. This was their goodbye.

She drove to the entrance to his wing. He turned to her as she pulled to a stop. "Have dinner with me tonight?"

"No. I'm going to spend this evening with Dad." She took a deep breath. "Adam, don't do this."

"So when I kiss you now you'll be kissing me goodbye?" His dark beautiful eyes were steady on her, drawing her inexorably toward him. Desperation for this one last kiss. It was the desperation that told her she couldn't allow even this kiss. Especially this kiss.

"No. Yes. I mean, I can't kiss you, but if I did I would be kissing you goodbye."

Rational thought disintegrated as he leaned closer. She caught his scent, saw his lips—lips she knew so well. Every cell in her body yearned for his touch. One kiss. One memory to take away. She wasn't strong enough to deny herself that.

"You want this, too," he said softly.

"No, I don't." She was inches from him and she knew everything about her contradicted his words.

He laughed, the sound low and rich. And more than anything she wanted those laughing lips on hers. She pulled back and looked straight ahead, anywhere rather than at Adam. Adam, whom she could never have again. "You should get out now. We both have things to do. Lives to get back to."

"I'm not getting out. Not until you kiss me."

"That's blackmail." She couldn't let him win. If he was going to be stubborn then she could be, too. She got out, striding round the car to open his door and hold it wide.

As he got out, she walked quickly to the rear of the car and removed his suitcase. She carried it to the recessed entrance to the palace. She turned and found him right there. He lifted his hands to frame her face.

Just that touch of his palms along her jaw rendered her immobile, stole her breath. Made her ache. Her lips parted with need for him. She felt the familiar insistent tugging low within her.

"Tell me you don't want me to kiss you, every bit as badly as I want to kiss you. If you tell me that, then I won't."

She fought for long seconds over her answer, drowning in his eyes, aching with the need to touch him. "I don't want you to kiss me."

He lowered his head and brushed his lips across hers.

"You said you wouldn't." The feebleness of her protest echoed the weakness of her willpower.

"You lied when you said you didn't want me to. So that made my lie okay, too. Tell me you don't want me to kiss you again."

His breath mingled with hers in the cool air. She swayed toward him, her body betraying her mind. "I don't."

"Liar." He kissed her again, this time the way she needed him to, his lips slanting over hers, tasting her deeply, and filling her with the taste of him. Her arms slid around him, pulling his body closer, holding him to her, and any last scraps of reason fled. She was lost to him, lost to the sensations. His warmth, his scent, the exquisite pressure of his lips on hers, the way his tongue teased.

Finally, at a nearby sound, they broke apart and he rested his forehead against hers. His thumbs stroked her jaw. "This is wrong." His words whispered across her lips.

She knew he had to see and admit it sooner or later. But still the admission, when she was blinded with the need stirred by his kiss, hurt. "I told you."

"I should be dropping you at your door, not the other way around."

"That's not how it works. I was the driver."

"No, you weren't. I fired you, remember. I was only letting you drive as a favor. I know how you like it. So get back in the car and I'll drive you to the gatehouse."

"No."

"Yes. Or we go inside." He glanced at the palace. "I have a big bed in there, Danni. And I can't stop thinking about having you in it. This is your last chance before I pick you up and carry you inside. Maybe then I'll have you worked out of my system and can let this be over."

Danni saw the calculation in his gaze and knew she had only seconds before he acted on his threat. She strode from him and got into the passenger seat, shutting the door behind her. If this was how he wanted to play it... If it made him feel better, gave him the illusion of control, she would do it.

He drove her to the gatehouse and cut the engine so that all was silent before he turned to her, his eyes darkening, soulful and sinful. "Kiss me again."

She wanted to do so very much more than just kiss him. He was some kind of sorcerer making her forget what was good for her, what was right. And she had to break his spell without giving him the chance to weave a new one.

She leaped out of the car, shut the door with hasty, choked words of thanks and goodbye and ran into the house.

"You're sure everything is all right?" Her father asked for the second time that evening as she looked into the fridge trying to decide what to cook for their dinner.

"Fine, Dad," she said as brightly as she could manage. But she was far from all right. Adam had said he was stopping his search and it was her fault. "I'm just a little tired. I'm looking forward to a quiet and early night." Her first night of getting used to not being with Adam. Given that they'd only had one night in each other's arms it shouldn't be that difficult. What was one night out of a lifetime? Even if that night had been blissful perfection. There was no reason for this awful weight pressing on her heart.

"Oh."

She didn't like the sound of that "oh" and looked at her father. "What's up?"

"I must have misheard him."

"Misheard who?"

"Adam."

A knock sounded at the front door.

"Dad? What's going on?"

"Adam called earlier. He said he was going to come around to see you."

Danni strode to the door, her father's voice catching up to her as she reached for the handle. "Is there something going on between you and Adam?"

Her fingers stilled and she turned back. "No, Dad. There's not." Not anymore. On one hand he'd think she was breaking ancient unwritten rules if there was something between them; on the other, there was probably nothing in the world her father would like better. It would be a dream come true for him.

But this was her life and she had to live it to best suit herself, not her father.

Danni pulled open the door and came face to face with the man she didn't want to see. And all the memories of what they'd shared and being with him came flooding back, swamping her. The oppressive weight lifted from her heart and it soared like a bird unexpectedly freed from captivity. She stared at his face and it reflected some of the same hunger she felt.

She'd missed him. Damn it.

She'd only been away from him for a couple hours and she'd missed him. It was so good just to look at him. And despite the fact that he was forcing her hand in coming here, there was a trace of uncertainty and need in his eyes as he watched and waited. She should have capitalized on it; instead, that uncertainty and need undid her.

"Adam." She meant to say his name without feeling. Instead her voice was filled with yearning.

She drank in the sight of him. A sight she had to deprive herself of. Soon. But not yet. She needed just a couple more seconds first. Time to imprint in her memory just how he looked—his eyes, his nose with that bump, his lips, his jaw. She had to clench her hands at her sides to keep from reaching for him.

From behind his back, he produced a bouquet of flowers.

"You shouldn't have." The gesture was romantic.

"You don't like them?"

She lifted the bouquet to her face and inhaled the fragrance. "They're beautiful. Nobody's ever given me flowers before."

He reached for her shoulders and pulled her toward him. His eyes searched her face.

She tried to be strong. Difficult when desire swept

through her, overwhelming good sense, overwhelming everything.

He pulled her closer still and waited. Leaving her anticipating. Wanting.

Finally it was she who gave in and closed the distance, needing the touch of his lips on hers.

He released her too soon from the kiss that should never have happened. His hands had traveled to loop around her waist and he kept them there, kept that bond between them.

She should pull away.

She stayed where she was.

On a soft sigh Adam kissed her again. This kiss was full of the promise of delight and pleasure. It was long blissful seconds before he lifted his head.

"I spent the entire meeting with the Spanish ambassador thinking of doing that."

"But we agreed," she protested. Too little, too late.

"We didn't agree to anything."

Danni laughed. A mix of exasperation and despair. Why did it have to be Adam? The one man above all others she could never have. The one whose whole existence was so far removed from hers. He needed a woman who was her opposite, cultured and sophisticated, diplomatic and beautiful. Someone who would make a good princess.

And she needed to forget about him.

But at this instant, cradled in his arms, she could only be grateful that he was making a liar out of her and taking what he—and she—wanted rather than what was right for him.

"Come out with me tonight. We need to talk."

"No. I have work in the morning. A press conference to prepare for later this week."

"Don't leave him standing out there, Danni. Ask him in." Her father's voice came from within the house.

"No." There was no strength, only panic, in her voice. She couldn't let him do this.

"Come and watch this, you two," her father called. "They've got coverage of the Brazil race."

Adam lifted an eyebrow. "Watching Formula One with your father, what harm could there be in that?"

"All sorts of harm."

A hint of a smile touched his lips. "Frightened of me, Danni?"

"No." Liar. She was terrified of what he'd done to her heart, of the havoc he could wreak.

"Good, then you won't mind."

"Why won't you take no for an answer?"

"It's a failing. Weren't you supposed to cure me of my flaws?" He looked over her shoulder. "Evening St. Claire."

Danni's heart sank. If her father was here, there would be no getting rid of Adam. "Evening, Adam. Are you two coming in or are you going to stand out there in the cold all night?"

Adam watched her and waited, appearing to leave the decision—now when it was too late—up to her.

"We're coming in," Danni said on a sigh. She had no strength to resist. Her earlier attempt had been a bluff—and he'd known it. There would be time enough for strength tomorrow. After just this one evening, in the company of her father. What harm could there be in it? A little voice in the recesses of her mind echoed her earlier answer—all sorts of harm. Because she wanted so desperately just to *be* with Adam—near him, able to watch and hear him, to laugh with him for one more evening.

Tomorrow she would leave. Go stay with a friend. Go somewhere Adam wouldn't follow her. She would force a clean break on herself.

"Have you eaten?" Adam asked as she put the flowers into a vase.

She shook her head.

"Takeout?" He pulled his phone from his pocket. "Is Chinese still your father's favorite?"

She nodded. Her acquiescence complete. She might as well just roll over and present her stomach for him to scratch. Oh, wait. She'd already done that.

He followed her to the living room. Her father sat in the armchair, leaving her and Adam the couch. They sat close, but not touching, which was its own kind of torture. As her father added his commentary to that of the announcers, Adam's hand, out of her father's line of sight, found hers and closed around it. And this touch was too much and not enough.

The three of them watched, intent, conversing only occasionally, shouting at the screen at times. And despite knowing that she shouldn't allow it, Danni found so much pleasure in sharing this with Adam and her father that it hurt, this taste of what could never be.

After they'd eaten, she made coffee, needing an excuse to get away, a chance to regroup, to grow a spine. But in the kitchen she stood at the counter and stared out into the night.

Adam came to stand behind her. His arms wrapped around her. "The times I spent here with you and your father were as close as I got to ordinary growing up and you have no idea how much they meant to me. I knew my father loved me but it was your father who spent time with me, who had no expectations. I've always been grateful."

"I liked how you were when you were here. You were so different from when you were with Rafe or the other kids. You were so serious, so remote, as though even with them you had to remember who you were."

"I must have been insufferable."

"We suffered you." She smiled, remembering those times. She'd seen the barriers he erected, they all had, but she'd seen the chinks and breaks in the invisible armor he cloaked himself with. She'd seen them when he'd been here, or when it had been just the two of them, and he'd thought she was too young to really understand what was going on, and too devoted to him to reveal the secrets he sometimes revealed to her. She'd reveled in her perceived status as his favorite. She wanted it still.

She stepped out from the shelter of his arms.

What if I fall in love with you? She wanted to scream the words, the real reason for her fear. Instead she locked them deep inside her. Because she knew the answer to that question. It would be a terrible, terrible thing.

Eleven

Something was off.

Danni had been coordinating the biannual press briefings since the start of the process of bringing a Grand Prix to San Philippe. The feel in the room today was different. And it wasn't just her and her confusion over her feelings for Adam and her sorrow over what could never be.

The last official press release two weeks ago, back when her life had been normal, had contained promising developments. But not promising enough to justify the crowd in the small room that usually had more empty chairs than full ones.

She caught an enquiring glance from Michael Lucas, the head of San Philippe motorsport, and gave a small shrug. As well as the usual motor racing commentators, and representatives from tourism, who expected a Grand Prix to have a major influence on visitor numbers, there were reporters and journalists she didn't recognize. There was also a new sense of energy and excitement in the room.

As she stood to the side of the stage, she reviewed her notes again, including the emails that had come in last night and this morning. Nothing surprising there. She could only be glad that, after a drop-off in interest over the last few months while proceedings slowed down in talks about safety and scheduling and disruption to residents, awareness appeared to be picking up again nicely.

She tried to keep her thoughts on task, tried not to think about Adam, who she had missed so desperately in her bed this last week. She'd ached for his presence, his scent, the weight of his body next to hers. Missed the way he made love to her.

The first thing she'd done at work the Monday after her ski weekend was to make arrangements to move forward her trips to other Grand Prix host countries. She was getting out of San Philippe. It was the only way.

The sound of Michael clearing his throat recalled her attention. The panel, including drivers, and manufacturers' representatives were all ready. Michael looked for her nod then began the conference with the latest updates, then opened the floor to questions.

He took a couple of questions about the race course then chose one of the journalists Danni didn't recognize to ask her question. Danni could see the woman's press accreditation but from this distance couldn't tell which publication she was with. But if interest in the

Grand Prix was spreading to mainstream media she could only be glad.

"I have a question for Ms. St. Claire."

All heads turned toward her. Danni hid her surprise, but suddenly she wasn't quite so glad. As she reached for the microphone the end panelist held out for her, she had a very bad feeling.

"Is it true that you're romantically involved with Prince Adam?"

Danni clamped shut the jaw that wanted to fall open. Not interest in a Grand Prix. Interest in a grand prize. A grand prince. Gossip about her and Adam.

She'd really thought they'd got away with it, a weekend of anonymity. But it had been naive to hope they might evade speculation and that their time together would be something she could treasure and keep to herself. Just one weekend. Did Adam not deserve that? Whether or not he deserved it, he wasn't going to get it.

Interest in the room picked up palpably. Journalists, presumably the ones who hadn't known already, sat up straighter. Initial surprise and disbelief turned quickly to curiosity. Danni glanced at Michael, who was frowning but whose head was tilted inquiringly, waiting for her to deny the accusation. Her breath caught in her throat. She looked back at the reporter. "That's not something we're here to talk about," she said with a brittle smile. She signaled for Michael to take the next question. They needed to divert the reporters' interest. A distraction like this one was the last thing she wanted.

But the journalist wasn't about to let it go at that. "How would you characterize your relationship with the prince?" She called out her question, not waiting to be asked.

Danni paused, needing to shut this down and move on. She was about to issue a categorical denial—after all what she and Adam had was over, it had to be—when she looked up and saw a solid, dark-suited man standing at the back of the room. Wrightson, one of the palace drivers. What was he doing here? He gave his close-cropped head the smallest of shakes.

No? No, what? Don't deny it? Do deny it?

Danni took a deep breath and looked back at the woman. "How would I characterize my relationship with the prince? To you, very carefully. And that's all I have to say on the subject."

A murmur of laughter spread through the room. The motorsport journalists were no more pleased about the presence of tabloid reporters than she had been. Imposters in their ranks. Though undoubtedly many if not all of them were scenting new angles for their stories, angles that might sell more papers or subscriptions or ad space on websites. They might not all like it but they knew what paid their wages. She just had to keep the focus where she wanted it. "Now let's move on. Robert?" Robert Dubrawski, a newscaster with a background in finance, would be wanting information on the economic impact of a Grand Prix.

Through a mix of firmness and humor, she kept the rest of the briefing relatively on track. And when the allotted time was up, she took a back exit from the room and into the side streets walking quickly, wanting to put distance between her and impending disaster.

She knew a quiet little restaurant in the old part of the city. She could get a corner table and figure out what was happening and what she needed to do about it. She was hurrying toward the restaurant when a sleek dark Jaguar pulled alongside her, slowing to a stop.

The window slid down to reveal Wrightson behind the wheel. "Prince Adam wondered if you could spare some time to meet with him?"

Only if Prince Adam could wind back time itself and stop this from happening. She was about to refuse when she heard her name called out. The reporter from the briefing and a photographer were running up the street toward her.

Danni hopped into the car.

The breaking of their story changed everything.

They had to come up with a joint strategy, an excuse for why they'd been seen together. And doubtless, if they needed it, Adam would have the very best PR advisers at his service.

She switched on her phone, found a message from Adam asking her to call him and another more recent message from the receptionist at work advising her not to come back after the briefing because photographers were swarming the building.

Danni didn't speak as the car rumbled over the cobbled streets, crossed an arching bridge and headed sedately for the palace. She did her best to tamp down the anticipation that seeing Adam inevitably stirred. Fifteen minutes later they drew up outside Adam's wing. Before the car had quite come to a stop, Danni opened her door and got out. As she looked around, unsure of what to do, the door to Adam's wing opened and he strode out.

And despite all her resolutions, her determination that everything had to be over between them and her annoyance that what should have been private had been made public, her heart leaped at the sight of him. So confident, so intense. The concern in his eyes for her.

He strode toward her and caught her shoulders. "You're okay?"

She nodded.

"I'm sorry about the press." Regret and anger tinged his voice. If the press had wind of their story, there were only two ways it could go. They'd revile her for stopping him from finding a suitable woman or they'd expect him to confirm it was serious with Danni.

He wouldn't accept either of those outcomes. He understood his duty.

"It's not your fault."

He pushed a lock of hair behind her ear. "Actually it is. It's because of me they're interested in you. I never wanted them to get to you." Along with the regret and anger she recognized resignation in his voice, his eyes.

He knew, finally, that what they'd shared had to be over.

Even with all her attempts to convince him of that simple truth, his acceptance of it opened up an emptiness inside her that filled with a great welling sorrow.

"As soon as my secretary told me there were pictures, I tried to get word to you. Your phone was off."

"I'd put it to voice mail."

"I know. So I sent Wrightson. I would have gone myself but…"

"Fuel to the fire. I get it. Thanks for trying though."

"I'd have stopped it if I could."

"I know. But you can't and so we need a strategy. Is it too late to say there was never anything between us?"

"They have photos of us skiing and photos of us

leaving the palace grounds together. The skiing ones have only just come to light. But combined with the others…"

"Can they be explained any other way?"

He lifted a shoulder. "They could be."

"Then let's—"

"It's best to be honest." He brushed his knuckles across her cheek. "At first you were labeled a mystery woman. Unfortunately, but not surprisingly, it didn't take them long to figure out who you were."

"No. It wouldn't have." She thought of the reporters' tenacious questions.

"I heard you handled the press well."

"I managed. I think. The questions caught me by surprise. I was about to deny any relationship when Wrightson shook his head."

"Like I said, it's best to stick to the truth. It always comes out eventually."

"If we have to stick to the truth," she said, "we tell them we had a weekend together but that it was a mistake."

"I don't make mistakes. And you definitely weren't one."

"Then we tell them that it…didn't work out."

"Seemed to me that it worked pretty well."

"It did." For that one isolated weekend.

"So have you come up with a way to handle the publicity?"

"I've spoken to the palace advisers."

"And?"

"I also spoke to my father and to Rafe."

"Oh." Of course it was inevitable that his father and brother would find out and have an opinion. She shouldn't be surprised or dismayed. "What did they say?" She held up her hand. "No, wait. Don't tell me. I know what they said." Adam had needed to hear their views, but she didn't. It was surely them who'd finally convinced Adam that there could be no relationship with her. She should be grateful for that. "What's the strategy."

"As unoriginal as it is, 'No comment' seems to be the preferred strategy. That combined with no further contact between us. When there's no fuel, the fire soon dies out."

His gaze searched her face and he shook his head. "I've missed you." He pulled her to him. Acting on pure conditioned response, she rose up for his kiss and welcomed the touch of his lips to hers.

How could this be over when he kissed her like that?

How could she walk away from him?

His kiss, as always, sent sensations spiraling through her, weakening her legs, trampling over rational thought. That was why she was having such trouble walking away from him, she thought with a half laugh—weak legs.

She'd been too long without him.

He was her addiction.

As her hands, of their own volition, slipped around his waist, he pulled her closer still. Enveloped her in his warmth. Warmth that turned rapidly to heat.

Once more, a voice whispered.

Once more before it was over.

"Can you do one thing for me?" she asked.

"I'd do anything for you."

"Make love to me once more." She would take this and then nothing more.

He pulled back. She read the hesitation in his eyes and then his capitulation. He caught her hand in his again and strode wordlessly for the palace. He hurried up to the second level, past the library and along a hallway hung with portraits. The next door they passed through led into a bedroom. Unmistakably masculine.

Her gaze took in the room. He hadn't been lying when he'd said he had a big bed. There'd be room to turn cartwheels across it. Or make love lying any which way across it. She could turn cartwheels but she'd much rather make love.

A lock clicked into place as Adam pushed the door shut behind him. For one long delirious second they looked at each other. Awareness and unbearable hunger hummed in the air between them. Then he tugged on the hand he still held and she went to him. With no thought of talking she reached for him, undoing buttons and belts and zips, finding her way inside his clothes, needing skin on skin contact, the male heat of him, her addiction needing to be fed. One last fix. This close she could breathe in the intoxicating scent that was his alone. The one that called every cell in her body to attention. And the touch of him, the warmth that spread through her, were enough to reassure her that satisfaction was close at hand. Her craving would be satisfied.

Her only consolation for her senseless weakness for him was that he seemed as desperate as she was—lost to the haze of desire. Tugging and pulling at her clothes, with none of his legendary finesse. He eased her back onto his bed and lay down over her.

All the world narrowed to this one moment, this one man. All her thoughts, every sensation was centered on him and what he gave her.

He rose up, his broad shoulders and corded neck straining. Ready for him, needing him, she arched against him. He accepted her body's plea and in one long stroke drove in deep and fast, filling her so that her "yes" came out as a low satisfied moan, mingling with a similar inarticulate sound from him.

So good.

He felt so good. So right. So perfect.

And then he was moving within her, slowly at first but she didn't want slow and he responded to her needs, driving in harder and deeper and she reached for his hips, clasping the bunching muscles, moving with his rhythm, pulling him still harder and deeper, her legs around his back. Because she needed this. She needed him.

They strove together, swirling into the same vortex of wanting, racing for a release that demanded completion. Sensation, like licks of fire, swept through her, curling her toes, setting her aflame for this, for him, carrying them to that other mindless place till sensation couldn't be contained and the power of it surged through them as it crested and shattered.

Leaving her shaken and spent.

He held her in his arms as their breathing slowed and minds and bodies adjusted to the fact that they were no longer one. Aftershocks rippled through her as sweat cooled on her skin.

"Funny," he said later as he pushed a lock of hair from her face. "Whenever I dreamed about making love to you here in this bed, I imagined it to be slow and exquisite. I thought we'd take hours."

The awareness of Adam losing his ever-present restraint with her, thrilled and humbled her. "At least you got the exquisite part right."

His arm tightened around her. "And maybe we could try…"

She didn't know where she would find the strength to walk away from him because she hadn't known, hadn't let herself believe, that they could be this good together. That she could want more than his body or to give him more than hers. That he could make such a deep impression on her heart.

No, not an impression, he owned it. All of it.

The heart in question sank with the dawning awareness.

Love.

She'd fallen in love with Adam.

He was like no other man she'd ever known. She loved his seriousness, his complexity, his kindness. She loved him and everything about him.

A man she couldn't have. The irony was that he was the one person she wanted to share the appalling realization with. The Adam who was her friend as well as her lover in whose arms she now lay. The Adam who understood her, who always had.

But she couldn't admit her love. All it would do would be to make him feel guilty. He'd never asked for her love. She'd been an interlude in his search for a wife.

Maybe she should just be grateful that they'd taken as much as they had. More than they should have been allowed.

It was hard to be grateful when her heart was breaking.

She sought the temporary solace of making love with him again.

A long time afterward, a long slow exquisite time afterward, she rolled out of his bed.

Love wasn't supposed to hurt like this.

She found strength along with her clothes.

It wasn't till she was dressed that she turned back to Adam to find him watching her. Those now serious eyes had been fierce with fire and passion. For her.

This was it. The end. They both recognized it.

She turned away from those beautiful brown eyes and crossed to the window. Seconds later she saw his reflection in the glass. He'd come to stand behind her. Outside, darkness was falling. Her life had once been so uncomplicated. She leaned her forehead on the window.

Fifteen minutes later they sat in a nondescript sedan belonging to the palace's head of security. "I did your one last thing. Will you do one for me? Will you let me show you something?" He'd asked and she'd agreed. How could she refuse him? They skirted the city, crossed the river and several blocks later turned into an industrial area on the outskirts of the city filled with warehouses and light manufacturing. "Where are we going?"

"You told me once there were rumors that I had a mystery woman."

"Yes. And you laughed."

"You'll see why soon. We're almost there."

At the entrance to a light industrial complex, he pressed a code into a keypad that opened an enormous gate. Inside, he drove slowly past a series of closed roller doors, finally stopping in front of one. He pressed a button on his key chain and one of the doors slowly rose. He looked at her. "I haven't shown this to anyone before."

"You don't have to show it to me now." She almost didn't want him to. She had no idea what was behind that door, only that it was deeply personal to him.

"I want to." He drove into the dim interior. Danni instantly recognized a workshop, tools neatly lining the walls, and saw straight away the shape of a low, covered car. They parked alongside it and the door closed behind them.

She looked from him to the covered car. "Why would you keep a car out here when you have all that space at the palace?"

"This is private. It's nothing to do with the palace or being a prince. It's my escape from both of those things. Through that door over there—" he pointed to a wall "—are stairs to the top level. I had it converted to an apartment, just a bedroom and a bathroom. It's utterly private."

He tilted his head toward the shrouded car. "Let me show her to you. My mystery woman." They approached the car and he peeled back the cover. Her first glimpse of gleaming wheel spokes confirmed what she'd suspected as soon as she'd seen the shape of the low-slung car. "Dad's Bugatti. You're the collector?" She looked from the car, its engine exposed, to him. "How is that possible?"

"Your father did so much for me for so many years. Especially after my mother died. I wanted to do something for him in return. I knew he was selling the car at least in part for your college fees and that he'd never accept outright financial help. So I bought it through an intermediary. Don't get me wrong, it wasn't truly altruistic, having the car to work on has given me peace and much pleasure over the years."

"Dad doesn't know?"

Adam shook his head. "I wanted to finish it and then give it back to him. It's nearly ready. I steal an hour here and there."

Danni touched his face—her fingertips to his beautiful strong jaw. "That's a lovely thing you're doing."

He opened the nearest door. "Hop in."

Danni let him hand her into the car. Into the driver's seat. He took shotgun. "Do you remember—" she began.

"Yes. And I'm embarrassed about it."

"You said a girl couldn't drive it. That girls weren't good drivers."

"Thanks for reminding me. Did I ever apologize for that?"

"Not as such. But you let me drive for you. I figured that meant something."

"It did. And if it will mean something to you now you can drive the Bugatti. The detailing isn't finished but it runs like a dream."

Half an hour later they were parked on top of a hill looking back over the lights of the city gleaming like diamonds strewn across the night. A full moon hung partially obscured in the sky.

"I could sit like this with you forever." Adam's low voice reached across the darkness between them.

Danni looked away and surreptitiously wiped a tear from her cheek. She tried to swallow the ache in her jaw.

"I hope you find a good man, Danni."

She turned to him. "Would you be insulted if I wished you success in your search for a suitable wife?"

"To my core."

"So, don't..."

"I won't." He reached for her hand, held it with a clasp more fierce than gentle. "But I want you to be happy."

"And I want the same for you."

He tipped his head back and closed his eyes. He opened them again and looked at her with that intensity that was unique to him. "You know that if I didn't love you as much as I do, I'd ask you to marry me."

"You love me?" The words reverberated within her, filling her with joy and sorrow, her greatest wish and her greatest fear.

"With all my heart. I don't know when or how it started. And I don't know how to stop. You can't possibly know how vital you are to me. But I couldn't ask you to share a life that would make you miserable. Rafe made me see that."

A silence stretched between them. He loved her. He loved her.

Finally, she spoke softly. "If I didn't love you as much as I do I'd accept."

"You love me?"

"With all my heart. And I do know how it started. It began when I was five and you got that book down from the shelf for me. And I don't know how to stop either, or believe that you can possibly know how vital *you* are to *me*. But I'm not what you need. I'd be a terrible royal wife."

His hand tightened on hers. "The constant glare of

publicity, the tedium of royal engagements. I couldn't bear to see your joy in life diminished."

She allowed another small silence, turning his words over in her head. "People cope," she said quietly. "I coped with the press today. But what about my lack of sophistication, my lack of diplomacy? I couldn't bear to discredit you."

He freed her hand, shifted his to caress her face. "There are far too many sophisticated and diplomatic people in royal circles. What I need in my life is vitality and plain speaking. Someone who's honest with me. Someone I can be with in the quiet moments. And I've been told I need to learn to have fun. To be more impulsive. I need a lot of work. I could use help with that."

She wanted so desperately to help him with that. "I meet none of your criteria for a royal wife."

"That's not quite true. You meet plenty of the criteria on that list. You're good with the press, you're good with children and you're beautiful beyond belief, but none of those matter anymore because I drew up a new list."

"A new list? When?"

"When you first tried to tell me that we were over. I thought it might be wise." He lowered his hand and pulled a folded and crumpled piece of paper from his pocket and passed it to her. "I didn't do too well with it. I couldn't come up with much."

Danni spread the paper out on the steering wheel. There was just enough light to make out that there were a few words on the paper but not enough to read them. "It's too dark. I can't read it."

"It says, 'Item One—she must be Danni.'" He blew out his breath. "And that's it."

The moon rose up from behind the clouds, shining enough light that she could make out her name on the paper. "You're right. It's not much of a list."

"It was the best I could do."

"I'd say you need help with it."

"I probably do."

"You should add to it that she must love you. Because if she loves you, whatever she has to give up will be less of a sacrifice than giving up on love."

"And I guess you'd tell me I should love her in return? With all my heart? And be willing to do whatever it takes to make her happy?"

"Absolutely."

"So that's three simple criteria." He turned in the seat and lifted his hands to her face. "She must be Danni, she must love me and I must love her in return? Will you help me find her and help me convince her to marry me, to never leave me?"

"Yes," she sighed. "But only if you kiss me now."

Epilogue

"Have I told you how beautiful you look tonight?" Adam stood and held out his hand to Danni.

"Yes." She put her hand in his, stood and walked to the dance floor with him, stepping gladly, gratefully into his arms.

They were the third couple to occupy the floor. The bridal couple, Rebecca and Logan, danced, eyes for only each other. Their wedding had been beautiful, full of pomp and splendor, but with human touches and laughter and most of all love.

Their love for each other had shone through every moment and every syllable of the service from the time Rebecca had taken her first step on the long walk up the cathedral's aisle.

Rebecca had looked amazing in her ivory silk and

lace gown and Logan had been visibly stunned as he watched her walk toward him.

Danni and Adam were among the very few who knew that beneath Rebecca's gown the first addition to their family already grew.

Rafe and Lexie danced now too, holding tight to each other. Their baby, Bonnie, had punctuated the service with her laughing gurgles, a delightful counterpoint to the beautiful solemnity of the occasion. Bonnie had stayed through the official luncheon but had been taken home by the nanny before this more intimate dinner and dance for a mere three hundred. But if they followed the pattern Danni had quickly become aware of, Rafe and Lexie would soon head home, too. Wanting to be with each other and their child had suddenly become a singular priority. The playboy prince had become a doting husband and father, completely besotted with the two women in his life.

At the head table, Prince Henri and Danni's father sat back in their chairs, sipping cognac and watching over proceedings with obvious fatherly pride.

Adam hadn't taken too long to bring his father round to the idea of their marrying. He'd had several meetings alone with him before bringing Danni to meet him officially. The main thing Prince Henri had wanted to be certain of was that they were resolute in their love for each other—because there would, he assured them, be trials. But once he was convinced of their love, he'd insightfully predicted that the country too would grow to love Danni. They would see her as just like them, an ordinary citizen, a commoner whom they could claim as one of their own and love. She would be the fairy tale come true.

And he'd been right. The press had quickly decided they were on Danni's side and made much of the work she'd done in bringing a Grand Prix to San Philippe. And they frequently pointed out how refreshing she would be for the royal family. Already it seemed that their prince, who they acknowledged could sometimes seem a little reserved, looked more relaxed and open. It helped that every photo they printed showed both Danni and Adam radiant with happiness.

Gradually, other couples joined the dance floor. So much had changed for Danni and Adam in the last month. They'd announced their engagement at Christmas. They'd considered waiting until after this wedding but speculation had been so intense that it seemed easiest to admit the truth, that yes they loved each other and wanted to marry.

Their wedding wouldn't be for another eight months. It was the soonest that it could be arranged given the pomp and ceremony that was apparently necessary, more even than there had been today. But, after all, it wasn't every day the heir apparent got married. The country wanted to celebrate, just as, after being robbed of a wedding by Rafe and Lexie eloping, they'd anticipated and then celebrated today's occasion.

Already a provisional guest list was being drawn up. Many of the names on it would be dictated by protocol and etiquette, with attention paid to international considerations. She and Adam were content to leave much of it to their aides, though they had made sure to insist that Blake be on it.

The only thing that really mattered to Danni was that she got to be with Adam. For the rest of their lives.

He danced with her, holding her closer than decorum suggested was proper, their bodies pressed together from shoulders to toes. Almost heaven, Danni thought as she swayed in his arms. Moving with him, being held by him. Every time she thought it couldn't get any better, it did.

"You look stunning in that dress." The dress in question had been made for her, a beaded evening gown, with simple flowing lines, in deepest purple.

"Thank you, but you know as soon as we get home I'll be kicking off these shoes and getting changed." She was gradually getting used to the formality of dress that was now often required of her, but she still liked her jeans best of all.

"You'll be getting out of the dress, do you mean? I'll be happy to help you with that." He pulled her closer still and spun her.

"So long as you're more help than you were when I was trying to put it on."

"The trouble is, as beautiful as it looks on you, it looks even better off you." He leaned down and whispered in her ear. "Though I guess you could keep the shoes on if you like."

Danni laughed. She couldn't believe she'd once accused him of lacking fun and spontaneity. In public he was seriousness personified. In private he was anything but. And she loved every facet of him.

* * * * *

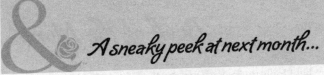

A sneaky peek at next month...

Desire

PASSIONATE AND DRAMATIC LOVE STORIES

2 stories in each book - only **£5.49!**

My wish list for next month's titles...

In stores from 15th June 2012:

☐ Ready for King's Seduction – Maureen Child

& The Cowboy's Pride – Charlene Sands

☐ A Breathless Bride – Fiona Brand

& Bed of Lies – Paula Roe

☐ The Wayward Son & A Forbidden Affair

   – Yvonne Lindsay

☐ A Secret Birthright – Olivia Gates

& Bachelor Unleashed – Brenda Jackson

Available at WHSmith, Tesco, Asda, Eason, Amazon and Apple

Just can't wait?

Special Offers

Every month we put together collections and longer reads written by your favourite authors.

Here are some of next month's highlights— and don't miss our fabulous discount online!

On sale 15th June

On sale 15th June

On sale 6th July

Save 20% on all *Special Releases*

The World of Mills & Boon®

There's a Mills & Boon® series that's perfect for you. We publish ten series and with new titles every month, you never have to wait long for your favourite to come along.

Blaze. Scorching hot, sexy reads

By Request Relive the romance with the best of the best

Cherish Romance to melt the heart every time

Desire Passionate and dramatic love stories

Have Your Say

You've just finished your book.
So what did you think?

We'd love to hear your thoughts on our
'Have your say' online panel
www.millsandboon.co.uk/haveyoursay

- Easy to use
- Short questionnaire
- Chance to win Mills & Boon® goodies

Visit us Online

Tell us what you thought of this book now at
www.millsandboon.co.uk/haveyoursay

YOUR_SAY